The Deep End

Nick Louth is a million-copy bestselling thriller author, and an award-winning journalist. After graduating from the London School of Economics, Nick was a foreign correspondent for Reuters, working in New York, Amsterdam, London and Hong Kong. He has written for the Financial Times, Investors Chronicle, Money Observer and MSN. His debut thriller, Bite, was a Kindle No. 1 bestseller and has been translated into six languages. The DCI Craig Gillard series and DI Jan Talantire series are published by Canelo, and in audio by WF Howes. He is married and lives in Lincolnshire.

Also by Nick Louth

Bite
Heartbreaker
Mirror Mirror
Trapped

DCI Craig Gillard Crime Thrillers

The Body in the Marsh
The Body on the Shore
The Body in the Mist
The Body in the Snow
The Body Under the Bridge
The Body on the Island
The Bodies at Westgrave Hall
The Body on the Moor
The Body Beneath the Willows
The Body in the Stairwell
The Body in the Shadows
The Body in Nightingale Park

Detective Jan Talantire

The Two Deaths of Ruth Lyle
The Last Ride
The Dark Edge
The Deep End

THE DEEP END

NICK LOUTH

CANELO CRIME

First published in the United Kingdom in 2025 by

Canelo Crime, an imprint of
Canelo Digital Publishing Limited,
20 Vauxhall Bridge Road,
London SW1V 2SA
United Kingdom

A Penguin Random House Company
The authorised representative in the EEA is Dorling Kindersley Verlag GmbH.
Arnulfstr. 124, 80636 Munich, Germany

Copyright © Nick Louth 2025

The moral right of Nick Louth to be identified as the creator of this work has been asserted in accordance with the Copyright, Designs and Patents Act, 1988.
All rights reserved. No part of this publication may be reproduced or transmitted in any form or by any means, electronic or mechanical, including photocopy, recording, or any information storage and retrieval system, without permission in writing from the publisher.
No part of this book may be used or reproduced in any manner for the purpose of training artificial intelligence technologies or systems. In accordance with Article 4(3) of the DSM Directive 2019/790, Canelo expressly reserves this work from the text and data mining exception.

A CIP catalogue record for this book is available from the British Library.

Print ISBN 978 1 80436 885 5
Ebook ISBN 978 1 80436 888 6

This book is a work of fiction. Names, characters, businesses, organizations, places and events are either the product of the author's imagination or are used fictitiously. Any resemblance to actual persons, living or dead, events or locales is entirely coincidental.

Cover design by Dan Mogford

Printed and bound in Great Britain by Clays Ltd, Elcograf S.p.A.

Look for more great books at
www.canelo.co | www.dk.com

For Louise, as always

Chapter One

Teignmouth, Devon. Boxing Day morning, 5:45. Still dark for another two hours.

Geoff Hutchinson eased himself out of bed taking care not to disturb his sleeping wife. At sixty-eight, the retired police constable remained as much of a lark as he had always been. Shift work, sea fishing, walking the dog, beach combing: he'd never had any trouble getting up early. And he wasn't alone. He could already hear the dog snuffling downstairs, her claws clicking on the parquet tiles. He dressed silently, eased open the bedroom door and crept downstairs.

'Quiet now, Sprocket.' The aged cross-bred spaniel pushed her soft greying muzzle against his legs, a tennis ball in her mouth, her paws skittering in excitement. Geoff always marvelled at the boundless optimism of dogs. Each new day greeted with joy and hope and excitement, even if the wind was howling or the rain lashing down. They had so much to teach humans. He peered out of the window. Dark skies and scudding clouds. Against the shed door he could see the thermometer in the light from the kitchen, swinging in the wind. Two centigrade. Seriously cold. But at least it wasn't raining.

He slid on his wellingtons, put on his thick quilted overcoat, shrugged on a small rucksack and wrapped a scarf around his neck. He reached for his cloth cap, but hesitated. Instead, he switched to his Santa hat. It was still Christmas, after all.

Sprocket could see all the signs and was whimpering and whining, her excitement reaching a fever pitch when Geoff reached for the lead and stuffed it in his pocket. He unlocked the back door and let the dog out into the garden. Sprocket sniffed the wind, screwing up her eyes.

The moment he stepped outside, Geoff knew that this wind had swept over Dartmoor. It wasn't the salt-laden easterly that blasted in from the sea, but a north-westerly, carrying a kind of peaty tang with a foretaste of sleet. An ill wind, as his dad told him, the day after Geoff's mother died. He gave a little shudder, as he opened the squeaky metal gate.

Sprocket knew where she was going, she always did. No lead required.

The streetlamps were still lit as Geoff walked side by side with the dog along Shute Hill, over the railway line, past the Lidl, and down to the promenade. The wind was absolutely freezing, the kind to get into your bones and make your eyes run. There was nobody about. A few empty beer cans rolled like post-Christmas drunks in the gutter, while the suspended illuminations swung back and forth between the ornate lampposts to some unheard tune. The first twilight glimpse of the sea as always made him catch his breath: a sheet of beaten pewter, scratched with lines of luminous foam, and the rhythmic sigh of the undertow. He'd lived here for twenty years, ever since meeting Molly, and regarded it as his home. Golden sandy beaches, lovely Georgian architecture and a Victorian pier, built in 1865, over two hundred yards long. The pier silhouette, all stilted legs like a metal caterpillar, heading out to the wild sea. Sprocket, walking stiffly because of her arthritic hips, led Geoff off the promenade at the first opportunity, down the steps onto the softer sand, towards the pier. There was a lot of gull activity there, considering how dark it still was. Sprocket sniffed the wind, then looked back to Geoff.

Far out, under the pier, there was something moving, silhouetted against the metal struts. Dark, curved, sliding. Screeching gulls circling nearby. A dolphin? No – no fin. A seal? Maybe. A basking shark? One had been washed up here a couple of years previously, but no, this wasn't that big.

He reached into his rucksack and pulled out a pair of compact binoculars. He walked down as close to the lapping waves as he could, where the piles of the pier departed from the sand to march into the sea. Whatever it was, some kind of weed-strewn hummock, was at least another eighty to one hundred yards away. But he could see the ravenous birds gathering on the struts and crossbeams. He tried his torch – a powerful LED job – and its light caught the slick reflection of the weeds, and dozens of flapping wings, but little else.

Something dead. Or nearly so.

He walked a little further, until the lapping waves swilled around his wellingtons. Sprocket came with him, and then retreated, whining, before running back to join him again. She barked into the darkness. She could smell something. This was a shallow beach, but there were deep pools swept by foaming waves in and around the pier supports. Geoff followed the torch beam, moved gingerly, holding onto the rusted metal as he sought firmer footing.

He tried the binoculars again, just as a wave swept the dark hummock, and turned it over. He glimpsed some glistening mermaid form, and then an arm, hung with thick tendrils of weed.

A hand, with dark nail varnish.

A woman.

She might still be alive. He pulled out his phone and rang 999. The operator sounded exhausted. He sympathised. The Christmas shift was often terrible. He started with the exact What3Words location: *blotches, eyelashes, memory*. A unique ten-yard square, used by emergency services. It was on a sign on the promenade, which he'd long ago memorised. He answered the tedious questions, impatient for a positive response. Yes, he was sure it was a body. No, not a seal. He'd seen a hand. He finally mentioned he was a retired PC. That sped things up a little. Police and Coast Guard, an ambulance too, just in case. She told him to stay where he was.

After he hung up, he realised that only he could make a difference to whether this woman lived or died. But only if he acted *now*. He slipped the phone back in his coat. Heedless now, he plunged on, water slopping over the top of his wellies as he traversed to the next rank of pier supports, five yards further out into the freezing sea. Molly had always said that he was naturally gallant, to the point of foolhardiness. If this woman hadn't yet drowned, he was the only one who could save her. His boots were now heavy with slopping, icy water.

Sprocket remained back at the shore, whimpering and barking. Whatever she wanted to say, it was good advice, surely. The next rank of stilts were just too far into the foaming tide, the body more than fifty yards beyond.

However, right here, there was a crossbar he could climb on, two feet above the water. He hauled himself up.

Once he was on the rusty, weed-strewn perch, he wrapped his torch arm around the stanchion, then looked through the binoculars he held in the other. Again, he saw only the roiling hummock, washed by foam. More gulls were arriving. Then a bigger wave came crashing through the stilts, sweeping the dark shape and its tangle of brown seaweed under a crossbar, through a pool and straight towards him. The knotted mass was driven hard against a nearer row of supports, and the backwash swept off great strips of brown blistered weed.

There, clinging to the metal, staring at him with bloody but empty eye sockets was a Medusa, with a mane of writhing seaweed dreadlocks, her hands caught in the metal frame. Unseeing, a cold pale mouth open. Silent words, an imprecation, a plea for help. She spun around, head back, one accusatory finger pointing at him before being dragged down by the next wave.

He screamed, octaves higher than his usual voice, and tumbled backwards from his corroded perch into the water. A freezing salty wash briefly closing over his head. Yelling with the cold, he struggled to regain his footing. In three stumbling, desperate steps he was in shallower water, spluttering, grasping a rusty pillar for support. As he emerged, he saw Sprocket gamely swimming towards him, barking. At that moment he loved the dog more than life itself. Her head was held high out of the water, paws working furiously. In two more steps, he met her in the shallows. Her teeth gripped his sopping trousers above the wellies, as if to pull him from the sea single handedly.

Now facing the land, he saw the first light of dawn reflected in the windows of the grand houses behind the promenade. His teeth began to chatter, and he knew he needed warmth. He scooped up Sprocket, pulling the dog close as he stumbled up the sand. Two other dog walkers were there, faces frozen in shock. Audrey and Keith, familiar faces on what they all liked to call the early shift.

'Geoff, what have you been up to? You're soaking!' Audrey yelled.

'There's a dead woman out there!'

'Is there? Oh God. You need to get into the warm,' Audrey said. 'My car is just here, hold on.'

'She didn't have any eyes.'

'What do you mean?' Audrey said.

'Just gory sockets. Blood was running down her face. And she called to me, for help.'

'I thought you said she was dead?' Keith asked, his white hair ruffled by the breeze.

'Well, I don't know. And I couldn't help. I'm so sorry. I just couldn't.'

Bundled inside Audrey's VW, wrapped in a smelly dog blanket, with Sprocket on his lap, the heating on full blast, the shivers turned to shudders, and then dissolved into sobs. Embarrassed to cry in front of Audrey, who sat in the driver's seat with her arm around him. It was the first time since his mother died. Cancer. He was fourteen and had never been able to say goodbye. She'd been wheeled away from the hospital ward by a porter, and he never saw her again. Now his great, shoulder-shaking convulsions gathered together every suppressed fear, every failure, every screw-up of the last half-century of his life. He had been unable to save his own mother in 1969, and he'd been trying to make amends ever since.

An hour earlier, the same freezing north-westerly was sweeping off Dartmoor carrying a few light flecks of snow down into Newton Abbot's least salubrious district. Detective Inspector Jan Talantire was in her unmarked Skoda with the lights off and the heating on maximum, the blower directed at the windscreen in an unequal struggle against condensation. Next to her in the passenger seat was Detective Constable Dave Nuttall. Behind her in the back seat were two uniformed PCs. Ian Fitch and Bob Latimer, the latter a hefty individual who, as a mouth breather, seemed to be largely responsible for the steamy windows and an unsavoury taint of male sweat. Latimer kept buzzing his window down, claiming he was hot, while Fitch, who protested he was freezing, kept reaching across to buzz it up.

'I could do with some breakfast,' Latimer said, sniffing.

'It's Boxing Day. There's nowhere open yet,' Fitch said. 'Not even the McDonald's on the bypass – not until ten, anyway.'

'I've got a cereal bar in the glove compartment if you're desperate,' Talantire said.

He was. Nuttall passed back one of the half-dozen bars secreted there. Latimer ripped off the wrapper and inhaled it noisily in three sizeable chomps.

They were parked half on the pavement on a B road, between a petrol station – normally open twenty-four hours but closed today – and the King's Head, a long-abandoned pub. Between those two fixtures were three grimy terraced houses. Behind them, a narrow street next to the pub led to a small cul-de-sac of 1970s social homes, badly in need of renovation. Dozens of wheelie bins crowded round the doors, a grey plastic congregation seemingly awaiting something. Deliverance, maybe? She smiled at her own joke.

A single white delivery van passed by, the first vehicle of any type for several minutes.

There was nobody about, and only a handful of lights on in any of the properties nearby. Nuttall was clearly getting impatient, checking his watch. This was his case. He'd been working on it for weeks, and now it was coming to fruition.

They had spent the last ninety minutes waiting for confirmation that their suspect was indeed in the property that they were staking out. Charlie Evans, forty-two, had been a minor criminal for years. Car theft, burglary, passing stolen goods, he'd done it all, and spent plenty of time inside. Evans had no history of violence, and though imposingly large, he suffered from diabetes that impeded his mobility. If he was at the property, he wasn't going to be sprinting away.

This time, Evans had been implicated in the theft of heating oil from rural properties in the north of the county, around Exmoor. He had been offering cheap oil top-ups for secluded properties on this side of Dartmoor, dozens of miles away from where it had been stolen.

He wasn't an idiot. He was very rarely in his own home, a rented flat on the other side of town near Wolborough. He moved sporadically between the homes of various girlfriends. Number 14, Enniskillen Walk, just a few yards away, was the home of one of them, Debbie Fenton and her two children, thirteen and nine. An informant had reported him there on Christmas Day, arriving loaded up with presents.

Talantire's phone pinged with an alert from the control room. Something had been found underneath the pier at Teignmouth. This wasn't the first message she'd seen about this incident. The initial report from a dog walker was that a dolphin or some other sea creature had become entangled in the rusted metal support structure. Then another call from an off-duty PC had identified it as a human body, entangled 'with tentacles'.

'That sounds interesting,' Latimer said. He had heard the first report on his radio.

'More interesting than waiting here,' Fitch said, morosely. 'Evans might have given us the slip.'

'I don't think so,' Nuttall said.

Talantire wasn't so certain. Evans' car wasn't there any more. It might have been parked somewhere nearby, but if so, they hadn't found it yet. Evans had clearly taken precautions, but not enough to completely hide his tracks. Digital Evidence Officer Primrose Chen had tracked down a burner phone that Evans had started using on Christmas Eve, bought from the very garage they were parked outside. But the service provider – thinly staffed at this antisocial hour – had yet to confirm which, if any, masts the phone had pinged in the last twelve hours.

They'd been wrong before. Just two weeks previously, staking out Evans' flat, Nuttall had disguised himself as a pizza-delivery driver, complete with moped, motorcycle gear and an empty pizza box. The door had been opened by a teenage boy who claimed to have no idea where his Uncle Charlie was. This time, they were waiting for definite confirmation of the phone's location. Nuttall had made clear that this time he didn't want, yet again, to bash down the door of yet another property to find that their quarry wasn't there.

Finally, Nuttall got the confirmation from Primrose. The phone had been on briefly at two a.m. right here in Enniskillen Walk. In all likelihood, he was still there.

'Right, let's go,' Talantire said. 'Dave, you take the back fence and alleyway, you others, come with me to the front. Make sure your bodycams are activated. There are two children in there, and it's Christmas, so we will go in gently. Don't break any toys. I'll judge this a success if the kids don't cry.'

They emerged from the car into a biting wind. Nuttall began whispering the words of 'Good King Wenceslas' as he slipped away past the wheelie bins and up the alleyway. There were no lights on in the house, but Talantire noticed a doorbell camera. Even more reason to behave calmly. She rang the bell and rattled the letterbox. Latimer shouted, 'Police! Open up.'

There was no reply.

Talantire knocked again and shouted through the letterbox that it was the police.

'Knock, knock, knocking on Evan's door,' muttered Ian Fitch. 'The fifth address for him in the last two weeks.'

'Shall I kick it down, ma'am?' Latimer said.

'Not yet,' Talantire said. She could hear some activity towards the back of the house. She and Latimer sprinted around to assist Nuttall, leaving Fitch behind at the front. A large man was waddling across the garden towards the fence at the back. Charlie Evans, wearing a tracksuit and slippers. He looked up to see three police officers staring at him across the fence.

'Bloody hell, don't you even take Christmas off?' he asked, holding his wrists up for the handcuffs.

Within half an hour, a police patrol car had arrived promptly to take Evans to Exeter for processing. Nuttall and Fitch went with him, leaving Latimer and Talantire at the scene.

They spent fifteen minutes inside the house with Evans' girlfriend, Debbie.

She lit a fag, sat back on the sofa and scrutinised Talantire head to toe through narrowed eyes, as if she were a rival. She then put on the TV. The softly, softly arrest had barely dented the family Christmas. The children, now awake and active, were far more interested in playing with their new toys than showing any distress about where their peripatetic 'uncle' had disappeared to. Latimer had even made them laugh, donning a Santa hat and doing a few belly laughs: *ho ho ho*.

While he entertained the kids, Talantire shrewdly assessed the family situation for a potential social services referral. There didn't seem to be any obvious red flags. Seeing as it wasn't clear that Charlie Evans was even a contributor – bar the odd toy – to Debbie Fenton's benefits-based household, it appeared his absence might not impact the family too much. Maybe he wouldn't be missed.

Talantire booked Debbie Fenton in to give a statement later in the day, then she and the others left the house, back into the cold.

'Shall I drop you back at Torquay then, Bob?' Talantire asked.

'Yes, but can we go and take a look at the body under the pier?' he asked. 'Then we can go into Torquay on the coast road.'

Talantire looked at the chubby, schoolboyish face. There are very few PCs that she felt comfortable spending time with on her own, least of all this one with his whiff of BO. But she had to admit that it probably wasn't a bad idea to take a look, just in case. Three out of every four reports of dead bodies at the coast turned out to be seals or in one case a basking shark. The fact that an off-duty PC had given the last report was a plus point. She had a basic forensics kit in the car, if needed.

'All right, Bob. Let's just make sure we got the keyholder to the pier there, unless you fancy wading out into freezing water on Boxing Day.'

'No, ma'am. I like my water hot, circulating round a teabag.'

Talantire rang the control room and said she was on her way.

Talantire drove down the A381 along the north bank of the River Teign, with the first hesitant rays of dawn turning into a broader glow on the eastern horizon.

'That's a lovely view, that is,' Latimer said. 'My mum and dad met on that pier and did half of their courting there.'

'So you're local, then?' she asked.

'They were, but I grew up in Plymouth. Dad was in the Navy.'

Talantire noticed the blue lights of three police patrol cars parked on the promenade and pulled up beside them. There were a few spectators around, a couple of them wearing Christmas hats and otherwise heavily wrapped up against the wind. The moment she left the fug of the car the morning's raw chill hit her again, colder here than it had been in Newton Abbot. She went to the boot and picked up a thick fleecy jacket and her forensics kit. With Latimer trailing in her wake, she made her way from the car and the beach towards a gaggle of male officers, who had managed to get steaming mugs of coffee from somewhere. A section of blue crime tape had been draped forlornly around the base of the pier where it joined the land.

She introduced herself and then asked, 'Is the RNLI coming? I see the station is only a few hundred yards further on.'

'Just waiting for the last volunteer to arrive,' said the oldest looking PC. 'Then they'll launch the Zodiac, which is just the size for this job.'

The pier keyholder arrived, a tall man in his seventies called Stan Nicholls. He unlocked the gate, led the group of officers past the pavilion and marched on a hundred yards to the left-hand side of the pier, below which the body was lodged. Talantire leaned over as far as she could on the rusting balustrade. She couldn't see the body, but the screaming flocks of gulls and crows showed where it was. She did notice a corroded ladder attached to the seaward side which descended towards the water.

'Is that ladder safe?' she asked Nicholls.

He shook his head. 'I used to go down it myself, back in the day,' he said. 'But there's no way it would pass health and safety now.'

'All right. Human tissues deteriorate quite rapidly in water, and we do need to confirm whether this is a human corpse or not.'

The noise of gulls was deafening now, the screech and scream bringing forth others, swooping under the decking, now there was reasonable light. A few bold ones balanced on the handrail, speculatively assessing the humans. After all, the fish and chip shops had been closed for a couple of days now. They must be starving.

'I'd like to volunteer to take a look, ma'am,' said the youngest of the PCs, a tall blond lad.

'Well, you can't go down in uniform; you'll be drenched in no time.' She looked down at the decking, some of which was in poor condition. 'Let's get a couple of these planks up, then at least we will be able to see.'

'You'll pay to put it right after, I trust?' Nicholls asked.

Talantire stared at this man, who'd just displayed his priorities. 'Yes, you can send us the bill.'

He nodded and went to fetch tools from a cupboard inside the pavilion. It took two uniforms five minutes with a couple of crowbars to lever up enough of the planking to shine a powerful police torch down. Talantire knelt on the edge of the hole and shone the light down into the water. There, masked by the flight of gulls back and forth, was a body, arms spread, face down, wearing what looked like a wetsuit. Her long, dark, tangled hair writhed in the foam, knotted with weed. A grey seagull was waddling up and down her back, working away with its beak, and fighting off rivals trying to edge onto its property.

A wave swept through, lifting the woman's arm briefly out of the water, where it affected a balletic arc as if she were still alive. 'Jesus Christ,' said Nicholls, backing away. Several of the PCs recoiled at the sight too. It was hard to believe that the woman was still alive, but they still needed to recover the body rapidly, before the gulls caused any more damage. Either way it was going to be a race against time.

Two hours later, Talantire was sitting in the crowded office at the RNLI station using her iPad, and warming herself with a Nescafé made by a volunteer. She had gone out with the boat and its crew in a borrowed wetsuit to take photographs. The body had been recovered from under the pier with some difficulty and slid into a body bag, while gulls swooped down over the boat and noisily contested the loss of their meal. Talantire certainly felt a keener appreciation of Daphne du Maurier's inspiration for *The Birds*.

She recalled the famous scene in Alfred Hitchcock's film of the book where Tippi Hedren fought off dozens of gulls, just as behind the scenes she had fended off the predatory director himself. Talantire's crime scene pictures today would undoubtedly be of keener interest to an ornithologist than to the forensic pathologist, as the birdlife was in much better and closer focus than the body she was there to document. An ambulance was now taking the corpse to Exeter, where the duty Home Office forensic pathologist would examine it tomorrow, or more likely the day after.

Talantire scrolled through the images. The woman was indeed wearing a wetsuit, with booties, but no hood. The tentacle-like hair was in fact very long hair extensions that would have reached her bottom, and which had clumped in the water, revealing the neat knots and beads which secured them. When they had pulled her into the boat, a mass of small crabs had emerged from the hair, and one from her mouth. She carried no ID, and when Talantire had unzipped the suit, she found she was only wearing a vest and a pair of Peacocks briefs. They had no idea who this woman was, but her distinctive hair might be a starting point.

No one was saying much in the RNLI station. The recovery of the body weighed heavily on the normally jovial volunteers. Unspoken questions about who might miss her, and how she came to be here, condensed like a cold mist in the room. She used the opportunity to take elimination DNA samples from the crew.

She checked her watch. Only half an hour left of her night shift. Normally, Richard Lockhart was the overnight duty DI, an onerous shift often covering the entirety of Devon and Cornwall, backing up three overnight detective constables in the region. Lockhart, known as the Prince of Darkness for his preference for working nights, was actually spending Christmas this year with one of his ex-girlfriends and their two children. Talantire had been happy to step in, seeing as her own home was now a de facto house share with fellow officer PC Nadine Lister. She wasn't happy about the situation, but at least now that Talantire had started seeing her boyfriend, Adam, regularly, she had somewhere else to go.

And all that was the fault of Brent West.

She banished the image of her former lover, but knew it would keep coming back, even though it had been seven years since they were together. In fact, he was becoming an obsession.

Admin, briefings and goodbyes took up the rest of her shift until she finally left Teignmouth at ten o'clock, leaving CSI to pick up the pieces. She headed north-west back to Barnstaple, along the eastern edge of Dartmoor. The overcast day had now cleared and the sky was a pale winter blue, etched with slender mauve clouds near the horizon. Using the hands-free, she rang the various officers she had worked with during the course of the night. Nuttall was already busy interrogating Charlie Evans in Exeter about the heating oil thefts, aided by PC Fitch.

She knew Latimer was at home after finishing his shift because she had dropped him off there as she left town. A courier would come to collect the DNA samples which she had left with the Teignmouth community police sergeant. He was also coordinating the missing persons inquiry, along with Moira Hallett of the Devon and Cornwall police press office at Middlemoor.

She'd done her job. All the boxes had been ticked, and she could go home now her shift had ended to take the rest of the day off. First, take the work car back to Barnstaple and drive home in her own Ford. Then a bath would be nice. A long slow soak in some hot bubbly water, something to get the salt out of her hair. She was seeing Adam tonight and that was definitely something to look forward to.

–

'She was already dead,' Molly said, sitting on the edge of the bath and watching Geoff soaking in the suds.

'I suppose she was, but I felt she was calling to me. She couldn't see.' He felt himself welling up again, inexplicably. 'I just wonder where she came from, if she was washed overboard from some boat. If there are people missing her.'

'I'm sure the police have got it all in hand, dear. Missing persons, all that kind of thing. I'll bring you a mug of tea in a moment.' She ruffled his remaining few wisps of damp hair and said, 'You could have killed yourself this morning. It doesn't take much on a freezing cold day in the water, especially at your age. Even Sprocket knew that when she tried to rescue you.'

'I suppose so.'

'You should have been born in the era of knights in armour. All that daring chivalry, for damsels in distress. Even dead ones. But I love you for it,' She caressed him again, kissed him on the top of the head and slipped out of the room.

Geoff lay back in the suds and thought again about that sightless face, the open mouth. Outside he could hear the shrieking of gulls that nested freely on his own roof by the chimney pot. It's one thing helping themselves to chips from holidaymakers, to the odd saveloy. But this was ghastly. Taking her eyes; it was unspeakable.

Chapter Two

Talantire arrived in her own street — the serpentine hillside of white lookalike homes which made up Cornwallis Avenue — and nosed the car up to the garage door on her drive. Then she let herself into the house with a certain amount of trepidation. The place was hot, with the radiators on maximum, but there was no sign of Nadine.

A quick trip upstairs revealed the spare room was still a tip: discarded clothing, shoes, a half-eaten box of chocolates, a plate with the remains of some kind of meat pie on it, glasses, cutlery and her own bottle of Drambuie, now two thirds gone. It had been unopened when Nadine moved in three weeks ago.

She turned down the heating and began to run a bath, but soon realised there was no hot water. In fact, there was still a rim of grubby suds at the tap end. Nadine had got there first. Annoyed now, and still a little chilled from her excursion first thing in the morning, she flicked the water heating back on and resolved to wait the half hour required. Returning downstairs to make herself a coffee, she found on the kitchen worktop a wrapped present the size of a cigarette packet with an extravagant red bow above it. There was a label with a picture of a robin in the snow, and on the other side a message:

> To Jan, Happy Christmas from Nadine, with
> thanks and appreciation for you letting me
> stay.

She unpicked the present to reveal a small jewellery box. She unclipped the lid to reveal a finely wrought silver necklace, hung with a single teardrop-shaped deep-blue gem. The pendant was the size and thickness of a two pence piece and edged in silver. Her jaw hung open. Ever the detective, she googled blue gems, and found it was lapis lazuli, a semi-precious stone found in Afghanistan. This was an expensive gift, no doubt about it. If Nadine had bought it, the cost would have been well over a hundred pounds, judging by what she'd seen online. Nadine was very short of money, so she said. It was a lovely if misguided gesture, a little too intimate surely for a colleague she had only known for a few months. Talantire would have been as happy if Nadine had just cleared up after herself occasionally and left the house tidy. And stopped leaving the heating on day and night.

She immediately texted Nadine to thank her for the gift, and also to try to establish when she was coming back. The crime-scene-like state of her room indicated a hurried departure. Nadine texted back quickly to say that she had been staying with her parents over Christmas, time with the kids and husband Rog. Talantire smelt reconciliation in the tone of the message.

She had been alarmed when Nadine had turned up on her doorstep in December with a nasty black eye, and had felt bounced into giving her refuge, while hoping that she would be able to find an alternative quickly. Maybe, finally, the family rift was healing. Though she was still concerned for Nadine's safety at the hands of a partner who had turned violent, she had her own selfish reasons for not wanting to share her home with someone who was no more than an acquaintance. All they had in common was a former lover, a dangerous, controlling individual who had damaged them both. That was harsh, and she knew it. But their shared bond through the ordeal of making a complaint against him was being corroded by the day-to-day difficulties of living on top of one another.

Talantire decided to follow up the text with a phone call. Nadine answered immediately, against a background of children's voices and the TV.

'Is this a good time, Nadine?'

'Definitely. I can get out of peeling sprouts.' The noise dwindled.

'That was such a lovely present. You really shouldn't have. You've got no money.'

'Well, I had to do something to show my gratitude, Jan. It was my aunt's.'

'Well, thank you anyway. How are you doing?'

'Much better. Rog and I had a heart-to-heart, though to be honest I think he's mainly tired of having to look after the kids himself.'

'Did he apologise for hitting you?'

'Not exactly, but I don't think he'll do it again.'

'Really?'

'I hope so, anyway.'

Talantire had heard similar refrains from domestic violence victims on a thousand occasions. Her own position was clear. If a man hits you once, he can and will do so again, if you give him the chance. Forgiveness is good, but makes it clear to the perpetrator that there was an escape route. He could get away with it. It established grim emotional habits that became ingrained and increasingly difficult to break for both parties. Nadine *must* know this; she was a police officer, for heaven's sake, and half the workload for uniforms was domestic violence. She had been on the same courses Talantire had, and surely more recently. *PC Nadine Lister, hold up a mirror up to your own life.*

'So what's the next stage?' Talantire asked.

'I'm going back to work in the New Year. I've spoken to my boss and to my doctor. I'm going to be more positive. I've signed up for therapy.'

'That's great news!' She meant it. Nadine was based at Camborne Community Police in Cornwall, a good two hours' drive away from Barnstaple, and had been off sick for a couple of months. If she was going back to work, she would have to move back down to Camborne. The domestic nightmare would be over. For Talantire, at least.

'I'll be back on Friday for just one more week, promise,' Nadine said.

Talantire's relief evaporated soon after the call ended. She and Nadine had been thrown together by circumstances, but there was little sign that her cohabitee was pursuing the task they had agreed to do, to take down the senior officer who had ruined their careers. Could she possibly do it alone?

–

As Talantire soaked in her long-awaited bath, and washed the salt from her hair, she realised that so much of her life was still in the shadow of Brent West. Commander West, now of Avon and Somerset Police, was a highly decorated and well-thought-of officer with a sparkling track record of catching criminals and reorganising failing departments within the police. With his chiselled good looks, West cut a dashing figure, but he was also a notorious womaniser with a decade-long string of conquests right across the four counties of south-west England.

Including her.

Levering herself out of the bath and wrapping a towel around herself, Talantire decided to review her complaint against him. Logging on to her computer, she re-read her submitted statement. Could she have worded it any better? It described how seven years ago she had had a brief relationship with him, and after a blissful first few weeks, she began to find him controlling and abusive. Worst of all, while in bed with him at his flat in Exeter, she had discovered a hidden camera in the headboard. She had stormed out, ignoring his insistence that she had never been filmed. Then, a few months ago she heard rumours that West was slated to become the chief constable of Devon and Cornwall. She was utterly appalled that he could even be considered, and concluded that she must make a complaint. 'This man is utterly unsuited to become chief constable of Devon and Cornwall Police,' she had written. And she stood by it.

What she hadn't mentioned was that before she had finally decided to make a complaint, she had heard on the grapevine that another officer had got there first, making a detailed anonymous allegation, also rumoured to be sexual abuse. It was clearly rife.

What was occupying her mind now, almost obsessively, was to try and find out who this person was, and why she had withdrawn her complaint. With the whole HR process being confidential, it had so far proved impossible. She still needed Nadine's help because she had contacts of her own.

She had to call Nadine back.

Talantire rang, but the call went to voicemail. Of course – she was probably sitting down to lunch with relatives. She had worked with Talantire on the Bodmin joyriders case, which was led by West. After the case, Nadine had rung Talantire out of the blue and confided in her that she had recently been in an extramarital affair with West, and during that had been repeatedly raped and abused by him. Nadine too had heard the rumour of West's promotion. She had been too terrified to make a complaint against such a senior officer without evidence, but assumed wrongly that it was Talantire that had made the initial complaint. Sensing her 'Me Too' moment, Talantire had filed a complaint, as did Nadine.

It turned out to be a disaster.

Talantire opened the box file she had kept all her printed documents in and slid out a well-thumbed envelope containing a transcript of a phone conversation; just three typed pages, but a deadly dagger to the heart of her complaint.

When Talantire went for her interview with the 'headshrinkers' – the human resources department at Middlemoor – she was told that the original complainant had withdrawn all allegations, admitting it was made up, and even apologising for having done so. If that wasn't bad enough, HR had been anonymously sent a sound file, a recording of Nadine and Talantire colluding against West, culminating in Nadine being heard to say 'we should work together.'

In the face of such evidence, the external panel of three male officers from Northumbrian Constabulary dismissed the allegations against West, instead putting Talantire and Nadine on a final written warning.

For Talantire, with a hitherto unblemished record, it was the worst moment of her career. She even considered resigning from the Devon and Cornwall force to take a job in the private sector. Nadine, on whose phone spyware was eventually found, turned her anguish inward. Her marriage, already rocky, began to disintegrate when her husband discovered her infidelity.

Now, after four weeks as uncomfortable cohabitees, Nadine would be going home. But Talantire wanted to emphasise to Nadine that it didn't mean the end of the campaign against Brent West. She was determined to bring him to justice and to clear her own name. She had already compiled a dossier of his rumoured ex-girlfriends and spoken to a few. None of them admitted to being the original complainant, or to know who she was. Much more work was required, on the quiet, not using work resources or time. She was still on that final written warning, and had to be very careful. But it made everything much harder.

Finally, Nadine returned her call.

'Hello, Jan. What's up?' She'd clearly been drinking.

'I forgot to ask, what progress have you made tapping your sources to find out who is the original complainant?'

'Jan, I don't want to talk about that now. It's still Christmas. I don't want to get stressed. Let's discuss it in a week, okay?' She hung up.

As Talantire submerged her head and ran her fingers through her dark tresses, she thought again about the woman they had found this morning at sea, with waist-length hair, floating in the water just as she was now. The Medusa, as Geoff Hutchinson had described her. Who was she? Somebody must be missing her. Did she need justice too?

Late that afternoon Geoff Hutchinson took Sprocket out down towards the beach. The wind was down and the sea was calm, though it was still very cold. There were fewer gulls about, but plenty of Boxing Day walkers, all wrapped up. They passed the pier, and the dog stopped to sniff the wind. The police divers had already paddled about in the water looking for clues, and the crime scene tape was now removed. Sprocket led him on their usual route, towards the skate park and the lighthouse, turning inland at the lifeboat station near the end of the promontory, towards the back beach and the wide calm Teign. Being protected from the force of the sea, the inland beach was full of small boats and dinghies drawn up on the narrow strip of sand. He wondered if Medusa, as he now thought of her, had her own small boat. She didn't seem to be a scuba diver, since she lacked a hood, mask or any of the other equipment one would expect to find. It was certainly possible that she was a Christmas holidaymaker and had come in on the train from London. It was all such speculation. The water was too high to allow them to walk on the beach, so he led Sprocket along the Strand and onto Morgan's Quay. There were no fishermen about, not even on the Fish Quay opposite. Sprocket knew this walk well and led him towards the Ferryboat pub, which Geoff was pleased to see was already open.

'I heard you and Sprocket had a bit of a shock this morning, Geoff,' said Bob Hill, whose three-legged rescue collie, Wobble, sat asleep underneath his bar stool. Sprocket looked up at the mention of her name.

'Nearly drowned himself, I heard,' said Harry Vickers. 'So, if as you say she looked like a Medusa, how come you didn't get turned to stone?'

'Those bloody eye sockets almost did petrify me, Harry,' Geoff said. 'Never seen anything like it. The hair, it was amazing; so long, and it seemed to be alive. Like snakes.'

'Were they hair extensions?' asked Liz, the barmaid.

'I don't know. How do you tell?'

'I've got hair extensions,' she said. 'Mine are taped Indian Remy hair.' She lifted up a hank of hair above her ear so that the three men could see the attachments.

'Well, Geoff, you learn something every day,' Harry said, his eyes sliding down the young woman's body. 'We could all do with hair extensions, couldn't we lads?'

'There's nothing on yours to extend, Harry,' said Bob, eyeing his mate's bald pate. 'But you could always get them to lengthen your deficiency downstairs.'

'Cheeky sod,' Harry muttered affably, before calling across to Liz. 'Don't believe everything you hear, love. It's all right as rain down there.'

She froze him with a look. 'I couldn't care less.' She turned on her heel and walked to the far end of the bar, noisily stacking the dishwasher with glasses, rattling the tray and slamming the appliance door shut, before turning to glare at them.

'Leave her alone,' Geoff hissed to Harry. 'You're eighty-one. She's *nineteen*.'

'Yeah, and ripe with it,' he said, cupping imaginary breasts.

'Look in the mirror, Harry,' Bob said. 'You're a bloody dinosaur.'

'Yeah, Tyrannosaurus wrecked, but I've still got the eyes of a young lad, and they go where they want.'

'Maybe the seagulls should have had yours,' Geoff said. 'Not those of that poor woman down at the pier.'

Talantire's original plan had been to see Adam in Tiverton, then spend Boxing Day night there because he was away over New Year seeing his family in the West Midlands. However, with Nadine's unexpected absence, it seemed a great opportunity for Adam to come over to Barnstaple, seeing as they would have the place to themselves. They could have a couple of drinks in town, at the Rising Sun, and then she would cook him a meal. That plan had entailed a deep delve into the freezer, because Nadine had somehow got through lots of her food supplies, including every single one of the frozen pizzas she kept as emergencies for quick meals after late shifts.

Despite the earlier bath, she now felt she needed some exercise, which would entail a shower afterwards. She took a one-hour run, Modge Hill and back, the last half hour of it in the dark, guided by her head torch. She hadn't been back long when Adam himself arrived. He was a good two hours early.

'I'm nowhere near ready,' she wailed as she opened the door to him wearing her running gear. 'I'm not even sure what I'm cooking.'

'I couldn't wait any longer to see you,' he said, embracing her and kissing her neck. They had met online more than a year ago, but it had petered out after a couple of dates when he went briefly back to his ex. They had only got back together again in the last few weeks.

'I'm all sweaty, Adam,' she complained, still enjoying the wetness of his lips and the scratching of his neatly trimmed beard.

'Horses sweat, men perspire and ladies merely glow,' he growled as he wrestled her down onto the sofa. She giggled as he pulled off her top, and kissed him back, passionately. They made love there and then, and the idea of a drink in town was forgotten. It was half past seven before Talantire, finally showered, was really able to consider what they would have to eat.

'Let's just order in a curry,' he suggested.

'Nowhere's open, but I could make a turkey biriyani, plus tarka daal with coconut. That won't take long. I've even got some fresh ginger root and, if it survived, a packet of fresh coriander.'

'Sounds great,' he said, reaching for her again.

'Adam, I can't actually cook it from bed.'

'That's a shame,' he said, releasing her. 'Especially now Nadine is moving out.'

On the way up to the bathroom, Adam risked peering into Nadine's room. 'She's such a slob, isn't she? As bad as some of the blokes I shared rooms with in college.' He closed the door.

'Yep. She seemed to be immune to subtle hints to do some housework, and I have been too busy at work to clear up after her. Except this morning, when I got back after the Medusa lady.'

'I saw the news online,' Adam said. 'Really weird. Do they know who she is?'

'Not yet. If there's nobody at home immediately missing her, it can take days or even weeks. Being discovered over the Christmas holidays, she is unlikely to be missed at work for a while, depending, of course, on what she did, if anything. It's always worth bearing in mind that Christmas is peak suicide time, when families expect to be together.'

'It's really sad,' Adam said.

'They're all sad, Adam; every single unclaimed body is a tragedy.'

'So you don't think it's murder?'

'It's far too early to say. The post-mortem won't be for a couple of days as the main Home Office forensic pathologist is abroad and being covered by the duty pathologist in Bristol. She's got to come down to Exeter, when her own workload permits. And as I've hinted, Christmas is often busy.'

Adam nodded. 'All the lonely people,' he said.

'Not us,' she said, embracing him. 'I'm not back at work until Friday, so let's not think about murder right now.'

Chapter Three

It was pretty calm the next morning when Harry Vickers piloted his Salcombe sixteen-foot launch from Back Beach through the Teign channel and out into the sparkling sea. He didn't go out much these days, his son Jack having taken over the half-dozen creels his grandfather had first used towards Dawlish. They were within the recreational potting licence that still only cost £24 for two years. He fancied a lobster for New Year's Eve if he could get one big enough, but it was an hour-long journey for paltry returns most of the time. Often there were only small crabs, and the odd tiny spiny lobster, which had to be released if it was less than about four inches long. Jack hadn't been out for three days, so there was a better than usual chance for one of the bigger ones.

Harry was dressed for rough weather with his yellow oil skin and waders, over a great big hairy pullover. With the big Atlantic swells at this time of year the weather could change in an instant, and he wasn't fooled by the watery sunshine and lack of wind. He'd been caught out many times before. The 7 hp Honda engine pushed the launch smoothly out, heading north-east, with a very slight Atlantic swell from behind. It was absolutely fantastic to be out here, blowing away the Christmas cobwebs, smelling the salt and the seaweed. He breathed deeply, and took in the encircling horizon and the boat's V-shaped wake. The marker buoy was two miles away, and Harry was surprised not to be able to see it. There was another launch out there, roughly at his destination. Binoculars revealed no activity or sign of life, which indicated that someone was diving to his pots. It had happened before, although not for years. He opened the throttle, a slight anger building in him. He was ready for a confrontation. Especially after last night.

Geoff had had a real go at him about the way he spoke about Liz. Okay, he'd had four pints on an empty stomach, but he didn't see what he'd done wrong. It was just a laugh, a bit of banter. Obviously, he knew that a girl of that age wouldn't be interested in him. Well, you can always hope, but still… Anyway, what's wrong with a bit of flirting with a harmless old widower like him?

Some of the female bar staff had a better sense of humour, that's all. Sue, who was the wrong side of fifty, had threatened to put him over her knee and give him six of the best for his cheeky remarks a week or so ago. That was the way to do it. Give as good as you get. Anyway, as everyone always said of him at the Ferryboat, Harry was just being Harry. For some reason, Geoff always seemed protective of Liz, but even Bob had rounded on him this time. Maybe the extra pint on top of the three was a mistake, and he had said a few things that today he probably regretted.

If someone's been into my lobster pots, there is going to be bloody trouble.

The boat was in better view. It was an Orkney launch, probably a sixteen-footer, and the engine had been lifted. It had been poorly maintained, that was clear. Mildew on the canopy, windows almost crazed with scratches, some damage to the hull. Just plain grubby. Nobody aboard.

As he circled the Salcombe around it, he saw a taut rope, snagged around his own marker buoy. The buoy was lying almost on its side, indicating the rope beneath to the creels was taut. He hauled the pots up and checked inside. One under-sized spiny, and a few crabs, too small to be worth bothering with. He put in fresh bait and lowered them back down.

He then circled the abandoned launch and lashed his own vessel to it. He stepped inside, into a three-inch puddle in the bottom, in which a baseball cap floundered. There was a netting sack of bivalves, a mixture of mussels, whelks and razor clams. Most were empty shells, the others dead and dry, indicating they'd been out of the water for a good while. He saw none of the evidence he would have expected if his creels had been raided. There was a plastic bucket, again full of shells, these being the best and largest and least damaged.

Given that Geoff had been wittering on about this woman whose corpse he found washed ashore, he thought he'd better call in the discovery of an abandoned boat. He searched the vessel closely to see if there were any clues he could find. There was a broken pair of women's sunglasses, the arm snapped off at the hinge. A very long dark hair was trapped in the other hinge. He fished out the soaking wet baseball cap. It was faded and bleached by the sun, but raised embroidered stitching at the back could still be identified: Brixham.

He climbed back into his boat, unclipped the radio and called it into the coastguard.

—

Adam was planning to leave first thing on Wednesday, but Talantire persuaded him to stay. He had his laptop with him and she said they could work side by side at the dining table. No need to go back home to Tiverton yet, she told him. He could manage client websites from her house.

'I thought you were off until this afternoon?' he asked, as she watched her bring down her own laptop from her home office.

'I am. This isn't work-work, its West work.'

'The avenging angel, sweeping in to dispatch Brent West,' he said, with a laugh.

'If only it were that easy. It's quite a puzzle.'

'How so?'

'As I've said, I need to find out which of his police girl-friends made the original complaint against him, which was then withdrawn. The withdrawal was bad enough, but according to the headshrinkers at Middlemoor, that communication, whatever type it was, included an extra allegation, and a particularly damaging one.'

'That you and she had worked together to try to bring him down.'

'Exactly. To me, it sounds like whoever wrote it was under duress, because it's the perfect way to undercut my own complaint.'

'You mean West made her write it?'

'Exactly. Now Fiona Hendricks, the chief head-shrinker, is no fool and must have been convinced that this was genuine. I'm not even allowed to find out if it was an email, a phone call or a handwritten letter. The whole thing is being kept under lock and key to protect the identity of the accuser, just as my own complaint is. Actually, it's not the complete disaster it sounds because when I was in a cubicle in the ladies' toilet, I overheard Hendricks on the phone to the new chief constable, trying to balance up the chances of the allegations against West being false against the possibility that he is still actually a threat to women. So they were quite happy for him to transfer back to Avon and Somerset. It seems like they have tipped them off at Portishead, so they can keep an eye on him.'

'Portishead?'

'Not the band. It's the big expensive seaside HQ of Avon and Somerset Police.'

'So why don't you let it drop? He is out of your hair now. Besides, he would be a powerful enemy, and you're on a final written warning.'

She rounded on him. 'Adam, why do you think I joined the police? What's the point of me investigating dozens of cases of domestic abuse or rape, most of which never get to court, breaking my head against the system to try to put these bastards behind bars, and then turning my back on one of the worst cases lurking within our very own force?'

'I'm sorry, it's just…' When she saw Adam shrink back, she realised her anger was getting the better of her again.

'I know what you're saying, Adam, but Brent West raped Nadine, he filmed me in bed, he took secret photographs and made videos of other women. I've seen some of them on WhatsApp. It's disgraceful. That kind of behaviour in the force is half the reason why we can't retain female officers. It's toxic, it's illegal and it's wrong.'

'Okay, okay, so how are you going to do it?'

'I'm gradually working my way down a list of all the women in the force he's been linked to in the last seven years. There's lots, unfortunately, and it's not just in Devon and Cornwall Police. It's much broader.'

'But when you get to speak to them, you're relying on them telling the truth. Whoever withdrew the complaint may claim never to have made one.'

'That's true, and I'm aware of it. But how else can I clear my own name, without exposing this pack of lies?'

He shrugged.

'Look, here's my list.' She turned her laptop around to reveal a spreadsheet with half a dozen names on it. 'These cells show the date of the relationship, the duration, the level of cooperation and whether any documentary evidence such as an image has been found. I need proof, and that's the toughest part.'

'What's this in the third column?'

'Those are my sources. For example, Ines Hidalgo, the Spanish translator, was mentioned by nobody except Catherine Ives. When West broke up with Catherine, she said she had already seen him with Ines, but no one else mentioned her.'

'And Moira Hallett – isn't she the head of PR? I've heard you refer to her before.'

'Yes, it's a rumour that nobody seems to be able to confirm and I'm not about to challenge Moira directly. I'm pretty confident she wouldn't be the complainant because she consistently backed West to be the new chief constable. Also, she hasn't changed jobs, which is what you would expect if she had made a complaint. But I can't get enough info to remove her from the list either.'

'Sounds like a nest of vipers.'

'It is. Most of the women I've spoken to so far seemed to assume that I was the original complainant.'

'Because you don't take any shit?'

'That's it.'

Adam blew a sigh and cupped his hands behind his head. 'Jan, I really worry about you, doing this. Your job is challenging enough as it is without going in as some gunslinger to bring down one of the toughest guys in the force. It could be really dangerous. If any of these women still have feelings for him and tell him, he'll get to hear about it. And then what?'

'Everything good in life is worth fighting for.' She leaned across to him and caressed his face. 'And Adam, I need your support.'

'But I'm a coward!' he said, laughing.

'I need you to be there for me, that's all. To listen and understand.'

'I'm here for you, Jan,' he said, kissing her. 'I've never met anyone quite like you.'

'Hah, that could be good or bad.'

'It's good, I promise.'

Adam went home early on Wednesday afternoon. They both admitted their attempts to work side by side had failed. They simply couldn't keep their hands off each other. They'd gone back to bed before midday, which was wonderful and exciting, but as Adam said, had done nothing to help him meet his deadlines. He had two separate websites which were supposed to be tested and running live by the first working day of the New Year, and he wouldn't get the chance to do anything once he was at the family home in Warwick.

Talantire felt a little wistful as she watched his car pull away. She certainly felt smitten by this good-looking and apparently uncomplicated man. He seemed genuinely interested in her, and understood the centrality in her of the fight for justice. She needed his solidity, for him to continue to be a good listener. Yet she didn't feel she had a good grasp on what made him tick. Maybe he felt the same about her.

She realised she'd never shown him her vulnerable side. Never talked about her childhood abuse by the babysitter, and only in passing mentioned her identical twin sister, Bella, oxygen-deprived at birth, and stuck in an institution. All that baggage, and so difficult for her to talk about. Perhaps now, just a few weeks back into their relationship, it was too early. There would come a time, though. She was sure of it.

She returned to her laptop and looked at the mysterious list of Brent West's known and suspected relationships, starting with Veronica Vaughan, West's ex-wife. She had been uncooperative when Talantire spoke to her and blamed the breakup of her marriage on what she called 'gold-diggers and whores'. She made it clear that she regarded Talantire as one of them, even though West had claimed already to be separated when he and Talantire had met. Moira Hallett, next on the list, was older than the rest and not supposedly his type physically, but West was quite capable of sleeping with someone in order to get a piece of information or some other favour. Then came Catherine Ives – a former PC, now working at Tesco, who had denied being the complainant – and the mysterious Spanish translator Ines. DC Samantha Mahoney was a recent complainant, according to Nadine, who had met up with her. But Talantire had watched this young and extremely attractive officer who worked closely with West on the Bodmin joyriders case. That was back in the summer. Samantha's body language with him, and her lack of deference, had broadcast quite clearly that they were in a relationship at that time. Nevertheless, while there could have been a nasty breakup since, Talantire didn't quite trust her. Not an inch.

Last on the list was the highest flyer: Detective Chief Superintendent Rebecca Crossfield, now working at the National Crime Agency, focused on drug gangs and organised crime in Merseyside. Talantire had met Rebecca years ago, as they were on the same intake at the Hendon Police College in north London. She was a larger-than-life personality, ferociously intelligent and strong-willed, and had been marked out for promotion very early in her career.

Talantire dug out Rebecca's work email and began to draft her a message. She deleted her first two attempts, realising that mentioning Brent West on a work email wasn't a great idea. If it ever emerged, it would sound like the continuation of her supposed collusion against him.

She needed to confect a subterfuge.

She googled recent big crime cases that the NCA had been dealing with in Merseyside, but there seemed to be nothing in the big-league drug world relevant to her own work in Devon and Cornwall. Drug crime in the southwest was dealt with by a separate department, based in Exeter. However, she had more luck when she looked at the vacancies. There was a DCI-level post within the NCA in Merseyside dealing with human trafficking. Although she had no experience in this field, it at least gave her an excuse for making contact. She typed out a brief email.

Hi Rebecca,

You might recall me from Hendon. I see you're doing great work up in Merseyside. I'm based in Barnstaple, so haven't quite reached your heights. I just wondered if we could have a chat, confidentially, about the human trafficking vacancy. My number is below.

Yours,

Jan Talantire (DI)

It was only an hour later when Crossfield rang her. Talantire's heart was beating fast as she answered the call. She had to do this very carefully.

'Nice to hear from you, Jan, and I remember you well, obviously. You were one of the standout achievers in the class.'

'That's very kind of you.'

'Not at all. I think you're being very modest about your achievements. You've had some very big cases, which I have followed with interest. I'm a little surprised to see that you are interested in the human trafficking position. I'm sure you'd be great, but it is a world away from your bread-and-butter experience. Are you getting jaded, down there in Barnstaple?'

'Well, there have been some issues.'

'The grass is always greener, eh? Well, the money is a lot better than I imagine you're currently on, and you'd have to move to Liverpool. That's no problem, is it? No kids, from what I've heard. No ties.'

Talantire thought of Adam, and then of her final written warning. It was tempting, no two ways about it.

'Look, Jan, why don't you come up and talk to me about it, if you've got a spare day?'

'I've only got tomorrow. I'm back on shift on Friday. Does that work?'

On the last day of her pre-New Year break, Talantire endured an interminably long rail journey, heading through Birmingham towards Liverpool Lime Street station. It started at Barnstaple before seven a.m., and – as is so often the case over the Christmas break – was crowded right from the start. By Bristol, it was packed solid, and it was more than six hours and three changes before she arrived at her destination. But, having treated herself to a first-class seat, she was able to work out en route what new chapter might now open in her life. She had originally contacted Rebecca with a view to unravelling the secret history of Commander Brent West, but it had quickly veered off in another direction. A new career in the NCA was certainly tempting, but she would probably have to apply for promotion to DCI first in order to get it.

She still hadn't mentioned to Rebecca the real reason for her call, but she was undoubtedly going to have to reveal it pretty quickly when they met face to face. It might be a difficult conversation because she was aware that Rebecca was married and had kids. If there was a past, as rumoured, with Brent West, she might be horrified to know that Talantire knew about it. Something like that could be dynamite to her home life. She'd already seen the damage it could do with Nadine.

Brent West was already making news in other directions, as Talantire's latest internet search for his name showed. Just before Christmas, he had cracked a rural diesel and heating oil theft and resale ring in Somerset. Fourteen arrests had been made. The breakthrough had been made in a sting operation, with West's team supplying farmers with tiny amounts of a dozen trace chemicals to add to every farm tank soon after fuel was delivered. One was a dye, which made it immediately obvious the fuel was stolen, but the other traces cleverly indicated whose fuel it was. Each farmer got a different recipe for mixing the chemicals, giving a unique signature. When stolen fuel was offered for resale, undercover police, posing as buyers, were able to test it and link a direct line back to the particular theft using the unique chemical combination.

It was simple, it was brilliant and it was all accomplished within a few weeks of arriving at his new post, as the glowing press release from Avon and Somerset Police made clear.

Talantire read the piece with a mixture of admiration and loathing for West. Inevitably, the Devon and Cornwall police and crime commissioner, the Hon. Lionel Hall-Hartington would be berating her own ad hoc rural crime team of DS Maddy Moran and DC Dave Nuttall for failing to come up with such an effective scheme. They would be under pressure to copy it. Worse than that, he was probably already questioning the chief constable's decision to let West depart for pastures new.

The ironclad truth was that the better a cop Commander West was, the harder it would be to bring him down. She needed several women to come forward to testify that he had abused, assaulted or bullied them. And given that her own testimony and that of Nadine had already been condemned as collusive, she would need entirely new allegations – something firm, ideally photographic or audio, evidence from a range of others – to stand a chance of nailing him. It was a massive ask, and she was far from sure that she could do it.

So far, the only ally she had on this gigantically ambitious enterprise was Nadine: slovenly lazy, unreliable and lacking in resolve. Talantire softened on this list of accusations when she considered how damaged and vulnerable Nadine was. It was easy to forget all that when she faced the unwashed dishes, casually discarded clothing, pilfered booze and other day-to-day difficulties of sharing a home with the woman.

Great news that she was finally leaving.

But the downside might be that if she was putting the past behind her, as she claimed, she might no longer be willing to press ahead on her part of the task they had agreed. Nadine was supposed to be combing her own network of friends for information about West's girlfriends past and present, but had produced little so far. The one connection that Nadine had claimed was an acquaintance with a young woman who worked in human resources in Middlemoor. Lakshmi Damina was very much a junior at the headshrinkers, and Talantire reckoned she probably wouldn't have access to the most confidential files that they needed if they were to discover the name of the original complainant.

Talantire was also far from convinced that Nadine would be able to persuade Lakshmi to even try, given their fairly distant connection. In any case, Nadine had not mentioned anything about Lakshmi since well before Christmas.

The train finally arrived at Lime Street at two p.m. They had arranged to meet at the Philharmonic Dining

Rooms, a grand and historic pub favoured by John Lennon, and when Talantire's Uber dropped her there, she found Rebecca already seated in a snug named The Brahms Room, looking at the pie menu. She was dressed down, in ripped jeans and a battered leather jacket, with her mass of corkscrew copper curls cascading over her shoulders. Talantire was particularly surprised by the number of piercings in her nose and eyebrows. She stood up and embraced Talantire as if they had known each other for years.

'Sorry to put you through such a long trip,' Rebecca said, as Talantire recounted her journey. 'There is a great job at the end of it, and I am sure you will be a shoo-in.'

They ordered food and a glass of wine, with Rebecca keeping a weather eye on the door into the snug.

'Liverpool is actually a much smaller city than you might imagine,' she said by way of explanation. 'My official face is known; this one not so much. All the piercings are easy to remove.'

'Have you had death threats?'

'Lots.' She smiled bleakly. 'One threatened to dissolve my kids in acid and gave their full names and the school they attended. I've had to move them on twice now.'

'Any idea who is behind it?'

'Jason Robbins, possibly. Kyle Mwani, maybe. They're both inside, but that doesn't make it any easier. Kyle seems to be able to post on Instagram every other day even though they've never found a phone on him. He's got thousands of followers.'

'Wasn't he the one live-streaming sex with a female prison officer?'

'That's right. Makes a mockery of the justice system. Even when you can put them away, it doesn't stop them running their crime empires. As for the prison officer, well, she's begun a new career on OnlyFans while awaiting sentence.'

Rebecca was interrupted by a text. She checked her phone, and her expression hardened.

'Something serious?' Talantire asked.

Rebecca blew a sigh. 'It's this bizarre case, which may well turn out to be the perfect murder.'

'Oh? Can you tell me?'

'I shouldn't, of course. But a great detective brain like yours would be fascinated.' She lowered her voice. 'So this is what happened. In August, someone broke into a private pet crematorium and cemetery while the owners were away and used it.'

'On who?'

'That's the point. We'll probably never know.' Rebecca grimaced. 'The clean-up was immaculate.'

'It's horribly clever, if you can do it,' Talantire said. 'But are pet crems big enough to burn people?'

'Yes, this one was. We should have predicted that someone would eventually figure out a way to do it. The couple who owned it were on holiday in the Algarve, and the husband got an alert on his smartphone, which flagged an unusually high gas usage. He rang a neighbour back home and got him to go round. The furnace was still warm.'

'That's terrifying,' Talantire said, trying to keep the shock out of her voice. 'You won't get much forensic detail from the ashes.'

'It's worse than that, Jan. By the time the neighbour had gone round it had been cleaned of all the ashes. There was literally nothing to go on.'

'Was there CCTV?'

'Yes, but it wasn't much help.' She looked at Talantire, as if about to say something, then thought better of it. 'You know, Jan, the worrying thing is that this could become a trend, particularly for gangland erasures. The current craze for dismemberment of gang rivals; you know the kind of thing where the hands turn up in one bin bag with the fingerprints burned off the, head found somewhere else without teeth, and the torso in yet another place. All that would be completely superseded by something much neater. No DNA, no bones, nothing. There would be no proof that anyone had even died. It's the kind of thing the Mafia already does in Italy.'

'That is very scary,' Talantire said, then asked: 'Where did it take place?'

'Rural North Wales. Look, I've already said too much, so not a word to anyone.'

'My lips are sealed,' Talantire said.

'So about this job. I have to say you'd be great for it,' Rebecca continued. 'Just the sort of person that we need who thinks outside the box and pursues leads with an unflagging determination.'

Talantire suddenly realised Rebecca was taking her interest seriously. She had prepared a back route into the story of her own relationship with West, and felt now was the right moment to use it.

'Look, Rebecca. The job is for a DCI and I'm not sure I'd get the promotion.'

'Why ever not? Look at your fantastic track record!'

'I'm on a final written warning.'

Rebecca's jaw dropped. 'How come?'

'I made a complaint against another officer – a senior male – as did another colleague. He's abusive and controlling in relationships, and in my view a sex offender. He raped my colleague.'

Rebecca's jaw was still open, but she leaned closer. Her eyes cut towards the door to make sure no one else could hear what they were saying. Talantire was waiting for Rebecca to guess who this was. If she'd had a toxic relationship with West too, perhaps she might put two and two together.

'Who are we talking about, Jan?' Rebecca had slipped back into her native Liverpudlian lilt. The woman was a chameleon. She looked barely thirty in the getup she was wearing, but Talantire knew she was the wrong side of forty.

'Commander Brent West.'

She stared at Talantire, her face stony. 'So that's why you're here.' The room had gone distinctly cold. 'Nothing to do with promotion.'

'Rebecca—'

'Where did you hear about him and me?'

'I just asked around and your name came up. Multiple sources. Sorry.'

She rolled her eyes. 'Comes of working with bloody detectives I suppose.'

'Rebecca, listen. I don't want to be here, digging into your life. I was stitched up by the headshrinkers at Middlemoor. West somehow managed to get spyware onto my colleague's phone and record her conversations with me, in which she suggested we should work together. Hence the collusion charge, and the dismissal of both of our complaints.'

Rebecca looked away and fiddled with a vape in her pocket. Stress. 'So it's Brent West you really want to talk about?'

'Yes. I hope you don't mind?'

'Well, I mind that you know. I'm not really used to discussing my private life with strangers.'

Talantire trod carefully. 'My understanding, and do correct me if I'm wrong, is that you had a relationship with Brent about five years ago?'

'I'm neither confirming nor denying at this point.'

'Well, I get that completely and I can assure you of complete discretion. I don't know if you are aware that there was an official complaint before mine, which led to him failing in his promotion to become chief constable of Devon and Cornwall.'

'He told me, but I don't know the details.'

This was a bombshell. She and West were *still* in contact. Talantire realised that she had to press on, even at the risk that this could get back to him. 'Brent secretly filmed us having sex during our relationship seven years ago.'

Rebecca was visibly shocked. 'Did you find the footage?'

'No. I saw the lens, and I have since found some stills from the same camera shared on WhatsApp. Fortunately, it wasn't me on this occasion but somebody else. I don't know who.'

'I'm completely appalled, and I have to say, it seems quite unlike the Brent West that I know.'

Talantire knew now, particularly with the use of the present tense, that she wasn't necessarily in sympathetic company. Rebecca was still a friend of West's. Why hadn't she even considered that possibility? Every word now had to be weighed carefully.

'I'm very pleased for you, and relieved that you didn't have such a bad experience,' Talantire said, with as much smoothness as she could manage.

'Well, it had its ups and downs, considering that we were both married. As you say, it was five years ago. We were on secondment to Interpol HQ and living out of suitcases in Lyons. He was quite gallant in fact, wooing me relentlessly, even bringing me home-made sushi as a surprise. He made his own liqueur chocolates too; quite an achievement when we were both living in hotel rooms.'

Talantire feigned being impressed. She'd had West's sushi, but never the chocolates. 'Did you not find him controlling or manipulative?' she asked.

Rebecca laughed. 'I'm sure that if you asked him, he'd say that I was the manipulative one. I worked against him in meetings, which was easy because I'm bilingual in French and picked up the nuances, whereas he was relying on the simultaneous translation which arrived a bit later. I networked more easily than he could. The upshot was that I outmanoeuvred him for the top job, which I really wanted.'

'Did you get it?'

'I did, and he was bitterly disappointed. Which is ironic, because I soon regretted it. I wanted to fight crime, to fight the corruption, to find out how organised crime always seemed to be one step ahead. I didn't want to be a bureaucrat, and that's what my prize job turned out to be. I left after eighteen months. But that's another story.'

'So what about him?' Talantire asked.

'He stayed there a while, mainly I think to pursue other affairs. That's how he operates. I could see right from the start that his attempt to seduce me was political, it is his reflex method of finding out what he wants, seeking out the feminine rung on every ladder he wants to climb. I spotted that almost immediately, but I don't think that he detected that I was outmanoeuvring him, networking and schmoozing the Francophone officials who control everything at the higher reaches of Interpol. I just knew so much more of what was going on than he did.'

Rebecca had out-Wested West, *amazing*. But it was what she said next that shocked Talantire.

'I finished with him when I got the promotion. You see, it came with expenses and a family apartment. When I moved my husband and two young kids over, it wasn't something I wanted to jeopardise through a casual dalliance.'

'But you're still in contact with him?'

'On and off.' The expression playing around her mouth when she said this made it clear that they were still sleeping together from time to time. Talantire was appalled, and angry with herself for just assuming that all women who had experienced Brent West would have come to the same view as she and Nadine had.

'So, just to be clear,' Talantire said. 'It wasn't you that made the initial complaint and then withdrew it?'

Rebecca shook her head. 'And don't bother to ask me who it might have been because I don't know. Brent can be managed, if you're canny enough. He relies on his looks and his charm, plus, well… I'm sure I don't need to tell you he is in a league of his own in one respect, but it's the same every time. You have to out-general him, contest his power, and then he'll respect you. He's a one-trick pony, or perhaps I should say one-prick.' She laughed again. 'He's brilliant and dim at the same time.'

Talantire's heart sank. More than six hours on the train in each direction to face this disappointment, and what now sounded more like relationship advice. She was long past trying to earn West's respect. She drained the last of her wine and put the glass down emphatically on the table.

Rebecca looked contrite. 'He used to talk approvingly about you, you know, Jan. I think he must have been quite upset when you ditched him.'

'He was filming me! And he's certainly filmed other women; I've seen the footage. The only thing I wounded in him when I gave him his marching orders was his pride.'

Crossfield gave her a very shrewd glance. 'But you are wounded too, aren't you?'

'I'm angry, Rebecca; that comes from a very different place. I'm not jealous or envious of who he is with now and don't give a toss about the might-have-beens. I'm angered that my privacy has been ruptured, and thanks to him, every Tom, Dick and Harry on WhatsApp was able to give their opinion of my performance in the bedroom. Having heard the testimony of others, I'm convinced this man is a danger to women.'

'Well, you have to do what you have to do,' Crossfield said.

'Rebecca, it's very clear that you and I have different views about him. I implore you not to tell him about my approach.'

'But you're planning to bring him down, Jan. You want to destroy him. Why shouldn't I warn him?'

'Because I'm asking you, as a woman, and on behalf of other abused women, not to. If you stay quiet, I will also keep to myself what you have told me about your relationship with him.'

Her eyes widened as she took in the implicit threat. 'I had taken that as read, actually.'

'And I took your discretion as read, too.' The two women stared at each other, sussing out each other's chess moves. 'Look, Rebecca, I'm going to tell you something that I was told in the strictest confidence. My colleague, the one who was raped, said she was locked in a freezing shed half-naked for three days, bound and gagged, and West came once a day to feed and abuse her. He made her beg to be released, and she did.'

'I knew he was into bondage and domination, but that's appalling.' Rebecca reached across the table and squeezed Talantire's hand. 'Look, I utterly understand where you're coming from. I shan't mention anything to him, so long as nothing about what I have disclosed to you goes any further.'

'Agreed,' Talantire said.

'You've given me a lot to think about,' Rebecca said, and then smiled. 'Hey, while we're here, you have to come and look at the famous urinals.'

'In the gents?'

'Absolutely.' She stood up looked around, checking the pub was still almost deserted. She led Talantire up to the bar, then round to the right and right again into the gents' toilet, which was empty. On the left was a row of magnificently ornate urinals in marbled caramel and cream, with a gully and brass fittings. 'Aren't they fantastic?' Rebecca said, stepping up onto the tiled plinth, leaning forward over the gully with both hands in front, wielding an imaginary penis.

Talantire's uncontrolled laughter masked the sound of approaching footsteps, and as the door opened, she only just had time to jump up onto the plinth, to stand side by side with Rebecca, as if she too was using the facilities.

A young man peered in, eyes wide, and said, 'Oh, Christ, sorry,' before closing the door again. The two women laughed uproariously, and after a whispered exchange while washing their hands, made their way out. The youngster, perhaps twenty, was dithering in the corridor, and stared at them. Both women mocked zipping up their flies: the look downwards, that slight male bend of the legs and then the raised jaw in time with the exaggerated lift of the right hand.

Rebecca then belched loudly, and said 'Ooh, pardon,' before they marched back to their snug, aware of male eyes upon them.

Chapter Four

Talantire was still chuckling about this experience as she was on the train on the way home. It was gone eight, and first class was much less busy than before. A call from DS Maddy Moran brought her back to the present. She connected her earpiece to make sure Maddy couldn't be overheard.

'There's quite a lot of developments about the Medusa lady, Jan. I thought you'd like to know. Has Wells rung you?'

'No.' Detective Superintendent Michael Wells was Talantire's boss. 'Any idea who she is yet?' Talantire asked softly, checking that she couldn't be overheard by other passengers.

'No. The DNA tests have come back, and she's not on the database; neither are her fingerprints. The post-mortem took place this afternoon at Royal Devon and Exeter Hospital.'

'Okay.'

'Also, an abandoned boat has been found, which might be connected to the case.'

'Where was it?'

'Half a mile offshore, towards Dawlish. Found by a retired lobsterman, tangled up with his creels. It's unregistered, and has no name, but enquiries are being made at all the marinas from Exmouth to Salcombe. It's an anonymous-looking craft, and nobody's come forward to say they've seen it, or worked on it, or anything.'

'I suppose you haven't any photograph that you can publicise.'

'Not unless we used your pics of the corpse, no. However, I've got a team of uniforms ringing round all the hairdressers from Sidmouth to Salcombe to see if they have supplied hair extensions and emailing photographs of them. That's all we can do for now.'

'Were you there for the PM?' Talantire asked. Always a good idea to use jargon if you might be overheard.

'No, but the pathologist was put through to me. She's a very nice woman from Bristol, Dr Hazel Williams. She said that even before she started, she could see there was evidence of poisoning.'

'What?'

'Yes, she said she took one look at the woman's toenails and said she'd need to order additional tests.'

'Toenails! What can you tell from toenails?'

A bald middle-aged man sitting three seats down appeared to be listening. He hadn't turned a page on his newspaper in several minutes.

'Search me. Anyway, the coroner has been contacted and the case referred to CID with a hurry-up on it.'

'Who's handling it?'

'I am, until you get back tomorrow.'

'Shouldn't it be run out of Exeter?'

'Geographically, yes. But Wells has taken it over.' Wells was based in Exeter but responsible for all of the CID investigations in North and West Devon, which were run from Barnstaple, Talantire's home base. He was a good boss, generally happy to let Talantire have her head without micromanaging. However, since the final written warning and the accusations of collusive allegations against West, he had interfered a lot more. It made the allocation of this case to her all the more surprising.

The phone indicated a call waiting from Wells, so after explaining to Maddy, she cut the call and switched to speaking to her boss.

'Just a quick heads-up, Jan,' he said. 'When you come in tomorrow I'd like you to—'

'—take over the Medusa case?'

The bald passenger was definitely listening now.

'Good grief, you're ahead of the game, Jan. Even on a day off. I'm impressed you already know.'

'I've had a long train journey, so I've been able to do some catching up,' she said.

'They are short staffed in Exeter CID because of the holiday period and it seemed a good chance for you to perhaps redeem yourself, to remind the powers that be of the quality of your work. This could be a high-profile case, and if you solve it quickly so much the better.'

'Thank you, sir.'

Wells cut the call. Talantire logged in to the Devon and Cornwall Police remote hub, and looked for messages from Dr Hazel Williams. There was a one-line notification at 7:30 p.m. of the completion of the post-mortem. It also mentioned that the deceased appeared to be about fifty and female. The full report would normally take another thirty-six hours, but Talantire couldn't wait that long. She noted the number on the bottom of the notification, then left her seat and went through the door at the end of the carriage into an empty vestibule. Then she made the call, away from prying ears. She got straight through to Dr Williams.

'I'd just like to introduce myself,' Talantire said. 'I'll be handling the case of the woman found at sea for CID.'

From the background noise it sounded like Williams too was on a train, presumably back to Bristol where she was based.

'Good to speak to you, Jan. I had a brief conversation with your deputy.'

'I heard, yes. Something about toenails.'

'Well, if she hadn't been wearing nail varnish I would have noticed it on her hands too. There is something called a Mees line, more formally leukonychia striata, which are white discolourations in bands across the nails. There are many possible causes, but it can be indicative of episodic and possibly chronic poisoning with heavy metals, principally lead, arsenic, thallium or selenium. There are certain other contaminants which may cause this effect, and we will have to look for the results of the blood tests tomorrow to know more.'

'You say chronic?'

'Yes. As the nail grows it is basically a record of the body's exposure to certain elements. It's true of the hair as well, except hair doesn't retain lead. Normally, you wouldn't expect to see exposure to these metals amongst those living in the UK. Environmental exposure, through paint, metalworking, landfill and so on, are much more common amongst those living in less developed countries where environmental safeguards are weaker.'

'Could this have been deliberate?'

'I cannot exclude that possibility, although as I say, the exposure as shown by the Mees line is indicative of weeks and months, not a single ingested meal for example. Deliberate poisonings are rare these days in the UK. Deliberate heavy metal poisonings are even rarer. Firstly, it is much harder to get hold of toxic substances, and secondly, the forensic detection regime is so much better than it was a hundred years ago when arsenic poisoning, for example, was quite common.'

She was aware that this conversation was following the usual route between investigators and pathologists. Investigators wanted firm and early conclusions to expedite the process of catching a culprit while the forensic pathologist, wary of eventual cross-examination in court, hedged and caveated to an infuriating degree.

The bald passenger had got up and was approaching. 'Hold on a sec.' Talantire muted the call as he opened the door, then she smiled perfunctorily as he moved past her into the toilet.

'There is one other possibility, which might aid your investigation,' Williams said when the call resumed. 'This woman may have had chemotherapy. Mees lines and the similar Beau lines in nails can be caused by some of the chemicals used in cancer treatment. As you know, this woman was wearing hair extensions. Her own hair was in relatively poor condition, and there were patches of alopecia. The fact she had hair extensions might in itself indicate she knew about it. Either way, it could be evidence of either chemotherapy or certain types of heavy metal exposure within the last year or so.'

'Is it possible to have a couple of the hair extensions to show hairdressers?' Talantire asked.

'Certainly. I was forced to remove them in order to cut the skull open to remove the brain. I shaved the head at those points so you can examine the extensions and the hair they were connected to, with the coroner's consent. I'm afraid in a couple of cases the beads came away, but I have bagged them for examination.

'That's great, I'll be over tomorrow.'

'As I say, we will know more tomorrow when the blood tests come back. Unfortunately, my formal report will be delayed until after the New Year because of my backlog; however I will flag up to you immediately any tox test results that may help your investigation.'

'That's brilliantly helpful, thank you,' Talantire said. After ending the call, she then began googling heavy metal exposure in the south-west, and came across one standout culprit:

Mining.

Many of the former tin and copper mines across the region produced heavy metals, particularly arsenic. In the 1870s the demand for arsenic for pesticides even delayed the closure of some mines in Cornwall. A study in 2020 showed potentially dangerous levels of arsenic in the soil in former mine sites along the Tamar Valley. The river flowed through Plymouth only forty miles to the west of where the woman was found. Perhaps that city should be included in the search.

Talantire's final call was to Adam. She was looking forward to hearing his voice. He'd been a bit disappointed that going to Liverpool had forced her to cancel the date they were due to have that evening. She had to admit to herself that she was at that stage where every sigh, every eyebrow inflection mattered. She tapped on his number, and it didn't take long for him to pick up.

'Hi, it's me,' she whispered.

'Hello you. I've missed you.'

'Missed you too.' Talantire realised that they were sounding like soppy teenagers.

'How was Liverpool?' Adam asked.

'Tough, actually. Politics, diplomacy, persuasion. The woman I went to see could be either friend or foe, and I can't tell which. She still sees West.'

'Whoops. I take it that was a surprise?'

'Yeah. I had thought his allies would all be men. Stupid of me. I should have known, or at least allowed for it, having discovered that Moira Hallett was a fan of West. It's a subtle game and I don't have long to learn how to play it perfectly. One screw-up, a single complaint about me to the headshrinkers and I'm toast.'

'So be careful.'

'I have been. I played for sympathy first, listing what West had done, particularly to Nadine. When that didn't work, I tried blackmail, which turns out to be a mutual blackmail.'

'Shit, Jan. This sounds scary.'

'It was the only tactic I had left: the tyranny of secrets. I could destroy her marriage, she could destroy my career. We both recognise the power each has over the other. The weird thing is, I really like her; she's my kind of a woman. In another life I think we'd be friends.'

—

When changing trains in Bristol Talantire took the opportunity to drop in and see her twin sister, Bella. The hospital where she had been living almost since birth was just a short taxi ride away from Bristol Temple Meads, and every yard on the journey twisted Talantire's insides tighter. Going to see Bella more often was a New Year's resolution, a promise to her mother Estelle after years of pretending that her identical sibling did not exist. The institution was small and comfortable, and resembled an upmarket nursing home, except for the unusually large number of staff. As Talantire signed in, she could feel her heart thudding. She was shown into the room where Bella sat on a specially modified chair, her thick masculine hands circling, fingers writhing as if conducting some unseen orchestra.

'Hello, Bella, how are you?'

As always, there was no reply, just a thick rope of saliva that leaked from the corner of her mouth and down her jaw. Wordless sounds emanated from Bella; groans and sighs and squeaks. Talantire was uncomfortable looking directly at Bella's face, a might-have-been mirror; the limpid blue eyes, the same nose, the same lips. It was as if her own features had been grafted on to Bella's bloated body, nestling on the thickened neck with its three chins.

'Let's wipe that up for you, Bella,' said the male nurse, Ahmed, as he knelt next to her and gently dabbed at the saliva. Bella stared sideways at him, and opening her mouth made a sound like radio static, switching her gaze back to her sister. Her arms stopped moving, and she uncurled her left hand as if presenting a flower to her sibling. The hand vibrated, as with some massive effort, Bella reached out up to the necklace, the present from Nadine. Jan reached forward so her sister could feel it. Bella then let go and held her sister's wrist. The hand was warm, hot even. Bella had never touched her before. Not once.

The brief strangulated sound that came next was from the vocabulary of unendurable agony, and Bella's eyes briefly closed to voice it. To Talantire, its only parallel was the cry of pain from a colleague when they had tested the discharge of a Taser during training. Unbearable, and unearthly. Bella's diaphragm pulsated with effort as she tried to focus this undeniable communication into something that might be understood.

'It's all right, don't be alarmed,' Ahmed said. 'She struggles to control her vocal cords.'

Talantire felt briefly ashamed that she was such a rare visitor that the carer had felt compelled to explain, as if she had never been before.

Bella's eyes widened, as if in denial. Talantire suddenly understood. Every single previous time that she had visited, she had projected onto her sister her own fears and guilt: that, but for the grace of God, it could have been her own umbilical cord that was twisted and trapped during birth, and not Bella's. That it could have been she who was deprived of oxygen. *You could have been me and I could have been you.* It was uncomfortable, but at least she knew what it was.

But this was different, something Bella was trying to articulate. The touch, the sisterly heat, communicated not just care, but something more. A warning; perhaps even a prophecy.

She was telling Talantire that her life was in danger.

Fifteen minutes later, a thoroughly spooked Talantire was in a taxi on its way to the railway station. The driver slowed in traffic, as they neared the drop-off point. They stopped at a pelican crossing to allow pedestrians to cross. Something drew her eye to the left and there, standing on the kerb, talking on the phone, was Brent West. He looked like he'd just stepped off the pages of GQ magazine: upright, handsome, with that chiselled jaw and easy smile. A red scarf was casually flicked over his raincoat, dark trousers below, polished black brogues. He crossed in front of her, not seeing her, heading towards the station concourse. Two thirty-something women, friends deep in conversation, going the other way, scanned him up and down, and then turned back to look at him after he passed. It was the Brent West effect. He glanced back at them, and in doing so, spotted Talantire. Their eyes locked for a millisecond, like an electric shock.

Two minutes later, Talantire got out of the cab, and paid the driver. The moment she turned round to face the station, she saw him right in front of her.

'Well, Jan, this is an unexpected pleasure,' he said.

'I've got nothing to say to you,' she said, walking briskly past him.

He kept step with her. 'Frankly, I think it's me who should be offended. You tried to torpedo my career.'

'You've done a good job of destroying mine,' she retorted.

She could see his smile out of the corner of her eye. She glanced up for a moment to look at the platform board, and he asked: 'Where did you get that?' He was looking at her necklace.

'None of your business.'

He smiled. 'Lapis lazuli. It goes beautifully with your eyes. A gift from your new boyfriend, perhaps?'

She didn't reply, so he asked. 'Are you heading to Paddington?'

'Thankfully, no. I'm on my way back to Barnstaple.'

'Well, have a happy New Year,' he said and headed off. As he disappeared into the throng, she stared after him. She vowed she was going to break him. That would be her New Year's resolution.

Once safely on the train, she went into the ladies'. Catching her reflection in the mirror, she looked haunted.

Her big eyes were pale blue in the harsh light, her mouth rigid; jammed with all the retorts she had thought of after he had walked away. The necklace was visible as a delicate silver chain, distinctive, yes, but the gem itself was partially hidden under her blouse.

How on earth could he have identified it?

She immediately knew the answer. *Nadine, you snake!*

Chapter Five

After a troubled night's sleep, Talantire was at work in Barnstaple CID by seven a.m. on Friday morning, raring to go. Just as well, as there was plenty of fresh information overnight on the public information line about the mystery body. She listened to a sample of the latest, received since the overnight case office had finished at four a.m. None had any apparent value. Speculation that the dead woman was an asylum seeker was a common theme – good riddance, some said – along with rambling drunken monologues. Given how little detail there was on the unknown woman, it wasn't surprising that most of the call-ins were a waste of time. They knew she was middle-aged, had dark hair and hair extensions, and may have owned a grubby sixteen-foot launch.

That wasn't much to go on.

The half-dozen uniforms assigned to the case had done a decent job of sifting through the earlier calls. She and Maddy had been copied in on the most useful calls and emails that came in the previous day and evening. Essentially, it boiled down to three women who'd been notified as missing, one of whom had already turned up. Separately, a man from Brixham thought he recognised the boat, and no less than two dozen hair salons had responded positively to the messages about hair extensions.

While she sat there, nursing a coffee she'd bought from home in a flask, she rang the overnight duty officer, PC Tim Caldwell, and after introducing herself asked: 'Do we have any pictures in of the two missing women?'

'Well, ma'am, it's only one missing woman now because another one has turned up. The remaining missing woman is called Sophie Hartnell, from Totnes. She was supposed to be coming down from London on Christmas Eve, by train, but hasn't shown up, and her phone's off.'

'Do we have an age for Ms Hartnell?'

'Thirty-seven.'

'That might be a bit young. Still, salt water is ageing, so they say. Height?'

'I didn't ask; sorry, ma'am.'

'There is some basic post-mortem detail on the case system, and you should look at it. She was measured on the slab at 1.70 metres, which is 5'7". So she's quite tall. If Ms Hartnell is short, it won't be her.'

'I did ask about nail varnish, ma'am.' He sounded young and eager to please. 'Ms Hartnell does wear nail varnish according to her husband, and she does like dark colours: chocolate brown, dark blue and red, of course.'

'Okay, very good, thank you.'

She hung up, then immediately got the call she'd been hoping for. Home Office forensic pathologist Dr Hazel Williams.

'I can confirm that the woman had been exposed to arsenic, lead and cadmium. These were chronic exposures, as I've already indicated, and the variety of metals that showed up indicate it's much more likely to be an environmental source than a one-off ingestion. Complete blood count and the kidney tests were quite in accordance with the Mees line, and I'm sure when I get back the hair tests they will show the same.'

'Were these lethal doses?'

'Probably not, though the cumulative effects would have been definitely very noticeable. This woman could well have been ill for quite a long time. These metals produce a lot of symptoms: headaches, listlessness, kidney and liver damage, behavioural changes, memory loss, anaemia, diarrhoea and vomiting. I'm sure she would have gone to her GP numerous times over the many months she had suffered. Her kidneys, particularly, were in a poor condition. If she lived with anybody, they would certainly have known about this. In fact, unless she was a complete recluse, there is bound to be somebody, a work colleague, a member of the family, who would be well aware of her deteriorating health.'

'That's great, thank you very much.'

'She had a considerable amount of alcohol in her system, too. More than the safe legal limit for driving.'

'So it could be suicide?'

'I don't want to speculate, but yes, it could be.'

—

Maddy arrived while the call was ongoing, and as soon as Talantire was finished, the two officers went downstairs to the kitchenette to make a fresh coffee and catch up.

'How was Liverpool?' Maddy asked.

'I'll tell you later,' she said, aware that this particular facility was used by many of the male uniforms. She didn't want to be overheard. 'How is the Medusa case? I see most of the public information stuff is rubbish.'

'Yes, not surprising. But we finally tracked down the bloke who reckoned he might have worked on that boat.

Duncan Athersmith is his name.' Maddy explained that the Brixham-based engine mechanic had left a message on the public information line on Wednesday afternoon from a landline. Calls back to it had gone unanswered, and there was no message facility. The case officers had misinterpreted his name, and it had taken a visit by a local uniform to a number of Brixham boat maintenance workshops before he was directed to Athersmith's home address.

'So what does he say?' Talantire asked.

'He recalls working on a seven hp Honda engine on a sixteen-foot Orkney launch owned by a woman, a couple of years ago. But he doesn't have her name.'

'Is there no paperwork?'

'He's not a paperwork kind of guy, is how he described himself. He works out of the back of his own van, probably just for cash. He did say if he could see the engine itself, he would know for sure he'd worked on it. The boat was recovered by the coastguard and is in a private dock in Teignmouth.'

'Let's get him there today,' Talantire said.

—

They arrived at Teignmouth at two p.m. to find Athersmith sitting on the bonnet of his van at the quayside, talking to a fresh-faced uniformed PC who turned out to be PC Caldwell. Talantire parked her unmarked Skoda behind the van and she and Maddy made their way over.

'Hi guys,' Athersmith said, giving a thumbs up, as Talantire introduced herself. He was a thick-set, bearded man in his thirties, wearing stained overalls, and had a baseball cap backwards on his head. He looked like he had all the time in the world.

The PC indicated that he had the keys to the private dock. Once Athersmith had picked up his toolbox from the back of the van, they all made their way along the edge of the water and, through a locked metal gate, down a staircase to a small gated dry dock, currently full of seawater. The launch was there, lashed to a capstan. It looked insignificant, and barely seaworthy. Athersmith clambered down and into the vessel, pulled up the outboard motor and undid the screws on the housing.

'Yeah, I recognise this,' he said. 'She brought it in because it wasn't sparking properly, and I did a compression test. It didn't have a rubber start button, and in fact it still doesn't. But this I do recall. It had the old, rounded Honda fuel connectors, and you can't get them anymore. They're all square.'

'So it's definitely the same boat?' Talantire asked.

'Yep, hundred percent.'

'Have you checked through your paperwork to see if there's a customer name?' Maddy asked.

'No, like I said, I haven't got much. I moved to a new workshop a year ago, and the old box of papers never turned up. I don't know what happened to it.'

'What year was it that you did this work?' Talantire asked.

'Probably 2021, based on the spark plugs I used.'

'Can you describe the customer?' Maddy asked.

'A woman, a bit of a hippie maybe.'

'Age?' Talantire asked. 'And what colour hair did she have?'

He shrugged. 'I don't remember stuff like that. If she was a babe I might remember her, so I guess she wasn't.'

Talantire rolled her eyes. She recognised this about some male brains: perfect recall of mechanical relationships, but only the haziest recollection of human ones, unless there was a hint of sex involved.

'Do you recall if she said whether she lived in the town?'

He shrugged again. 'My girlfriend says I'm terrible at customer management.'

'She's not wrong,' Maddy said, with glance at Talantire, 'but thank you anyway for your help. If you remember anything, let us know.'

—

The detectives returned to the car, and Talantire sealed up an elimination sample of DNA from Athersmith.

Now it was time to tackle the hairdressers. Surely they would be better at record-keeping than the mechanic. Given that the boat gave a link to Brixham, it seemed a logical place to start, allowing them to prioritise the huge list of salons who would come back to them about hair extensions. The inquiry team had already notified the hairdressers about in-person visits, so when Talantire and Maddy Moran turned up at Clouds by Danielle in Bolton Street, they were expected. It was the second of the three salons in the town.

The salon was busy, but Danielle Simpson showed them into a quieter back room where there was a table with a selection of hair extensions already laid out. Danielle was in her mid-twenties and seemed very switched on. 'We keep detailed client lists, so we know all of the ladies who have had hair extensions in the last six months since we opened here. Most of them wouldn't be due to come back to have them refitted for some weeks or months.'

Maddy brought out a clear plastic evidence bag in which was one of the dark hair extensions found on the dead woman. 'We emailed you the picture a couple of days ago, but this is one of the actual extensions,' she said. 'Are you able to tell me if it's one of yours?'

Danielle looked closely. 'This is a secret weave, and uses a row of nano beads for the thread, one above and one below, so the beads can't be seen. This would be suitable for somebody whose natural hair couldn't take too much weight. We use beads like that, but there are so many types so I can't be absolutely sure. If I could feel the extension itself, I could tell you whether it's Remy or not. Either way, it's one of the better quality ones.'

'How long would it last?'

'These sewn-in ones last six to eight weeks for someone with fragile hair, two weeks longer otherwise. We think they're better than the glue-on ones and obviously better than the clip-on ones, but your hair needs to be strong enough for the attachment with the threader.'

Danielle opened a hefty appointments book and flicked through. 'I did two dozen dark hair extensions in the three months running up to Christmas, but only six with a secret weave. Let me see.' She jotted down several names and phone numbers and passed across the note to Talantire. 'There you go.'

'Normally we would ring, but in this case I think it would be easier if you did,' Talantire said. 'You can ask your clients if they are ready to schedule an appointment. There's a lot more to explain if I ring, and we don't want to alarm people.'

The two detectives waited while Danielle rang the six numbers. Three of them replied and there was a conversation. She left messages on the others.

'Much appreciated,' Talantire said. 'Perhaps you can pass those names and unanswered numbers to me, and at least we can check the location of the phones.'

By early evening, they felt they were narrowing down their search. The missing woman, Sophie Hartnell, had turned up at Totnes, so they were now solely tracking down hair extension customers. Talantire and Maddy sat in an office at Brixham's small but modern police station on Rea Barn Close with PC Caldwell, who briefed them on visits to two addresses in the town, both of which corresponded to the names of those who hadn't replied to phone messages.

'Deborah Robinson turns out to be a student at Norwich University,' Caldwell said. 'We spoke to her parents, who said she had hair extensions put in before the start of term – to make an entrance, so to speak. She lost her phone in the first week, but now has a new one, so it's no wonder we didn't get a reply. Her mother gave me the new number, and I rang and spoke to the young lady in question, who confirmed the details.'

'What about Mrs Katarina Lezcano?' Talantire asked.

'She certainly has lived at the address we have,' Caldwell said. 'It's a top-floor flat with a view over the harbour, and there was post for her on the vestibule doormat. We couldn't get into her flat, but we understand the place is empty. The whole house has been decorated recently; looks like holiday lets. I spoke to the landlord, a Rodney Weskerton, who said Mrs Lezcano had left before Christmas. I asked her if he had a forwarding address, but he said unfortunately no, because she had left the place like a tip and he'd have liked to have had a word about it.'

'Well, it's a very unusual name, so that will help on the appeal for information,' Talantire said. 'We still don't have a photograph, so I'd like to take a look inside the apartment this afternoon.'

'I'll arrange it directly,' Caldwell said.

The apartment was at the top of a very narrow staircase, which smelled of fresh paint, and in daylight would have been rather beautiful. There were windows front and back, and a fine if distant view of the harbour. The landlord, who lived in Sherborne in Dorset, had arranged for a local keyholder to let them in, and this woman, a Mrs Shaw, acted as if they were about to buy the place, showing them the features.

'Did you know Mrs Lezcano?' Talantire asked.

'Vaguely,' she said. 'She was a bit exotic, some kind of artist; she worked as a part-time cook at the seafood shack.'

'Do you have a forwarding address for her?'

'No, but Felipe, the man that runs the restaurant, probably has.'

'Did she have a car?'

'No idea.'

'Did Mrs Lezcano go fishing, to your knowledge?' Maddy asked. 'If she worked at a seafood restaurant, she might have an interest.'

'No idea. Again, you should speak to Felipe.'

There seemed to be nothing in the apartment, except some new furniture still with the labels on. Talantire had hoped to find some trace of the woman so that she could do a DNA swab. This place looked like it had been thoroughly renovated and all trace of its previous occupant had gone. Even the bathroom, normally a good place to look for DNA, had been given a makeover. A clearly new washbasin and shower unit had been installed with fresh tiling and pristine grouting. Inside a louvred cupboard was a brand-new gas boiler.

However, the common parts of the building were little changed. In the entrance hall was a shelf for post, with a small mirror above and a large doormat, near which three sets of wellingtons, a pair of perished rubber shoes and a set of slippers languished. Opposite the mirror was a sculpture of a boat with a sail made from driftwood, scraps of canvas and seashells, hung within a driftwood frame two feet square and four inches deep. Movements of the sea were cleverly reflected in broken mussel shells glued on to the backing, and which spilled thickly forward, almost tumbling from the frame, as if the sea were escaping from it. Clearly heavy, the sculpture hung from the wall on brass hooks from four screws. The initials KL were painted on the prow of the boat.

'That's one of hers,' Mrs Shaw said. 'Not to my taste.'

Talantire reckoned the hallway and its contents would be rich in hairs, fingerprints and plenty of DNA from all and sundry. She took swabs from inside the footwear, some gel lifts and swabs on the shelf, mirror and artwork, and finally shook the mat into a bin bag. Mrs Shaw looked at her as if she was mad, an expression that changed very little even after she explained what she was doing.

'I'm sure the landlord would be happy for you to do the entire house; it would save him a fortune on cleaners,' she said.

There was one afterthought. 'Tim,' Talantire said, nodding at the sculpture, 'let's take this, if we've got a big enough evidence bag. Her DNA is bound to be on the back.'

The PC went back to the car and returned with a large paper evidence bag. While Talantire held it open, Caldwell grasped the sculpture gingerly in his blue nitrile gloves and manoeuvred it off the wall. Something was dislodged within the artwork, and as he turned it round to look, something fell heavily to the tiles, with a metallic bang. Talantire crouched to look and saw an oily cloth, with two elastic bands around it. She eased off the rubber restraints to reveal a pistol wrapped inside.

'Oh my word,' gasped Mrs Shaw.

'Please don't say anything about this,' Talantire urged her. 'Confidentiality of evidence is important.'

'I won't say a word,' she said, one hand on her chest for emphasis.

Talantire gave her a tight smile as she left, knowing the woman would probably be on the phone to her friends within two minutes of their departure. Back at the car, Talantire and Caldwell scrutinised the back of the sculpture. The gun had fitted neatly into a cavity behind the hull of the boat, secured by a piece of dowl. The pistol was small, finished in black steel, with the manufacturer's name, Beretta, on the grip.

'I don't know anything about guns,' Caldwell said.

'Neither do I,' Talantire said. She carefully took DNA swabs and fingerprint lifts from the weapon, before sealing it in a plastic evidence bag. 'And I can't imagine what it was doing there in a public space in the back of our dead woman's artwork. This is the procedure: I'll send it off to the National Ballistics Intelligence Service in Birmingham. They will test-fire some ammunition and see if it has ever been used in a recorded crime.'

Caldwell's boyish expression reflected his enthusiasm at this exciting turn of events. Talantire dropped the young officer off at the local police station before returning to Barnstaple with the evidence bags, which would be dispatched by courier that evening to the relevant labs.

She knew that a few of the uniforms who worked downstairs from her had a working knowledge of firearms; an unhealthy interest in some cases, but one that might prove useful today. As soon as she arrived, she walked into the uniforms' coffee room, which was the usual masculine mess of discarded cups, crumbs and magazines. The only officer there was Sergeant Ken Venables, one of her least favourite officers, who had racially harassed her colleague Primrose Chen soon after her arrival. Somehow he had escaped with only a warning for his behaviour. Venables looked up from his phone as she walked in.

'Can I help you?' he asked. He should have, by rights, addressed her as ma'am, but never did.

'Actually, yes you can.' She showed him the plastic evidence bag containing the Beretta. 'Word has it you're a bit of a gun enthusiast. What can you tell me about this, without getting it out?'

He leaned forward and held the plastic bag. 'Where did you get this?'

'I hoped you would be answering the questions, Ken, not asking them.'

He rolled his eyes. 'All right. As you can probably already see, it is a Beretta pistol, 9 mm, Italian made, very popular in the US military.' He started googling on his phone and quickly found a website that told more, much of which was of no interest to her. 'If you let me look at it, I can tell you if it's loaded.'

'There's no way I'm going to let you look at it before it gets to forensics. Let's look at the website.'

Venables handed the phone to her, and she saw the figure she wanted: weight.

'Right, thank you for that.' She returned the phone, headed upstairs, then turned left into the CSI office, which was unstaffed. She went to a desk and pulled out a set of digital kitchen scales. She first weighed an empty evidence bag of the same size as that containing the weapon and then weighed the full one. It surprised her. The net weight was two percent below the technical spec for the gun. That was a bit of a mystery, but at least proved to her it was unloaded. Making her own web searches, she was able to identify the safety lock, which was on. Satisfied now, she made her way back into CID, where Maddy was working the phones. Talantire waved the evidence bag in front of the detective sergeant's, face which produced a look of alarm. She ended her call quickly and then asked: 'Where the hell did you get that?'

Talantire told her. Maddy, after all, was on the case, unlike Venables.

'Not in the apartment, then?' Maddy asked.

'Nope. In the vestibule, which by any standards is weird, even though it was concealed in the back of an artwork.'

'So are you assuming it belonged to the dead woman?'

'Not necessarily. It seems to be unloaded, but if she possessed bullets, and was suicidal, why didn't she use the gun?'

'And why didn't she keep it in her apartment?' Maddy asked.

'These are all good questions. So any progress your end?'

'Not much. The seafood shack is closed until New Year, the owner is abroad and I've left a message for him. I've found that the dead woman did own a car, but we don't know where it is. Have you found a phone for her?'

'Not yet, but I think once we do, it will tell us a lot that we don't know. We just need to find out where she moved after vacating the flat. Then I'm sure we will get some answers.'

—

When Talantire got home at nine that evening, feeling hungry and with a clear plan for what she was going to eat, Nadine was already there, sitting watching TV in pyjamas with the central heating on full blast and a glass of wine on the table. They exchanged greetings before Nadine's attention was drawn back to some celebrity programme.

Talantire went into the kitchen, and opened the fridge, looking forward to eating one of the two salmon fillets that she had bought yesterday evening on the way in from the station. But they weren't there, and neither was the asparagus she'd bought to go with them. She looked in the recycling box but didn't see the packaging. Then she looked in the main kitchen bin and saw the wrappers there. Her anger flared, and she only just stopped herself saying something. She counted to ten.

While she could make herself feel better by rowing with Nadine, the woman was about to move out. Just a few more days. Besides, Talantire needed Nadine to help with her campaign against West. That was the priority. *Swallow your anger*, she told herself.

'Have you chased things up with Lakshmi?' Talantire asked casually, as she came back into the lounge. She had to repeat herself over the TV.

'No, I thought I might try in the New Year.'

'I think you have to strike while the iron is hot,' Talantire said.

'Mmm,' Nadine muttered.

Finally losing patience, Talantire grabbed the remote and turned the TV off.

Nadine rounded on her as if shocked. 'What's up with you,' she said, taking a swig of wine – undoubtedly Talantire's.

'Do you remember, Nadine, it was you who first suggested working together against Brent West? I was against it, but thanks to you downloading some malware from him, he got to find out we had been talking, and sent a recording anonymously to the headshrinkers.'

'Yes, I remember,' she said defensively.

'Thanks to that, our complaint against him failed, and now we're both on final written warnings. I'm trying to find out who had made the original complaint, but frankly, I don't think you're pulling your weight.'

'Oh, here we go,' Nadine said, rolling her eyes.

'Let's sit down now and plan what we're going to do over the first week of the New Year to reach the objective we set.'

Nadine steepled her hands over her face in exasperation. 'We can't win, Jan. I'm going back to work next week and I need to leave all this shit behind me. I can't function if I'm carrying all this baggage. I need to look to the future, but you seem to be stuck in the past.'

'The future? Okay, let's just think about the future. If we do nothing, Brent West will carry on abusing women right across the police force. We will have abdicated our responsibilities. I already feel guilty that we haven't been able to stop him.'

'We've done our best.'

'Nadine, your best isn't good enough. Where's the fire in your belly?'

'I'm not as strong as you, Jan. I was raped, remember? My marriage is in tatters and I'm trying hard enough just to hold it together.'

'And that, obviously, is the only reason I've let you stay here, eating all my food, running up my gas bill, leaving your discarded clothing all over the place. I felt sorry for you – anybody would. I've made endless allowances, but honestly, it's too much.'

Even as she said it, she knew she'd gone too far. She was tired, she'd had a long day and she just wanted to be able to relax in her own home.

Nadine was on the verge of tears. 'When I came here, I had a black eye, remember? I thought of this place as a refuge, somewhere I wouldn't be criticised and attacked and made to feel useless and small. Clearly I was wrong. And I gave you my aunt's most precious piece of jewellery, to say thank you and to say sorry. Would you like more? I'm sure I've got some other jewellery.'

'No! I don't want your bloody jewellery,' Talantire retorted, as the wave of guilt swept over her. 'In fact, it's not your aunt's, is it? Brent West gave it to you, didn't he?'

'No, that's not true!'

'You just off-loaded it to me as part of "moving on". Your so-called New Year's resolution.'

'No.'

'I saw him at Bristol Temple Meads station, and he bloody recognised it!'

Nadine steepled her hands over her face. Found out, even as she kept repeating the word, 'no'. She began to cry.

'All right, Nadine,' Talantire said, taking a deep breath. 'You lied to me. But let's put that behind us. I'm setting a few house rules for your last few days. Buy your own food, don't eat mine, don't alter the thermostat settings, don't use up all the hot water just before I get home. And for God's sake please tidy your room.'

'I'm not a child,' she whispered, 'and I only ate the salmon because it was past the sell-by date, and I thought it might be wasted.' And with that final flourish she drained the last of the wine, stormed out of the room and thundered upstairs. The door into her bedroom slammed.

'It was on special offer,' Talantire muttered to herself. 'On the day I bought it, because of the date it was marked down, you stupid woman.'

She went back to the fridge to find out what else she could eat. She settled on the remains of a pasta salad, which was much further past the sell-by date than the salmon had been. It tasted fine, but because her stomach was so knotted with irritation she could only eat a few spoonfuls. There was half a bottle of white wine, actually not one she had bought. She recognised the brand; it was one of those from the bottom shelf at the convenience store. She poured herself a glass and sipped it. Cheap, yes, but not that nasty. She swigged it down in one.

Midnight. DI Richard Lockhart was sitting in the CID office at Barnstaple, playing Tetris on Talantire's computer. After five exhausting days over Christmas with his kids, shuttling between the homes of his ex-wife, ex-partner and current girlfriend, he was more than glad to be back on the night shift. Friday nights were normally busy, and because of the timing of the shift he had attended more knifings, domestic incidents, aggravated burglaries and general violence than most of his colleagues. Tonight, as with most nights, he was the only officer of his seniority on duty for the whole Devon and Cornwall region. The mileage on his unmarked BMW was way higher than Talantire and her team had ratcheted up.

But tonight was deathly quiet.

Not a single call across the region that required his immediate attendance. The lunatics were clearly saving their mayhem for Sunday, New Year's Eve. For uniforms, that was always one of the busiest shifts of the year. He was off that night, having booked it months in advance. Instead, he had chosen the guaranteed quiet night shift the day after, national hangover day, Monday January 1, when he was likely to be able to catch up on paperwork.

He set the Tetris aside after five minutes and logged in to Talantire's caseload. Progress was being made on identifying Medusa Woman, as she was dubbed in the press. Mrs Katarina Lezcano, aged fifty-three. They had an address for her in Brixham, but she no longer lived there. They had located her employer, but the owner of the restaurant where she worked was currently abroad in Portugal. The discovery of chronic heavy metal poisoning was fascinating – and not disclosed to the press – but to Lockhart's experienced eye, the fact that her boat had been discovered, and she had a high level of alcohol in her system signified to him that she had taken her own life. It had been Christmas, after all. Then the discovery of a gun. That intensified the mystery.

The phone rang. It was the overnight operations team on the Medusa case, two officers based in Exeter. He was technically their SIO until Talantire arrived for her

Saturday shift at eight a.m. He was told a that a woman was on the line who claimed to have significant information, but refused to give her name. She had demanded to speak to the head of the inquiry team. Was he happy to take the call?

'Okay, put her through.' He heard the click of connection and then said: 'Hello, I'm Detective Inspector Richard Lockhart. I believe you have information about Mrs Katarina Lezcano?'

'Yes, I am her partner.' The voice was tremulous, and close to tears.

'May I take your name and address?'

'Mary Stuart Davies, non-hyphenated.' She gave an address in Oxford, and had an accent to match those dreaming spires. 'The body you found, is it her?'

'Before I answer that, I need to verify some details. Can you tell me her address?'

'Yes, it's currently care of Hilditch Farm, Newton Abbot. She was in a bloody caravan in a paddock.'

Lockhart saw that it didn't match the address details. 'Was there a previous address?'

'Yes, but the ghastly landlord evicted her. She had a lovely flat, but was turfed out two months before Christmas so this dreadful tyke could turn her home and all the others into Airbnbs.' The woman read out the address in Brixham and it matched the records he had in front of him.

'Thank you for that,' he said. 'I am sorry to have to tell you that although there is no forensic confirmation as yet, it does seem likely that it is her.'

Her voice gave a little catch, and a gasp. 'That is so cruel, so horrible,' she sobbed.

He waited for the tears to stop, gave her his gentlest condolences, then said, 'So you didn't live together?'

'Well, therein lies a tale.' She gave a bitter chuckle. 'We were going to. I was planning to retire down to the West Country and we were going to put our savings together to buy a place, well, mine mainly. She didn't have much. Anyway, we had arguments. She had some mental health issues, and they had become worse in the last year. She had become a little paranoid, and I have to confess I had second thoughts. We had a row, and I decided not to come down at Christmas. She was bitterly disappointed.'

Lockhart could feel the guilt oozing from the woman's voice. He could also tell she'd been drinking, probably quite heavily, her voice slurred, and she paused occasionally to sip something. It was a fact of life, taking calls from the public at this time of night.

'Did she own a boat?'

'Yes, a tiny grubby thing, and I wouldn't go on it.'

'Are you aware that a boat was found, snagged on some lobster pots?'

'Yes, I had read that.'

'We would like to formally interview you, Ms Davies.'

'*Miss* Stuart Davies. I'm a Miss, not a Ms and definitely not a Mrs. Or you can just call me Mary; everybody does.'

'I've made a note, Mary. Did she have any family?'

'Just a son, Alex. A lovely young man, but he fell out with her some time ago, and they stopped talking. It was agonising, actually; it put Katarina in a deep depression because they had been very close. She tried everything, but he went off travelling in September and hasn't been in contact with her for months. But he'll be gutted when he discovers this.' Prompted by Lockhart, she read across the son's contact details. 'About this interview, I want to come down to Brixham anyway. Can I come tomorrow?'

'Yes, I'll notify DI Talantire, who is in overall charge of the case.'

'Why the detectives? Isn't it just an ordinary police inquiry?'

'It might turn out to be that way, but there are some question marks over the case that I'm not at liberty to disclose.' He wasn't going to tell her about the poisoning or the gun. He'd pass on that particular chalice – poisoned or not – to Talantire.

When Talantire arrived the next morning, she almost ran into Dave Nuttall. She had opened the double doors into CID while he was on his way back from the gents, staring at his phone. 'Morning, boss,' he said. 'Bloody hell! I don't believe this. I've got to see this on a bigger screen.' He hurried across to his chair and logged into one of the large-screen PCs used for CCTV.

Talantire followed, sensing that there was something dramatic going on.

'I've just been sent this by a mate in North Wales Police,' Nuttall said, pulling up a video on to the screen. 'This is CCTV from a pet crematorium on the night of a break-in.'

'I'd heard about this,' she said, remembering her conversation with DCS Rebecca Crossfield. 'But I haven't seen the footage.'

'This is going to blow your mind.' He hit play. She watched over his shoulder as on the screen, the beams of headlights broke into an otherwise black background from the right-hand side. In the beams they could see a wooden gate which closed off a driveway to the left, and a low building on the far left. The background showed an area of extensive woodland. The camera was from a high vantage point, and as the light intensified it showed the front of a Ford Transit, its number plate masked, nosing up to the gate. This then triggered a proximity light which bathed the entire driveway and the woodland behind in light. After a few seconds a figure emerged dressed in a hooded head-to-toe coverall, and wearing a dark baseball cap under the hood. Clearly male from his build and gait, he had in his gloved hands an angle grinder which made short work of the padlock on the gate. The van was then reversed through, and the image switched to another camera. The transit was reversed up to a set of double doors of the low building beyond, lit by a proximity light. The same individual opened the rear doors of the van.

'You can't see this, but behind the van he's working on the locks of the crematorium,' Nuttall said. 'Now watch this.'

Talantire looked closely at the man as he lifted out something very heavy from the Transit. It was a bulky army-style kitbag, which he lowered to the ground while he closed the van doors.

'It's moving!' Talantire said, and placed a hand over her mouth.

'That's right,' Nuttall replied. 'I couldn't see it properly on the phone screen.' He zoomed in further on the bag and ran last the few seconds of footage again. The kitbag was writhing and wriggling. The man kicked it, hard, then bent over and appeared to speak to it. The bag stopped moving, and he hefted it with difficulty onto his shoulder and made his way into the building opposite.

'The poor bastard in the bag is about to be burned alive,' Nuttall said.

'It's horrifying. No wonder the NCA kept it secret,' Talantire said.

'Far too shocking to reveal. There's more footage of him coming back the next morning to clear up. He even has an industrial vacuum cleaner with him. The last thing you see is him wiping down the gates, the locks, the doors, the handles, you name it. The crime scene was so tidy you could eat your dinner off it.'

'That's taking forensic awareness to new heights,' she said.

'There is a huge National Crime Agency investigatory team on this, and my mate is part of it.'

She hadn't mentioned to Nuttall that she had visited Rebecca Crossfield in Liverpool, so let him continue to bring her up to speed.

'But he told me they're just going through the motions,' Nuttall said, 'Because there's absolutely nothing to go on. It is a diffuse mass of small rural roads leading up to the crem; no ANPR for miles. No phone mast pings that match the expected movement of the vehicle, and of course no DNA or prints.'

'It's the perfect crime,' Talantire said.

'Glad it's not on our patch,' Nuttall declared, shaking his head.

'Definitely,' she said. She could now fully understand Rebecca's concerns about the changing nature of drug turf wars. These people were terrifying enough as it was, but now they could genuinely threaten to erase somebody. To rub them out entirely, as if they had never existed. She didn't envy Rebecca her high-profile role at the NCA, with the threats that it brought. A married woman with kids trying to protect her family from these kinds of people. The job in Liverpool had a deadline in the middle of January. She'd have to have a real think about it, but right now she wasn't keen. Besides, she still had scores to settle here. She couldn't go and leave that unfinished.

—

Mary Stuart Davies looked completely out of place in Brixham police station's only interview room. She appeared to be in her late sixties, had short neat dyed blonde hair, and long dangly earrings. She was wearing a glorious hand-knitted rainbow cardigan, green woollen tights and flat Mary Jane T-bar sandals. Her intelligent green eyes roamed the battleship-grey décor.

'I suppose it's the sheer stultifying dullness of these places that makes criminals confess,' she declared, as she took a seat opposite Talantire.

'It would have to be even more boring for that to be true,' Talantire responded. 'Most of the people that I bring in here are pigheadedly determined to deny even that which is blindingly obvious.'

'I can assure you that I will not be one of those.'

Talantire set up the tape, and was at pains to ensure the correct name and title as per Lockhart's underlined notes. She would call her Mary.

'Uniformed officers this morning visited Mrs Lezcano's caravan at Hilditch farm and have taken some DNA samples which may confirm the identity of the body we found.'

Mary nodded, her face grave. 'I really can't believe it, and I feel terrible for not being there for her.'

'Perhaps you can tell me how you got to know her?'

'Well, I came down to Brixham with friends and went into a gallery where some of her work was exhibited.'

'What kind of work?'

'Paintings, though in some ways these were more like sculptures. They had thick impasto, oil pigment embedded with seashells and found objects from her beachcombing. They were quite gloriously colourful and passionate, as indeed was she.'

'When was that?'

'The third of May, 2019. I fell in love with the work and then I fell in love with the artist.' Tears were now running freely down the woman's face and she made no attempt to wipe them, even though Talantire slid a box of tissues across the table to her. 'I bought four paintings on the first day, then commissioned some directly from her to save on the gallery fee. We had lunch at the seafood shack where she worked part time and then spent the rest of the day in bed in her apartment.'

It was a fuller and a more precise answer than Talantire had requested, but she felt it prudent to let the woman continue her tale. In police work there is no such thing as too much information, so long as it was accurate.

'Our love affair flowered quickly, but was unfortunately sporadic because I still had commitments at Balliol during term time, and some podcasts that required me to be in London at least two days a week. I miss her terribly.' At this she finally did grab a tissue.

'What do you teach?'

'History. Mediaeval history, history of art. The podcasts are about renaissance sculpture, part of a series commissioned for the Australian Broadcasting Corporation. I've got an oenophile sideline, too.'

'Wine?'

'Yes, I write a column for a couple of magazines.'

Talantire made some notes. 'How often did you get to see her?'

'Christmas, Easter and the summer holidays always, except during lockdown. The odd weekend here and there. I urged her to come and spend time with me in Oxford, but she wasn't happy being away from the sea for long. Her connection to water is quite intrinsic to her, as an Aquarian.'

'When did you last see her?'

'We had a weekend together in North Devon in the middle of October.' She brought out a hardback diary and gave Talantire the dates. 'We Zoomed twice a week and spoke on the phone most days. I rang her on Christmas Eve, at around seven p.m. That was the last time we spoke.'

'I gather from your previous statement you said you had planned to spend Christmas together but changed your mind?'

Mary Stuart Davies nodded and wiped her eyes. 'We'd had a big and quite uncharacteristic row on the phone the previous week, and I told her I wouldn't be coming and slammed the phone down.'

'What was the argument about?'

'She claimed that I didn't love her, that I only loved her work and was trying to make money out of it. These were very hurtful allegations. It is true that I did sell one small piece of hers to a friend of mine, but as I told her, only for the same price that I paid for it, which was of course to my mind far less than I felt it was worth. But to her it felt like a betrayal, even though it wasn't actually a gift from her to me.'

'So just to be clear, you weren't there at Christmas?'

'No.'

'Where were you?' Talantire stopped writing and looked her in the eyes.

'Golly, you've just asked me for my alibi!'

'These are routine questions, Mary. Don't be alarmed by them.'

'Well, I am a little alarmed. I spent Christmas with my sister and her husband in Suffolk. I can give you all the details if you want to check.'

'Yes please.'

After she'd given the address, she leaned forward. 'If you want to know what killed her, detective inspector, it was being evicted by that malign landlord from the flat she had lived in for three decades. It was a place she loved and which had such magnificent views over the harbour. She'd had a lovely studio there, space to work on her sculptures too, and even access to the flat roof, with space for an easel. Katarina had no money to pay the scandalous rent increase she was presented with in April, so she and the other tenants downstairs were evicted so that the landlord could finish having the place tarted up and rented out to holidaymakers. Katarina was there all year round, not just in the summer,' Mary said, tapping the table with her finger. 'She was a local through and through.'

Talantire was indeed intending to interview the landlord, but she had other questions to ask Mary that were more urgent.

'You mentioned that Mrs Lezcano was unwell. Was she aware of her illness and her changed mental state?'

'Yes, of course. She had terrible headaches and would sometimes just vomit for no reason. She was anaemic and had kidney problems, combined with the terrible lassitude which sometimes meant she went to bed for days at a time. But she also had surges of enormous energy, working on one particular sculpture all night, sometimes. Sadly, it was never finished.'

After thinking long and hard about whether to disclose it, Talantire said: 'Toxicology tests have shown that your partner had chronic exposure to arsenic, lead and other heavy metals.'

'Oh my goodness!' She steepled her hands over her face, eyes wide, then said: 'Well, that would explain everything, wouldn't it?'

'It might well. Did she know?'

'I don't think so. She never mentioned it to me. She'd been to the doctor's a couple of times, but she preferred to follow her own alternative medicines. That's another thing we rowed about.'

'We traced her through the hairdresser she used to get hair extensions,' Talantire said. 'The pathologist noted that she seemed to have weak and patchy hair. Had she had chemotherapy at all?'

'No. She was aware that her hair lacked the vigour and bounce it used to have. I paid for the hair extensions; they were a gift from me.'

'You mentioned she didn't have much money. Was she in debt at all?'

'She never mentioned debts to me. She was quite frugal. She earned very little, but her outgoings were pretty low too, until the eviction. She was horrified, I knew that, when she looked around to try to find somewhere else to rent in Brixham. There was absolutely nothing at the rent she had been paying. Most of the places weekly rent was more than she'd been paying for a month. They're all going to people from London, who only come down for a few weekends a year. It's wrong.'

Mary paused, as if considering something. 'I wonder if she was poisoned by the seafood at the shack.'

'It's something we will look into. Historically, there's a lot of heavy metal in the soil in Devon and Cornwall too, in areas where there have been mine workings.'

'But she didn't grow up here. She's originally from a rather grand Italian *familia*, but spent her childhood in Buenos Aires with her mother, who fled an overbearing patriarchy. Then in her twenties, she herself met a British artist, Royston Brown, who brought her to live in Britain. That was in the early 1990s. When Alex was born. She went back to her own name when they divorced in the early noughties.'

'Do you know where he lives?'

'In Eastbourne, I believe. He's in his eighties now, but still working.'

'There's one final thing I want to ask you, Mary. Were you familiar with her sculpture in the vestibule of her previous apartment? A driftwood boat with seashells?'

'Yes, a rather splendid piece. She was going to take it when she moved, but one of the other tenants bought it, for the ridiculously cheap sum of twenty pounds.'

'Do you have the name of the tenant?'

'No.'

'Were you aware that the artwork contained a gun?'

The woman's jaw hung open. 'You mean a weapon, actually inside it?'

'A Beretta pistol.'

'Well, it wouldn't have been hers.'

'So you never saw the weapon in her flat or heard her mention it?'

'No. Never. If it was in the common parts of the building, it must belong to somebody else.'

Talantire thanked her for the information. The Prince of Darkness had been right when he'd said in his notes that he felt it was a suicide, notwithstanding the mystery of the gun. Mary Stuart Davies's account rang true, and she was clearly upset. There didn't seem to be any financial motive for anyone to kill Mrs Lezcano. Probably not even for the landlord, who had succeeded in getting her out of the flat. The financial report on the woman's bank accounts was due over the weekend, but might well be delayed given how thinly bank security departments would be staffed over the New Year holiday.

'So Mary, a few formalities. As you identified yourself as Ms Lezcano's partner, do you regard yourself as next of kin?'

'Well, apart from Alex, who is actually a blood relative.'

'In his absence, we need someone to formally identify her body, which is in the mortuary at the Royal Devon Hospital in Exeter. Would you be prepared to do that?'

'Yes, I would.'

'I'll give you a lift and will be there with you. Just to warn you, it's not a pretty sight.'

'Well, naturally. She'd been in the sea.'

'Yes, for over twenty-four hours, but worse than that. The post-mortem has already taken place, so there will be an incision visible across her skull, and some of her hair will be missing. I'm afraid the seabirds had taken her eyes too.'

She grimaced and then sobbed. 'That's horrible,' she said.

'It only needs to be a quick glimpse; it is simply a formality needed by the coroner,' Talantire said, with a sympathetic smile.

They arrived at the mortuary office where they were greeted by a lugubrious male technician, so pale and slender he looked to have just emerged from his own fridge. Mary paced about nervously while the paperwork was prepared. The smell of antiseptic and other miscellaneous cleaning products never quite masked the chilled meat taint. The technician led them through to a sizeable chamber, lined with steel-doored cabinets and a series of metal examination tables. The body had already been pulled out onto a gurney, under a white sheet. A cardboard disposable vomit bowl was already in place on a small wheeled table. Mary was already shaking, audibly swallowing, wringing her hands. Talantire reached out to hold her hand, which was clammy, and nodded to the technician to lower the sheet.

A brief glimpse can still be a horror remembered for a lifetime: the partly shaved head where the circular saw incision was looked like the outline of a pair of headphones across her skull, despite the bone segment having been replaced. Worst of all were the empty eye sockets, black with dried blood, peck marks around the mouth.

Mary turned away, gripping Talantire by both arms, and heaved. Talantire prayed the woman wasn't about to be sick on her. The unearthly sounds were a bad omen, so she steered Mary away, and grabbed the cardboard bowl. She was only just in time.

Talantire spent ten minutes waiting outside the staff toilet, waiting for Mary to emerge. She kept back the crucial question until the woman was fully recovered, but never got the chance to ask it.

'I couldn't even tell if it was her,' Mary said, still wiping tears from her eyes. 'She was so... mutilated.'

'I'm so sorry we had to put you through this, Mary,' she said. She took the woman for a coffee in the hospital refectory and, only when she was fully composed, arranged for a taxi to take her back to the station for her return to Oxford.

No sooner had Mary Stuart Davies departed than Talantire got a call from PC Caldwell, who was at Hilditch farm.

'Ma'am, I think you'd better come and see what we found over here,' he said. 'It's amazing.'

Chapter Six

Hilditch Farm was wedged into a muddy valley just north of the Teign. A cramped dairy place, scattered with rusting farm equipment, plus a surprisingly large number of Post Office vans from the 1960s. A thick mist hung over the place, and the stench of cow muck was overwhelming. The farmer, Tony Conybeare, was straight out of central casting with an accent as thick as clotted cream and a ruddy, weatherbeaten face that mapped his eighty-five years. Talantire was pleased she had brought her wellies because wading down the track to the caravan meant negotiating ankle-deep slurry, which in the rain had leaked from a steaming pile the size of a double-decker bus behind a hedge on the land above them. PC Caldwell, in boots borrowed from the farmer, trudged behind miserably.

'Kat knew my wife through the seafood shack business. When she heard that she was desperate for somewhere to stay because she was being evicted, we offered her the caravan,' Conybeare said. 'Fortunately, we also had some sheds where she could store her artwork.'

The caravan was a reasonable size, mildewed in green, except where the windows had been scrubbed. It was wedged into the corner of a paddock, adjoining three sheds and a heap of rusting harrows. It did have a rather lovely view across meadows down to the distant sea, a few miles away. Talantire wiped her gumboots on the thick nettles which grew around and under the caravan and ascended the steps.

She pulled open the door, sat on the doormat to remove her wellies, then put forensic booties over her socks. Talantire turned to look at the dark and dingy place where Katarina had spent the last few weeks of her life. There was a sagging settee, a fold-down bed and a folding table. Each of them was covered with brightly coloured ethnic throws, but did little to disguise the fold-down and fold-away life the poor woman had descended into. After the airy flat in Brixham, this would have been spirit crushing, particularly for a woman who was already of delicate mental health, and quite ill. Add in an argument with her lover and difficulties with her son, and it seemed quite easy to see why she might have wanted to take her own life.

'It's in the shed, ma'am, what I want to show you,' Caldwell said, with boyish impatience.

Talantire switched back to her wellies, and was shown to one of the sheds, which was unlatched. She opened the door and flicked on the light.

The room was dominated by an extraordinary life-sized sculpture, seemingly made from tens of thousands of mussel shells, which depicted a woman on her knees, leaning back with hands around her own throat as if she were being strangled by an invisible assailant. The quality of the work was extraordinary, and the woman's haunting eyes, made from a lighter type of seashell, had rolled back in her skull. The balance and poise of the piece was amazing, she really seemed alive. The rest of the shed was full of paintings, mostly unframed, bearing the same thick impasto colours that Mary Stuart Davies had described.

At the far end were boxes, electrical and woodworking tools, and much artistic paraphernalia.

'You think she knew she was being poisoned, ma'am?' PC Caldwell asked, pointing at the piece. 'Felt it was strangling her, like?'

'This could mean so many things,' Talantire responded. 'It could be a response to her own illness, it could be attempting to describe her personal relationships, it could be describing the position of women in history or in the present day.'

'A feminist piece, then?'

Talantire nodded. 'Quite possibly.' Maybe she too had run into someone like Brent West.

—

Talantire had planned an afternoon incident meeting at Brixham police station, but just as she was starting to organise it, Detective Superintendent Wells messaged her. Her boss assumed she was winding down the investigation, now that the woman had been identified, and suggested it could run with one officer manning the phones in Exeter plus PC Caldwell on the ground in Brixham. To her, it seemed a bit premature, and she rang him up to contest the decision. After all, what about the gun? He hadn't heard about it, but still remained sceptical, even when she told him.

'I'm sorry, Jan. There is no evidence the firearm has been used, is there?'

'Not as yet—'

'—This isn't really a job for you any more, it's well below your pay grade.'

'There is also the issue of the heavy metal poisoning.'

'I know, but that's likely to be accidental, isn't it?'

'Probably, but—'

'Okay, well get DS Moran to wind up the loose ends ASAP. I've got a request from the NCA in Merseyside about tracing a stolen vehicle which originated in this neck of the woods. They specifically asked if you could help, as apparently you know the background to the case. Something to do with a crematorium.'

'All right,' Talantire said. She felt a frisson of excitement. Rebecca Crossfield must have asked for her. 'I'll tie things up here on the Lezcano case by the end of the day.'

Katarina's car was one of those loose ends. It was already dark by the time she got to see it. The aged VW Golf was found illegally parked on King Street by the harbour, where it had already attracted a parking ticket. Talantire went along with PC Tim Caldwell, who had tracked the vehicle down through DVLA records. Even though the case looked like it was going to be winding down to an accidental death report, Talantire still insisted on taking fingerprints and DNA samples from the door handles and boot lock.

'Why are you bothering, ma'am?' the young officer asked, as he watched her working away with her forensic kit and gel lifts.

'Think of it as detective insurance: we both believe there wasn't any foul play, but if we later discover there was, and the car is already towed away by some Herbert in a truck, dumped at a garage awaiting next of kin, touched by all and sundry, it will be much harder forensically to work out who was in it when it was parked here. Five minutes spent now might save hours of hard forensic work later on. That is particularly true of any traces that we get on the inside.'

Caldwell nodded. 'I hadn't thought of it that way.'

With her gloved hand, she tried the handle. 'Ah, unlocked. Interesting.' She leaned inside and found the car keys in the glove compartment, along with a mobile phone and a postcard, plus paperwork for the car. She kept an eye open for bullets, too, ones that would have fitted the Beretta. There was no sign of any.

'An unlocked car. What does that say to you, Tim?'

The young PC scratched his head. 'That she was in a hurry and forgot?'

'Possibly, but what would the hurry be? My best guess is that the car was left here on Christmas Day some time while she went down onto the quay to her launch. Now anyone who was planning to return to the car and use it again would have locked it, wouldn't they? And they'd take the phone.'

'I guess so.'

'But if you are planning to take your own life, what would be the point?'

'I see what you mean.'

'Now if you go into that shop opposite and check their CCTV, you might be able to find out what time the car arrived here.'

'Yes, ma'am.'

She looked at the postcard. It was stamped and postmarked from Morocco in October, starting with 'Dear Mum', followed by a cheery scrawled message and signed 'love Alex'. She dropped it into a paper evidence bag.

'Tim. Have you ever dealt with a death before?'

'No, but we covered it on the course last year.'

'Right. Just remember that unless we can show foul play, you'll be working principally for the coroner now, not me. She'll want a precise timeline of the deceased's movements. There will be an inquest and you may well meet this young man, the deceased's son.' She waved the evidence bag with the postcard at him. 'It's your job to track him down and let him know the news as gently as possible. Don't mention the gun to him, or the poisoning. At least not for now.'

'Okay.'

'There may be a coroner's liaison officer available to assist you in conversations with the family.'

'Right. The coroner will want to know about the poisoning and the gun though, won't she?'

'Absolutely. The post-mortem paperwork will go to her directly, but keep in close touch with DS Moran, who will be marking your homework until it's done.'

Talantire bagged up the phone for Primrose to take a look at and left the young constable to sort out the rest of the scene.

—

Talantire was back at Barnstaple by seven and was relieved to see that Primrose Chen was still at her desk. The digital evidence officer, who could equally have been called the diligent evidence officer, was at the Aceso Kiosk, a desktop device which was able to rapidly strip the information out of mobile phones. Up until a few years ago, getting a look into a locked mobile phone would have required days and weeks of work with the service provider, something that would inevitably be slow over the Christmas holidays.

'What are you working on there, Primrose?' Talantire asked.

'It's a case for the child protection team.' She gave a grimace. 'Some horrible images.'

'If you fancy a break, do you want to look at this one? Technically it's not urgent because it's probably a suicide, but I'd like to get it wrapped up tonight.'

'No problem,' Primrose said. She removed the current device from the machine and picked up the evidence bag that Talantire offered her. Rapidly extracting the SIM card from the casing of the device, she pressed it into the slot of the kiosk, worked the controls for a couple of minutes and then came up with a list of images and videos.

'Shall I put these on a data stick for you?' she asked.

Talantire nodded and watched as Primrose ran all the files through virus-checking software before uploading them onto a USB stick. Talantire thanked her and took the stick over to her own machine, where she started on the images, most recent first. Christmas Eve, a stark self-portrait, full of sadness. Katarina Lezcano in the caravan, her face lit by flash. An imperious, exotic and handsome face, deep dark eyes and a strong nose above expressive lips. The luxuriant hair, attachments in place, was there in its full glory. It was easy to project onto this face what Talantire knew would happen in the next day or so. There were other similar pictures, and as she delved back into the hundreds on the phone, she found selfies taken with Mary Stuart Davies, and older still, ones with her son, who looked to be around about thirty.

Then she turned to the videos. The most recent was just a few minutes before the final selfie, again taken in the gloom of the caravan.

> 'I'm going to go out fishing now. It seems the best way to spend a lonely Christmas, with the sea, my one true friend. She may sweep out but at least she always comes back in again.'

Something of a poetic suicide note, Talantire thought. The previous one, made while walking in woods, was more closely targeted.

> 'Alex, I cannot believe that our relationship has deteriorated so much. The blunt, horrible, rude things you have said to me. I just cannot believe that you are saying this to me, your mother. Every year you used to come and stay with me at Christmas. But now you are away, still. Morocco, why Morocco? I have torn myself apart trying to work out what it is I have done to offend you so much. I'm ill; you know this. I have awful migraines. I know I have a temper. But we are a family. You are all I've got.'

She turned away, shoulders shaking, and the video ended. The spiral to suicide was clearly illustrated: the estrangement from her son merely the epicentre of the gradual implosion of her life, eviction from her beloved flat, the ill health and the arguments with her partner.

There was another video, Katrina looking disconsolately into the lens in a darkened room. She was sitting at a table, and there was an object on the table which looked like the Beretta.

'*Is this the end?*' she asked, her voice slurring. '*How fate twists me, even now when I stare into the abyss.*' She picked up the gun and pointed it at her right temple. '*This little devil came into my life just to taunt me. But even there I fall short.*' Her left hand swept the phone off the table, and the video ended.

Talantire took a quick flick through the remaining images. There were quite a number of Alex and his mother in happier times, sharing a cream tea or a meal in a pub. There was clearly affection. The young man was well turned out, often in chinos and loafers and a pastel pullover, with a nice smile and a skin fade cut in his sandy hair.

She knew him.

The realisation hit her like a bullet from nowhere. The face was vaguely familiar – someone she had seen, perhaps only once or twice, and probably not talked to. Somehow, she felt he was gay, an impression formed from whatever previous encounter they had had. He didn't look like a police officer, not at all, but neither did he look much like the kind of person she banged up in prison. That accounted for most of the people she ran into day to day. Perhaps it was somebody in Barnstaple, in the locality. This, she knew, was going to bug her for the rest of the day. She had an excellent memory for faces, and she always got there. In the end.

A ping on her phone interrupted her reflection.

The DNA tests from Ms Lezcano's flat were back. As expected, there was very little from the renovated apartment itself. However, emptying the vestibule doormat into a plastic bag had turned out to be an act of inspiration, and had produced twenty-five DNA matches, including Ms Lezcano's. One other seemed worthy of further study. A single hair trapped within the fibres of the doormat had been identified as being from James Ferguson Garrett, a man who was on the database because of a criminal record. None of the others were. As expected, the artist's DNA was all over the sculpture, and the gun. There were no other traces on the weapon, but the edges of the artwork frame had traces of other DNA, including Garrett's.

Talantire quickly checked into the national criminal record listings and discovered that Garrett had a record as a small-time local dealer, mainly in cannabis, who had done a total of three years inside in the previous decade. He had no previous in firearms. She quickly checked against the address details for other residents in the shared building. No, Garrett wasn't on the resident list. However, after further checks online, she discovered that Garrett ran a man-with-a-van removals service; one that was still operating. He could of course have had a legitimate reason for being in the building, if he helped any of the residents to move out, indeed even if he had helped Ms Lezcano. But it was clear that the van business gave him a legitimate cover for drug distribution.

Did Garrett know Ms Lezcano? He had certainly touched her artwork, as the DNA records showed. But it could have been innocent.

It was definitely worth a closer look. She texted Maddy with the details, and messaged Primrose asking her to look for any communication from Garrett on the dead woman's phone.

—

She should have finished an hour ago, but there was still more to be done before she could return to what remained of her Saturday night. Talantire turned to the vehicle that the National Crime Agency in Merseyside had asked her to look into. It was a silver Audi saloon which had been found burned out in North Wales in September. Licence plates had been removed, but it was identified by the chassis number and turned out to have been stolen two weeks earlier in Plymouth. So far, so routine. There were thousands of vehicles stolen, used for crime and set ablaze every year. This, however, was an unusually long journey. What was particularly odd was that the car seemed to have been stolen twice. Originally nicked in Plymouth, then found abandoned in Newton Abbot and then stolen a second time from the garage in that town where it was being held pending forensic tests to establish whether it had been involved in a hit-and-run on a pedestrian.

Talantire frowned. That was very unusual, but she couldn't see why the NCA was particularly interested in it. She rang DCS Crossfield and got straight through. 'Hi Rebecca,' she said. 'That's a very odd case you've sent me. Is it related to the gangland killing?'

'It could be.'

Talantire could hear a TV and family noises in the background and waited while Rebecca moved into a different room.

'To be honest, Jan, we're so short of clues that we're chasing down anything, however much of a longshot it is.' Rebecca laughed. 'We've been trying to identify the Ford Transit used to transport the body to the cemetery and have basically taken every single ANPR hit on that make of vehicle in a fifty-mile radius on the night of the killing in August. As you can imagine that is hundreds and hundreds of Transits. We are gradually crunching down the numbers, the ownership, and so on. A dozen of those caught on ANPR turned out to have been reported stolen, and in each of those cases we have followed their entire journeys on cameras as far as we can, by mapping the entire network. In most cases, it is clear that those stolen vans were not in the right place at the right time; the ANPR hits too early or too late. But three of them couldn't be eliminated.'

'So you have three stolen Transits whose movements might fit with a trip to the crematorium on that night.'

'Yes, it's not much, is it? But curiously, one of the three was originally blue, not white. At least it was that colour when it was reported stolen but had magically become white by the time it showed up on ANPR.'

'So you're thinking that for a meticulously planned job like this, stealing a distinctive vehicle and making it bland will be the kind of thing that the brains behind the killing would employ.'

'Precisely, Jan. And this blue Transit was stolen from a small village just a week before the cemetery incident, and only ten miles away from where the Audi was found burned out a week later.'

'It could be coincidence, I suppose,' Talantire said.

'Like I said, we are clutching at straws. Because that's all that's left. The other problem is we are trying to find out who in the whole gangland world might be missing. Obviously if we know who the victim is, we have a fighting chance of working out who might want to kill them. And again with limited visibility we have into known gangs, there are always dozens of individuals who slip off the radar for weeks and months at a time.'

'That's really difficult,' Talantire said.

'Yes, and between you and me, we're getting nowhere. Of course, the people who really would know are the gang leaders, but obviously we can't get into their minds. We have undercover officers out there, with their cars to the ground, but we've got no names. Only that something major is in the offing. A European crime organisation flexing its muscles in the drugs trade, settling some scores. Probably the Calabrian mafia, the 'Ndrangheta.'

—

Talantire got home at 8:15 p.m. There was a car on the drive, a VW, which she presumed to be Nadine's. It was a newer model than her previous car, which had been repossessed in December. She let herself in and saw that Nadine was there, watching TV as usual. She'd had her hair cut, in a layered style not dissimilar to Talantire's own. After they exchanged greetings, she asked: 'Nice car; how did you manage that?'

'Dad lent me some money, without telling Mum. She's still angry with me.'

However, it was clear that housework had been done, and in the fridge were two salmon fillets and some asparagus. Both well within date. That was nice.

'Thank you, Nadine,' she said.

'You're welcome. I'm sorry, I've been such a slob. I got you a load of pizzas for the freezer, too.'

'Look, Jan, let's go out. There's a new cocktail place in town, which is open until midnight, and it's supposed to do fantastic espresso martinis. The evening will be on me.'

On your dad, more like, Talantire thought. Her knee-jerk response would have been to say 'no'. She was tired, and it had been a tough shift. However, tomorrow was New Year's Eve, and she would be working, covering for the Prince of Darkness who, cunningly, had booked the night off months ago. So, tonight in fact, would be her last chance for a bit of entertainment before the New Year. With Adam away, what could be the harm?

'All right, Nadine. Book a taxi for nine?'

While Nadine sorted out the arrangements, Talantire rushed upstairs for a quick shower. She then dug out a black lacy cocktail dress she hadn't worn for years and was pleasantly surprised she could still fit into it, just. She went a bit heavier than usual on the make-up, guessing that Nadine would be dolled up too. Talantire assessed herself in the full-length mirror of her bedroom. Not bad at all. With her highest, most impractical heels, her legs look shapely. Something about being 5'8" tall. One worry was her hair. Nadine's new style, a layered cut with a loose fringe, was just a little too much like a shorter version of Talantire's own cut, and a similar dark shade. She didn't want to hide her hair away in a ponytail, as she often did at work, but she didn't want to look like Nadine's sister either. Far too creepy. She got out the curling tongs and spent ten unpractised minutes putting in as many waves as she could. It should last an hour or two, so long as it didn't rain.

The doorbell rang, indicating the arrival of the taxi. Talantire went down to get it while Nadine shouted from upstairs that she was nearly ready. In the end, there were ten minutes on the meter before she arrived, in a black mini dress a good six inches shorter than Talantire's own. And Nadine too had been tonging her hair. It looked even more like her own. And the lipstick was a similar shade too.

'Snap,' Nadine said, as she got in next to Talantire.

Misgivings were gathering in Talantire's head, like hooded yobbos around a late-night shop. She was feeling claustrophobic, smothered, observed. *Nadine, please leave my life, and soon.*

They headed off to Pandemonium, an aptly named place on a side street, near the old Market Hall. It had only been open three months, and she recalled the Prince of Darkness had already attended a stabbing outside on one occasion. The theme was pandas and bamboo. Artificial floor-to-ceiling stands of the latter were dotted around the black-and-white tiled floor. Though it wasn't early, the place was quiet, with the mainly twenty-something demographic clearly reserving their financial firepower for tomorrow night. Talantire spotted a booth where they could talk, if they could make themselves heard over the warbling of Christina Aguilera. However, Nadine plonked herself on a bar stool, saying she wanted to see the cocktails being made. She opted for the espresso martini while Talantire, initially tempted by the house cocktail bamboozle, instead went for a known quantity – the Long Island iced tea.

The drinks were superb; they hadn't stinted on the alcohol. If Talantire had expected to be able to have a conversation with Nadine, she was disappointed. Her eyes roamed around the floor over Talantire's shoulder, shrewdly assessing the male talent. Inevitably, it was no more than a few minutes before a couple of twenty-something lads slid up to the bar and sat on adjoining stools, peering across at them. Nadine's body language was completely obvious, crossing her legs so her skirt slid up, holding her shoulders back to reveal even more decolletage and fluffing out her hair extravagantly behind her.

Christ. I should have guessed.

Talantire sipped her drink and caught the eye of one of the two men.

'Hello, ladies. Two pandas out to find a mate?' he asked, chuckling to his friend. Original at least. And direct. He was nice-looking, in a tousled boyish way, with a mop of unkempt hair and a nose ring. His mate was skinny and nervous, tattooed all over, with a white shirt that was too big for him and drainpipe trousers. He was fiddling with a vape almost the size of a clarinet.

'No, two cunning foxes ready to raid the henhouse,' Nadine replied.

'You look like identical twins,' the nervous mate said.

'I'm a twin, but not with her,' Talantire said, stung by a pang of guilt. Poor Bella, in her institution.

'I'm the third twin,' said Nadine, laughing. Talantire felt suffocated by the comment. When they turned away to order drinks, Talantire rolled her eyes at Nadine, before leaning in to whisper in her ear. 'Too young even for you,' she said.

'I've had younger,' she said.

'You should see this place tomorrow night,' the nervous lad said. 'It'll be crazy busy.'

'I'm working tomorrow night,' Talantire said. 'That's why we're here now.'

'Working on New Year's Eve!' nervous exclaimed, then leaned over to tell his mate.

'What do you lovely ladies do?' asked the tousled boyish one.

'We're police officers,' Talantire said. The lads look like they'd been given electric shocks. Talantire was sure the tousled one's hair stood on end.

'What did you say that for?' Nadine said, she watched them back away.

'Oh come on, were not on the pull. And you're married.'

'I just want to have a bit of *fun*, if you know what that is. This is like spending the evening with a bloody nun.'

Across the room, Talantire saw a face she recognised. A dark-haired mid-thirties individual with a watchful look that she had put away for running a car theft operation about eight years ago. He had an unusual name. Voss – that was it. Stefan Voss. She could remember names when she needed to. Two years, he'd got, when he was twenty-eight. He was talking to two other men. They were all dressed in T-shirts and tight jeans. When Voss looked in her direction Talantire looked away, but she felt his eyes on her. She'd been spotted. This was annoying, because it put her back at work. It was one of the reasons why she very rarely went to this kind of place any more.

Uh-oh. He was coming over. *Shit*. It was too late to make an escape, and Nadine had just ordered another round of drinks.

'Well well well,' Voss said. 'If it isn't Detective Sergeant Talantire. How are you doing?'

Nadine rolled her eyes: they wouldn't score with this lot, either. 'Jan's a detective inspector now,' Nadine corrected.

'I'm fine thanks, Stefan, and how are you?' Talantire said, smiling tentatively, though annoyed that Nadine had revealed her first name. Voss was swaying slightly, and his eyes were a little bloodshot.

'I'm doing okay, actually,' he said, looking around him to check no one was listening. 'Gone straight, since I got out. I'm installing double glazing these days. It's all right. Steady money.' He smiled back, his eyes sliding to Nadine's cleavage, a kind of gravity that seemed to work on every male in the entire universe. Talantire was relieved that Voss didn't seem overtly hostile. Drunk, yes, but seemingly at the happy stage, not the belligerent one.

His two mates, sensing an entrée, wandered over to join him, pints in hand. 'Do you know these two lovelies, Stef?' asked the shorter of the two, in a broad Devon accent.

'This one and me go a long way back, don't we?' Stefan said, resting his arm on Talantire's shoulder.

'A few years, yes,' Talantire said, looking across to a baffled Nadine.

'You shouldn't have let her get away, Stef,' the mate said. 'She's well out of your league. They both are.'

Voss smiled towards his mate.

'But you moved away, didn't you Stefan? To the other end of the country.' Talantire was actually enjoying sharing this fictional version of their shared past. HMP Durham wasn't anyone's idea of a good move, and he'd clearly kept it secret from these two.

Voss grinned back at her, and his arm slid more proprietorially around her shoulder, his beery breath and slightly slurring words enveloping her. 'You actually did me a big favour though, Jan, back then, didn't you, love?' His thumb was rubbing her neck, and she felt a little uncomfortable, even though she appreciated this maudlin confession.

'Blow job?' This was muttered by one mate, leaning towards the ear of the other, who immediately laughed. Talantire could read lips pretty well.

'Just some solid advice, actually,' she said, shrugging off the arm, which he was happy to let drop. Nadine was fascinated by this coded exchange, her eyes flicking from one to the other.

'Thanks to you, Jan, I'm in a better place now,' he said. He got out his phone and showed her pictures of his two kids. 'These are my little ones and that's my partner, Sonya. We've been together five years now.'

'They're lovely,' Talantire said. This conversation was going in a completely different direction from what she expected. His mates were baffled too. 'Are you an online influencer, or something?' asked the taller mate, who hadn't addressed her so far. 'TED talks and stuff?'

'Not exactly.' She glanced at Voss, whose expression betrayed the fear that she would spill the beans.

'Careers advice, basically,' he said. 'I remember when you told me in that first interview, those two ways I could go. I thought of that. A lot.'

'You were in an industry with no future,' she said.

'Right, Jan,' Nadine said, checking the time on her phone 'We got to meet the guys over at Secrets.'

'Are you going?' Voss asked, clearly disappointed.

'I'm afraid so, Stefan,' Talantire said, draining the last of her cocktail. 'But well done. That old job was no good for you anyway.' She rested a hand briefly on his shoulder, and was then surprised he pulled into a hug, and whispered into her ear. 'Honestly, it changed my life. I discovered who I am. If you hadn't got me, I just would have gone on forever.' He kissed her gently on the cheek as she extricated herself.

His mates were obviously baffled, and one of them asked if he could get Nadine's phone number. She ignored him and led Talantire out of the nightclub. Once they were outside, Nadine said: 'Bloody hell, Jan, let's write it up for the Ministry of Justice: prison *does* rehabilitate.'

'Sometimes,' Talantire said. 'Only sometimes.' She turned and gave Voss a cheery wave.

'He was off his face,' Nadine declared.

'Still counts.'

Secrets, in line with its name, was certainly a well-hidden piece of information, particularly on that night. The nightclub was half-empty, and the music seemed louder with fewer bodies to absorb it. It was clearly more down-market and less sophisticated than Pandemonium, and the clientele correspondingly rougher: older, more shaven heads, more tattoos. And that was just the women.

Talantire knew this was a place where females had been drugged in the past, but Nadine had an answer. She ordered lime daiquiris, but specified tall highballs, not the shallow coupe glasses, so they could dance with them in their hands without spillage. They fended off a whole series of older males who would approach with their own dad-dancing techniques, then try to lean in and speak to them after a couple of minutes. Meaningful communication was impossible, and the bellowed approach lines were even older and more careworn than the Victorian building Secrets occupied.

No, she didn't come there often. No, they weren't sisters. No, she didn't want a drink, thank you. While on the floor she mainly drank water from a bottle that Nadine had in her Dior knockoff bag, at their feet. It did feel good to lose herself in the beat, and Nadine was certainly a great and energetic dancer. They were the centre of attention from circling men, some of whom had already tried their luck, but seemed not to be giving up. It was like being eighteen all over again.

By three a.m., after a particularly dull conversation with a man who was old enough to be her father, Talantire had had enough. But when she turned around, Nadine wasn't there. Her handbag was still on the floor, so she scooped it up as she went off in search of her. She went up to the bar and turned her head towards the exit. It turned out she was standing outside, talking to a man.

In the glare of the streetlamp, the dab of white powder on Nadine's left nostril was obvious.

Talantire probably shouldn't have been shocked, but she was. Cocaine, or possibly ketamine, and Nadine a serving police officer. Her opinion of her accidental housemate sank still further.

Chapter Seven

It was eleven when Talantire emerged gradually from under the bed clothes on Sunday. She and Nadine had got home at half-five in the morning. She didn't have to be at work until the afternoon, but the shift would finish after midnight, and she wasn't looking forward to it. She had a reasonably clear head because she drank water after the first two cocktails, a precaution that Nadine hadn't taken. She'd clearly been drunk, and Talantire once again felt responsible for her. Worse still, she had been texting her husband and sending pictures of them both dancing. 'Just to show I can still have fun,' she had announced.

She levered herself out of bed, threw on a bath robe and went in search of coffee. She passed a pair of Nadine's discarded knickers on the stairs and opened the door into the lounge. It looked like a bomb had hit it. Nadine's cocktail dress and shoes were on the settee, and two apparently stolen cocktail glasses with Secrets monograms were on the kitchen table. Talantire now vaguely remembered that Nadine had brandished the glasses in the taxi as some kind of trophy. With that and the coke snorting, how the woman had ever decided to join the police was beyond her. They had to be returned, and if Nadine didn't do it, she would. She almost tripped on Nadine's red Dior imitation bag, which was lying on the kitchen floor. Picking it up, she found Nadine's phone inside. Talantire had watched her use it many times and reckoned she knew what the code was: her birthday in November.

Talantire went to the bottom of the stairs to listen. There was no sound from the spare room. She logged onto the phone and checked recent messages. Nadine had sent a blizzard of short and incoherent messages, with pictures, to her husband and her daughter, who was only eleven. Roger, who was on the nightshift in Camborne police at the time, had simply replied 'WTF Nadine', with an angry emoticon. Talantire could see his point of view, to some extent. Nadine had gone on long enough about how hard up they were, and here she was living it up in nightclubs, surrounded by other men. Imagine his reaction.

She scrolled down, past a particularly vindictive exchange between Nadine and her mother about childcare and responsibilities, and then came across a bombshell. A message from Brent West on Christmas Eve. It was quite simple and direct.

'You still haven't signed, Nadine. Forwarding it again. Last chance.'

Talantire knew exactly what this document would be. Her heart beating fast, she switched to Nadine's emails. There, on Christmas Eve, was an email from West which forwarded a document and attachment drawn up by a prominent firm of London solicitors. She opened the attachment and read it with a rising sense of horror. Using her own phone, Talantire photographed the letter and the crucial paragraphs of legalese.

> My client disputes entirely your version of events, but in order for him to get on with his life and for you to move forwards, out of a charitable sense of understanding of

your ongoing marital and mental health difficulties, he is willing to offer a substantial staged payment to help you put your life together. These payments in no way act as an admission of liability for any of the damaging, defamatory and hurtful allegations that you have made, which are entirely untrue. They are also made on the strict understanding that no reference to the existence, contents or terms of this agreement shall be made by you to any person, in writing, orally, via any medium electronic or otherwise, including those which have yet to be invented. This includes communication to friends, family, colleagues – current or previous – medical or therapeutic practitioners, or legal representatives whether here or abroad. Transgression of any of these terms will be vigorously pursued in the UK High Court and you may be subject to unlimited damages and costs for damage to him, his career and his reputation.

Talantire could hear sounds of movement upstairs, so she rapidly scrolled down the document, photographing each intimidating paragraph, until she got to the crucial appendix which detailed payments. Five grand a month, for a year. Sixty thousand all told, each payment conditional on performance against the terms.

She turned off the phone and put it back in the bag. She had started by being horrified but now she was angry. She had trusted Nadine, at least to tell the truth, but she had let her down by going behind her back to make this deal with West. Her only ally had been bought off.

So *this* is where the money came from. *This* is where the new car came from, their night on the cocktails, too. It felt dirty, the proceeds of crime. Truth laundering. The tentacles of lies seemed to be encroaching on Talantire from all directions. The last day of the year, and the last real hope of nailing Brent West seemed to be evaporating, like the coke that had disappeared up Nadine's nose the night before.

She couldn't face Nadine without the risk of a massive row, so took her coffee upstairs while she dressed into running gear. To dissipate her fury she was going to go on her toughest run: the steep track through the centre of the Forestry Commission area, too muddy year round to attract many of the dog walkers, then onto the hard stony track as it rose over to Oxcombe and a long haul up Modge Hill. Finally, down to Ferrecombe towards Gunn, through the meadows and back round by the side of the B road. The full loop was a little over seven miles, seven tough miles.

The steep ascent was hard after the heavy night, and she felt her energy was low. She was overtaken by a man on a mountain bike, and struggled on in his wake, drawing strength from her anger and determination more than from the body. *I will not be defeated. I will not. I will see this thing through to the end, even if I have to do it on my own.* She couldn't wait to see the end of Nadine's occupation of her home, even more so now that she might be a Trojan horse. Perhaps she was even feeding back to West details of her own campaign. She hadn't told Nadine everything, perhaps out of some premonition, but at the time it was more because of the woman's flakiness than any suspicion of her being a spy in her midst.

She was five miles in, exhausted and desolate, when her phone rang. She stopped by a stream to answer it and saw a flash of blue dart low over the water as she put the phone to her ear. A kingfisher. It made her smile, but not as much as hearing who the call was from.

'Hi, Jan, it's Holly, finally returning your message. I'm so sorry it's taken me months to get back to you.'

'That's okay,' Talantire said, breathlessly. 'Excuse the heavy breathing; I'm out on a run.'

'Good for you. I'm stuck at work, but everyone else is out at the pub, so I thought I'd ring.'

Holly King was a detective chief inspector in fraud based in Exeter, and a rumoured former girlfriend of Brent West. Talantire had messaged her a few months earlier, saying she was pursuing a discreet enquiry into 'the treatment of women in Devon and Cornwall police', but had heard nothing back. She had been meaning to follow up again but needed a way of doing so diplomatically. It was thin ice when she wasn't sure what each woman thought of their former lover. It would be too easy to press too hard and risk being reported for pursuing a vendetta.

'I made my own enquiries, and I gather this is about Brent West,' Holly said.

'You've got me bang to rights,' Talantire said, laughing. The two women had occasionally been on the same teleconference, or working peripherally on the same case, but had rarely been in the same room at the same time. Holly was a spirited, tomboyish individual, who had originally been a forensic accountant, and in her youth was a promising pole vaulter. This led to lots of jokes about shattered glass ceilings and soft landings. But she'd done well for good reasons. There was no fooling this woman any more than there had been with Rebecca Crossfield. Both smart cookies, with a good network of contacts. 'As you must be aware, there are rumours circulating about you and him in the past.'

'Yes, and I'm pretty annoyed about it,' Holly said. 'I'm incredibly discreet about my love life, and it annoyed the hell out of me that he bragged about me as a conquest. "Turning over one from the other side", is what I heard.'

'He boasted about me, too,' Talantire said. 'It's all over WhatsApp. And he filmed me in his flat in Holloway Close. I spotted the camera lens in the headboard.'

There was a gasp at the other end of the line. 'The bastard.'

'Was he abusive towards you?' Talantire asked.

'Well, he abused his position: he was my boss's boss, and he was running a big case in which I was at that time just a small cog. However, he arranged a meeting just with me behind my boss's back, then we went out to dinner, ostensibly to discuss the case. I figured out immediately what he was after, but not why. He promised me a promotion; I was at DI at the time.'

'So you got the promotion?'

Holly ignored the comment. 'It turned out that he had a room booked in the hotel where we ate, and, yes, I let him seduce me. It had been a while since I'd slept with a man. He was very charming, but he just turned out to be a manipulator.'

'Tell me about it. My relationship with Brent was about seven years ago, for a few months. He was pretty good at the big romantic gestures, at least at first. He brought me a tray of home-made sushi to the balcony of my top-floor apartment, on a cherry picker, while I was sunbathing.'

'Huh, I never got that,' Holly said. 'I was a little curious why he went for me. Then I realised he wasn't actually attracted to me; he was just trying to set up a threesome. He had some other woman in Cornwall, a community policewoman who swung both ways, as it turned out. He just wanted to set up his fantasy.'

Talantire had a clue who that might be, although Nadine hadn't mentioned anything about it. 'Did it happen?'

'Not with her, no. With someone else.'

Talantire was struggling to keep up with this. 'Another officer?'

'I'm not going there; this is private.'

'Well, you did return my call.'

Holly paused. 'Yes, because I heard that you made a formal complaint about him over the summer and then withdrew it.'

'That wasn't me,' Talantire said. 'I made a complaint only when I'd heard that there was one already made, the one that stopped him being appointed chief constable.'

'Oh, everybody said it was you. That only you would have the guts to take him on, to humble Devon and Cornwall's own Harvey Weinstein.'

Talantire laughed. She had heard this now a few times. 'No, Holly. There were two of us who made complaints, *after* this first one. But when it came to the formal hearing, we were told that the original complaint had been withdrawn, with an apology, believe it or not. This woman also claimed that she and I had cooked up the allegations together to bring him down!'

'There was no proof of that, was there?'

'Not with her, no. But unfortunately, there was some evidence of collusion with my co-complainant. Her phone was bugged by West. Somehow, the tribunal had been sent a recording of us talking about "getting him" from her phone.'

'Oh, Jan, what a colossal fuck-up.'

'Yes, the bastard has run rings around us, frankly, and he still is.' She was thinking about Nadine's legal deal. The latest blow.

'Who was the first complainant?'

'I still don't *know*, Holly. That's the thing. Unless I can get to this woman and get her to admit that she lied about colluding with me, my own complaint remains on ice.'

'West must have put pressure on her; it's the only explanation for such a volte face.'

'I agree. He can be very scary. He threatened to kill my co-complainant.'

'Who is she?'

'I'd rather not say, if you don't mind.'

Talantire had been tempted to name Nadine, but felt it would be more sensible to hold the name back for now until she knew for certain that Holly was an ally. This delicate harvesting of confidences was a subtle skill, so different from a formal police interrogation, and she was still feeling her way. This process was not backed by law, but by alliance, by sisterhood, by affinity and experience, and even by trade: I'll tell you mine, if you tell me yours.

There was a long pause and then Holly said, 'Well, anyway, to get back to the reason for me finally returning your call after all this time: I've been toying for many months with the idea of reporting West for the abuse of his position, particularly since I'd heard that you and others had weighed in first. It's my New Year's resolution.'

'Do you have any actual evidence?'

'No, it's just my word against his.'

Talantire sighed. 'The trouble is, if all you have is a senior officer taking advantage of his authority to shag a junior, then most of the top brass of the entire British police force is in trouble. We really need much more.'

'I can ask around.'

'I've already been doing that,' Talantire said. 'There are some who are just too frightened, and for good reason. And by the way, do get your phone checked. West has access to some of the best mobile phone spyware around. He's like the spider crouching at the centre of a web, his feet on all the threads, just waiting to feel a vibration.'

'I don't want to be the fly that he catches next,' Holly said.

'I've got a meeting in Exeter with my boss a week on Friday; the dreaded annual review,' Talantire said. 'Let's meet up for lunch afterwards.'

'Good idea.' They arranged the details and Talantire hung up. The call had restored her mood somewhat. She had a spring in her step as she approached home.

She arrived to find Nadine sprawled on the settee looking at the TV, sporting a monster hangover. She had cleared up her clothes and handbag, but there were plenty of dirty dishes where she had cooked herself scrambled egg. Talantire had to wash them, including scrubbing the pan, before being able to make her own much-delayed breakfast. Fortunately, there were plenty of eggs left, to which she added mushrooms, bacon and chorizo, all on two slices of toast. She wolfed down her food, staring resentfully through the double doors from the kitchen at the back of Nadine's head. Only three days to go of this torment. Until she got rid of her. Thank God!

It was a relief for Talantire to arrive at CID in Barnstaple: the office wasn't generally a humming model of efficiency, but it was a lot tidier than her own home, with the exception of Maddy Moran's workstation, which was festooned with Post-it notes. The woman herself was there, with piles of files to either side.

'Hello, Jan,' Maddy said. 'Have a nice relaxing break?'

'I'm not sure about that,' Talantire said. 'I feel ready for a holiday.'

'Well, Nadine Lister posted videos and pictures on Facebook of you two dancing away at Secrets last night.'

'Are you a Facebook friend of hers?'

'Nope, but her settings allow anyone to look at it.'

Talantire rolled her eyes. 'You would have thought after what happened to her...'

'Yes, you would, wouldn't you,' Maddy said tartly. 'This will be all over the place now. And by the way, what's with the she-and-me matching hairstyles?'

'I know; it makes me very uncomfortable.'

Maddy laughed. 'Not that uncomfortable; you both look like you're having a great time. Considering this twisted sister appears to be your live-in stalker.'

'She's moving out on Wednesday, thank God. I can't wait to get rid of her.'

'About time, too. Speaking of pains in the arse, PC Tim Caldwell and I interviewed the dead woman's landlord in Brixham yesterday. Rodney Weskerton, and a right piece of work he is too. Let me show you.'

Maddy primed the CCTV feed from the interview room. Weskerton was a tanned fifty-something in a white shirt and smart jacket, who wouldn't accept that the death of the woman had anything to do with his commercial decisions. Maddy, who had her own problems with bad landlords, had given him a hard time over the eviction, but he resolutely denied harassing the woman. There was quite a testy exchange at one point:

'She had the place for years at below-market rent,' Weskerton said. 'I was fed up with subsidising her.'

'Were you making a loss?' Maddy had asked him.

'Not as such, but I was missing out on the holiday market. It's been booming all across the South West.'

'It's not quite the same as subsidising then, is it?'

'I thought you were enquiring about a woman's death, not quizzing me on the rights and wrongs of the property market. This was simply a commercial decision. I needed to invest in the property, to modernise it.'

'What to you seems like a commercial decision can be life or death for somebody else, can't it? There aren't enough homes for people down here, are there?'

'That's right,' added Caldwell, his first contribution to the interview. He was still living with his parents.

'The market decides; it's nothing to do with me,' Weskerton said with a shrug.

'It seems highly relevant to me that her state of mind might have been influenced by the loss of her home,' Maddy persisted. 'It might well have been the last straw.'

Weskerton rolled his eyes. 'Listen, Ms Lezcano wasn't a good tenant. She left an awful mess when she departed. Paint, rubbish bags overflowing, bits of bloody seashell everywhere, glue stains, you name it. I'm shocked and saddened that she died, but it was nothing to do with me, alright?'

'When did you last see her?'

'I've not seen her face to face for many months. As you know, I live in Sherborne, and don't get down to Brixham that often.'

Maddy clicked off the video. 'I didn't like him.'

'It shows, Maddy.'

'Well, people like him, they make me angry. Pricing the locals out of the market, and then their properties stay empty most of the year.'

'We can't put that right, and the interview room isn't the place to try. I hope for your sake he doesn't make a complaint, because you won't have a leg to stand on. We should only be interested in whether he had any direct involvement in her death.'

Maddy shrugged. 'I can't see he did, unfortunately.'

'What about James Garrett? Have you managed to track him down?'

'He wasn't at the last address we had for him. Caldwell is working on it. He's spoken to several of Garrett's mates, but they are being very cagey. He may well have had legitimate reasons to be in the entrance hall at the victim's address.'

'Is there any progress on how she got the heavy metal exposure?'

'Some. Chemical analysis of her hair has been forwarded by the forensic pathologist. Her notes say it shows that the victim's most recent hair growth was largely free of contaminants. Although you can't be precise about these kinds of things, the improvement seems to coincide with her moving out of the flat.'

'I wonder if it could be lead pipes, or something like that?' Talantire suggested.

'Maybe. I could put in a request to the water company for analysis. I did manage to make contact with the owner of the seafood shack where she worked. His name is Felipe Gomes, and he is currently staying with his parents in Lisbon. He was absolutely distraught to hear of her death.

She was a first-class cook apparently, although she had to have quite a lot of time off work because of ill health in the last few months. Gomes echoed the opinions of the victim's partner that the eviction was a massive blow to her.'

'Have you got other agencies involved?'

'Yes. I had to notify Gomes that the local authority food hygiene people would be visiting the restaurant when it reopens next week, and any samples will be sent for analysis. He was very cooperative, but of course did make the point that if it is a problem with the food, it's the customers who normally fall ill, not the staff.'

'How has young Tim been doing?'

She smiled. 'He's rather lovely, quite keen and enthusiastic, is PC Caldwell. And he's worked very hard. He tracked down the ex-husband, Royston Brown, who is in his eighties. He remarried and claims not to have seen Ms Lezcano for twenty years. Brown had a text from his son in Morocco and is hoping to speak to him when he gets back from the trek. But here's something interesting: Caldwell also got through to Ms Lezcano's aunt in Italy. She was part of a very wealthy family. The Lezcanos own a huge vineyard and estate in Piedmont. I've seen the website. There's lots of property, too. So while the financial report showed the woman was in overdraft and had no savings, she might eventually have been in line for some serious wealth.'

'Do we know that? Is there a will or anything?'

'I don't know. Katarina is the eldest daughter, and the winery is run by the oldest son. There is bad blood between her and the brother, apparently, but she got on fine with her younger sisters.'

'Still, there's a potential motive here,' Talantire said. 'Mary Stuart Davies is a wine writer, so it's reasonable to assume that she would know the rough value of the Lezcano estate.'

'I agree,' Maddy said. 'We haven't found a will for Katarina, and it's a matter of conjecture whether the family would consider a lesbian partner to be a spouse. It depends how traditional they are.'

'Yes, it's a bit of a stretch. I don't think we are quite at the stage where we could justify getting a warrant to look at Miss Stuart Davies's computer search history.'

Maddy laughed. 'That's exactly what young Tim wants to do. He's quite keen to become a detective. He tracked down some CCTV which shows Katarina parking at Brixham Harbour and getting into her boat.'

'Let's have a look,' Talantire said.

Maddy found the footage fairly quickly and played it on her screen. It was from an external camera above a harbourside shop, giving a view of the harbour. Katarina's car was seen approaching the harbour side on Christmas morning at half past ten. She parked illegally on a hatched area near the boat ramp, then emerged from the car. She was dressed in a wetsuit and had a small rucksack on her back. She spent a long time looking out over the water and running a hand through her thick hair, before she made her way to a set of stone steps which led down to a mud bank. At this point, Maddy switched to a different camera from a shop across the other side of the harbour, which gave a more distant view, but clearly showed Katarina clambering into a launch. A few minutes later the vessel set off, Katarina at the helm, and exited through the mouth of the harbour.

'And that,' said Maddy 'was the last anyone ever saw of her.'

'We didn't find a backpack,' Talantire said. 'I wonder what was in it. It must have been something important, and she didn't have it with her when she got washed up under the pier.'

Maddy shrugged 'I don't think we'll ever find it. Tim is still going through the pictures and messages but he's been off the last few days. It's not considered a high enough priority for anyone else to pick up on.'

Talantire went to her own terminal and logged on. She went into the shared file system for the case and pulled up the folder of videos and images extracted from Katarina's phone. She could see from the timestamp that only a small proportion had been looked at by PC Caldwell.

There was a brief exchange of emails in September, between mother and son.

> Alex, darling, I haven't heard anything from you. You haven't confirmed about Christmas. I know you had this thing going on at work, but can you just let me know?
>
> I'm not coming, sorry, I'm going to be busy. I'm not sure how long I'll be staying here in Morocco.
>
> Alex, don't be like this. You always spend Christmas here. It's unlike you to be so cold and distant. We only have each other, remember?
>
> I'm fed up with you. I'm not coming. Just leave me alone.

It seemed fairly clear evidence of the deteriorating relationship. She pulled up the image of Alex and called Maddy over to look at it.

'Ah yes, that's the elusive Alex,' Maddy said.

'Do you recognise him?'

'Nope.'

'I've seen him somewhere before, and I'm racking my brains try to find out where.'

'He has an address in Exeter, but is still in Morocco, according to his last message.'

'Is that since he was notified of her death?' Talantire asked.

Maddy returned her own terminal and opened a document 'Yes. Here it is: "OMG, can't believe it. On trek in Sahara, sporadic signal, give me a number and I'll ring when I can. Am so shocked." That was four days ago. Nothing since.'

'That's all?' Talantire said. 'Even allowing for the difficulties of being in the Sahara...'

'Well, they had already fallen out,' Maddy said. 'Maybe he just felt he had to go through the motions.'

'Okay, keep trying with him. We need his input.' She looked down at her phone, which had just pinged with results from the DNA lab.

'Oh wow!' she said. 'Garrett's DNA has turned up inside the victim's caravan.'

Chapter Eight

Geoff Hutchinson always enjoyed a New Year's Eve lunch at the Blackbeard Inn in Teignmouth. He and Molly stood together at the bar, waiting for their table at the restaurant to be free. They enjoyed the atmosphere here, and the press of people drinking on the last day of the year, greeting each other in the warm fug against the gentle hubbub in the background, was warming to him. But as he ordered a pint of Dartmoor ale, he detected a familiar voice to his left. Turning, he spotted a man that he had arrested in the last month before he retired five years ago.

James Garrett.

Garrett had filled out since Hutchinson had last seen him, and his mass of curly dark locks was turning grey above the ears, but his distinctive baritone rumble hadn't changed at all. Hutchinson was sure that this man was unchanged despite his jail time: an opportunist with a short fuse, a man who would today be called 'differently moraled'. A bad 'un. He'd heard that Garrett lived in Brixham, so it was a bit of a surprise to see him here. Up to no good, undoubtedly.

Molly had been trying to get her husband's attention. 'The table's ready now, Geoff.' As he turned to her, Garrett caught him with a quick glance.

The meal was as good as ever, but Hutchinson was preoccupied and Molly complained that he was being more than usually taciturn. After finishing the main course, Hutchinson made his way to the toilets, which were at the far end of the bar. Neither Garrett nor his mate were standing there. Hutchinson tried to get into the gents, but the door banged into someone who seemed to be leaning on the other side. 'Jesus, 'old on a sec,' came a familiar voice. There was only a few seconds delay, but when the door opened, Garrett's mate bustled out nervously, his hand still stowing a plastic bag into his back pocket. Garrett was standing at one of the two cramped urinals. Unwilling to squeeze in next to him, Hutchinson shot him a dark look and went into the cubicle.

'I remember you too, mate, don't worry,' Garrett called across. 'Just stay out of my way.'

'Then you'd better stay out of mine,' Hutchinson replied.

Garrett's laugh was low, and contemptuous. 'A bit tasty are you, grandad? Black belt Zimmer frame?'

Hutchinson heard him step away and leave the gents. There was no sound of running water and no sound of the dryer. When he had himself finished, he washed his hands and soaped down the metal door push, before leaving. He didn't want Garrett's germs on him. When he got back to the table he borrowed some of his wife's sterilising gel and wiped his hands on a napkin. He still had plenty of friends in the force. He'd let them know who he'd run into, and what he appeared to be doing.

He got out his phone and went to the car park.

—

James Garrett was proving elusive. By the time PC Tim Caldwell had turned up at the Blackbeard Inn, his quarry had disappeared, along with the two mates he had been drinking with. None of the bar staff seemed to know the men, and most of the customers had since left. However, with the helpful details supplied from retired officer Geoff Hutchinson, he had photographs of all the registration numbers of the vehicles in the car park at the time. He emailed them on to Detective Sergeant Moran for checking and entered them into the dashcam on his patrol car. He then drove south into Teignmouth.

And then a stroke of luck.

Caldwell spotted Garrett just forty yards ahead, emerging from a convenience store on the right-hand side of the street. He was carrying a carrier bag and, judging from his stance, it was heavy. Booze. Garrett was wearing the same rugby shirt and jacket that Hutchinson had described and was staring down into his phone. Caldwell eased the car across the road and drew it up by the kerb along which Garrett was walking. Only then did Garrett look up and spot the police car. His face froze for half a second, then he pocketed the phone. As Caldwell was opening the car door, Garrett lifted the bag to his chest, ran past and turned left into an alleyway. Caldwell was after him instantly, calling in his location as he began to run.

Caldwell may have been a junior and inexperienced police officer, but he was young and fit, and he was confident that he would quickly catch this overweight thirty-something; a man who had spent the last three hours in the pub and was lugging some heavy shopping.

No contest.

He sprinted up the alleyway and saw Garrett go left at the end, fifteen yards ahead. Caldwell raced up and round the corner, straight into Garrett's waiting fist. The agonising blow knocked him back against the wall, blood spurting from his nose. It was followed by a kick aimed at the groin, but which actually connected with his knee and toppled him to the floor, with the pain trebled. He tried with his arms to protect himself against a kick to the face, and largely succeeded, but when he saw Garrett break a bottle of wine against the wall above his head, his bowels turned to water, and against his own better instincts he curled up into a ball.

But Garrett didn't stab him with the bottle. He merely pressed it against Caldewell's neck, making soft but utterly believable threats before he snatched the police radio and smashed it under his heel. He then picked up his shopping, walked nonchalantly past the trembling policeman and back out of the alleyway in the direction he had come.

The manhunt started immediately. The case was given the high priority that an attack on a serving officer always gets. All six local PCSOs on the community team, plus five uniforms drafted in from Plymouth, where they had been preparing to police that night's New Year celebrations. Talantire and Maddy blue-lighted it down to Teignmouth, with an impromptu incident room meeting arranged for six p.m. at the Exeter Road police station in the centre of town. On the way, they rang PC Caldwell on the hands-free. He was being treated in A&E at Torbay.

'Tim, how are you doing?' Talantire asked him.

'I've been better, ma'am,' he responded thickly. They'd heard that his nose was broken, and he sounded like he had a heavy cold.

'You shouldn't have tackled him on your own,' Maddy said. 'You know the rules.'

'I had no idea he was going to be violent; he was running away. He seemed unfit, and I thought I could take him.'

'Convicted criminals being violent, who would have thought it?' Maddy said.

'Well, it's a lesson learned,' Talantire said. 'And we are really sorry to hear that you got hurt. We will get him, I promise you.'

'I've been trying to trace the cars from the pub car park,' he said. 'But my personal mobile isn't verified, so they won't talk to me.'

'Leave it to us, Tim. You just concentrate on getting yourself better,' Talantire said.

'The worst thing is my knee. It's agony. The doctor says I've got a cracked patella. It might take six months to get better. I can't walk.'

'We'll have you driving a desk, then,' Maddy said.

'We'll look after you, Tim,' Talantire said. She thanked him again and hung up.

By the time the incident room meeting began, Maddy had established that none of the cars Hutchinson photographed at the Blackbeard pub car park belonged to James Garrett. It would take far more checking to be sure that he wasn't borrowing a vehicle from a friend. His van was found in Brixham, not far from his rented flat, and the CSI unit was called in to check it for drug residues. Enquiries with his neighbours revealed that nobody had seen Garrett since before Christmas.

Talantire pulled up a whiteboard as the uniformed officers in the team made their way inside. The most senior of the eight who could make it was a sergeant, appropriately named Hunt, given the nature of the operation. Hunt was a stickler, a lean, formal and unsmiling individual with metal-framed glasses and a piercing gaze. He had twenty years in the force in Plymouth, and was most particular on his Christian name, Michael, which given his surname was not to be shortened, ever. Naturally, behind his back, that was the only way he was ever referred to.

'Thank you, everybody,' Talantire said. 'I'll keep this brief. James Ferguson Garrett is, as you all know, a person of interest in connection with the death of Ms Katarina Lezcano, who was found dead beneath a pier on Boxing Day morning. His DNA has turned up not only in the hallway of the shared house where she had an apartment up until December, but also inside the caravan where she lived for the last month of her life. This enquiry has become more urgent since the assault on PC Caldwell. A Beretta pistol was also found inside one of her artworks in that same hall.'

She then pointed to details she had jotted down earlier. 'These are all the fixed points of Garrett's life that we know about: his address, his friends and so on. I hope you have all read up on his criminal record. Given the level of violence he managed to exhibit today, I would say he's got off lightly so far. That is about to change. What I need you to do is to call in all of the street CCTV, doorbell cameras, anything covering his movement as a pedestrian since he left the alleyway where the assault on PC Caldwell took place. If he got into a vehicle, I need to know the number plate.'

'What about his phone?' Hunt asked.

'Our digital evidence officer found a number for someone called Jim on the dead woman's phone, which hasn't been rung since June. If he has a new number, it's not been stored under that name. So, yes, we are working on it.'

'There are no formal accounts of any kind for his man-with-a-van business,' Hunt said. 'There's a website, but no legal information, and there's nothing on Companies House. I should imagine the entire business was run in cash.'

'What about the phone on the website? Can we trace that?' Talantire asked.

'That phone's not been used for a while. He must be using a burner,' Hunt said.

'Okay, crack on with that,' she said. 'There's a public appeal with a picture going out this evening. We're warning the public not to approach him.'

—

New Year's Eve was as busy as any other, and Talantire's night shift seemed an endless litany of liaisons with a hard-pressed uniform branch across Devon and Cornwall over assaults, domestic incidents and sexual assault. There were three other detectives on the night shift, all DCs: one in Penzance, one in Plymouth and one in Exeter. She left the office twice: once to help the rape team, who needed forensic and investigatory backup after an incident in Lynmouth on the North Devon coast, and the second time for a complex road traffic accident on the Okehampton bypass, which had led to a fight between the occupants of two vehicles. There wasn't a moment to pursue the manhunt for James Garrett, which was just as well because even if they had found him, she would have been scrabbling for resources to make an arrest.

She didn't get home until seven in the morning, almost comatose with tiredness. She was relieved that Nadine's car wasn't there. She had been planning a grand reconciliation with Roger and her family the previous evening. Talantire hoped she would be better at finding peace and understanding on New Year's Eve than most of the inhabitants of the country. She had an exhausting shift as fresh evidence of the power of alcohol to destroy relationships. She took a long hot shower, washed her hair and went to bed.

She awoke at half past eleven, hearing noise and conversation on the landing outside her bedroom. She heard a young girl's voice exclaiming: 'What a dump!'

Pulling on a bath robe, she opened the door to see Nadine and a girl of about eleven in the doorway of the spare room. 'Oh, hi, Jan. Sorry if we woke you.'

'What's going on?' Talantire asked woozily.

'Dad's turfed us all out,' said the girl, who was looking at Talantire as if she was something she had trod in. 'So we've *got* to stay here.'

'I don't think…' Talantire began.

'Just for a day or so,' Nadine said hurriedly.

'Thank God,' said the girl. There was a thundering on the stairs and a stocky lad of about eight burst onto the landing. He was wearing a Manchester United football shirt and carrying a foot-high plastic gorilla in his hand. 'Mum, where's my PlayStation?'

'No, no, no, sorry. This has got to stop,' Talantire said, trying to herd them back down the stairs. 'You were leaving, Nadine, as I recall.'

'On Wednesday, Jan,' Nadine said, as if explaining to a small child. 'Today's Sunday.'

'You can't bring your family here. There's no space.'

The daughter nodded vigorously. 'And it's a shithole.'

'Millie, shut up. Auntie Jan is being very kind to let us stay.'

'I am *not* letting you stay!'

'She's a complete witch, I knew it,' Millie said, pulling her mother's hand. 'Let's go.'

'Nadine, why didn't you at least ask?' Talantire said.

'I did, two hours ago. I messaged you twice.'

'I was asleep; I'd just got in after the nightshift.'

'Are you unemployed, Auntie Jan?' the boy asked. 'Our Uncle Malcolm is. He wears his dressing gown *all* day.'

'Daniel, shut up!' his mother said.

Talantire tried as best she could to ignore this wave of insults. Looking past Nadine into the spare room, Talantire spied an additional suitcase, and a large rucksack.

'Mum, where's my PlayStation?'

'Nadine, this is not happening,' Talantire said.

'It already happened; get over it,' Millie said, pushing past into the spare room and slamming the door.

'Mum, *where's* my PlayStation?'

Talantire was trying to pinch herself, praying that she was still asleep and that this was just some horrendous nightmare. But no. She had to stop it; she had to stop it *now*.

'Downstairs, everyone,' Talantire ordered. She even clapped her hands, something she never imagined she'd have to do in her own home. The boy responded immediately, and Nadine followed. There was no movement from the spare room. Talantire turned the handle and walked in.

Millie was lying on the bed wearing sunglasses with heart-shaped lenses. 'Jesus, don't you knock?' she asked.

'This is MY HOUSE! Get downstairs.' She advanced into the room, shaking with rage.

'I've got a migraine.' Millie rested the back of her hand on her forehead. 'And I've got mental health, so don't you *dare* touch me. I'll call social services.'

She couldn't believe what she was hearing. How she had been ambushed in her own home. She couldn't touch this child, even here. Final written warning. It wouldn't take much. The correct way to do this would be through social services, care professionals, uniformed police. And it would all take hours and hours, and if the alternatives for the children were worse, she would be persuaded to let them stay, at least until the start of term. Eviction would require a court order, and that would take weeks if not months.

Talantire retreated and closed the door behind her, heading down towards the kitchen where the boy was looking through the fridge. 'What's for lunch, Auntie Jan?' he asked.

'Bread and pull it,' she replied, a phrase from her own grandmother, plucked from memory. 'And I'm not your auntie.'

Nadine had the TV on. Talantire walked over and turned it off. 'Nadine we are having a conversation.'

The woman was trembling, barely keeping it together. 'I'm so sorry about this.'

'So what happened?'

'Rog and me had a row. He threw everything back in my face, all the accusations. He said that the kids were feral because of me.'

'What's feral?' asked the boy, a biscuit half-wedged into his mouth.

'Shut up, Daniel.' She turned back to Talantire. 'He called me a whore and a slut, shagging anything that moved.'

The child didn't ask for an explanation of those terms. Probably the only one he wasn't familiar with was the word 'moved'.

'What about your mum? Can't she at least look after the kids?' Talantire asked.

'She had a heart murmur two days ago and is being kept in hospital under observation. Dad's with her.'

'Your sister in Portsmouth?'

'Not that bitch.' This came from Millie, who was standing at the bottom of the stairs, still wearing the sunglasses.

'My sister doesn't understand children,' Nadine said.

Talantire sympathised. Even battalions of professionals might struggle with these two. 'When does term start?' she asked hopefully.

'At Daniel's school? On Wednesday. Millie is on suspension.'

'I have complex needs,' the child added helpfully. 'I have ADHD, and exhibit challenging patterns of behaviour, including inappropriately sexualised behaviours. I'm a bully. The root causes are a chaotic home life, poor parenting and bad choices by the relevant adults, and my witnessing of domestic violence. I need a safe space, free from exposure to domestic disharmony.'

'Sometimes I think she's too intelligent,' Nadine said, ruefully.

'Not an accusation that can be levelled at you,' Millie responded, and flounced out of the room, back upstairs.

'Auntie Jan,' Daniel asked. 'You know Wolverine?'

'The animal?'

'No, the superhero.'

'I'm afraid I'm not familiar...'

'Could he beat a crocodile, do you think?'

'What, at swimming?'

'No, fighting. Would a crocodile kill him?'

'If it was hungry.'

'Can a crocodile beat a tiger?'

'I really don't know.'

'Sorry about this, Jan,' Nadine said. 'He's always on about this stuff.'

Talantire took a deep breath and turned back to Nadine. 'So where are you going to go? I'm serious, you really can't stay here.'

'I've got a furnished place to rent in Camborne. The tenancy starts next Wednesday.'

'This Wednesday? The day after tomorrow?'

'No, it's the tenth, the week after.'

'Nadine, you said you'd leave on *Wednesday*.'

'Yeah, sorry, I made a mistake about the weeks.'

'You'll have to find somewhere else to stay. I can't have the kids staying here.'

Nadine shrugged helplessly. 'Where can we go?'

'I thought you had money? From your dad? And there's your police pay. Take them to a caravan site for a few days,' Talantire said, wondering if Nadine would own up about the pay-off from West.

'I'm really short at the moment. I *will* pay you some rent.' Nadine's voice went really small, as if she was pleading.

'The thing is, Nadine, I can't trust you to tell the truth, can I?'

'You can.' Her voice was now barely a whisper.

'You're getting a pay-off from West, aren't you?' She leaned in closer, checking that Daniel wasn't within earshot. 'Five grand a month, for keeping your mouth shut, and pretending the rapes never existed. Enough to rent a pretty good place, I would say.'

Nadine began to dissolve into tears. 'How did you find out?' she croaked, through a thickened throat.

'It doesn't matter. What matters is that you have sold out, and you've made it impossible for me to continue to go after him.' She thought she might as well float her own deceit. 'So it's over. He's won, we've lost and you've got your money. Good result, Nadine, well done. And you're still in my bloody house.'

'I'm so sorry, Jan.'

'Sorry you got found out, yes.'

'I don't have any money.'

'You spent the first five grand pretty quickly, then, didn't you?'

Nadine nodded, tearfully. 'I'll pay you three hundred rent on Friday.'

Talantire was on the verge of losing it entirely. 'Is that when West's payment clears? No, I'd rather starve than take his money. Where's your self-respect? Today's Monday. You've got until first thing Wednesday morning. I want you out.'

'You're being cruel to my kids.'

'You ain't seen nothing yet.' Talantire thundered upstairs into her room and slammed the door. She changed into running gear.

She was due to meet up with the Black Bull Harriers at Hartland Quay. But she had something to do first. She had a plan. She checked the weather forecast on her phone.

Yes, it was going to be getting colder for the next few days. Good. She thundered downstairs into the kitchen, where Daniel was occupying the table with his PlayStation. She grabbed the small set of kitchen steps, slipped through the internal door into the garage and disconnected the gas boiler. She opened the steps so she could reach the fuse boxes high up on the garage wall. She angrily pulled out every fuse and slipped them into a plastic bag, which she hid in her sports bag. She made an exception for the kitchen socket circuit which supplied the freezer. That had to stay running. She returned to the kitchen, found all the internal house keys in a drawer and, after locking the door to the garage, pocketed them.

She retrieved the remains of a sliced loaf from the fridge and made herself a large breakfast of toast and Marmite with coffee, nudging Daniel aside so she could get some space to eat it. Nadine was slouched on the settee, muttering to herself and clicking the remote at the TV, while she balanced a plate of something on her lap. There was no sign of Millie.

'The telly stopped working,' Nadine complained.

'The remote is old,' Talantire said, as she finished off her toast. 'Try some new batteries.' The woman was too stupid to even notice that the TV's tiny red light had gone off. How did she ever get into the police? How long before she realised that the house was getting colder and that nothing worked? This cuckoo family might last a few hours, but by four p.m. they'd need lights, and that's when it would hit them. She had a feeling that when Millie was uncomfortable, that would force the issue. She could clearly wrap her mum around her little finger. Once Millie couldn't stand it any more, they'd be gone. Hopefully.

Talantire grabbed a change of clothing and all the torches in the house and loaded them into her sports bag. She was able to lock her own bedroom door, one benefit of the house having previously been a shared student rental. After a brief goodbye to her Midwich cuckoos, she jumped into the car. She fired up the engine and pulled out into the road, accelerating hard to get out of Cornwallis Avenue as soon as possible. The day was clear and bright, with a keen northerly wind. She was looking forward to the run, her first sociable event with the Harriers since before Christmas. She had some anger to sublimate, but she also needed distance from the suffocating domestic disaster of Nadine and her brood.

New Year's Day. Fresh starts, fresh thinking, fresh ideas. She took a deep breath, then released it slowly.

Chapter Nine

Talantire arrived early at Hartland Quay, and after parking overlooking the cliffs, used the time to ring Adam, relaying to him everything that happened with Nadine.

'Jan, poor you! This is unbelievable. Them just arriving and taking over your home? Couldn't you have called the police?'

'Well, seeing as both Nadine and I are the police, it would have seemed strange to any young cop who turned up to witness the cat fight. The interests of the children would be paramount in safeguarding terms. Seeing as I couldn't deny I had given Nadine a set of keys, it would be classed as a civil matter between us.'

She told him about turning off the heating and electricity, and he cackled with complicity. 'It's brilliant; it's bound to work.'

'I think so, but I dread to think what state they'll leave the place in.'

She was planning to ask, but he got there first. 'Why don't you come and stay with me for a few days? Until they've gone?'

'I'd love to,' she said. 'I've really missed you, Adam.'

'I've been thinking about you the whole time,' he said, 'worried about you out there, policing the nutters on New Year's Eve.'

'The worst nutters are the ones at my house, my little nest of cuckoos, trying to push me out and just about succeeding.' She sighed. 'This whole Brent West thing has got out of hand too, and I feel I can't trust anyone. But I'm also determined to push it through to the end.'

'Jan. My home is your home. My mum and dad are looking forward to meeting you at some stage. My sister can't believe I landed such a heroic woman.'

'Heroic? I hope I can live up to the stories!'

'Of course you will.' He paused. 'I love you, Jan. I want you to know that.'

She had a catch in her throat, and fierce tears squeezed through her closed eyelids.

'Oh, Adam,' she sobbed. 'I feel the same way.' Two familiar cars arrived, one parking into the next slot to hers. 'The harriers have arrived, so I'd better go. But thank you.'

'For what? I haven't done anything.'

'You have, more than I could tell you.' She hung up and tried to suppress the sobs of happiness that were shaking her shoulders.

—

It was just getting dark when Talantire got home. She'd had a good run followed by a late lunch at the Black Bull with the rest of the Harriers. Now she was returning with a due sense of dread. That Nadine's car was absent from the drive cheered her up hugely. Maybe they'd gone. She reversed up to the garage door and retrieved a torch from her sports bag. A dark car, parked a little way further up the street from her home, reversed away, just using sidelights. It was a strange manoeuvre, and her cop brain clicked in, memorising the number plate when it passed a street lamp. She jotted it down before leaving the car.

Cornwallis Avenue had its own climate, colder and windier than the rest of Barnstaple, as if it was somehow a few degrees further north. The air had a polar feel, and she realised she would have to put the heating back on before she could take a shower.

She opened the front door and shone the torch within. She gasped: the place was a complete tip, as if it had been burgled. It was cold, too, enough to see her breath in the beam. Her two leather sofas, the only really quality furniture she possessed, were lying on their fronts, face to face. From beneath there was a flash of light.

'Are you a burglar?' Daniel called. 'Don't hurt me.'

'No, Daniel, I live here. It's Jan. Where are the others?'

Talantire now realised that the boy had made a fort with the two settees and cushions, the backs of the sofas a roof over the top. When she pulled aside the front cushions, she realised he had made a nest for himself with duvets and blankets and had within his precious PlayStation.

'They've gone to buy some heaters and extension cables, 'cos it's freezing in here.'

'It's meant to be, Daniel. I thought they might enjoy a game of polar bears.'

The boy emerged, and she realised he was wearing one of her coats; a rather fashionable, white three-quarter length quilted job. She noticed knitting needles were protruding from the sleeves.

'What are you doing with those?'

'I'm Wolverine,' he said, and growled, moving his spiky hand towards her face. She caught his arm and pulled up the sleeve to reveal the needles gaffer-taped to his fingers.

'So you're ready to defend yourself, are you?'

'Yeah.'

'Have you eaten anything?'

'Pizza.'

Yes, in the torch beam, she could see the crusts distributed across the floor and the countertop, and some more trodden into one of her throws. She took a deep breath and kept her temper. She made her way upstairs, unlocked her own room and packed a suitcase with everything she would need to stay at Adam's for a couple of weeks, including her laptop. She looked at her phone, seeing a dozen messages from Nadine. She glimpsed the last one which said: 'Jan, it's absolutely freezing. I can't believe you are treating my kids this way.'

Ignoring the message, she walked round the house and photographed the mess with crime scene precision. She even found an unused packet of yellow numbered plastic crime scene markers, reserving the last one for Daniel, who proudly held it up as he was photographed wearing her coat and knitting needles. All this would come in very useful if she ever began civil proceedings for the damage. But she couldn't imagine doing it. Nadine was a rape victim, damaged and struggling to save her marriage. She didn't need any more worries. Talantire had just finished loading the car when she realised that she couldn't legally leave an eight-year-old on his own.

She risked ringing Nadine, who answered from her car.

'About time, too,' Nadine shouted.

'You can't leave your youngest alone in the house, Nadine. Why didn't you take him with you?'

But even as she asked, she realised she knew the answer. With him in the house, she could always get back inside. No one could lay a finger on either of those children without official approval. This was clearly going to be a fight. After a short and bitter argument with Nadine, she hung up to call social services on the emergency out-of-hours number and settled down in her car to wait.

A call on her work phone surprised her. It was from a duty uniform on the public information line. 'I'm sorry to disturb you ma'am, but this gentleman claims to be the brother of the dead woman, and was able to give her date of birth and address. He insisted that he would only speak to the officer in charge. I know you aren't on duty for a few hours, but are you happy to speak to him?'

'Yes, that's not a problem.'

The man who was put through spoke with a vaguely Italian accent, but his English was perfect. 'My name is Carlo Franco Lezcano, and I am Katarina's older brother. I think you have been expecting my call.'

'I was hoping to speak to you, yes. My deepest condolences for the loss of your sister.'

'Thank you. I am at Milan airport and expect to be in Exeter on Tuesday. Perhaps we can arrange to meet? I think I need to identify the body.'

'That won't be necessary; her partner has already done it.'

'Her partner?'

'Mary Stuart Davies.'

'What? I don't know this person.'

'Well, we are satisfied—'

'Mary, is a woman's name, yes? She cannot be her partner. I am a lawyer and there are certain legal standards to uphold. Have you spoken to Alex?'

'Well, I'm sorry Mr Lezcano. Alex has not been in touch and we understand he is still in Morocco. Have you spoken to him?'

'No. He does not return calls.'

'Ours neither. Miss Stuart Davies met the legal thresholds that apply here.'

'Do they live at the same address?'

'No, but we have many photographs of them together, and messages on her phone. It was important for us to assist the coroner at the earliest possible opportunity.'

'And what about my sister's bank accounts? Does this woman have access—'

'There is no need to be alarmed. We have not given her anything that she did not have before. She has not been allowed access to your sister's possessions.'

'I'm very upset; this is not right.'

'If you give me your telephone number, I will encourage her to call you, to put your mind at rest.'

'But this woman is a total stranger. How can I be reassured?'

'Mr Lezcano, I know this is a very stressful time, but if this woman made your sister happy in her final months and years, I think this should be a source of comfort to you and your family.'

'But you are a detective, no? Why would you be involved if she had not been murdered? Or the victim of some fraud?'

'CID was brought in on a precautionary basis, but I have to say that the evidence points to suicide. I realise that may not be any comfort to you, but we see ourselves as working on the family's behalf to provide facts about her death.'

The man's grumbling continued for some minutes before Talantire was able to finish the call. He seemed to be hinting that his sister had money, but there was no evidence of that. They may have only looked back at six months of her financial records, but her lifestyle over a longer period seemed to hint at a very basic standard of living. If Katarina Lezcano had money coming down the line, she certainly didn't seem to be counting on it.

—

It was four hours later when Talantire headed off for the nightshift, with a boot full of all the overnight things she would need to stay with Adam for at least a couple of nights. Social services had been brilliant in the end; they had found a static caravan for Nadine and the kids in Sunnysides, a seasonally underused mobile home park on the edge of Barnstaple. It would tide them over until the start of the tenancy in Camborne. Urgent reports, referrals and so forth would be triggered, along with counselling for both Nadine and her husband Roger. Sorting all that lot out had taken hours, as she had predicted.

Only after Nadine had returned her keys did Talantire replace all the fuses. Nadine got the children to say 'thank you for having me' and apologised for the disruption. 'I'm sorry we've got no time to clear up,' she said, as they wheeled out their luggage.

Daniel had revealed to her in the last few minutes that they had kept themselves warm by running the oven on max with the door open, and taking it in turns to press down the toaster and hold their hands over the top. That was the price of leaving the kitchen socket circuit on. There would be quite an electricity bill to pay.

She slid her Ford into the Barnstaple police car park and went up into CID. Maddy Moran was at her desk on the phone, so Talantire simply logged in to see the latest. She was hoping that James Garrett would by now have been tracked down, but there were no sightings on the record. However, there were more forensic details emerging about Katarina Lezcano. Toxicology tests on her brain and other organs confirmed the damage that exposure to heavy metals had done to her. But it was still unclear how she had been poisoned and if it was deliberate or an accident. Police had gained access to the seafood shack in Brixham where she worked, and with the help of the local authorities had taken samples of the foodstuffs in the freezer for testing. Results were awaited.

The ballistics report, however, had arrived. The email was concise.

The Beretta was a deactivated weapon, with no firing pin and some permanent damage caused to the interior of the barrel. That explained it being lighter than the spec. Its origin was unclear, though the deactivation was in a style used by the Dutch government.

Talantire was relieved that it wasn't a workable weapon, but she was still alarmed that something like this could turn up in the hands of a vulnerable and troubled woman like Katarina Lezcano. It was only legal to own such a firearm with the correct certificate, and none had been found. The Beretta wasn't on the official register. How on earth had she got hold of it? Through Garrett, perhaps? That would be something to ask him, if they ever found him.

She turned back to the photographs on the case, including those of the artworks that had been found at her caravan. The amazing sculpture of the woman, holding her own throat, was so prophetic and so significant that it demanded further investigation. She rang PC Tim Caldwell and spoke to his mother. She told her that Tim was with the physiotherapist and was off duty until

Wednesday. He would be on crutches for six weeks. She made it sound like Talantire's fault.

'I'm really sorry to hear that,' she responded.

'I hope they get that bastard soon. Tim was only doing his job. He didn't deserve that, did he?'

'No, he certainly didn't.'

Talantire hung up feeling vaguely guilty.

Maddy was off the phone and greeted her. 'How's the domestic mayhem?' she asked.

'Better, hopefully. They've moved out to a caravan park. I would be happy never to see any of them again. They left my place like an absolute tip. The daughter is a total nightmare.' She regaled Maddy with the details.

'My sympathies.'

'I'll go back and tackle it in a day or two, but I'm staying with Adam until Thursday.'

'Well, that will have its advantages, I'm sure,' Maddy said with a salacious grin.

'So no signs of Jimmy Garrett?' Talantire asked, anxious to change the subject.

'Nope,' Maddy responded. 'We weren't getting anywhere on the vehicle trace. However, we have got some CCTV which appears to show someone dressed like him on an illegal e-bike in Teignmouth, so that's how he could be getting about.'

'When was that?'

'Three days ago.'

'So before the assault on Tim?'

'Yes.'

'I took that call from Katarina's older brother, who's never heard of Mary Stuart Davies. He seems quite irate about her identifying the body.'

'He wouldn't talk to me,' Maddy said. 'Has he heard from the son?'

'No. And I think it's very fishy,' Talantire said. 'Why wouldn't he have returned home?'

'I haven't had chance to think about it,' she responded. 'We had fifteen arrests last night, and I've been pulled in all sorts of directions.'

'I'll give you a hand, if you like. But I want to check some of these details on the Lezcano case, because you're too busy and Tim Caldwell is off sick and time is moving on.'

'Right,' Maddy said.

'I mean, what if her son poisoned her, Maddy? That would explain why he's in no hurry to come back. She had written about falling out with him.'

'It's plausible, I suppose.'

'What kind of work does he do?'

She looked at her notes on the system. 'Secretarial. He's a temp, with SelectStaff in Exeter.'

'Did you ring them?'

'Tim did. There are a few notes. He's not taken up any placements since September. That seems to coincide with his absence abroad.'

'Okay leave it with me.' Talantire looked into the records PC Caldwell had made, which looked fairly thin and amateurish. He seemed not to have checked up on the young man's passport to see if he was genuinely abroad, nor was there any attempt to trace his phone, whose number had been recorded on his mother's own device.

Talantire decided to make a few broader checks into the woman's death, including further investigations into her partner, Mary Stuart Davies. Looking again at the messages on the woman's phone, her plight seemed obvious. Worsening health, mood swings and estrangement from family and friends. It was no exaggeration to say that the poisoning was the trigger which caused her life to unravel. So how had these heavy metals got into her system over such a prolonged period?

Talantire had a theory, and if there was time enough at the end of her shift, she might be able to check it. Of all the nights in the year, the tail end of national hangover day might be one quiet enough.

—

It was still dark at seven a.m. when Talantire arrived at Hilditch Farm. She had rung the farmer, Tony Conybeare, the evening before to say that she planned to visit early, if she got time. Conybeare said he was always up before six, and any time after that would be fine.

It was a cold, blustery morning, with sporadic heavy rain, and Talantire made sure to don her wellingtons and waterproofs before she made her way down the muddy track. The torch beam caught the jagged branches of hawthorn and blackthorn bushes that lined the path. The caravan, four hundred yards beyond the main farm buildings, was just visible behind a screen of straggly bushes, still displaying tatters of crime scene tape. Conybeare had confirmed that nobody had been down here since the police search the previous week. The only footprints Talantire saw were the deep rain-filled hoof marks of cattle which had crossed the path between two barns.

She fished in her pocket for a bunch of keys which worked all three police padlocks: one for the caravan and two for the sheds in which the dead woman kept her artwork. She was aiming for the largest shed but noticed that the caravan's padlock appeared to be missing, as was the hasp to which it had been attached. She played the torchlight over the steps up to the caravan door, which revealed fresh mud.

Someone had been here recently, and she had a pretty good idea who it might be.

Wary of the experience suffered by PC Caldwell, she backed away behind one of the sheds so she could call in for assistance without being overheard. As she was making the call she saw, against the back of the shed, an electric bike partially covered by a tarpaulin. She played the torchlight on the ground and saw from the muddy tracks that it had been brought in from a different direction up the hill from the far end of this meadow, rather than past the farmhouse up the hill. If there was a way in from the lower part of the meadow, that would explain why Conybeare wasn't aware of the unexpected visitor.

She had just called in the discovery of the e-bike when she heard the rattle of the caravan door. She killed the call and clicked off her torch, making her way as silently as she could across the muddy ground to the next shed. Light, from a mobile phone, was playing across the other end of the hut where she was standing. Aware of Garrett's record of violence, she considered her own weapons: she had in the pocket of her anorak a pair of handcuffs and a PAVA spray, plus in her hand a powerful lightweight torch. Not much, but something, if it came to a fight. She stood with her back to the wooden shed, breathing as lightly as she could as slurping, sucking footsteps approached unseen. The phone light illuminated the opposite shed, and the reflection from the shed window dazzled her. Her enemy was just around the corner, to her right. The rules of engagement dictated that she should declare herself as police and demand her opponent surrender.

She had a different plan, but then the control room ruined it.

Her phone rang, and she tossed it far into the darkness. The phone light followed the splash it made in landing, trying to find the source.

She could see his silhouette, a male, stockily built, facing away, towards the ringing phone. 'Do you want some, copper?' he whispered, turning from side to side, unsure where she was.

'Yes.' She took one step towards him and kicked sideways at the back of his knee. The man staggered and yelled, but did not fall. She flashed the torch on for a moment, enough to be clear as he turned to her that this was indeed James Garrett.

She saw he had a knife, serrated, six inches, made for steak, but not bad for penetrating guts. He went for her, and she vanished into the darkness behind the shed. She heard the slop of his muddy footsteps, and waited with her PAVA spray just around the next corner.

He wasn't stupid; he lunged with his knife arm around the corner, and found the sleeve of her anorak, and a sting of flesh penetrated beneath. The pull of the knife made her fumble the spray, which discharged into nowhere, then fell to the ground.

With her anorak snagged by the knife, she rounded the corner fully and braced against the shed side with her other hand. She kicked backwards and high, her boot connecting to something hard, the side of his head or jaw. He staggered back and swore, his breathing heavy, and his light fell into the mud, face down, leaving only a faint halo on the ground. She hoped he would reach for it so she could kick again, with more power.

But he backed away, breathing heavily, until she could no longer see him.

They were fighting blind, but she rated her chances.

He was less fit than her, that was obvious. But he was probably stronger. She could play for time if she could keep out of his reach. But waiting until backup arrived – that would be a long combat. And her PAVA spray and phone were in the mud somewhere. She took two quiet backward steps into the open before briefly clicking on the torch in her left hand. His face was caked in mud, and there was blood, but the knife glinted as he waggled it backwards and forwards in his hand. She clicked the torch off for the safety of darkness, as he advanced cautiously.

'Garrett, just lie down, you're under arrest,' she shouted.

'Arrogant bitch! I'm going to slit your throat. No copper arrests me. No woman, neither.'

She stumbled into some rusted piece of agricultural equipment in the mud behind her, half-buried, tines exposed. She corrected her balance and stepped backwards over it, as Garrett advanced. She could feel the rusted structure, a harrow perhaps, and took one more step backwards to be free of the heavy frame. She felt the edge of its contours with her boot and felt sure that her enemy was unaware of it.

'Come on then, if you've got the bottle,' she taunted, clicking on the torch and shining it into his face. He rushed for her and immediately tumbled down onto the harrow. He screamed in pain, and she could see him face down, spreadeagled on the triangular frame. She couldn't see the knife, but did see that he was trying to pull himself up with his left arm, not the one the knife had been in. That other arm, somewhere below him, couldn't help him unless he dropped the weapon. She jumped onto his back, and fighting to keep her balance, stamped his head hard onto the metal, which brought a new cry of pain. Kneeling down now, she grabbed his left wrist and slid the cuffs over it, then clipped it on to the harrow. She then jumped off, as he wriggled himself around. When she next got to play the torch over him, she could see he was knotted, his left arm behind his back, one leg badly twisted and the glint of the knife in his right.

'Not so impressive, James. Brought down by an unarmed woman.'

He swore at her, bellowing his frustration, as he attempted to free himself. She let him struggle breathlessly for a minute, while she regained hers and called in for backup. Then, using the torch, she found and picked up her phone and PAVA spray. She waited out a minute of threats and swearing, until his movements slowed and his cursing deteriorated into breathless acceptance of his predicament. Time to ask a question or two. She stood over him, a boot resting on his knife arm, until he took the hint and dropped it.

'Did you poison Katarina?'

'No way! She was my friend. I liked her.'

'Did you supply her with a gun?'

'What gun?'

'A Beretta, which we found in the back of a sculpture.'

'I don't know anything about that.' He didn't sound quite surprised enough at the revelation. Talantire assumed he was lying.

'Did you supply her with drugs?'

'Only weed, as a painkiller. She was suffering a lot.'

'So you didn't charge her anything?' Talantire said, folding her arms.

'I gave her a big discount. I didn't do anything wrong. My whole life you bloody coppers never leave me alone.'

'Try going straight, it usually works.'

'I did, but you lot never, ever believe. Once a crook always a crook.' He tried to throw her off, and she stepped away watching as he once again became furious, rattling the handcuffs as he tried to stand.

'It's up to you to prove us wrong,' she said.

'Yeah, right. I saw that old git, Sergeant Huchinson, in the pub. He started this whole thing up again.' Rain was pouring across his face now, and a mixture of mud and blood ran diagonally down his cheek and jaw.

'He's long retired now,' Talantire said. The rain intensified, and she pulled up her hood.

'Unlock me!' he yelled, rattling the handcuff. 'I'm in agony.'

'So was PC Caldwell after your assault on him.'

'Good. I'm glad. I think you broke my leg.'

'You should look where you're going, shouldn't you? I'll unlock you when help arrives.'

—

Garrett was in a police interview room by ten a.m., fortified by a strong cup of coffee and a Greggs sausage roll. His leg had been bandaged and there was a dressing on his cheek. He was a picture of sullen disappointment, still in handcuffs, and eyed Talantire with smouldering anger. The doctor in A&E had diagnosed a hairline fracture of his eye socket where Talantire had kicked him. As she sat opposite him, she was flanked by PC Caldwell, who had come in specially, on crutches. On the other side was a duty solicitor, a bored-looking woman.

Garrett steadfastly stuck to his story that he was a friend of Katarina Lezcano, having originally met her at the seafood shack, for which he had done some deliveries. After hearing of her illness, he offered to supply her with cannabis, of which she was a small-scale user already.

'So, Mr Garrett, why did you so violently resist arrest?' Talantire asked, while PC Caldwell nodded his head vigorously. 'This could all have been a very civilised discussion.'

'Because I'm sick to the back teeth of you lot. I get stopped and searched at least three times a year when travelling around in my van.'

'Well, you continue to be a drug dealer.'

'No, I'm *not*. I gave it up, except for the odd bit here and there, like I gave to Katarina.'

'We can argue the toss about that if you like, James, but your attack on PC Caldwell is going to put you back inside.'

He shrugged extravagantly, seemingly accepting the logic of that statement.

'Tell me about the gun, James.'

'Don't get your knickers in a twist. It's deactivated. There's no firing pin.'

'It's not registered either, so that makes it illegal.'

'Come on, it's a technicality.'

'Maybe, compared to the rest of the sentence you will be looking at. So why did you give it to her?'

'I didn't, really. I just left it at her place, because I didn't want any awkward questions when the plods came to search mine.'

'Why did you need it?'

'I had some old scores to settle, people who needed to see that I couldn't be pushed around. I just warned them off, that's all.'

'Where did you get it?'

'In a car boot sale.'

'Come on, I wasn't born yesterday,' Talantire said.

Garrett shrugged. He clearly wasn't going to tell her any more. She had one final question.

'Did she know that it wouldn't fire?'

'Yes. I'm sure she wouldn't have had it on the premises otherwise. I don't know what she did with it after she moved. She didn't return my call.'

Talantire told him where they had found it and he rolled his eyes in incredulity. 'In the hallway? That is so stupid.'

'Like you say, she didn't want it in her home. It was well concealed.'

She left him to the desk sergeant to be charged and held in custody. Now it was light, she wanted to return to the caravan and the sheds to look again at the artwork Katarina had left behind. Talantire had a growing hunch that this was where the clue to her poisoning would be found.

—

She returned down the muddy farm track and saw that a rather miserable-looking police constable was posted by the door to the caravan. He was standing on the bottom step looking down upon a sea of mud, blowing on his hands to keep warm. He let her into the larger of the two sheds in which the life-size seashell sculpture dominated. She had seen before some of the tools which the artist had used, stored in boxes.

Using nitrile gloves, she carefully unpacked the boxes. There was a grinding wheel with a ceramic sanding disc, as well as tubs of glue and a variety of other artists' tools. It was perhaps a little too much to expect PC Caldwell to have taken samples of all this for toxicology, but it was an obvious step on the road to establishing what exactly had poisoned her. She already had a theory about that. She'd googled it, and it did seem possible. She took samples of everything, including a dust mask, and stashed everything in carefully labelled evidence bags. She'd have these tested urgently. Getting to the bottom of the poisoning was well overdue, and she knew it could come from the coroner's budget if necessary.

Before she left, she went back up to the farmhouse to thank Tony Conybeare for his cooperation and, in the warmth of the farm kitchen, she requested a big mug of coffee which she then delivered back to the PC.

Then, five hours later than scheduled, she signed off from her shift, and after depositing the evidence bags at Teignmouth Police Station ready for the courier, drove off to her afternoon Pilates course in Barnstaple. After that, she would stay the night at Adam's house, where he had just got back from his break. She could hardly wait to see him. In just a few short weeks, he had become a pillar of her life.

Chapter Ten

'I'd like you all to stand with your shoulders relaxed and just breathe in gently through your nose and exhale with your mouth,' said Tina, standing svelte and poised in front of the class 'After the excesses of Christmas and New Year, you might be feeling like dinosaurs, ready for extinction. But we'll deal with that aching back with a trip to thoracic park, where we will be freeing up all of those sticky vertebrae.'

Talantire was standing amongst sixteen other women and two men in a gym in Barnstaple, in the first Pilates class of the New Year. It was a little crowded, with plenty of New Year resolutions in evidence from the new faces she saw. But among those were two latecomers, who were grabbing her attention and threatening to destroy any hope of relaxation in one of the few periods of me-time in her life.

PC Nadine Lister, her former live-in stalker, and Samantha Mahoney. *What on earth?*

DC Mahoney was, to Talantire's knowledge, Brent West's most recent girlfriend. Blue-eyed, dark-haired and shapely, she was the classic West girl, and perhaps prettier than all the rest of them. She also seemed to be sporting a tan, which made everyone else in the class look pasty. Nadine had been insistent that Sam had broken up with West for exactly the same reason that so many other women had: his overbearing and controlling personality, and his manipulative and domineering nature. Talantire wasn't so sure. The two women were in the row behind her, and she felt their eyes upon her as Tina urged them to lie on their mats.

At the end of the class, Nadine and Sam made their way over.

'A bit of a surprise, seeing you here,' Talantire said.

'You mentioned the class,' Nadine said. 'So I thought I'd enrol, and I let Sam know about it, too.'

Talantire had hoped she was shot of Nadine. She could hardly bear spending more time in the woman's company. 'How is Sunnysides?' she asked.

'It's alright. Daniel is happy enough, but Millie seems to think it's a prison camp.'

'And how are you, Sam?' Talantire asked, tentatively.

'Been a bit rough the last couple of months,' she said. 'What with one thing and another.' She seemed to be hinting at the breakup.

'But you managed some time in the sun, I see?'

'Yes, that was a couple of months ago, but I've been topping it up on the sun bed.'

'That's quite a workout,' Nadine grumbled, staring at the class teacher, who was now collecting up various bits of equipment. 'Is she an influencer or something?'

'No, she's a former prison officer. Anyway, you should be alright, you're both nearly a decade younger than I am,' Talantire said, as she gathered up her mat and headed to the door.

'God, all those back movements, everything creaks and cracks,' Nadine said. 'I think my pelvic floor needs sanding down,' she said with a laugh.

'So what are you doing in this neck of the woods, Sam?' Talantire asked, as they made their way to the car park. She knew Sam lived in Crediton about twenty miles west of Exeter.

'My mum lives in Barnstaple, and I'm staying with her until tomorrow,' Sam said. They said goodbye and headed off to their respective cars. Sam's was parked next to Talantire's, and just as she was getting in, she said: 'Jan, I've got a contact in human resources, so I think we can find out who the original complainant was.'

'Oh, who?' Talantire asked, standing up again with the car door partially open.

'She's fairly new in post, but she's on our side.'

Our side? Talantire wasn't even sure whose side Sam was on. Sam was probably referring to Lakshmi. Talantire wasn't going to reveal how much she knew about the staffing at the headshrinkers at Middlemoor. Devon and Cornwall police headquarters was a nest of vipers at the best of times. Anything Talantire said might get back to West. It was imperative that he didn't get to know everything she was up to.

'Do you have a minute?' Talantire asked, gesturing to her passenger seat. Sam nodded, and got in.

'Look, Jan, I know you probably don't trust me, but...'

'I've been burned before, Sam. Let's see your phone.'

The detective constable offered up her Samsung. Talantire turned it off and placed it on the dashboard. 'Just a precaution, Sam. You appeared to be in a relationship with Brent during the Bodmin Moor joyriders case, during which he spent a lot of time trying to undermine me.'

'Was it that obvious?' She seemed surprised.

Talantire gave a sharp laugh. 'Blatantly: the lack of personal space between you, the informality and the fact you never took your eyes off his face except to looked daggers at me.'

'Oh, sorry about that,' she said, looking out of the window. 'I really fell for him.'

'It's a large club, Sam, with enticing membership deals, but no one ever renews.'

Sam looked at her, before staring away again. 'Brent really shafted me, you know.'

There were plenty of ways to take that comment, but Talantire softened a little when she saw Sam was on the verge of tears. She rested a hand on Sam's shoulder while awaiting further revelations.

'He got me pregnant and made me have an abortion.'

'He *made* you?'

'Well, he already had kids, and persuaded me how embarrassing it would be for him, and how it might damage his career because people would put two and two together if they saw me walking around with a swollen belly.'

'It was all about him, then.'

She nodded. 'He made it clear it would be over, too, if I kept the baby. And I couldn't bear that.' She began to weep, tears rolling down her cheeks. 'I was in love with him.'

Talantire dug out a box of tissues from the glove compartment and handed them to her.

'Were you in love with him yourself, Jan?' Sam asked.

'I was smitten, certainly. But I have this guarded nature, and I don't…' She realised that she was revealing things she had never mentioned to any colleague. The steel door came down. *I'm not going down this path with her.* Sam could be using her own apparent vulnerability to draw out mutual confidences, that very same tool Talantire herself had used with other exes.

'So how did it end?' Talantire asked.

'He went back to one of his previous girlfriends – some high-powered woman at the NCA – soon after he moved across to Avon and Somerset.'

Talantire tried to hide her shock. Rebecca Crossfield! It couldn't be anyone else. Rebecca herself had hinted that she was still sleeping with him when she visited her in Liverpool. From her description, it had sounded like a dalliance. Fuck buddies, even. But West was apparently taking it seriously enough to have dumped Sam Mahoney, rather than stick to his normal MO, running both relationships in parallel. It certainly reinforced Rebecca's own story, that she was the only one to have tamed him. But could she believe it? She wasn't sure.

'So when did you last see him?' Talantire asked.

'Not for weeks and weeks.' Her eyelashes flickered a little as she said this, and broke eye contact.

It was a lie.

Talantire knew immediately. She had spent thousands of hours staring across the interview table at habitual liars, professional perjurers, fabulists, fabricators and fantasists. Some were absolutely brilliant, weaving threads of untruth into broad and verifiable canvases of fact. DC Samantha Mahoney was not one of them. There might be plenty of truth in what she said, particularly the pregnancy and abortion, but it was blatantly obvious to Talantire that Sam had been consorting with her enemy very recently. In which case, this whole approach to her, offering a mole at Middlemoor, might be a ruse.

Her job now was to hide her own realisation, not to let Sam know that she knew. If Sam was West's Trojan horse, she must appear to bring her within the walls of the citadel of trust, where Talantire could feed her lies of her own that would get back to West. Disinformation. The meat and drink of espionage.

'So do you think we will be able to get him?' Sam asked.

'No. I think he is too clever. My New Year's resolution is to give up on this whole charade. He's got too many friends in high places, and my own credibility is shot, thanks to a certain person not a million miles away.' Talantire's eyes followed Nadine's Volkswagen as it left the car park. She could only hope that Sam would be taken in by this deceit. She doubted whether West would, when he heard about it. But she had to try.

'I think you should press on with it; that's what I want to do,' Sam said. 'I won't rest until he is in jail.'

'Well, good for you. I have to move on with the rest of my life. I'm on a final written warning, so I've got to be careful.'

'Yes, Nadine told me.'

Thanks, Nadine.

'I've got to go now, but thanks for making contact,' Talantire said. Sam took her phone and got out of the car and into her own.

'By the way, where was it you were on holiday?' Talantire called across.

'Morocco. It was lovely.'

Morocco? Seemed a popular place at the moment.

Talantire started the engine and reversed out. She watched carefully to see if Sam started to make a phone call. She didn't. It would be too much of a giveaway if she immediately rang West.

As she drove home, she turned around in her head the conundrum she was caught in. DC Samantha Mahoney was clearly a clever woman, but what was she thinking? Granted, she must still be completely in thrall to West. She must have spent ages rehearsing this story with him. The courage required to come out here with Nadine, to Talantire's home turf, to the Pilates class, and tell this raft of lies would be substantial. But even as Sam weaved this tale, pretending to hate her former lover, she must simultaneously be aware of the verifiable truth of the allegations about his behaviour. How could such contradictory positions exist in one person's mind?

Talantire still hadn't figured it out by the time she pulled into Adam's drive. She had so much to tell him, and she craved his touch, his warmth and support.

―

The first Wednesday of the year dawned, crisp and cold. Talantire awoke in a strange bed, and her first action was to hug the sleeping man next to her. The warm cuddle: a much-underrated pleasure. She wanted to stay in that warm cocoon, but she couldn't. She was back on day shifts for the next month, so she made sure she was up good and early. Last time she had stayed at Adam's she had been horribly late for work, something that was quite out of character. As she drove in on the nearly hour-long journey to Barnstaple, she got a call from Primrose Chen.

'Good morning, ma'am. You asked me to check on the mobile phone belonging to the victim's son.'

'Alex Brown, yes.' Talantire knew that, despite not possessing the phone, they could find a great deal of information within it from the service provider on whose network it ran, simply by having the phone number and a warrant. Less that they had got from Katarina's device perhaps, but useful, nonetheless. Messages, texts, emails, pictures; all stored on a backup server on the cloud.

'I've only just started on it a few minutes ago, but I can already tell you one thing: six days ago, at the time he sent a message to us saying he was still in Morocco, the phone was actually in the UK. It had been in Morocco, back in October, because I can see the roaming carrier data. It's mostly been off in the meantime.'

'So Alex Brown is lying to us.'

'It seems that way, ma'am.'

'That makes him a very clear suspect. We've been slow on this, but I think we need to know a great deal more about him.'

The son might have had all sorts of reasons for wanting his mother dead, and there had clearly been a falling out. They'd been slack on this, she acknowledged to herself, but things were going to change now.

—

On arriving at the office at eight a.m., Talantire looked across CID. There was a pretty full complement of staff, the best turnout since before Christmas. She exchanged New Year greetings with those colleagues who hadn't been in on the two previous days and felt good and ready to tackle her workload. She logged into the system and checked to see what was new. Dave Nuttall had had a success with a confession from Charlie Evans about the heating oil thefts, while Maddy was still knee-deep in various New Year's Eve incidents, including two particularly nasty domestic assaults of the he said, she said variety where forensic investigation was required to support the victim's case.

Consequently, nothing more had been done about the Katarina Lezcano case, which Maddy had already assumed to be a suicide and could await the return to work of PC Tim Caldwell.

Talantire was going to change that. She rang Alex Brown's mobile and found she was unable to leave a message because the mailbox was full. She put a call in to Select Staff and asked for the full details on all the jobs and notes on file for Mr Brown. The receptionist she spoke to said they could do it by midday, when the manager came in. Talantire then applied for an extension to the warrant they already had for Brown's electronic and communication devices to allow them to get a financial order and to enter his home address in Exeter. It was granted without any quibbling. She pulled up all the pictures that Primrose had already extracted from Ms Lezcano's phone and flicked through the various images of her son. He was definitely someone she had seen before. Not a cop, not a criminal and no acquaintance she could think of. If he was a temp, there were all sorts of places you could have run into him.

There was a simple answer to this, and it took only a few minutes. She created an internal 'wanted' notice, a copy and paste image of Alex Brown and a brief background to the case, and distributed it on the daily newsletter which went to all frontline officers in the region.

It had only been out there five minutes when she got a screen-top message, followed in quick succession by half a dozen others. Alex Brown was well-known to dozens of officers. He had worked at Middlemoor for four months in the summer and resigned in September. He had been the PA to the assistant chief constable, Jeremy Noone.

Talantire was staggered to find this coincidence. Someone with close connections to the police had been lying to his mother, fair enough – who hasn't done that – but wasn't sufficiently worried about her death to get in contact with his former employer. He still hadn't turned up. This was getting very strange indeed. She had a very bad feeling about it.

For the next half an hour, the revelations came in thick and fast, including one from her own boss DS Wells, who not only messaged her but rang shortly afterwards.

'What are you doing, digging into this, Jan?'

She explained Alex Brown's connection to the case. 'We still haven't got to the bottom of how she was poisoned, sir. Alex Brown is the next of kin and has been telling us porkies. He claimed to be in Morocco when we informed him of her death, but his phone was in Gloucestershire.'

Wells was silent for a while. 'Well, Jan, as usual, you seem to have a good reason for what you're doing. But don't proceed any further. It's very delicate.'

'Sorry, sir, I don't get—'

'Just leave well alone, do you hear me?'

'Yes, but—'

She could hear him typing. Clearly sending someone else a message. 'Jan, I think I'm going to have to get back to you on this.' He cut the call.

What on earth was going on? Wells seemed quite troubled. She barely had time to give it a thought because other messages were coming in. The next phone call was from a PC Giles Cadwallader.

'Hello, ma'am. I think I might be able to help you shed some light on this,' he said cagily.

'Go ahead, Giles.'

'I'm a friend of Alex's. It's quite sensitive, so I'd prefer to do it face to face, if that's all right?'

'Are you at Middlemoor?'

'Not any longer. I asked for a transfer, as I couldn't bear it there any longer. I'm in Axminster.' That was the far eastern end of the county, a good ninety minutes away.

'Look, I don't think I can get over there today,' she said. 'You could ring me at home this evening. Would that be all right?'

He thought for a while before agreeing and she gave him her personal mobile number. 'Giles, do you know where Alex is?' she asked.

'Not exactly. He's abroad; Morocco, I think. But I think what happened gave him a nervous breakdown.'

Before she could ask another question, he said: 'Sorry, got to go.' The line went dead.

Confirmation now came thick and fast. The manager of the staff agency rang her. The woman said they hadn't heard from Alex since September. 'That was such a shame, as he got such great feedback from clients. He was really one of our most reliable and well-thought-of contractors.'

'Can you send me his file in its entirety?'

'You should already have it,' she said.

'I'm sorry?'

'Devon and Cornwall Police requested it formally in October, I think.'

Talantire was shocked. 'Was there some disciplinary issue?'

She laughed. 'Well, you'd know better than I. So, are you not calling from HR?'

'No, as I said to your receptionist, I'm from CID.'

'Oh God, what's happened?'

'I'm afraid I'm not able to tell you at this time,' she said hating herself for having to be so opaque. 'But I think by the end of the day I might be able to tell you more. Inquiries are ongoing. Can I ask you one final question. Who was the signatory to the formal request from HR?'

'Hold on a minute.' Talantire could hear the riffling of papers. 'Yes, I thought so. It was the head of HR, Fiona Hendricks.'

'Can you send me the letter she sent, plus your reply?'

There was a short pause. 'Look, if you have the authority of pursuing a case, surely you can get this directly from your own HR department. All the letters have "Confidential" plastered all over them, so it's really not up to me.'

'Of course. Thank you.' Talantire hung up and steepled her hands over her face. Damn! The woman was being sensible and following protocol. She wouldn't have any idea why Talantire couldn't possibly get the documents from HR. Even making the request would be incriminating. Hendricks would assume it to be part of her private vendetta against Brent West. She mentally kicked herself for being so stupid. Assumptions, assumptions, assumptions. The enemy of all good police work. She now suspected exactly what had happened. Everything was falling into place. Wells's reticence, the cat-and-mouse game with Brent West's former girlfriends, it all made sense.

As Talantire put the phone down, Maddy looked across at her, seeing her hands still steepled over her nose and mouth.

'You look like you've seen a ghost,' she said.

'I have,' Talantire replied, letting her hands fall. 'I've discovered something truly incredible. But I have this horrible feeling I'm not going to be allowed anywhere near it.' She looked around to check whether anyone was close enough to overhear. Unfortunately, a couple of officers were already staring at her. That's the trouble when you recruit based on sharp eyes and an enquiring mind. There is no such thing as a secret.

Talantire glanced towards the ladies' toilet. 'Got a moment?'

Maddy nodded and followed her, past Dr Crippen the coffee machine, past the CSI glass box and into the bathroom. Talantire checked that none of the cubicles were taken and then turned to Maddy.

'No end of people recognised our Alex Brown, Maddy. He worked for months at Middlemoor.'

'You're kidding!'

'He was a temp at first, then once he gained his security clearance, he took on what was to be a permanent role as the PA to Jeremy Noone. Then one day in September he just didn't turn up for work. He signed off sick by text but never filed a fit note. He just kind of dropped off the face of the earth. Those are the facts. But here's what I think.' She lowered her voice and said: 'There was some kind of personnel issue about Alex requiring Fiona Hendricks, no less, to write to SelectStaff, the agency that employed Alex in October. Now I don't think it was a complaint about his work. The agency manager in fact let it slip that he was one of her best employees. So what was it? I think the only conclusion is that he had *made* a formal complaint, not received one.'

'Against who?'

When Talantire said the two words, Maddy's jaw nearly hit the floor. The entry of another officer into the ladies terminated the conversation, but she had put her point across.

The two detectives left, and huddled by Dr Crippen, still staring at each other. The implications were massive. This revelation completely blew open her attempts to nail Brent West for his treatment of women. Because the original complainant, the woman Talantire had spent weeks trying to uncover, whose allegations had sunk West's attempts to become chief constable, was not a woman at all, but a man. The assumption she had made was completely wrong. Which meant that she had wasted months heading down a cul-de-sac looking only at the women who might have had relationships with West. Now, finally, here was the answer: Alex Brown. And now nobody knew where he was. If he was in Morocco, then somebody else in Britain was using his phone to pretend that he was still abroad. All roads, all enquiries, all suspicions came back to the same man.

Brent West.

Back at her desk, Talantire wondered how she was going to get any closer to the truth. She needed to find the exact nature of Alex Brown's complaint against West. She thought she knew her former lover pretty well, and was certain that West was not bisexual. Even though he was quite capable of sleeping with those he wasn't attracted to in pursuit of some other advantage, it seemed to her unlikely. Men like him were up for threesomes, okay, but only as the filling in a female sandwich, not the other way round.

None of the other women that she had talked to had mentioned any such proclivities, either. Of course, there were literally hundreds of other ways in which Brent West could have upset a PA, male or female: bullying, rudeness, attempts to overreach his authority – that could be a good one – or simply being a complete arse in some other way. Talantire couldn't believe that she had just *assumed* that the only type of complaint that HR would take seriously against West was one related to sexual conduct. Just because of the way he had treated *her*. She had framed her campaign against West in the image of her own experience. Idiot!

This entirely explained why Wells was so equivocal about her pursuing Alex Brown. He must have known that he was the original complainant against West. Only a small number of senior officers would know the details, including Fiona Hendricks, chief head shrinker. So the search for whoever poisoned Katarina Lezcano led to Alex Brown, a man who everyone in HR thought had conspired with her to bring down Brent West. That inevitably meant the Lezcano case would be given to somebody else. She had a precious few hours before senior management cottoned on to this, and one great opportunity. The one place where she would undoubtedly get a copy of the original complaint against West was on Alex Brown's own computer in his flat in Exeter.

She already had the warrant, so now she needed to get down there immediately. Brown's flat was over an hour away, so the sooner she started the better. She jumped up from her terminal, waved a quick goodbye to Maddy and raced downstairs to her unmarked Skoda. She roared out of the car park, past the Travis Perkins yard, and only at the roundabout on the edge of the industrial estate did she put on the blues and twos. At the first traffic lights she turned off her personal and work mobiles. She didn't want to be hauled back, and if she didn't know she was off the case, it wouldn't matter.

She drove like a demon, hitting 110 mph at one point as she raced along the A361 towards Tiverton. Cars pulled off the carriageway to make way for her; she was like a woman possessed. The satnav kept updating her arrival time, gradually improving it, as she squealed around the first Tiverton roundabout, then slowed to navigate the busy centre of the market town. Once on the A396, she accelerated again towards Exeter. Brown lived in the Heavitree section of the city, in a quiet suburban street on the first floor of a converted Victorian house.

Talantire left the blue lights on as she parked the car, then rang both doorbells – ground and first. There was no reply. There was no time to arrange for a locksmith. She just had to keep her fingers crossed that she could effect an entry without too much difficulty.

She saw a young woman with a toddler in her arms looking out of the next-door window at the blue lights, and beckoned her to the door. Talantire showed her warrant card and explained that she was looking for Alex Brown. Had she seen him?

'No, not for months.'

'What about the downstairs occupant?'

'She is staying with her granddaughter in Huddersfield.' The woman looked up the street. 'My husband reckons Alex has moved in with a boyfriend, but we still keep watering his plants.'

'Ah! You've got a key? Fantastic. So do you know the boyfriend?'

'We've never seen one here. We just made the assumption. The place is so neat, he's got be that way, hasn't he?' She rolled her eyes knowingly.

Talantire smiled. 'We try never to jump to conclusions.'

Alex Brown's flat was indeed neat and modern, tastefully furnished and full of an extensive array of plants that had clearly been lovingly cared for in his absence. His bookshelves were heavy with Russian literature. The fact that the neighbours had been keeping an eye on the place at least removed one worry that she'd had – that the man himself would be found dead within. Nevertheless, Talantire donned booties and blue nitrile gloves in order to explore. The place did smell a little stale, but she detected nothing worse. The dishwasher was full of clean crockery and cutlery, and the fridge was clean and tidy too. In the freezer were some frozen vegetables and oven chips, along with some ice cream.

The bathroom still had toiletries, toothbrushes and a comb, and these last items she bagged for evidence. There was only one bedroom, the bed neatly made, and a foldout desk, on which was a Hewlett–Packard printer/scanner and a Wi-Fi router. There were plenty of charging cables and plugs, but no sign of a laptop or PC. She opened cupboards, drawers and under-bed storage containers. Back in the lounge she saw on a bookshelf a Russian matryoshka doll. This one resembled the Russian President, Vladimir Putin.

She smiled to herself and grabbed it. She twisted Putin, who opened at the waist to reveal another doll within. Medvedev. She opened this doll, and found Putin again, working backwards through time. Then Yeltsin, Gorbachev, Chernenko, Andropov, Brezhnev. Finally, a gap, with only a finger-sized doll there inside Brezhnev

– Lenin. Beside Lenin was a computer data stick. She slipped it into an evidence bag.

She risked turning on her own mobiles, work and home, to find a message had been left for her by Wells on both devices. His message was plain: because of the potential conflict of interest, the Lezcano case was being handed to DCI Fred Winterflood from Exeter. Maddy had also been removed from it. Winterflood himself had left a message for her on her work mobile.

She rang him back, and he picked up immediately.

'Hello, Jan,' he said. 'Thanks for getting back to me. I really hope you could brief me on this one because it's a little baffling. As far as I can see from the notes we're talking about a suicide, so I don't understand what all the fuss is about, or where the assistant chief constable's former PA fits into it.'

'I'm afraid I was quite late to get the message so I'm actually standing here in the living room of Alex Brown.'

'Ah, are you?'

'Yes, and I'm very happy to tell you that there are no dead bodies here.'

'Well, I hadn't been expecting that, but I'm very glad to hear it, all the same.'

She then gave him a summary of the case, from the discovery of Katarina's body in the sea and the heavy metal contamination of her body, through to the awkward correspondence between her and her son, as well as the involvement of her current partner, the formidable Mary Stuart Davies. 'So yes, we are leaning towards the idea that this lady took her own life, but I am very worried about Alex, who claims to be in Morocco while his phone is here in the UK.' She decided to say nothing about her suspicion of the involvement of Brent West, at least for now.

Winterflood had a reputation as an affable and thoroughly reasonable cop, a safe pair of hands, who treated all his subordinates well. He was short and wide, in his late fifties, and she had heard that he had recently taken six months off to get over prostate cancer. He was so happily married that none of her female contacts had ever heard of him misbehaving. By no means a typical career policeman. She'd seen him across meeting room tables and over Zoom, but had never had the time to chat. Despite this, he had been generous enough to send her congratulations on some of the big cases she had cracked.

'So why are you being taken off it, Jan? What is this conflict of interest?'

'If they didn't tell you, that's interesting in itself. It concerns a personal matter, indeed a personnel matter. I'm sure being such an experienced detective you can dig it out for yourself, and if you do, I'll then explain to you why it's a load of tosh.'

'Very mysterious!' he exclaimed with a laugh. 'So did you find anything of interest at the flat?'

'I've got toothbrushes and combs for elimination samples, but otherwise it's pretty tidy.'

'So, nothing to give an insight into his disappearance?'

'No,' she lied, thinking about the data stick. 'I'm not quite done yet, but no. I guess if you ask HR to open up to you about his correspondence with them, you might find some answers.'

Chapter Eleven

Talantire arrived at Adam's house at seven o'clock that Wednesday evening to find him still enmeshed in a website design, the deadline for which was the next day. He gave her a welcome hug, invited her to help herself to a glass of wine, which she did, then returned to his upstairs office. She then unpacked her own laptop on the kitchen table to look at the treasure she had recovered from Alex Brown's flat. There was no password protection on the data stick and a scan revealed no viruses. She opened the folder marked 'Middlemoor', and immediately struck gold. A letter, dated August 3:

> To whom it may concern,
>
> I would like to report an incident of unprofessional conduct by a senior serving male officer and an apparently more junior female officer which took place on Easter Sunday, April 9 2023 at 4:15 p.m. in the vacant office of the chief constable, and indeed on his very desk. I was working next door in the secretarial office, which sits between the assistant chief constable's room and that of the chief constable. I was quietly catching up with a backlog of correspondence on overtime when I first heard laughing and giggling

along the corridor, then the sound of the lock being opened in the next-door office. Shortly afterwards I heard the unmistakable sounds of female sexual pleasure. There is an adjoining door between the secretarial office and the two senior officers' rooms, and through the gap in the sliding door I was able to confirm what I had heard. I recognised the senior officer as Commander Brent West, but I did not know who the female was.

As a temp at the time, and still awaiting my security clearance, I did not feel that I could challenge them directly. However, I did exit the room quietly, and sat in the ground floor reception area, which I knew they would have to pass at some stage. Only then did I check that there were plenty of cameras in that area which would have proven their presence on that date and time. I made a point of asking the security personnel at the desk whether all footage from these cameras was routinely recorded and they affirmed that it was. It was forty minutes later when Commander West left, in full dress uniform. A few minutes after that the female officer in plainclothes also departed. She looked notably flushed. I took a photo of her as she passed and am happy to send it to you to assist in identifying her. I made no mention of any of this until I heard in July that Commander West was being considered for the role of chief constable.

Although I remain a very lowly employee within the hierarchy of Devon and Cornwall Police, I do my best to uphold the very high standards of honesty, integrity and professionalism required within the force. I also feel that such standards should be applied equally to officers of all ranks and particularly the most senior. I think therefore that my witnessing of this particular act reflects badly on the candidacy of Commander West, and renders him unsuitable for high office. I also trust that under the human resources whistleblower policy, my confidentiality will be protected. I would like a specific assurance on this point.

Yours faithfully,

Alexander Brown

PA to Jeremy Noone

The first response was a full two weeks later, a staggering delay considering the gravity of the accusations:

Dear Alex,

I do apologise for the delay in response to your letter. I was away on holiday, and no decision could be made in my absence. We take the allegations you have made extremely seriously and will look into them. We will, of course, completely protect your privacy; I personally guarantee it. I have copied in the assistant chief constable, who will undoubtedly be taking a particular interest.

I would like to arrange an appointment for you to come in for us to take a fully detailed statement of the events you witnessed. It is quite possible that the activities you describe are not only of a disciplinary nature, but may cross the boundary into criminal activity.

Once again, thank you very much for bringing this to my attention.

Sincerely,

Fiona Hendricks

Head of Human Resources

The data stick contained various other short letters, administering the complaint process, and a follow-up to an apparent actual interview that took place at the end of August. Most of the space on the device was devoted to downloads of reams of regulations gleaned from the Devon and Cornwall Police personnel handbook. Nowhere on the USB was there any letter withdrawing the allegations that he had made, or indeed the apology. There was also nothing which hinted at the identity of the female police officer caught in flagrante with West. Annoyingly, there was no sign of the photo which Alex said he'd taken of her. The last document on the data stick was dated 26 August. It was only a few days before he went off sick.

This underlined Talantire's suspicions that the withdrawal wasn't a change of heart on Alex's part, but something forced on him by West. After all, she had vaguely recognised Alex, but they didn't know each other. While he might, for whatever reason, have wanted to withdraw his own allegation, there could be no reason for him to confess to a non-existent collusion with her, someone he demonstrably didn't know. The only person who would benefit from the withdrawal was West himself, who must have been aware that Talantire had made her own complaint. How he had found out, she didn't know, but she had her suspicions.

She was still mulling what this might imply about subsequent events when her phone rang. She was expecting a call from PC Cadwallader, Alex's friend, but it wasn't him.

She recognised the number, marked in her contact list as Nadine's second phone. It belonged to her daughter, and it was one that they had conversed on after Talantire discovered the spyware on Nadine's main mobile. She answered with a due sense of dread.

'Hello, Nadine.'

'It's Millie.'

'Oh, hello, Millie.'

'Do you know where Mum is?'

'I've no idea. I saw her last yesterday evening after Pilates.'

'She went out this morning to the supermarket and hasn't come back. Her phone is switched off.'

'Are you and Danny there on your own?'

'Yep. It's like a prison here. I've cooked some baked beans, but there is no bread and no Coke, nor nuggets.'

'Is there anybody at reception?'

'Nah, the whole place is basically dead.'

'Did you ring your dad?'

'Yeah, he's at work. He rang Gran at the hospital, who basically went off on one.'

Nadine's parents lived in Camborne a good ninety minutes' drive away from the Barnstaple holiday park where their grandchildren were living. They would probably be beside themselves that the kids were being left to fend for themselves.

'Did your gran ring social services? You're not supposed to be on your own.'

'I rang them myself; they said it's fine.'

'Oh, come on, Millie. Social services would never accept a child of eleven left in charge of an eight-year-old on her own.'

'They were okay, honestly.'

'Millie, if you didn't ring them, I will.'

'I did. Are you calling me a liar?'

'I'm afraid I am, yes.'

The child called her a bitch and hung up. Talantire immediately rang Nadine's phone, which was indeed turned off. With a heavy sigh, she climbed the stairs to Adam's office and updated him on the latest.

He shook his head with amazement. 'Nadine is a tragedy magnet, isn't she? Everything that could go wrong, will go wrong.'

'I'm going to ring social services myself,' Talantire said. She spent the next half an hour talking to a very concerned woman on the out-of-hours helpline who said she'd treat the case as a matter of urgency and asked Talantire to officially report the mother missing.

'Given Nadine's track record, I'm not sure she would be treated as a missing person unless she's gone overnight,' Talantire responded.

The woman seemed shocked, but Talantire was only speaking the truth. Police resources were not easily allocated to a missing adult, even a police officer, after just an eight-hour absence. She wouldn't officially be classified as vulnerable, either, despite her tender state of mental health. The care of the kids was another matter. She wondered if they would end up in care. It was certainly possible.

As soon as she put the phone down, it rang again, an unknown number. It was Roger, Nadine's husband. She'd never spoken to him before.

'Hello, Jan. I hope you don't mind me calling, but I'm a bit worried about Nadine.'

'Me too.' This was interesting coming from a man who'd given her that mother of all black eyes.

'Millie rang me to say she hasn't been back since heading up to the supermarket at 10:15,' he said.

'That's what she just told me,' Talantire responded.

'We both know how ditzy Nadine is, so I just wanted to check that she's not at your place.'

'I don't think so, Roger. I have the keys back, so she couldn't get in. I'm not there at the moment; I'm in Tiverton. I'll ring a neighbour to see if the car is on the drive.'

'Thank you.' He paused. 'So I guess you wouldn't be able to keep an eye on the kids.'

She had suspected that he was working his way round to asking this. 'No, I'm more than an hour away, and am on shift from eleven. But I have rung social services.'

'Shit, have you?'

'It seemed like the only reasonable thing to do.'

He sighed, and then said: 'Look, I probably should have rung before, but I'd just like to say, I really appreciate you helping her and providing her with somewhere to stay, and letting the kids stay too for a couple of days.'

'Happy to do it.' It seemed neither the time or place to let him know that she had felt bounced into providing Nadine somewhere safe to stay, and had had no say whatsoever in the arrival of the children. Still, she was impressed he thanked her. He then explained about Nadine's mother being in hospital, something she had already heard, and reeled out a list of reasons why there was nobody who could look after the kids until the start of the school term.

'It sounds like you are going to have to take some time off, Roger. Social services are going to be all over this, eventually. You being a police family isn't automatically going to get you off the hook, you must know that. Especially now that there has been some verified domestic violence.'

'What verified domestic violence?'

'Roger, when she came to me on December 16, she had a massive black eye and claimed that you inflicted it on her.'

'The lying bitch; I've never laid a finger on her.'

'There are *photographs*, Roger. I took them myself; there's no point denying it.'

There was an exhalation of wordless anguish at the other end of the phone. 'It's a lie,' he said thickly. 'I promise, Jan, I promise on my life. I never, ever, hit her.'

It was a heartfelt defence, no doubt about it. Talantire swiped through to the pictures on her phone, as if to prove to herself that they really existed. And they did. Nadine, sitting on the edge of the bath in Talantire's home in Cornwallis Avenue, pallid in pale underwear, looking miserable and slumped and dejected with a black eye the size of an apple, her eyelid swollen closed. She had a large crescent-shaped cut across the bruise, and purple finger marks on her neck, throat, shoulders and arms: the classic signs of being gripped, shaken and strangled. It was textbook stuff, straight off the courses every police officer had been on. Looking at these pictures stirred anger within her.

'Shall I send you a sample image, Roger? I'm really not making it up.'

'Okay. She didn't report it, or I would know.'

'I wanted her to, believe me. I worked on her for *hours*. But she is terrified of losing the kids, scared of being rejected by her own mother and couldn't face the public humiliation. You share a police house, right? You'd be fired, but you'd probably both lose the home. Above all, she still loves you, Roger, but she's in denial.' She attached the picture and hit send. There was silence for a few seconds then a sob, at the other end of the line. The assailant faced with the consequences of his own actions.

'I didn't do this, Jan, this... is not my doing.'

'Well, she hardly did it to herself, did she! What would be the point?'

There was a short silence, then: 'So that you would take her in, perhaps. Make you feel sorry for her.'

'I *already* felt sorry for her!' Talantire gave a short bark of a laugh, amazed at Roger's sheer effrontery, but then stopped. The hairs on the back of her neck stood up. God, he might be right. Nadine was a superb manipulator of others' emotions; she'd made her feel guilty so often. But if she had done this to herself, of course it would have worked. It couldn't have failed. Who could possibly turn away someone bearing such bruises? The stigmata of a violently failing marriage.

She didn't know what to say in answer. 'Well, Roger, the important thing is to find her, isn't it?'

'I couldn't agree more.'

'I'll be back home tomorrow morning. I've got some clearing up still to do before I go to work. I'll give you a ring then.'

'All right,' he said, and added, 'Thank you.'

She put the phone down and blew a sigh. She sat, stunned, with her hands steepled over her face. If Nadine could do this, hurt herself to create an impression, could anything she said ever be trusted? Had she really been raped by Brent West? Had she really been held captive in a shed in freezing weather against her will? What if she'd made it all up? Maybe she'd been taken in completely. Talantire prided herself on being able to see a lie a mile off, but it just could be that Nadine had this one ability, the one that Sam Mahoney certainly didn't have.

Bewildered, Talantire went to the fridge and helped herself to another glass of white wine. She couldn't help thinking about the NDA that she had seen on Nadine's phone. A non-disclosure agreement offered by Brent West and presumably since signed by Nadine. He wouldn't have offered it if he didn't need to buy her silence, would he? It was the smoke that proved the fire.

Talantire tried to imagine if anybody would agree to pay money to buy off an unfounded allegation. Actually, it did happen. She could recall a few cases, particularly to forestall allegations of child abuse. None of her doubts were laid to rest by this conjecture.

She only realised she was wandering around the kitchen when Adam came down and looked at her. 'What's up? You look stressed.'

'Nadine has gone missing. I've spoken to her kids and her husband, and suddenly I don't know what to think anymore.'

He took the glass of wine from her hands and put it gently on the kitchen table, then pulled her into a big enveloping hug. She surrendered to the warmth of his arms and rested her head against his.

'Leave it to somebody else to sort out, Jan; you've *got* to take time away. You finished work hours ago but still look so stressed.'

'I don't know what to do,' she said. 'But I feel I should be doing something.'

'Not every buck stops with you,' he said. 'Just remember that. There are people on duty now whose job it is to chase all this up. There are plenty of good detectives and keen minds. You can't carry the whole world's troubles on your own shoulders.'

—

That night, she had a dream where her twin sister spoke to her and warned her about something. But she couldn't hear what she was saying, because Bella was confined behind a thick sheet of glass, which gradually turned into a window of a car in which Talantire was sitting, and her sister standing outside. Bella receded into the distance as the vehicle pulled away. She awoke with a start, relieved at the passing of the nightmare, and snuggled into Adam's warm body, beneath a protective arm which slid around her. She lay awake for some time, listening to the susurrus of his breathing, like gentle surf on a pebbly beach. She kissed his shoulder, and lay with her ear against his chest, drawing sustenance from the steadiness of his heartbeat.

She awoke while it was still dark, with pins and needles in her arm where it was trapped under his body. She eased it gently out without waking him, massaged some feeling back in, then reached across to turn on the work phone. She had been hoping to see messages indicating that Nadine had turned up.

Nothing. Just a text from her neighbour confirming that Nadine's VW wasn't there.

—

A chill January Thursday morning, still dark, and Geoff Hutchinson was up early again, long before the central heating kicked in. He and Molly had arrived yesterday evening to stay for a few days with Molly's sister and her husband, at Burnham-on-Sea on the Somerset coast. Sprocket was already waiting for him, wagging her tail, at the bottom of the stairs as he tiptoed down. They had stayed here before, but not for several years. Leaving the house quietly while everybody else was still asleep was more challenging in a home that wasn't familiar. Geoff picked up the key on its string by the back door and let the dog out. He had in mind to go through the arboretum toward the coast, head north then return via the sandy beach. Sprocket would enjoy the soft sand on her arthritic feet. Checklist: lead, dog bags, dog treats, torch, phone. Yes, he had everything. Even his favourite small binoculars.

The moment he was outside in the garden, Geoff felt the cold, crisp air and inhaled deeply. He turned left out of the house up the lane to the slight rise which gave a view over the sea. He gazed out to the west, seeing the sparkling fairyland of lights that marked out the new nuclear power station being built at Hinkley Point. Gazing north, he could see the dark edge of the South Wales coast and the calm pewter sea, and below him the still-dark town of

Burnham. He opened the gates and went along a country track, between low hedges, taking in the view. The arboretum was to his left, shrouded in darkness and mist. The track turned west towards it, a 200-acre private estate, and beyond it a woodland burial ground. They made their way down through a well-maintained forest track, helpfully covered in bark chippings and past stands of mature trees. These included a group of immense sequoia, which reached high into the sky. Sprocket stopped, and lifted her head, ears pricked. Yes, Geoff could smell it, too. A taint – not so much a smell of bonfires as a sickly reek. Not pleasant at all.

They had talked about it last night over dinner, and Geoff had remarked how appropriate it was to have a private crematorium just outside a town called Burnham. 'Willows is a pet crem, now,' Keith had said. 'Willows Equine and Pet Memorial Centre.'

Geoffrey had quickly leaned down to clamp his hands over Sprocket's ears. 'Shh,' he said. 'She might get upset.'

'Aw bless,' said Anne, and looked down at the elderly dog. She and Molly had exchanged a smile.

Geoff now moved to slightly higher ground underneath a cedar, and trained his binoculars further down the hill, beyond the bottom edge of the arboretum. At the centre of a cluster of buildings was the Victorian detached house from which Willows was run. A light was on downstairs. There was a horsebox and Land Rover, a white van and a car all parked on the apron by the house, and behind the house, a squat building with a tall chimney.

The crem itself.

There was a wisp of smoke coming from the chimney. Was the furnace on now, before 7 a.m. on a Thursday? That seemed strange. Geoff led Sprocket lower until they came to the gate which would take them out to the lower path, which Keith had reminded him ran along the bottom edge of the arboretum between there and woodland burial site. There was a sign on the gate, saying 'Private', and next to it a yellow planning notice about the diversion of a public footpath. Keith hadn't warned him about this, so it must be new.

Sprocket was making whining noises, and kept turning to go back, hoping Geoff would follow. But Geoff had other plans. He led Sprocket along the hedge which bounded the lower path, until he found a gap that he could squeeze through onto the track he had intended to follow. Sprocket joined him and scampered ahead into the darkness. The path descended until they were within thirty yards of the gravel apron which encircled the house. Geoff turned off the torch and just listened. If the furnace had been operating, he would have expected to hear some kind of a hum, but there was nothing. He could see no signs of activity, so, mentally shrugging, he headed off right, along the path which would lead further north to the beach. He'd gone about a hundred yards past the back of the building complex and the smell was stronger here: horrible and rancid. Sprocket stopped to do her business, and he risked clicking on the torch to clear up after her.

And it was there, in the beam of light, that he noticed: it was snowing. Tiny dusty particles, swirling and billowing. Ash, from the chimney. He shone the beam into the air, and caught myriad motes, drifting north-east towards Weston-super-Mare, Portishead and Bristol.

—

Back at the house, Geoff told his hosts what he had encountered as breakfast was being prepared. 'I had to force my way through the hedge to get onto the footpath, and then to get onto the beach, I had to climb over a locked gate at the end. Luckily, Sprocket was able to slide through the gap underneath.'

'There's new people who seem to be running it now,' Anne said, as she worked the grill, from which delicious smells of bacon and sausage emanated. 'They bought the arboretum as well as the crem business. My hairdresser's husband works there part time on the garden maintenance, and he says they're from London. Certainly not from round here.'

'There's a lot of money in pets,' said Keith, looking at Sprocket, who was lying on the settee, staring at them. 'Gourmet pet food, ice cream for dogs, vets' bills through the roof. And specialist cemeteries.' He sipped his coffee and winked at the dog. 'You don't know how lucky you are, do you, Sprocket?'

Geoff laughed. 'I still feed her the basic mix; none of the bloody pouches. And she likes it well enough, don't you, Sprocket?' The dog looked from one to the other, knowing that something relevant to her was happening, but not what. 'She didn't like that smell, and neither did I.'

After they finished breakfast, Geoff and Keith retreated to the lounge. Geoff had his laptop with him and logged on to Companies House. He looked at the listing for Willows Equine and Pet Memorial Ltd. The company had been set up only six months ago, and had a single director by the name of Lyndsey Smith, born in May 1981, whose address was given as that of the memorial centre. She'd never been a director of anything else. Geoff was a little surprised that there were no other directors. He switched to the company's website, which had no mention of the woman. It was, however, slick and full of the unctuous parlance used by undertakers about 'absent friends' and 'dignified individual cremation treatment' for everything from gerbils to ponies, with prices to match. The crematorium was closed to visitors all day on Thursdays, when the cut-price communal pet cremations took place.

So that was what he had witnessed.

The first Thursday of the new year dawned with a watery sun as Talantire drove back from Tiverton to Barnstaple. She just had time to spend two hours at home before beginning her shift. She arrived there just before nine. Everything looked normal, but as she let herself in, the enormity of the mess still to be cleared up hit her with force. She attacked it with vigour, discovering various pieces of clothing left behind by the children, discarded tissues, scratches on the worksurfaces and a thumb-sized green plastic arm on the stairs, which must have come off one of Danny's toy figures.

She had texted Roger to ask if there had been any news on Nadine, and at 9:30 a.m. he called her back.

'Hi, Jan. No sign of her. But I've been relieved of normal duties to help look for her.'

'Where are you now?'

'I'm just at the end of Cornwallis Avenue. I'll be with you in two minutes.'

She looked out of the window and could see a patrol car approaching. It looks like he had the kids with him, too.

Not wanting anyone to see the state of her place, she stepped outside to meet him. Roger was in uniform. A fit-looking fellow, average build, dark eyes. She couldn't help imagining him hitting Nadine. Emotions rush to judgement, even when the intellect hesitates.

'Nice to meet you, Roger,' she said, offering a hand which he shook firmly. Millie had emerged from the car too, leaving Danny in the front passenger seat. She was wearing a hooded top with her hands thrust deep in the pockets, and was making teeth-chattering noises and rubbing her arms.

'Can we come in for a moment, Jan?' Roger asked, glancing at his daughter.

'It's a bit of a mess, but yes.'

'But it's *our* mess, so the kids are going to help, aren't you, Millie?'

She gave an expansive shrug, and thrust herself even deeper into her hoodie, her head bowed. Talantire led them in, hearing Millie's loud tut as she saw the state of the place. In truth, it was already a lot better than Talantire had found it. The furniture was the right way up, but there were binbags half-full of rubbish at the bottom of the stairs, and it still had a stale smell. Danny joined them, with an Action Man in his hands.

'I was thinking that Millie could mop the kitchen and clean the work surfaces while Danny cleans the bathroom. By way of saying sorry,' Roger said.

'It's a nice offer, thank you, but it's not necessary. I don't have long before my shift starts.' Both kids scarpered out of the door, straight back into the patrol car.

'Ah.' He looked around. 'Nadine's car triggered two ANPR cameras on the way to Tiverton, including the one on the roundabout at the end of the A361 where it meets the A396, but nothing beyond. So that's where I'm heading, once I pick up the children's aunt at Barnstaple station. She has come down from Manchester to babysit at the caravan park.'

'That's a relief, that someone will look after them.'

'Absolutely.' He stared out towards the car. 'Those injuries on Nadine, by the way, were self-inflicted.'

'How do you know?'

'I questioned Millie about it, about when she first saw the bruises. She said that Nadine hit herself with a hammer. She managed to do it a few times on her own body, but... well, I'll get her to tell you in her own words.' Roger went out to fetch her from the car, and the girl stood with them in Talantire's entrance hall.

'Millie, tell her what you told me,' Roger said.

Millie shrugged and turned to Talantire. 'Yeah, well basically, I heard a shout of pain in the bathroom and saw Mum with a hammer in her hand, and she'd whacked herself on the arms and shoulders, and was sort of strangling herself to make bruises on her neck. I asked her what she was doing, and she said "Trying to get us somewhere to stay with Auntie Jan." Then she told me: "I need a black eye, but I haven't got the courage." She was waving this hammer around. I told her she was being stupid and she'd give herself brain damage if she hit herself on the head with a hammer. I looked around and reckoned I had the answer. I got a tin of beans, wrapped it in a face cloth, then stuffed the whole lot in a sports sock. I gave it to her, but she still couldn't do it. So she says: "Would you, Millie? Sorry to have to ask." So I said yeah, no worries. Lie down and close your eyes. And I smacked her with it really hard. She screamed so loud that Danny even came up and left his PlayStation.' A smile played across her face.

'How could you *do* that to your mother?' Talantire asked.

'She asked me, didn't she?' Millie rolled her eyes as if it was obvious. 'I'm an obedient kid, basically.'

Talantire looked at the child and realised she had found a bone fide psychopath; intelligent, cold, rational and without a hint of mercy. She'd grow up to kill, she was certain of that. Maybe she already had. She then looked at Roger, who was staring at his eldest child, as if to ask *did I really spawn this creature?* He and Talantire exchanged a look as weighty as a report for child referral.

—

After the Lister family had driven away, Talantire rang the control room to ask for a patrol car to check the last ANPR sightings of Nadine's Volkswagen. It turned out that Roger had already requested it, which was something of a relief. She then rang Sergeant Beatrice Dodds, Nadine's boss and the head of Camborne community police. The two officers knew each other well, having worked together on the Bodmin Moor joyriding case.

'Hi Beatrice. Can I ask, did you give PC Roger Lister permission to look for his own wife?'

'Not exactly. I gave him time off to go and see his kids. Why?'

'He arrived at my home in a patrol car and seems to think he's got permission to try to track her down himself. Obviously, if she's found dead, he would be—'

'—the prime suspect, I agree. I notified her as a missing person this morning. I believe DS Moran has been assigned the case, as it's on Barnstaple's patch.'

That was good news. A good officer, an ally, a friend.

'Suspicion of the husband isn't just theoretical, either,' Talantire said. She described the bruises on Nadine,

Roger's denials and the almost incredible explanation that the daughter had confessed to helping her mother make them.

Beatrice blew a long sigh. 'Do you think Roger coached his daughter to give that confession?'

'It crossed my mind, but I have to say it seemed like a voluntary, indeed almost enthusiastic, revelation on the part of the child. I genuinely think Millie enjoyed it.'

'Well, we are in wild speculative territory here, Jan,' Beatrice said. 'Let's just find the woman ASAP.' It was exactly the kind of robust and practical suggestion that Talantire would have expected from her. She readily agreed. After the end of the call, Talantire looked around her untidy home. She sealed the bin bags, dumped them in the wheelie bin outside and decided to leave everything else until later. She wanted to find Nadine herself. It suddenly seemed a very important thing for her to do.

If Nadine was dead, there were three people in the frame. Husband Roger, of course. He had argued with her for months over her affair. Brent West, who thought he had silenced her with the NDA. Finally, Nadine's own daughter had to be considered. That would be dark territory indeed.

She arrived a few minutes early for her shift at the office and immediately filled in a docket for the evidence bag with the data stick which she had taken from Alex Brown's flat. She had already copied across all the data stick files onto her own personal laptop, but registered it as unread when filling in the docket, and on the case file. She copied the most crucial files onto a new data stick, intending to hide it at home, just in case. DCI Winterflood, who had taken over from her on the Lezcano case, would get it later that day through the internal post.

Seeking confidentiality, she went into a meeting room, sat down and then rang PC Tim Caldwell, who was working now in Exeter. She asked about his broken patella, and softened him up with some small talk, about 'driving a desk'. He laughed. 'I'm actually really enjoying the interactions with the coroner and the Crown Prosecution Service,' he said.

'Enjoying the CPS? Well, it'll soon wear off, I guarantee it.'

She found out plenty about the case that she dared not try to get from Winterflood directly. First, that the small-time drug dealer James Garrett seemed genuinely to be a friend of the dead woman. He'd been interviewed numerous times now, and his consistent line had actually checked out. Mary Stuart Davies had met him too, apparently. Second, that the seafood at the restaurant that Lezcano worked at was not the source of her poisoning. Analysis of the seashells found in the caravan and of the dust around her grinding machine revealed that it was the shells themselves that were the source of the heavy metal poisoning.

'I had a feeling that that was the root of the problem,' Talantire said. 'I read up about a real-life case in Canada of a woman, also an artist working with seashells, who became sick from the contaminated dust.'

'That case was mentioned in the lab's report,' Caldwell said. 'It said that even though the mussels were probably safe to eat in normal quantities, the shells concentrated the toxins found in the waters, and inhaling the dust got it straight into her lungs and bloodstream.'

'That's exactly the same, then.'

'So there was no foul play; that was Winterflood's conclusion,' Caldwell said. 'It was definitely suicide.'

'Maybe it was, but it was triggered by the absence of her son, Alex Brown. And as far as I can see, there is nothing new on the case files about him. Has he been in contact?'

'No, ma'am. The coroner is very disappointed, seeing as he's next of kin.'

'You are aware that his phone was in the UK when he was claiming to be in Morocco, aren't you? He texted messages to us, saying he would be in contact on his return.'

'Yes, but DCI Winterflood doesn't think it's significant.'

'Really? You know that Alex Brown worked at Middlemoor as a temp in the office of the deputy chief constable?'

'I had heard that, yes. I never met him.'

'And he's *disappeared*, Tim.'

'Look, do you want to talk to Winterflood? He's sitting right here.'

'Yes, all right.'

The phone was passed over and Talantire heard the baritone rumble of the DCI's voice. 'What can I do you for, Jan?'

She laughed at the informality. 'Look, Fred, I know I'm banging on about the same thing—'

'—what a surprise—'

'But I'd like to suggest to you that this whole case is completely the wrong way round.'

'Go on then. Give us the Brent West angle, because I'm sure that's where you're heading.'

'All right. You're looking at the probable suicide of a woman, found washed up on the south coast of Devon, agreed?'

'I'm with you so far.'

'But as a result of our inquiries, we have discovered that her son's unexplained and uncharacteristic absence, particularly over Christmas, may well have contributed to Ms Lezcano's decision to take her own life.'

'Possibly, yes.'

'He claims to have been in Morocco, and we know his phone was there, for a while—'

'—and he sent a postcard, which is in our possession,' Winterflood added.

'But he still claimed to be there in the last week, while the phone from which that message was sent was definitely in the UK.'

'Jan, there are all sorts of reasons why the relatives of the dead may want to lie to us.'

'I know, but Alex Brown was the original complainant who kiboshed Commander Brent West's attempts to become chief constable of Devon and Cornwall.'

'How on earth do you know that?' Winterflood whispered. The change in noise indicated he had moved away from his desk. A door closed, and the background hubbub diminished. 'That is information you should not have. Even I only got a glimpse of it. I'm not allowed to keep a record of it on the case file.'

'I'm a detective, Fred. It's my job to know these things, and I have impeccable sources.'

'You found something at the flat, didn't you?'

Talantire realised Winterflood was pretty shrewd.

'No comment.'

'You could be sacked for this, Jan. You know you are *off* the case. Final written warning and all that.'

'I wasn't off the case at the time when I was at the flat. You know, Fred, isn't it funny how everybody seems to know what's on my personnel file and yet I can't find important information on anyone else's file, even though it may be a murder.'

'Jan, please. I've indulged you pretty well on this so far. You have a terrific reputation and your brain is second to none, but this obsessive hatred of Commander West is going to be the downfall of you, honestly. I've heard it from many sources that you'll just stop at nothing—'

'— what sources?'

'You tell me yours, I'll tell you mine. But you won't, of course—'

'My source? Okay, I found a data stick in Alex Brown's flat, detailing his complaint, mentioning Brent West was caught screwing a female officer on the chief constable's desk, while wearing most of his full dress uniform, on an otherwise quiet Easter Sunday. Probably some juvenile dare.'

'It was all made up, Jan. I shouldn't tell you this, but as you are already a friend of Alex's you will know—'

'I've never met the guy!'

'He said otherwise.'

'It wasn't *him* saying it, Fred, it was—'

'Why this obsession, Jan? Look, whether you know it or not, Alex Brown is gay, and he made a pass at Commander West, who is, I think we can all admit, a very good-looking fellow. And when he was rejected, he took it out on the man by inventing this tale.'

'That might be Brent West's story but—'

'It's Alex's story, Jan, not Commander West's, though he did corroborate it. Alex himself told HR when he withdrew the complaint on September 12.' Winterflood was speaking slowly, as if explaining to a petulant child why their upset was so unreasonable. It just inflamed her anger.

'Fred, you're not thinking this through. Brent West *wrote* Alex Brown's apology and sent it from Alex's phone, so he was corroborating his *own* story. That is not corroboration—'

'How could—?'

'Because I'm convinced Alex Brown is *dead*. Brent West murdered him, then electronically impersonated him, pretending to be in Morocco when he was back here in the UK.'

Winterflood laughed, softly but dismissively. 'Brown's phone *was* in Morocco, at least for a while. And explain the postcard, which we can prove has Alex's signature, because I checked it myself, and also bears a bone fide Moroccan postmark. Answer me that, and then I'll take it seriously. Against my better judgement, I'll pretend this phone call never happened. Luckily for you, Wells won't get to hear about it.'

He hung up.

Shit. She had said far more than she had intended to. As Winterflood had hinted, if he told Wells, she'd be fired. She emerged from the meeting room, feeling that all eyes were upon her. But in fact, it wasn't true. Maddy Moran and Dave Nuttall were standing around a terminal talking earnestly to two uniformed PCs. They looked like they had far more important things on their mind.

'What is it?' she asked as she made her way across.

'They found Nadine's car, at Knighthayes Court, the National Trust place.'

'Any sign of her?'

The two uniformed cops shook their heads gloomily.

'Let's go,' Talantire said. 'Right now.'

Chapter Twelve

Knighthayes Court was a grand Gothic Revival house standing in 262 acres of parkland just off the A361, a mile or so north of Tiverton. Talantire had passed fairly close by herself just yesterday, on the way to Exeter. Nadine's Volkswagen was found away from the main car park, on a side road off the main driveway near a private cricket pavilion, which was closed for the winter. Talantire arrived as the back passenger with Maddy and Nuttall in the spare unmarked car, a Vauxhall estate. A steady rain beat down as Nuttall eased the car up towards the VW, next to which was a CSI van and three Tyvek-shrouded technicians working away on the outside of it. There were three patrol cars up near the main house, and they'd heard over the radio that a search of the grounds was being organised with the aid of National Trust volunteers.

Venka, the CSI team leader, came over to speak to them. A divorced former pharmacist from Southall, Ragavati Venkatagiri was based in Exeter, enjoying a second career in her fifties, and with a good reputation for thoroughness.

'Got anything so far?' Dave asked her, through the open car window.

'Plenty of prints, but there should be more. The car is a mess inside. Hamburger wrappers, chicken nugget boxes, stains on the seats, a hairbrush, so we should get plenty of forensic.'

Talantire buzzed down her window. 'Venka, Nadine had only owned the car for a couple of weeks, so there may also be DNA from a previous owner. Are there any tyre prints from other vehicles in this lane?'

'I'm sure there are plenty from ours, and from the patrol car which found it,' Venka said. 'But is there anything specific you are thinking of?'

'She may have left in another vehicle,' Talantire said.

Maddy and Dave both turned to look at her. 'Why do you say that?'

'I don't think she knew this place. There was never a National Trust sticker on this car, nor her previous one, so I doubt she's a member. She lives in Camborne, two hours away. She came here only because somebody told her to. It's a great place to meet: the house is closed every winter, there is no CCTV on the entrance and vehicles would not be visible, parked here on this service road. It's a perfect deserted spot. So while I reckon it's worth combing through all the woodland, my money is on her not being here at all. We should get the ANPR from the main road cameras from an hour each side of the rendezvous time.'

'We don't know what the rendezvous time was,' Nuttall said.

'Well, we do know that, according to the daughter, Millie, Nadine left to go to the supermarket just after ten yesterday morning. Those kids guzzle ice cream like there's no tomorrow – I know because they stayed with me – so it is pretty certain she would only visit the supermarket on the way home from whatever other meeting she had in mind. She wouldn't want to risk frozen produce melting. It takes an hour to drive here from Barnstaple, so I reckon she would be here at eleven or thereabouts, so we need to examine the cameras from ten until, I don't know, one p.m. to find out what the other vehicle was.'

'That's a lot of assumptions, boss,' Nuttall said. Venka nodded in agreement, then signalled she was returning to join her colleagues.

Talantire watched her go, then said: 'I agree, but I know a few things about Nadine that perhaps you don't.'

'Well perhaps it's time you told us,' said Maddy.

Talantire nodded. 'I know it's not my case and I'm only a witness, but I still want to do this by the book.' She stepped out of the vehicle and headed along the lane away from the crime scene. She rang the main number for the headshrinkers at Middlemoor and asked to speak to Fiona Hendricks, the head of HR. She was put straight through.

'Fiona, I need to ask your advice.'

'Go ahead.'

'As you may have heard, PC Nadine Lister has gone missing.'

'Yes, how awful.' Her concern sounded genuine.

'It's not my case, because of the way that she and I were entangled over the Brent West allegation. However, I am a witness, because Nadine and her two children actually lived at my home for several days, and there are things that I know about her and things that she told me which may bear on this case.'

'I see.'

'I just need your official permission to reveal to the investigative officers something that they might otherwise not ask about.'

'You're referring to her complaint about Commander West, I presume.'

'Yes. Not just its existence, but the details that she told me. In addition, I need to disclose other things that I have discovered which bear on the case, which to my knowledge nobody else knows about but me.'

'Well, it's absolutely clear that the investigative team need to know everything that they can, and that overrides the duty of confidentiality that we owe towards Nadine, and indeed to the accused. The safety of the missing officer must be our top priority.'

'That was my reading of the rules, but I'm glad you agree. Would you be so kind as to ping me over something in writing to that effect?'

'I see you don't trust me.'

'It's not that; I think you are highly professional. But I've got to cover my arse, just in case those bastards from Northumbria get involved again.'

Hendricks permitted herself a small laugh. 'I do see your point.'

'As you know, Fiona, as indeed everyone in the entire force seems to know, I'm on a final written warning and I can't take any chances.'

'I hear you, and you're on safe ground here, I guarantee it. Look, would you be kind enough to tell me what those "other things" are that bear on this case?'

Talantire had guessed that Hendricks wouldn't be able to resist the temptation to ask. 'I'll tell you just one, and that's because it's relevant to the nature of Nadine's complaint. She was offered an NDA by Brent West, which includes £5,000 a month for keeping quiet about the allegations.'

'Before she submitted her complaint last summer?'

'No. After it had been dismissed, along with mine.'

'That doesn't make sense,' Hendricks said.

'That's what I thought, initially. But she had hardly told anyone about what had happened to her. Certainly none of her colleagues, because down in Camborne they worked with her husband, who didn't know either. When she confessed to me, it was in the spirit of the secrets of a fellow victim. She was desperate to tell somebody who wouldn't judge her for having had an affair, even if it was one in which she was raped. I was an obvious choice because I was in the same situation. The details of her complaint are pretty powerful.'

'I know, I've read them. Absolutely horrific, if true.'

'At the moment they are confined within the confidential computer system at HR. I think Brent West is terrified that they may get out.'

'They don't have to be true to be damaging, remember that.'

'I think they *are* true, because of my own experience with him, but either way an NDA from his perspective does make sense. The fact she turned up in a nearly new VW indicates to me she got money from somewhere.'

'That's hard to prove.'

'What you have to realise, Fiona, is that the disclosure of the allegations is going to blow this investigation sky high. I'm a witness, West is a witness, it's all going to come out. I don't think Fred Winterflood is going to know what has hit him. He's already aware that Alex Brown made allegations against West and has now disappeared. Winterflood apparently doesn't seem to think that's important because he's concentrating on our Medusa lady.'

'I read about her.'

'Well, two of the three known complainants against Commander West are missing.'

'Good grief, I hadn't thought of it that way,' she said. 'I thought Alex Brown was still on holiday.'

'You were meant to think that. I think he's dead. Murdered.'

'Is there any evidence of that?'

'No, not yet. He's simply missing, as is Nadine. Both complainants. Fiona, I'm the only one left. Can you protect me? Can anyone?'

'Look, I think you might be overreacting—'

'Am I?' Talantire cut the call, then walked back to the car and told Maddy and Nuttall everything she had just told Fiona Hendricks. The two officers, Talantire's subordinates, were absolutely staggered by the tale. Nuttall was particularly shocked because he hadn't ever heard Talantire's allegations against West, whereas Maddy Moran had been to some extent her confidante in the hard days after her complaint was dismissed by the headshrinkers at Middlemoor.

'So you genuinely believe that Brent West is on a campaign to murder everyone who's made a complaint against him?' Nuttall asked.

'Originally, I didn't think so, but I do now.'

Maddy and Nuttall looked at each other, as if they believed their boss had finally lost all grip on reality. Jan leaned forward between the two front seats of the car, and asked: 'Why did she come here, when she was supposed to be shopping an hour's drive away in Barnstaple for her children? Why come to such a lonely, secluded place, and not even park in the main car park?'

'To save the cost of parking?' Maddy suggested.

'It costs £1.10 an hour,' Talantire said. 'Leaving the car here, illegally, risks a bigger fine.'

Nuttall made a couple of phone calls and passed on the information that the search had come up with nothing so far. 'There are no lakes to drag, just one small pond. So it's mainly walking all of the woodland trails.'

'They're wasting their time; she's not here.'

'Where is she then, boss?' Nuttall asked, looking at her in the mirror.

'I don't know. But not here.'

Two hours later, back at Barnstaple CID, Talantire confronted her workload: a special request from Police and Crime Commissioner the Hon Lionel Hall-Harrington, aka Bagpuss, to implement in Devon and Cornwall the same heating oil and diesel theft prevention scheme that they had used with such success in Avon and Somerset. In other words, to roll out Brent West's chemical tagging scheme. Ever since DCS Crossfield had told her about it, she had known it would happen, but it was adding insult to injury that this task would fall to her. To pay homage to Saint Brent, as some saw him. Besides, she simply wouldn't be able to concentrate on it. She was just waiting for the moment when the bodies of either Nadine Lister or Alex Brown turned up.

Then she realised. Of course! Maybe she could pursue it, because it would give her the excuse to go up to Avon and Somerset, into the lion's den. She'd be able to meet Brent West's team and find out exactly how it was done, but perhaps she'd also be able to undertake some espionage. She made a couple of calls and then emailed the Avon and Somerset rural crime team leader, DCI Jez Crawley, formally making the request and copying in the commissioner. That did the trick. Bagpuss's name was certainly good for something. Her appointment was almost immediate, noon tomorrow at Avon and Somerset's Portishead HQ.

She checked her phone messages and discovered that while she'd been busy she'd had a call on her personal mobile from PC Giles Cadwallader. He'd promised to call her days ago with information about his friend Alex, but hadn't done so, and her messages to him had gone unanswered until now. She rang him and he picked up. He was apologetic for the delay and added, 'I'm really sorry, ma'am, but can you come to Axminster? I'd really prefer to do this face to face.'

'Actually, I can,' she said. 'I'll be passing by your neck of the woods on the way to Bristol tomorrow. Can you meet me at Taunton Deane motorway services on the M5 at ten? That's not too far out of your way, is it?

'No, that will be fine,' he said.

Next day, Cadwallader was early, already waiting in a patrol car in the car park at Taunton Deane services when Talantire arrived at ten minutes to ten. She parked nearby, and as she approached, he pointed to the passenger side door. She got in, relieved to finally have this conversation. He was a tall, sandy-haired individual, and clearly nervous.

'I just want to check, ma'am, that this is completely off the record?' he said, as she settled into the passenger seat.

'I guessed it had to be, from the cloak and dagger nature of our meeting,' she said. 'It's not a problem because I'm not on the case looking into the death of Alex's mother.'

He nodded. 'It's DCI Winterflood, isn't it?'

'Yes, and he will do a good job once we can get him to accept what the investigation is really about. First of all, I have to ask you, have you heard from Alex?'

'No. Nothing. None of his friends have. His phone voicemail is full, and we're really worried.'

'When did you last hear from him?'

'There was an email, saying he was going on a trek in Morocco. That was in the middle of September. None of us friends have heard anything. There were a couple who got text messages. He claimed he was having a great time. I was surprised that he didn't message me.'

'Why is that?'

Cadwallader looked at her. 'We were close.'

'Partners?' She glanced at his hands, with a wedding band in evidence.

'Not exactly. We saw each other, off and on, for a few months, then broke up. But we were still friends.'

'I take it the secrecy about all this is because you're married to someone else.'

'You do your homework.'

'You've not come out?'

'Look, I've a two-year-old son and I adore my wife. But you need an escape valve, don't you?'

She smiled in agreement. 'Look, Giles. You give me the information you have and I can take it and feed it into the investigation one way or another.'

'Our mutual friend Sally reported him as a missing person in November, and I took it up on her behalf. But since he messaged in response to the death of his mother, which was only a week or so ago, we can't get anyone to take it seriously. First off, I spoke to Border Force, and his passport hasn't been used that we know of for over a year. There are no end of flights booked in the name Alex

Brown, but none have used the passport number we have for him at that address. It's a little complicated because he has Irish citizenship, and I believe an Argentine passport too. He could be travelling under either of them.'

'So you reached a dead end?' Talantire asked.

'Well, he's on the missing persons website, but that doesn't automatically attract any resource to look for him.'

'Did Alex ever tell you about his complaint against Commander Brent West?'

'Oh yes, starting with the incident itself, last Easter. Initially, he just thought it hilarious. He was kicking himself for not filming it on his phone; even though the crack in the door wasn't wide enough for a proper picture, he would still have got the full, apparently dramatic, sound effects.'

'Did he find out who the woman was?'

'Yes, but I've forgotten the name. She is a serving detective constable.'

'DC Samantha Mahoney?'

Cadwallader clicked his fingers. 'That's the name, thank you.'

'So no complaint was made initially?'

'No way. At that time, he was very new but was still aware how senior West was. It was only much later when he heard that West was in the running for chief constable that he reflected on it and thought he should make a complaint.'

'I saw the letter,' Talantire said. 'And I saw some of the earlier acknowledgements and replies, but not the formal response.'

'I don't think he got one, at least he never told me about one. He went off sick, didn't speak to anyone then just disappeared off on holiday.'

'Did West threaten him?'

'I believe so, because he just stopped talking about the whole issue, just a few days after we heard that West wasn't going to get the job. He was pleased about the appointment of the new chief constable, Hamid Sharif, and hoped to get the job as his PA.'

Talantire, too, had been delighted. Not just because it meant West didn't get the job, but also because Sharif was a vigorous and effective leader, openly gay – for which he'd suffered acid burns in his youth after an attack in his native Pakistan – and definitely not part of the white, male patriarchy which had previously ruled Devon and Cornwall Police.

'But there was no news about it?'

'No. It was about the time he went off sick.'

'It's possible that West forced him to sign a non-disclosure agreement. He did that with a fellow complainant, a female officer who accused him of raping her.'

'Is that the officer who's disappeared, PC Lister?'

'Yes, between you and me. It was Nadine Lister. I see that you've been keeping up to speed on developments. West offered to pay for my silence, too.'

'What did he do to you?' Cadwallader asked.

Talantire shrewdly assessed him before replying. 'I was in a brief relationship with him seven years ago. He used a concealed camera in the headboard to film us having sex.'

'Ugh.'

'I'm not the only victim. I've seen images of others.'

'How disgusting.'

'Has Brent West contacted you at all?' she asked.

'No. I don't think he knows of my existence.'

'I would strongly suggest you keep it that way. Some of us don't have that luxury. Alex has disappeared. Nadine has disappeared. If I disappear, you'll know who's responsible.'

Cadwallader's face was frozen in horror. She thanked him and got out of the car. She got into her own, then started the engine and drove off, onto the M5 heading north. Destination Portishead.

The Portishead campus of Avon and Somerset police headquarters looked like a spruced-up version of Devon and Cornwall's own Middlemoor. It was aided by its location in a pleasant seaside town ten miles from Bristol, rather than in the middle of the city. As she entered the car park, she couldn't help noticing a huge black Ford Ranger, identical to Brent West's vehicle. Just the sight of it made her heart beat faster. She edged past in her Skoda to check the number plate and found that it wasn't his. That was a shame because she had just that morning signed out from Barnstaple CID stores an official magnetic GPS vehicle tracker. She had used the heating oil investigation reference on the paperwork, which was credible, but had other ideas of how to deploy the device.

She parked, and made her way into the thoroughly corporate HQ, where she checked in and was handed a security lanyard. DCI Jez Crawley came down to greet her and took her up to a large and modern briefing room, where he and two other male officers gave her the full PowerPoint demonstration of their chemical kit.

'What's so brilliant about it,' Crawley enthused, 'is that with just three trace chemicals in tiny amounts, combined in different proportions, we are able to give a unique chemical signature to every single tank of heating oil, diesel or other valuable liquid. We can do spot-checks on tankers, and on those who bought supplies informally, and using gas chromatography find out exactly whose it was. In fact, it's a solution to the traceability of many other types of crime involving liquids.'

Talantire had noticed Brent West's familiar features on a series of posters on the wall of the room, which looked to be part of a campaign encouraging farmers and rural home dwellers to get their tanks authenticated. 'In some ways,' Crawley explained, 'it's like the campaign to have bicycles marked, but this is a criminal market worth a great deal more than cycle theft.' His eyes flashed enthusiastically behind his spectacles.

'I understand that it's something Commander West came up with,' she said.

'Yes, it dates from his days in Interpol in France and Italy, and he adapted the technique, which had been used to trace and identify heroin. We've since adapted it, and the most recent versions allow farmers to just drop in a few tablets, which dissolve in hydrocarbons, whereas the earlier versions used drops from an eyedropper.'

He handed her some publicity leaflets, again with a prominent picture of West. The whole place seemed to be a shrine to her mortal enemy, and she felt she couldn't take too much more of it. But she had come here, into the heart of enemy territory, to get information. And that's what she planned to do.

'Is Commander West still working on this project?' she asked.

'No, I think he is working on a drone strategy for vehicle pursuits. It just seems to be one good idea after another,' Crawley said, rubbing his hands together.

'Did you personally work with him in the last few months?'

'Yes, it was a great privilege. Everybody seems to want a piece of him, especially, it has to be said, female officers.' He laughed, then looked at her meaningfully. 'But he is on site today, I believe, for a commendation from the chief constable at two p.m. If you'd like to meet him, it's possible it can be arranged. Would you like me to text him?'

'No, it's fine thank you. I have to be back in Barnstaple,' she said. Crawley was an obvious West acolyte; not a safe repository for any information about her mission. She was not on the kind of ground where she could disclose what her actual interest was. But over the next few minutes some casual questions about the project that Crawley had worked on with West turned up useful information. Crawley described a hard-driving, seven-day-week schedule in September and October to get the chemical signature scheme up and running. She realised that meant West wouldn't have had time to be out of the country on holiday at that time, to get to Morocco to dispatch the postcard to Alex Brown's mother. The card that was currently in possession of DCI Winterflood. There was, after all, a much more convenient courier available to him.

DC Samantha Mahoney.

Sam had admitted being in Morocco. Talantire had already suspected that West's allegedly estranged ex-girlfriend was playing the role of double agent. But her self-confessed Moroccan tan was strong evidence that she was more deeply involved in the plot to eliminate West's accusers than simply being a spy. Complicity in Alex

Brown's disappearance, by laying a false trail, indicated knowledge of what had really happened to him. However besotted she might be with West, she would surely wonder why West wanted her to post a card signed by someone else.

Crawley asked Talantire if she could stay for lunch, and she said yes, as long as it was quick. He led her out of the administrative building and in through one of the other two square buildings to the police restaurant, which was crowded with officers in full uniform, ahead of the awards ceremony. She followed Crawley to the self-service area and picked up a quiche and a coffee. While she was waiting to pay, she saw across the crowded room the unmistakable figure of DCI Winterflood, just setting down a tray of food. Not wanting to be spotted, she turned her head away and quickly paid. She then followed Crawley to a table which was thankfully at the opposite end of the large refectory.

What was Winterflood doing up here? It could only mean one thing. He was here to interview West, and to put to him some of the allegations she had made. Good old Fred Winterflood, diligent and open minded, following leads however wild he thought them. She found it gratifying. If only she'd got something more concrete to offer him to buttress her accusations.

She sat down with Crawley, making small talk for fifteen minutes as she ate her quiche. Crawley wanted to know about her background and why she was so interested in rural crime. He might well have been aware of her reputation in high-profile murders, and this was his way of trying to find out what happened to her career. And she could have told him: screwed, basically.

Crawley looked over her shoulder and stiffened somewhat, as if to stand. 'Hello, sir,' he said, with a full helping of nominative determinism.

'Do you mind if I join you?'

The voice came from behind, and it was utterly familiar.

'Jan, so delighted to run into you again, and here, of all places,' Brent West said, as he made his way around the four-person table to sit down diagonally opposite her.

'Ah, so you *do* know each other,' Crawley said.

'Of old, I'm afraid.' She turned to West. 'I'm here for Jez to show me your initiatives around dealing with thefts of heating oil.'

'So I heard,' West said. He was in full uniform except his cap, exuding from every pore confidence and poise and annoying amounts of desirability. And of course, he knew it. His tray included a bowl of what appeared to be tomato soup and spaghetti bolognese. The desire in her to hurl them both over his carefully pressed white shirt was almost irresistible. He unfolded his large white paper napkin and tucked it in at his collar, as if he could read her mind.

'I hear you're getting an award,' she said. *Sadly, they don't give awards for the kind of deceitful cruelty and abuse that really marks you out from a typical officer.*

'Yes,' he said, with an expansive sigh, as if such things were a necessary but tedious distraction. He took a spoonful of soup and said: 'We've got the high sheriff of Bristol and the commissioner, as well as the press. It's pretty hard to keep a low profile these days.'

Crawley laughed, as of course he would. Talantire could feel indigestion coming on.

'If anonymity is what you want, you could make a start by stopping your toadies putting your picture on every leaflet and poster,' she said.

Crawley watched her, slack jawed. West himself seemed to find her outburst funny.

'So, Brent, what happened to Alex Brown?' she asked him, as casually as she could. 'Do you see much of him anymore?'

West spilled a spoonful of soup that was on its way to his mouth, spattering the napkin. 'I don't know what you're talking about.'

'It's *who* we're talking about. Not what. We're two team members down on the awkward squad at the moment, Alex and Nadine.'

Crawley's eyes popped even wider at this public attack on a senior officer. His gaze shuttled between the two of them. 'I've just got some emails to return in the office,' he said, standing up. 'Nice to—'

'Jez, sit down,' Talantire said, firmly. 'No woman is safe on her own with Commander West, so I'd like you to stay as my chaperone.'

Crawley looked across at West, who nodded as he supped another spoonful of soup. Crawley looked like he'd prefer to be anywhere but here, blinking rapidly, unsure what to do with his hands.

'DI Talantire has a history of making outrageous and unfounded allegations,' West said, calmly. 'So I'm also glad that you're staying to hear them. There isn't a shred of truth in anything she says, but this is an aggressive piece of stalking even by her standards. Using an invitation to meet your unit, Jez, as a pretext to publicly humiliate me.'

'You don't look very humbled, actually,' Talantire said. 'You never did. And as for stalking, can I just remind you that it was you who came to join us, at this table. Not the act of a man who seems determined to avoid my presence, is it?'

'I really do have to be going now,' Crawley said, standing and picking up his tray. He looked across at West and mouthed the word 'sorry'. She watched him go and then turned her gaze to West.

'What are you trying to do, Jan?'

'Trying to get you to take responsibility for your criminal acts.'

'I really don't know what you're driving at.'

'You tried to get Nadine to sign an NDA. I've seen the document; it's there, on her phone still, recorded on computer servers that even you can't get at.'

'She's a troubled soul, Jan. I felt sorry for her. I felt I could make her life easier and more financially independent just so long as she stopped this series of nonsensical allegations that you and she cooked up together. She signed the deal, made the truce, accepted that her allegations were untrue and we are now friends again. If only you had shown the same common sense.'

'You can't buy me off.'

He shook his head. 'I simply saw it as an opportunity to make peace.'

'Where is Nadine? Your good friend, who has disappeared, leaving her kids in a caravan park. Where is she?'

'I don't know.'

'Where is Alex? A principled young PA, who had the balls to point out that you would not be the right man to lead Devon and Cornwall police. What have you done with him?'

'I don't know what you're talking about.'

'Let me lay it out for you. On Easter Sunday last year, Alex Brown witnessed you and DC Mahoney having sex on the chief constable's desk—'

'Nonsense.'

'On August 3, aware you were in line for that job, he wrote a letter of complaint to HR. On August 17 he got a response, then on August 26, he had an in-person interview in which he detailed what he'd seen to Fiona Hendricks. Shortly afterwards, your candidacy was terminated, and on August 28 Alex emailed in sick. No one saw Alex Brown after the end of August: not his friends, not his mother, not his work colleagues. No phone messages were returned. I think by then he was already dead. On September 12, he withdrew the complaint by email, apologising for having supposedly conspired with me against you—'

'And quite right too. I was shocked by that, I have to say.'

'It wasn't true; I never met the man. Anyway, on September 14, he resigned from the police, and from SelectStaff. In October his mother received a postcard from Morocco, postmarked Marrakesh and signed by him, which I think he wrote when you were standing over him—'

'Jan, your imagination is astounding.'

'—just before you killed him. That card was then taken to Morocco and posted there by your girlfriend, DC Samantha Mahoney, to establish the fiction that he was on holiday in the country. Messages sent from that phone to Alex's mother amongst others claimed that he was still on holiday there in October, yet we can prove the phone was back in the UK.'

West leaned back and laughed gently.

'Oh, poor Jan. You could have gone on to great things. A fantastic detective brain, tremendous insight... but this paranoid episode you seem to be enduring needs treatment, urgently. You come across as unhinged, don't you see it? The fact that you went to the trouble to fabricate allegations against me is very sad, all because you are still struggling to come to terms with the end of our relationship seven long years ago.'

He knew exactly how to make her lose her temper, and she was close to it, her fists balled on her tray. She inhaled as slowly as she could, counting to ten. Here he was, right in front of her, impregnable, unassailable.

She got up and walked away, heading to the bathroom, feeling West's eyes boring into her back. She really *had* to learn to keep her cool. This all came back to her childhood. When her mother had refused to believe her story about the babysitter Mr Pye interfering with her. Her mother had belittled her in almost exactly the same way as Brent West had, and had pressed all her buttons.

Her outburst in front of Crawley wasn't going to do her any favours at all. It was quite possible that either he or West might complain to the chief constable of Devon and Cornwall Police, and if that happened, well, she might be suspended. It was hard to see how even her generally sympathetic boss Detective Superintendent Michael Wells could protect her.

She needed evidence: firm, factual, concrete evidence. But how was she going to get it? Instead of going to the ladies, she took the lift to the top floor, where the executive offices were. Sure enough, West had an office there with his name on it, right next to the chief constable. A short stepping stone on the route to power. The door was open, and two officers, one male, one female, were talking about computer upgrades, with their backs to her. The office had a great view of the distant Bristol Channel, and a desk as large as a double bed.

She was sure he must have used it as such.

If she'd even dreamed she might get access to his office, and had Primrose's preparation, she might have been able to breeze her way in as a techie, wave her visitor lanyard, spout some technical guff, and install a piece of spyware on his computer. But that wasn't the kind of thing you could wing. And these two officers sounded like techies themselves. She dismissed the idea, but took the opportunity to visit the ladies' toilets on this floor. Senior officers only.

The place was pristine. She retreated to a cubicle and texted Maddy to ask if there'd been any progress in finding Nadine. While waiting for a response, she finished up, then took a swab from the top of the toilet paper dispenser. The perfect height for snorting cocaine from. She wouldn't be at all surprised if it came up positive, one of the many things West might do for a dare. Especially in the ladies. As she was sealing the evidence bag, she got a call back from Maddy.

'Jan, I'm not going to be able to keep you up to date,' Maddy said. 'You're a tenable suspect, so I'm afraid I'm not going to return any of these messages. I know it's hard, but you have got to stay away from the investigation.'

Talantire was affronted at this but knew Maddy had no choice. They were the rules.

'But Jan, between you and me, we haven't found her. We've had a hundred volunteers combing Knighthayes Court and the surrounding pastureland.'

'Any forensic in her car?'

Maddy sighed. 'Jan, if we find anything, you'll undoubtedly get to hear. Bye.' She cut the call, leaving

Talantire in a state of shock. She felt she had so much to contribute to the case but was shut out of it. And her own detective sergeant hanging up on her. Maybe everyone was right about her. Maybe she was losing the plot. Getting paranoid. Having a nervous breakdown, as West had hinted. She really wanted to cry, but she wasn't going to. She rang Adam and left a brief plaintive message, saying that she needed to hear his voice. Then she took a deep breath, left the cubicle, washed her hands and made her way out towards the car park. In the corridor coming the other way was DCI Fred Winterflood, looking shocked to see her.

'Hello, Jan,' he said. 'What are you doing here in darkest Portishead?'

'I've been learning about the chemical marker system for heating oil thefts. What about you?'

'A bit of this and that,' he said.

'Well, when you do get to speak to Brent West, do ask him about the Moroccan postcard. I think you'll find that it was dropped into a post box in Casablanca by none other than his girlfriend, DC Samantha Mahoney, who happened to be on holiday there, as she confirmed.'

Winterflood's mouth opened, but no sound came out. He was clearly thinking about what she had said.

'She's the weakest link, Fred. Anyway, got to go, urgent business in the rural thefts department.'

She walked off, hoping that Winterflood would heed her advice.

—

Driving home improved her mood, powering down the M5 in some unseasonable sunshine with the radio on.

Things got still better when Adam returned her call, and they had a long talk on the hands-free. She relayed the details of her confrontation with West, and he was full of solid advice and reassurance, and said all the things that any woman would want a supportive partner to say, until the end: 'Jan, you've got to learn to control your temper. You made it so easy for him, by rising to the bait.'

'I know, I know. But I just can't help myself.'

'You're so fiery, which is wonderful, but you're in a chess game, not a cage fight. Your professional detachment – that great insight you have – has deserted you.'

'It's because it *is* so bloody personal.'

'Not to him, though, by the sound of it. He's outplaying you, encouraging you to make these unfounded allegations in front of others.'

'Adam, for fuck's sake, they are not unfounded!'

'Okay, okay, Jan,' he soothed. 'I know, but the evidence is… not readily available, is it?'

He let her blather on angrily for a couple of minutes, then asked. 'Do you want to come and stay at mine tonight?'

'Oh, I'd love to,' she said. 'But I've still got some clearing up to do first, so it won't be until later on. And I'm working tomorrow too. Is that alright?'

'We can just get a takeaway.'

'Sounds perfect,' she said. 'I'll bring one in on my way over. I can't tell you how much it means to me to be able to hear your kind voice on the end of the phone. It's been a truly shit day.'

'I'm sending you a big hug,' he said.

She got back to Barnstaple by three o'clock to find an email from Crawley with ten attachments of promotional bumph for the chemical signature scheme. He mentioned nothing about the refectory scene he had witnessed between her and West, and she crossed her fingers that he hadn't reported it. Maybe her luck would hold. When her boss rang her, she was on tenterhooks, but again she found Detective Superintendent Wells in a relatively cheerful mood.

'We're reorganising the caseload a little bit,' he said. 'As you know, we can't have you getting involved in the investigation into the disappearance of PC Lister. I've moved Winterflood across to be SIO on that, with DS Moran and DC Nuttall reporting to him.'

'What about the Alex Brown case? Isn't Winterflood doing that at the same time?'

'There is no Alex Brown case, Jan. There is however a Katarina Lezcano case, which is being removed from CID. PC Caldwell will tie up the loose ends.'

'What?'

'It's a suicide Jan. It's increasingly obvious.'

'The woman took her own life because of the breakdown in the relationship with her son, who didn't come to stay with her for Christmas. He didn't stay for the very good reason that he was dead, and had been for months, for having dared to report Brent West to HR.'

'Bring me the evidence, and we will look into it, or more precisely Fred Winterflood will look into it.'

'Sir, how can I bring you the evidence when I'm not on the case?'

'And how, DI Talantire, can you lobby everyone for this conclusion *without* any evidence?' Getting no reply he said: 'It's been clear for a long time that you are too heavily emotionally involved in this case for your judgement, or should I say, prejudices, to be taken seriously.'

'Where is Nadine, sir? Tell me that. Two days missing now.'

'We are trying to find her. I don't think I'm breaking any rules to let you know that Winterflood informally interviewed Commander West this afternoon at Portishead, shortly after he received an award for innovation in policing. The main upshot of that is a cast-iron alibi. Commander West was teaching a course at Portishead all day, in front of thirty-five officers, on the Wednesday that PC Lister went missing. He was not involved, do you understand? Now, please, stop wasting any more time on these ridiculous conspiracy theories. If you raise them again, there will be consequences. The final written warning is still there. Do I make myself clear?'

'Yes, sir.'

'Now, your task is to pursue this rural crime epidemic with full vigour, aided by the chemical signature scheme. I'm sure I can get you some manpower.'

'Sir, honestly, it's mainly a PCSO leafleting job, raising awareness. It's not—'

'Jan, it's my decision, and I'm sorry you think it's beneath you. You might be surprised at the difference you can make to this if you put your mind to it.'

Talantire got back to Barnstaple to find that her desk and computer terminal had been moved into one of the small meeting rooms at the far end of the room, behind Anorak Land, as the techie station was known. In fact, two young male technicians from that department were still connecting up the equipment.

'What's going on?' she mouthed to Nuttall, who seemed to be waiting with a phone clamped to his ear for somebody to come on the line.

'Middlemoor,' he mouthed back, shrugged and then returned to his phone call. Talantire stalked up to the technicians and asked them the same question.

'Ma'am, we got a job order from Exeter,' said one with a *don't blame me I only work here* tone to his voice. She watched with a sinking heart as her wheeled set of metal drawers, complete with distinctive fridge magnets, was jammed into a narrow gap at the back of the meeting room. She went into the room, unlocked the drawer, took out a stack of case files on the heating oil thefts and stowed them in a shoulder bag. Unwilling to watch this slow-motion humiliation, she scrawled a note and left it on Nuttall's desk. It said: *I'm working from home for the rest of my shift.*

Her heart sinking, she descended the stairs from CID, went out into the car park and unlocked her Ford Focus. She felt everyone she passed was looking at her, the mad bitch who finally went too far. On the way home she stopped off at B&Q and got herself a doorbell camera, and a couple more proximity lights for the garden. She lived alone, after all. It was like the old joke: just because you're paranoid doesn't mean they're not out to get you.

She drove into Cornwallis Avenue in the gathering dusk, reversed up to her garage door and glanced right.

There it was again. The same black BMW that had been there a few nights ago. Same number plate, definitely, no lights. There was someone sitting in the driver's seat. A man in silhouette. She must have lingered in her gaze long enough to alert him, because he did a quiet three-point turn, flicked on the lights and headed away down the other end. The whole thing just ratcheted up her level of unease. She let herself in as if conducting a raid, PAVA spray in hand, going from room to room. The place was still a tip, but didn't seem to be any different kind of a tip from how it had been when she left it. That was the problem when you had a housemate who left the place looking like it had been burgled. It was hard to tell if you actually had been.

She started step one of her survival plan: she rang Adam and dictated to him the number plate of the car she'd seen. 'If anything happens to me make sure Maddy gets that registration number,' she said. She passed across Maddy's personal phone number to him. He seemed really worried, but she said she had lots of things to do and would get back to him really soon.

After hanging up, she logged on to the remote portal for the DVLA database of drivers' details. She once again cited the rural heating oil investigation on the online form, before hitting 'Search'. The registered owner's address came up as a lease company in Falmouth. That would be a dead end without a formal inquiry.

Bemused, Talantire then set to work installing the doorbell camera, linking it up to her laptop and phone, then downloading some additional virus and spyware checkers. She went to the shed to get out the large stepladder so she could reach to install the proximity lighting.

Someone had broken in.

The shed lock was broken, the hasp levered off and away from the flimsy wood so that the still-locked padlock hung uselessly on the metal clasp. She grabbed the outward-opening door and flung it wide. There was no one within. Nothing obvious seemed to have been stolen, though she struggled to remember what junk she kept in there. She went back into the house and dug out her backup forensics kit which had been locked inside a cupboard in her bedroom. She took fingerprint gel lifts and DNA samples from all around the house, doorbell, garage door, light switches, rear door, handles and even the boot and door handles of her own car. She meticulously photographed everything she did, using plastic crime scene markers, and loaded them all onto her own laptop. All the pictures she saved across a series of email drafts, which by saving she knew would appear on servers that could later be scoured for information by investigators. She wrote up a brief description of what she had done and saved it to the cloud, then downloaded everything onto a fresh data stick which she put into her pocket.

She realised she was preparing for her own death, and for the investigation that would follow her disappearance. A ripple of terror rose in her. She felt so sure this was going to happen and seemed unable to do anything about it. Nobody believed her; even Adam had seemed a little unsure about her conviction that West was responsible for all this. Planning for catching him after she'd been killed was all very well, but it also seemed defeatist. As she cleared up inside the house, tackling the room where Nadine herself had slept, she took some more DNA and fingerprints samples. Nadine had not been abducted from Cornwallis Avenue, but it was possible that someone had visited her there when Talantire herself was away, and at work.

Seeing the room where her colleague and erstwhile friend had stayed was a poignant reminder that she had been missing more two days now. Could she still be alive?

Talantire struggled to find a scenario that would fit it. The case had made the newspapers and regional TV, and her picture had been widely distributed. She was a very attractive woman, and the sunny portrait of her at the beach in a dress, presumably chosen by Roger, made her look dazzling: smiling into the camera, big blue eyes and perfect teeth, an hour-glass figure. Happier times, certainly, and presumably long before she ran into Brent West.

Talantire bagged up all her results, carefully filled out the labels and logged them on the evidence system for Maddy's attention. She would drop them off at Barnstaple on her way to Adam's, ready for the courier drop next morning.

What else could she do? She could get one of those phone apps for tracking kids, put the trace on her own phone as if she was the child and give Maddy the parental control. There was one other thing she could do, too. She had a fitness tracker, a present from her mother which also included GPS and could therefore be traced. The model she had was one of the cheap ones and quite ugly, which is why she rarely wore it. She took it out of its box and inspected it. It wouldn't stretch around her ankle; it was designed for the wrist. But West would spot it there. He was far too smart not to realise the implications. However, she fiddled with it and managed to remove the strap so it was merely a two-pence-piece-sized metal disc. She used a transparent plaster to tape it inside her sports bra, under the webbing by her shoulder blade. The device was waterproof, too, so even if West drowned her, there would be a good chance of some signal.

So long as somebody was looking for her.

She had just finished this when Maddy rang. 'You're sending me a lot of forensic samples, Jan. What are you up to?'

'If I should die, think only this of me: that she prepared her mates with everything they would need to find who did it.'

'Jan, really,' Maddy said.

'I'm under surveillance, Maddy. I spotted this black BMW outside a few times. And someone's broken into my shed.'

'Have you reported it?'

'Not yet. But there are photographs and forensics.'

Maddy said nothing for a while. 'That wasn't the reason for my call, Jan. I'm just giving you a heads-up. I'm sorry to be the bearer of bad tidings. You're going to be called in for questioning tomorrow and taken down to Exeter.'

'Arrested?'

'Not at this stage. But Winterflood wants to put some questions to you, in connection to the disappearance of Nadine Lister, following the discovery of some evidence which may connect you to the case.'

'What evidence?'

'Come on, Jan. You know I can't tell you. A patrol car will come to pick you up from home at nine.'

She spent the rest of the evening taking precautions, copying all the sensitive data from her laptops and phones onto a data stick. She rang Adam and explained that she had to cancel coming over to see him. Instead he readily agreed to come to hers, and to smuggle out data sticks the next day when he left.

When he arrived, bearing a takeaway, she set it carefully down on the table, and held him close. He enfolded her in his arms and caressed her hair, and they slid together onto the sofa. She allowed herself to weep, gently. Eventually, after eating just a little, they retreated together to her room, and he held her in the darkness until she eventually surrendered to the oblivion of sleep.

Chapter Thirteen

'Detective Inspector Talantire, you are not obliged to say anything, but it may harm your defence if you do not mention when questioned something which you later rely on in court.' The standard police caution was read out to her, as she sat the wrong side of the interview room table in Exeter police station on Saturday morning.

On the other side was DCI Fred Winterflood. There was no one else in the room, but the tape recorder was turned on. He didn't look comfortable, but she felt worse: utterly humiliated. She was relieved the interview was being conducted down here, where Winterflood was based. To be dragged in front of the desk sergeant in Barnstaple, in front of colleagues she knew well, would have destroyed her.

Winterflood began. 'As you know, we are investigating the disappearance of PC Nadine Lister, who was last seen by her children at 10:15 a.m. last Wednesday, leaving the caravan park in Barnstaple where she was temporarily lodging. Previous to that, she had been staying with you, is that correct?'

'Yes, I took her in before Christmas when she arrived on my doorstep bearing injuries that looked like the result of domestic violence.'

'I see, and according to a witness statement given by the eldest child, you and Nadine argued all the time.'

'I wouldn't say "all the time". She was a hugely disruptive influence in my household, especially on those days which she spent there with the children as well. I told her I was willing to give her a place to stay for a short while, but it seemed to take a lot longer for her to leave than I expected.'

'Did you try to throw the family out on the street on New Year's Day morning.'

'No. Nadine arrived with her children without even telling me, while I was still in bed after an exhausting overnight shift. Of course I wanted them to leave; I'd never given her permission to bring them in the first place. But as it happened, it was me that ended up leaving.'

'You were angry, weren't you?'

'I've course, but I also sympathised with Nadine, what she'd been through.'

'You're referring to the "alleged rape".'

'Alleged? It's multiple rapes, by her account. Look, where are you going with this?'

'Have you ever been inside Natalie Lister's Volkswagen?'

'No.'

'Then how do you account for your DNA being found within the vehicle? I know you were there soon after it was located at Knighthayes Court, but officers present at the scene say that you didn't approach the vehicle at that time.'

'No, I didn't. I've never been inside the vehicle; never driven it, never been a passenger. I can't explain why my DNA is inside, unless it was contamination on one of the many objects that were moved out of my house when she and the kids moved out to the caravan park.' Talantire leaned across the table and said, 'Look, I liked Nadine, I sympathised with her predicament, I felt for her—'

'Interesting that you used the past tense, there, Jan.'

'Yes! Because I think she's dead! Murdered by—'

'You?'

'No!'

'Well, you have a motive, and as all your colleagues will attest, you have a temper. Isn't it possible that you arranged to meet her, had an argument, put your hands around her throat—'

'How dare you accuse *me*, the person who was done the most to support this struggling woman, of attempting to harm her! Yet the person who I am convinced has killed her is swanning around, utterly free, getting awards—'

'I have interviewed Commander West. I also interviewed Nadine's husband. They both have unimpeachable alibis. You, however, do not. On Wednesday morning, at the time of her disappearance you turned off both your work and personal phones. Why did you do that?'

'Look, I went to search Alex Brown's flat in Exeter and didn't want to be called and taken off the case. I didn't have much time.'

'Turning off your phones is highly incriminating. Especially because on that same morning your unmarked Skoda triggered cameras on the A361 between Barnstaple to Tiverton — at an illegal speed, I may add. The last camera before the roundabout turnoff to Knighthayes, you passed just two minutes after Mrs Lister's VW did. That seems like quite a coincidence.'

Talantire folded her arms and stared at Winterflood. 'It is. But unlike hers, my car would additionally have triggered cameras from Tiverton all the way to Exeter, showing where I was actually heading.'

'Some time later, yes.'

'Look, I didn't go to Knighthayes until much later, with other officers.'

'So you say. Motive, means and opportunity, Jan. You are the only person who has all three.'

'This is ridiculous,' she said. 'You are shooting the messenger. In this whole investigation, it is me who brought out the connections between the crimes, the disappearance of Alex Brown and that of Nadine.'

'Where did you leave Nadine's body?'

'No one is trying harder than I am to find out where she is.'

He glanced at the clock, then tapped his papers together before addressing her. 'Detective Superintendent Michael Wells is in the adjoining office and has been watching this interview.' He nodded at a camera high up on the wall of the interview room. Winterflood then winked at her, subtly. 'Sorry, it's come to this, Jan,' he whispered. 'Only doing my job. I'm sure you'll come out the other end unscathed.'

'Unscathed! Fred, this is like something from Kafka.'

Wells walked in as Winterflood left and took over the seat that he had vacated.

'I'm being stitched up here, sir,' she said. 'I wouldn't harm, Nadine. You know that.'

Wells shrugged expansively. 'I've been having discussions with HR this morning and the verdict is unanimous. I'm sorry, Jan, but I can't have you on active duties with an allegation of this severity against you. You are suspended, with immediate effect.'

'What! While Commander West, with even more serious allegations against him, continues to work as normal.'

'You are entitled to a police friend,' Wells said, 'who can be from the Police Federation or a colleague, to support you in this disciplinary process.'

She was shaking as he led her out to the desk sergeant, who brusquely took her name, address and rank, then, after writing it down, held out his hand. 'Warrant card, lanyard, police phone.' No please, no ma'am, no deference. Nothing that her rank would normally require. She took the lanyard from around her head and the warrant card from her pocket and placed them on the counter.

'Are you in possession of PAVA spray?' he asked.

'I have one at home, and a pair of handcuffs in the car.'

'After we've taken you home, the constable accompanying you will come in and remove all items of police equipment. You will no longer be able to access any of the police databases and all your online privileges and security door access to police premises will be revoked. Do you understand?'

'Yes,' she whispered, fighting back tears.

'As part of the inquiry we need to look into all personal phones, laptops and computer equipment from your home,' the sergeant continued.

'Oh, hell, come on!' She turned to Wells, beseechingly.

'Jan, it would be easier if you gave us permission rather than us having to get a warrant,' Wells said. 'You know the drill. Look, this could be over quite quickly. Once Nadine gets back in contact, I'm sure all this will be forgotten.' He smiled sheepishly.

'It won't be forgotten by me, I can assure you of that,' she said. 'In the meantime, if you need to get hold of me, I'll be staying with my boyfriend.' She gave Adam's address, and his mobile number. There was no way she'd stay at home, without communications, when she felt so unsafe. It was almost like her employers were facilitating her abduction and murder.

—

'This is getting out of hand,' said Detective Sergeant Maddy Moran. She was sitting in Barnstaple CID's meeting room with digital evidence officer Primrose Chen. They had just heard about Talantire's suspension.

'It just seems so harsh,' Primrose said. 'Jan was really trying hard to help Nadine in her case.'

'Damn right she was,' Maddy responded. She herself had earlier that day been told she would no longer be working with DCI Winterflood's team on the Nadine Lister missing person case. Detective Superintendent Wells had told her she had a potential conflict of interest, because of her friendship with Talantire. He said it was sensible to separate all of Talantire's former colleagues from the inquiry, which was now being led from Exeter. Even Primrose had been told she was removed from the digital evidence team for the case.

'However, I still have access to the case files, and I've been sneaking a look at the ANPR timings,' Primrose whispered. On her iPad she showed Maddy a series of images from the road safety partnership, which managed speed cameras. 'Jan certainly had her foot down, registering 75–85 mph on all the cameras, bar the one in Tiverton town centre, which had a thirty limit. She hit forty-two on that.'

'Winterflood says she was only two minutes after Nadine's car on the last one before the turn off to Knighthayes Court,' Maddy said.

'Yes, and she took fifteen minutes to reach the next one, on the A3126 through Tiverton, two miles after the

Knighthayes turnoff roundabout. That's fifteen miles, so the average speed drops to 60 mph, because the last two miles are in a 30-mph zone. I can't see that gives enough time to turn off to abduct or otherwise interfere with Nadine.'

'Show me,' Maddy said.

Primrose pulled up a map. 'The stately home is nearly a mile off the A361. Let's assume she was driving like Lewis Hamilton—'

'Or Dave Nuttall.'

'—and averaged sixty miles an hour on that windy, twisty country road. That is one minute each way. Let's further assume that she managed to abduct Nadine, and dragged her out of her own car, presumably tied her up, and put her in the boot or back seat of the Skoda in three minutes flat. Which is going some.'

'Agreed.'

'So that's five extra minutes, at least, off the time between the two speed cameras.'

'Run that by me again,' Maddy asked. 'Maths was never my strong point.'

'A to B in fifteen minutes, right?'

'Yep.'

'But if you have a detour in the middle to point C and back that takes five minutes; that means you covered the measured distance from A to B in the remaining ten. And fifteen miles in ten minutes is—'

'Bloody fast,' Maddy said.

'It's an average speed of 90 mph.'

Maddy squinted across at her. 'You did that in your head?'

'It's not rocket science! But don't you see the problem reconciling that with the observations we have?'

Maddy shrugged.

'We have four observations of her actual speed, right?' Primrose said. 'But the average speed required to make the abduction timings possible is higher than any of the speeds her Skoda actually registered at the cameras. What is the probability of that?'

'Ah, but drivers often slow for cameras and then speed up afterwards,' Maddy said.

'She didn't need to, she's exempt.'

'True. But it might be a reflex.'

'I don't buy it. Maddy, don't you see?' Primrose said. 'This changes everything. The fact that Talantire's car was only two minutes after Nadine's tripping the nearest camera to Knighthayes was seen as incriminating, because of the proximity. But in fact, it's an alibi. She couldn't have abducted Nadine, because there was no time.'

'Well, we could try putting this all to Winterflood, but I don't think it's enough to get her suspension lifted. Besides, he's no more a mathematician than I am.'

'Here's something else,' Primrose said. 'Winterflood and his crew remotely downloaded the contents of Nadine's phone yesterday, unfortunately onto a confidential server in Exeter that I can't access. However, the main evidence file does say that the last location of the phone was at Knighthayes Court at 11:26 on Wednesday morning. It was turned off there, three minutes *after* Jan's car had already been caught on camera in the centre of Tiverton.'

'That's pretty conclusive then,' Maddy said. 'She was already past, if that's the moment of abduction.'

'Assuming the phone and its owner were in the same place,' Primrose said. 'It can't have been Jan.'

'Are we going to wait for Winterflood to come to the obvious conclusion?' Maddy asked.

'We might have to, because I'm not supposed to have access to the case file.'

'But we've got to do something,' Maddy said. 'Alright, I'm going to ring Jan, to let her know what we have.'

She punched out the number and then realised. 'Ah, Winterflood's got her phones, of course,' she said, putting the receiver down. 'If we email her, the message will be seen by the investigatory team, and we'll be in hot water.'

'Do you have Adam's phone number?' Primrose asked.

'No, but he is a website designer, so must have his own website. We should be able to contact him through that.'

Talantire was sitting in a steaming hot bath at Adam's home, with a gin and tonic, while he sat on the edge, drinking a beer.

'I'm screwed, Adam. They've got me exactly where they want me. Out of the way.' She had told him every detail of what happened to her and Adam was horrified. Now she was virtually incommunicado. She had bought a burner phone on the way over to see Adam and could use the data stick onto which she'd downloaded everything she needed. But everything she had found out was via her phones and devices, now in the hands of police in Exeter. Everything that she had uncovered about Brent West, all the messages that she had sent to her ally Georgie, and the WhatsApp threads that he had copied her into. All these were now exposed to the investigation. Georgie was a motorcycle cop, and a passive member of some of the more extreme male police WhatsApp groups. He would now be exposed as the mole in the group: the snitch. She had promised him confidentiality, but had let him down. It would take quite a long time for them to find everything, but would they draw the same conclusions she had? There was no way of knowing whether West had allies inside Winterflood's team who could tip him off.

Adam's phone pinged. 'Jan, I've just had a message from Maddy, through my website. She's giving you her personal number to ring.'

Talantire stepped out of the bath and grabbed a towel. Within two minutes she was talking to Maddy, listening to what she had discovered.

'You look pleased,' Adam said, after the call ended.

'I am. Primrose has managed to prove with ANPR camera timings that I couldn't have abducted Nadine. Winterflood and co. haven't come to the same conclusion as yet, and of course she can't let them know that she has been accessing forbidden data. I can't risk her getting fired, just to clear me a day or two early. It's just such a relief to know that they can't draw out my suspension much longer. I should be back at work on Monday.'

That weekend Talantire prowled Adam's house like a caged animal, waiting for the call that never came. On Sunday she and Adam went for a long river-side run, which they curtailed after seven miles because Adam couldn't keep up. But he was firm that she shouldn't run alone. Back at the house, she scoured the data she had earlier downloaded from Alex's USB stick onto her own. She needed to uncover West's plot, but deprived of police resources, she couldn't chase up any of the leads that she had got. On the TV evening news there was a story about Nadine's disappearance, which after four days was now beginning to get national attention. Devon and Cornwall police were sticking with the simple line that they were very concerned for her safety. Any viewer coming cold to the story might have imagined that they were simply expecting it to be suicide. There was no link made to the disappearance of Alex Brown, nor the death at sea of his mother.

Only at seven o'clock that evening did the call come.

Adam passed the phone across to her. 'Detective Superintendent Wells,' he said.

'Hello, Jan,' Wells said. 'I've got some good news for you. I'm ending your suspension because a closer look at the timings makes it obvious that you couldn't have been involved in Nadine's disappearance.'

'Thank you. I feel vindicated.'

'If you want to return home this evening, a police van will meet you there with all of your personal equipment. Your passwords have now been reactivated, although you will still not be working on this case, nor have access to the case files.'

'I'd still like to be able to feed information in.'

'You can do that through DCI Winterflood, or DS Moran, who is now back on the case, too.'

'I saw on the BBC that there are plans to send divers to some of the rivers in the area,' Talantire said. 'It seems to me that the case is being characterised as a probable suicide.'

'All avenues remain open; we've got an open mind.' Getting no reply, he added 'Jan, I'd like to offer a personal apology for the obvious hurt and distress this suspension has caused you, but I think you realise we had no choice.'

'I'm not so sure about that, sir.'

'Well in any case, I'd like you in tomorrow morning, first thing. Rural crime, I'm afraid. Someone has helped themselves to several tons of diesel from a large farm on Exmoor. The farmer had, off his own initiative, secured one of the chemical tracing kits, so there's a good chance of finding the culprit.' Wells said goodbye and cut the call.

'Can't wait,' Talantire said to herself.

—

Talantire was driving back home to meet the police van, which was due at eight. She passed the Esso garage on the main road just two hundred yards before the turning to Cornwallis Avenue. There was only one car at the pumps, a black BMW seven series. Having seen one in surveillance mode near her home twice in the last few days, she had made a habit of watching out for them: black, 2022 registration. There were so many, and she rarely had the time to read the registration number before she passed, as in this case. The first three letters of this one were the same as the car she'd seen in her own street. She slowed down and did a quick U-turn at the entrance to Cornwallis Avenue, before returning to the main road. She was able to find a space across the road from the petrol station, and parked to take a look. In the bright lights under the canopy, she was able to see a man emerging from the minimarket, with what looked like a bag of sweets. She recognised him immediately. A sergeant from the Penzance-based police firearms unit, Colin Donnelly, who had left the police after she made a complaint against him last summer, during the Bodmin joyriders case.

Donnelly had been on the same WhatsApp group as Brent West, on which her sexual history with the senior officer had been sniggeringly discussed. Then, while on operation with the firearms unit, he'd said to them, in her hearing: 'She used to be one of Commander West's bitches. Gives good head, apparently.' He'd never been formally disciplined, leaving the police before proceedings had begun.

She watched as he got into the car, and apparently oblivious of her presence, drove off, away from her home. So it was Donnelly that had been keeping surveillance of her house. Donnelly and West working together perhaps, it might make sense. If Donnelly had abducted Nadine, then that would have allowed West to have that essential alibi.

Chapter Fourteen

She was home in two minutes. The police van was waiting. Everything was returned in cardboard boxes, bar the paperwork. Nonetheless, the process of setting up her home office and re-inputting passwords took another hour and a half. All that, and the place still looked a tip.

It was now 9:30 p.m. The first thing she did was to run as many checks as she could on Sergeant Colin Donnelly. Like many firearms officers, he'd joined from the military, worked at the Met in London, then had an undistinguished six-year career at Devon and Cornwall Police. There were three complaints logged against him in that time, which was not an unusual number. She couldn't see his personnel file to discover what they were, but was able to cross-reference them on the Independent Office for Police Complaints website by date and location. Only one of them was serious enough to appear on the IOPC log, and that involved a female complainant in Penzance, who said she was sexually assaulted after being arrested in possession of cannabis in 2019. The case was eventually dropped due to lack of evidence.

Talantire turned back to WhatsApp. Donnelly had been far more active in posting misogynist content than West himself. The tone of the contacts between them on the messages that Georgie had forwarded to her indicated that they knew each other reasonably well. But in the last two months, neither of them had posted anything.

Talantire logged on to the ANPR system and requested a regional download of all the cameras that the black BMW had triggered in the last two weeks, and pegged it to the rural crime enquiry to give herself some cover. She then realised that the van which had been waiting outside her home to return the computers would be equipped with a dashcam, possibly one linked to ANPR. She would have to ask Maddy to get that for her. Still, it was a start.

She heard a noise and looked up. It sounded like a door banging. She looked out of her home office window, the front bedroom, which had previously been Nadine's bedroom. She could see no movement, so went to her own bedroom at the back. There, she could see the shed door, banging in the wind. She knew for a fact she had tied it up with baler twine when she was clearing up a few days ago.

Her heart started hammering. Here she was, at home, alone, at ten o'clock at night. She'd still not found time to properly re-set the doorbell camera on her laptop. Adam had offered to come and stay with her tonight, but she had declined. She had an early start tomorrow, but he also had a meeting with a client first thing, back in Tiverton. He was clearly just being gallant.

Perhaps it was justified.

Seeing the open shed door as an indicator of an intruder, she wondered if perhaps she'd been too blithe about it. She texted Adam to say she had some indications of an intruder, telling him that if she hadn't texted again within five minutes, to raise the alarm. She headed downstairs, armed herself with her largest adjustable spanner from the toolbox, put on all the exterior lights, then opened the back door. There didn't seem to be anybody else about. She made her way down the path to the shed and saw that the baler twine had been cut.

Gingerly, she grabbed the shed door to stop it banging and peered inside. Nothing seemed out of place. She had already taken DNA and fingerprint samples the last time an intruder messed with the shed and sent them off to Maddy. She had no idea whether Maddy had already sent them to the lab or was merely holding into them. She tied up the shed door, went back inside the house and locked the door, then texted Adam to say she was okay. She logged on to the Barnstaple CID system and was pleased to see there was an incident number opened at her address, linked to the case of Nadine's disappearance. She wasn't allowed to access the case, but at least it would mean that all of the photographs she had taken, inside and out, after Nadine's disappearance, and all of the forensic samples would be logged on the case file, and might eventually be looked at. Even if it was only because the person they had been investigating was her.

Adam rang her, and seemed relieved to hear her voice. 'What's going on, Jan? You're not safe there. I'm going to come over.'

'I'm not going to say no, Adam. It's very kind of you. Hopefully by the time you get over, the doorbell camera will be properly set up again, along with the other camera over the back door.'

'It's still not exactly Fort Knox, is it?' he said. 'I'll be with you in an hour.'

'Adam, I love you for this,' she said.

'I just want to protect you,' he said.

After some extended and heartfelt goodbyes, she hung up and looked at her resources. Although she'd been given back her own computer equipment and phones, most of her police kit hadn't been returned. Her forensics go-bag, handcuffs, PAVA spray and even her hefty police-issue torch would still be in a cupboard somewhere downstairs at Barnstaple police station. If only she had made more of an effort to get to know the neighbours. She knew a few by sight: the elderly couple next door on the left, the young family opposite and the builder whose van was always parked half on the pavement on the right. Her shift work and the nature of her policing job made it very hard to make local connections, but the real reason was her workaholism. She pretty much only came back to Cornwallis Avenue to sleep.

Right now, she was dog tired. She would be back to work in the morning for the eight o'clock shift, and it was important to get some sleep. She managed to hold on until Adam arrived, and then locked all the doors, before snuggling up in bed with him.

Talantire awoke shortly after six, entwined with Adam in her own bed. It was still fully dark as she wrapped herself in a towel to slip into her home office to survey the night's footage from the doorbell camera. Nothing but the odd cat, and no BMW passing in the street. The shed itself was still as she had secured it with the remains of the baler twine.

She swept into Barnstaple CID fifteen minutes early, feeling that the weekend's suspension had been simply a bad dream. Various colleagues who had distanced themselves from her on Friday and Saturday now made a point of coming over to say how glad they were she was back, and fully exonerated. DC Dave Nuttall arrived a few minutes later with a bag of doughnuts and two coffees from the posh Italian place.

'One of these is for you,' he said. 'I guessed you'd be in early.'

'Thank you. I much appreciate it. So what about Nadine?'

Nuttall checked that they weren't being overheard, then said: 'We're running out of places to search. Husband Roger is in the clear, seeing as he was with his boss on the day she disappeared. The homes of all of her relatives have been searched, including the sister in Portsmouth, even those further afield in the Midlands and North-East. We've had access to her NHS records, and although she had been prescribed antidepressants, she wasn't considered a suicide risk.'

'She was told to go to Knighthayes Court, Dave. That wasn't a suicide trip.'

He sighed. 'I know.'

'So what about other vehicles?'

'We've got 473 number plates on both ANPR cameras that straddle the turn off to Knighthayes within half an hour each side of her arrival. The same calculation that Primrose made to put you in the clear applies to most of them. They were on through journeys and wouldn't have had time to abduct her.'

'My guess is any intelligent abductor would have avoided all the ANPR by arriving from the north on back roads and returned the same way,' she said.

'I agree. We found a couple of doorbell cameras on that route,' Nuttall said. 'All we picked up are a couple of delivery vans, white vans. No number plates visible.'

'Well, I have my own suspect to add to the mix. Colin Donnelly, a former sergeant based in Penzance.'

'I've heard of him. Wasn't he in the firearms unit?'

'Yes. You'll find all kinds of evidence about him in the WhatsApp screenshots I sent in. He is a mate of Brent West's.'

Nuttall looked up at her sceptically at the mention of that name.

'Look, Dave, I'm sure that nobody has got round to looking at all the stuff that was taken off my phones when I was suspended, but seeing as I've effectively waived my anonymity, you will find all kinds of detail there that link comments about me and Nadine and other female officers to a group of misogynist cops, who seem to be led by West.'

'Boss, you put me in a really awkward position,' he said. 'Winterflood is SIO, and he's far from convinced that Nadine is dead. All that stuff you sent is on the backburner because it's such a can of worms. I'm sure eventually—'

'Someone will find me dead, having ignored all the clues.'

Nuttall took a sip of his coffee and swung his chair gently from side to side.

'Look, Dave. Just do one thing for me. This is the registration number of Donnelly's leased black BMW. It's a 2022 seven series. See if it's turned up anywhere near my house, Nadine's temporary caravan home or at Knighthayes Court in the last two weeks. The police van which brought my stuff back yesterday has a dashcam; it's worth checking that too, because I saw Donnelly at the garage near my home last night.'

'I promise I will,' he said.

'Check for his DNA on the samples that I sent in from my home and shed too. That was broken into; if it was Donnelly, he was probably just trying to freak me out.'

'Anything else?' he asked, with a hint of sarcasm.

'If you need me, I'll be off in darkest Exmoor, visiting the site of some tedious heating oil theft,' she said.

—

It felt great to be back at work. Even an investigation into rural crime allowed Talantire the opportunity to drive along some of the most beautiful country lanes in Britain. She turned off north at South Molton, enjoying the low, watery sunshine. Edgecott Home Farm was on a single-track road, at the centre of the maze of small lanes just beyond Withypool. The satnav told her she was just three quarters of a mile away. She had already spoken by phone to the farmer, Martin Jackson, who, as it turned out, had served on Devon County Council with Lionel Hall-Hartington many years ago, and shamelessly namedropped the commissioner right from the start. She fully expected he would try to leverage his friendship in order to get more resources. The fact of her attendance was probably evidence of that. The commissioner had probably had a word with Wells to make sure she was sent. At least old Bagpuss still had high regard for her, even if this was used to further his own agenda.

Within a mile of the farm, the single-track road was blocked by a white van, its four-way flashers on. It was parked at a dip in the road between high overgrown hedges, rear doors partially open, washing machine and dishwasher boxes visible within. There seemed to be no one about, and her honk of the horn elicited no reaction.

There was no address nearby to deliver to. So where was the driver? Behind the hedge having a pee? But why leave the rear doors open? She consulted the satnav for alternatives, but the only other route would add six miles, the first three of which would entail reversing down this narrow lane to the main road. She stepped out of the car and, peering past the van, noticed a passing place just ten yards further on. Why on earth had the driver stopped here? She began to make her way forward the five yards between the front of her car and the back of the van, calling out again.

She was still two yards away when the rear door flipped open, revealing a crouching man in dark overalls and a ski mask with a yellow police-issue Taser in his hands. She leapt back, turning to run, when she heard the Taser discharge.

The pain was immediate, unendurable, paralysing. The world flashed black and white, and she spun around like a marionette, screaming. She fell on the bonnet of her car, her limbs not functioning, and her face hit the metal, hard. The man was on her in an instant and after a brief but intense struggle, there was once again a terrible pain, the Taser pressed into the small of her back.

'That's just the start, bitch,' he said.

Colin Donnelly: she knew the voice, his London accent. Too stunned to resist, she couldn't stop him manhandling her into the back of the van. But when he paused to fold her legs in, she, from somewhere, summoned the energy to kick out sideways with her heel and caught him in the face. He swore, punched her in the belly then said: 'I'm going to enjoy this.' He gave her three more unbearable jabs with the Taser, pressed right into her, each one seemingly more painful than the last.

She blacked out, feeling she was about to die. *Please no, please no.* Thoughts flashed through her mind of Adam, her lover and protector, her sister Bella, who had uncharacteristically reached out to her, as if she had known, and then the shadow of Mr Pye, the abuser from her childhood. And that's when the terror really began. She came round, bound up completely in the back of the van, wrists tied with cable ties behind her, a rubber ball gag being forced into her mouth, buckled behind her head. She didn't recall it, but she'd been stripped of her jacket, shoes, belt and wristwatch, leaving her with blouse and work trousers over tights and underwear.

'You just thought you could get away with it, didn't you?' Donnelly said. 'Slagging me off in front of my unit, making an official complaint. My boss gave me the choice: resign or face a disciplinary, all that shit with the headshrinkers.'

She could hear him unzipping something and was rolled into what felt like a kitbag. In a millisecond, she realised. This was exactly what she'd seen on the video, from the North Wales crematorium. *Oh God, no! No!*

She stretched herself out as much as she could, making it hard for him to squeeze her limbs into the bag. After failing time and again, cursing and swearing, he gave her another jab with the Taser, and this time she really did think her heart would explode. Tears and snot poured out of her face, and she struggled to breathe, unable to stop him pushing her into the bag. The closing of the zip made her panic. The total darkness, no air. *Please no, please no.* She couldn't help wondering if this was what Nadine had faced, and whether she could have endured it. The same with Alex Brown.

Burned alive. *No!*

'Done this before, you know,' Donnelly said, as he manoeuvred the kitbag around in the van and slammed the doors. 'Extraordinary rendition, they called it. I was in special forces, for a private contractor. We nabbed some guy from a hotel in Kandahar, bagged him up just like you, took him on C-130 to Morocco and then waterboarded the shit out of him. MI5 officer standing by all the while. He's still in Guantanamo, poor sod. That was work, but ones like you, well. Bit more fun, bit more of a hobby.'

He started the van engine and then drove off. The vibrations of the engine and the chassis drowned out whatever else Donnelly was saying. Talantire had to use every ounce of self-control to focus her mind against hopelessness and despondency. She wasn't going to die. She was going to survive. She had everything to live for. There were four chances, each of them slender, that she would be discovered as missing.

One, the control room would soon know that something was up. Talantire had been expected at the farm. The alarm would be raised within half an hour at most. This was not like Nadine, who was missing for many hours before anyone knew, nor like Alex Brown, who had been assumed to be abroad for weeks but had probably been dead for a long time by then.

Two, the tracker watch was still underneath her bra strap. Maddy already had the app on her personal phone.

Three, Maddy also had the family locator on Talantire's personal iPhone, which would give her instant updates on its position, so long as it was switched on. There would be a timeline of journeys and locations. All the way to North Wales, if that's where he was heading. That would be five hours, at least, maybe six.

Finally, the unmarked Skoda's dashcam would have captured a rear image of the van, and its registration number. It might be a false or cloned plate, but still. Even if Donnelly set the car ablaze, that data would still be on the cloud and could be retrieved by her colleagues.

But the one poisonous thought Talantire could not get out of her mind was the video she had seen with a live victim being taken to a crematorium. *Burned alive.* Try as she might, she couldn't eradicate from the brain the terror of being consumed by heat and flame. Turned into ashes. It was a long way to North Wales, but that still might mean she only had a few hours left to live.

Then an unimaginably horrible death.

Chapter Fifteen

Detective Sergeant Maddy Moran was at that moment sitting in a meeting room at Barnstaple CID with DCI Fred Winterflood and DC Dave Nuttall, with PC Caldwell and press chief Moira Hallett on Zoom. They were halfway through an incident room meeting about the disappearance of Nadine Lister.

'I still think on the balance of probabilities we're talking about a suicide,' Winterflood said. 'We've simply no evidence of anything else.'

'But why would Nadine go to Knighthayes Court, sir?' Nuttall said. 'She wasn't a National Trust member, and it's quite a long detour if she only went out to buy groceries.'

'I appreciate the assignation or rendezvous angle,' Winterflood said. 'But there's nothing on her phone to back it up. Yes, there is the NDA with Commander West, but she signed it.'

'Maybe she went to collect the money in cash?' Maddy asked.

'That doesn't make sense. A sum from his bank was already in the process of being transferred to her account on the day she disappeared. They had reached an agreement. Why would he even need to do anything as extreme as this? Besides, he wasn't there: he has a cast-iron alibi.'

'With or without the NDA, Nadine represents a threat to West, sir,' Maddy said. 'The payment is a kind of cheap alibi, isn't it, if he intended to kill her all along?'

Maddy heard a ping on her phone, one of several she had received during the meeting so far.

She ignored it.

'PC Roger Lister and the family are now back together again, and being supported by a family liaison officer,' Winterflood said. 'Despite the turbulent family history, he is in the clear.'

'If I may interrupt,' Moira said, 'The greatest difficulties of course are that we don't have a coherent story to tell the press. They simply don't understand how a serving officer can go missing for five days, with no body found, no suicide note, no apparent lines of enquiry, no people of interest, nothing. The public will begin to feel that if we can't protect our own, how on earth can we protect them?'

Winterflood sighed. 'We can't manufacture evidence just for the sake of a media strategy, Moira. We've still got quite a lot of electronic material still to go through, and I was wondering, Maddy, if we could get your digital evidence officer Ms Chen involved. The team in Exeter is overstretched. Now that Talantire's in the clear, there's no conflict of interest.'

'I'm sure she'd be keen to help,' Maddy said.

'She can start with the social media accounts; we've barely begun with those. And look through the older material on both her phone and that of the daughter.'

'Right.'

It was only at the end of the meeting, after Winterflood had foolishly distributed to the team cups of coffee from Dr Crippen, that Maddy looked through her notifications and saw that Talantire's personal phone had forty minutes ago triggered a location alert. It had exceeded the 'normal distance' she had set up of fifteen miles from her work base. That wasn't in itself unusual. It was something likely to happen several times a day when Talantire was out and about. Maddy followed up the notification to see the timeline, expecting it to be Adam's home in Tiverton, but saw the last entry was in rural Exmoor half an hour ago.

Winterflood began talking to her, and she put the phone aside for a moment. When she got back to it, she looked more closely and could see that the phone was now turned off. Instead, she rang Talantire's work phone, which prompted her to leave a message.

'Wasn't Jan doing a rural crime visit today?' she asked Nuttall, who was sitting at his terminal.

'Yep, a farm in Exmoor after a heating oil theft,' he replied.

'Both her phones seem to be switched off,' Maddy said. Then she remembered the fitness tracker. She worked her phone, accessing the app. There was no current location, but a couple of pings from ten minutes ago put the tracker in the middle of Exmoor, heading north-east towards the Brendon Hills. But that last notification was seven miles away from the last location of the phone. And the health display was pinging out heart rate alerts, showing extreme exertion.

'Dave, I think this could be serious,' Maddy said. She rang the control room and asked them when was the last they heard from Talantire.

'Funny you should ask that,' the operator said. 'We just had a complaint from a farmer that she's forty-five minutes late for an arranged meeting. We tried to check in with her fifteen minutes ago and couldn't get through.'

Maddy alerted Winterflood, who seemed reluctant at first to take it seriously. 'She's been out of contact for less than an hour,' he said.

Maddy explained about the fitness tracker and the family location app on her iPhone. 'I can't think of a single good reason why she should be seven miles away from her phone.'

'Come on, she may have mislaid it.'

'Sir, Jan *specifically* asked me to track her for just such an eventuality. She knew this would happen.' Maddy looked down at her iPhone and saw a new tracker location. She was now eight miles from the last phone location.

Winterflood turned away to deal with another officer.

'Never mind,' Maddy said to herself, and rang the control room again. She asked for them to give her a location for the GPS inside the unmarked Skoda. A screenshot of that map was pinged over to her within two minutes. It was the final piece of evidence that Maddy needed, to get her boss's attention. 'Sir, her car is still at the same location as her phone last was, but she is moving north-east, presumably in another vehicle, according to her fitness tracker.'

Winterflood, not the most digitally savvy police officer, looked over Maddy's shoulder at the contradictory positions given for her tracker and the unmarked car.

'All right, let's get some resources on this,' he said.

'And what's this?' Maddy said, bringing up the tracker's health dashboard. 'Several massive spikes in her heart rate about forty minutes ago, when she was close by her car. Something terrible must have happened! We've got to help her.'

'All right, DS Moran, take DC Nuttall and head to the location of Talantire's vehicle. I'm going to try to persuade

Wells to let me have a helicopter from Exeter, and a drone unit too. It would perhaps be a good idea to get a firearms team out there as well.'

As Maddy rushed out of the office, she could see Winterflood, busy on the phone, trying to drum up some manpower. Now, finally, they were waking up to what might have happened.

—

Inside the kitbag, Talantire was unbearably hot and could hardly breathe. She was tied in a foetal position, resting on her knees, with her wrists crossed behind her back. The ball gag was on a thick strap around her head, buckled at the back.

She had worked really hard to still her anxiety, to slow her breathing as she fought against the darkness and the claustrophobic tightness of her confinement. She reckoned she'd been in the bag for fifteen minutes, and from the movements of the vehicle they were still on rural roads with plenty of stops and turnings. She couldn't hear much above the vibration of the van floor and the noise of the transmission, but it was clear the vehicle rarely got above third gear.

The biggest problems were pressure pains on her shins from the hard floor, periodic cramps in her calves, which were agony, and the tightness of the cable ties which cut into her wrists and ankles. These slim, tough plastic straps were a favourite of abductors, as they could be looped and then tightened on a one-way ratchet. Years ago, she'd seen training videos about escaping them, which was possible when your hands were tied in front, and you could see what you were doing. But in reality, no one was ever tied like that. Every gangland dead body had their hands secured behind them. That underlined the grim reality. Most such prisoners ended up dead.

She worked her hands backwards and forwards, hoping to loosen the ties enough to be able to slide her hands over her bottom and down towards her calves where she could at least get to work on the ankles. But it was anatomically impossible, without dislocating her own shoulders, to be able to reach over her hips. She was several inches short of it. The only progress she made was to topple the bag sideways when the van went round a sharp bend. It eased the unbearable pressure on her knees and shins, and seemed to give a little more space.

She had no weaponry beyond teeth and fingernails. But with the ball gag, she couldn't use her teeth, and her fingernails were cut short. She explored as best she could inside the fabric of the kitbag behind her with her fingers. It felt like robust army-style canvas, with a chunky metal zip which ran over the back of her head, down her neck and along her back, where it was very tight against her. There was some kind of lock, a hard metallic lump, immediately above her skull. It brought to mind the notorious case of the GCHQ intelligence officer Gareth Williams, who had been found dead in 2010 in a bag very much like this one, padlocked from the outside. Despite his DNA and fingerprints never having been found on the padlock, indicating that he hadn't locked himself inside, no one had ever been charged for the crime.

He'd not been able to get out. Could she?

She couldn't reach either end of the zip, but determined to make sure that every part of her body picked up information. She explored the individual teeth of the metal zip along her back with her fingernails, scratching and probing and pushing to find an area of weakness. She tried again and again, seizing the material in finger and thumb on each hand and trying to pull the zipper apart. But she couldn't get a purchase on it. However, being on her side had certain advantages, and one was that she could feel with her cheek that there were irregularities on the floor of the van. The bag had briefly snagged on something sharp, like a rivet, or even a screw head. She braced herself for the next corner, and tried and failed to invert the bag so that the zip would be pressed against this sharp point. When she did finally succeed in this manoeuvre, she immediately toppled over to the other side. It seemed desperate, hopeless, but she had to keep trying.

―

Maddy and Nuttall soon found Talantire's abandoned car, blocking a country lane. They pulled up behind the Skoda, and Nuttall emerged for a closer look. The driver-side door was still open, the keys in the ignition. The dashcam had been wrenched off, leaving only the mark where the sucker had been on the windscreen. Maddy and Nuttall stood and surveyed the scene. There was no sign of an accident, no tyre marks, no broken glass.

Maddy began peering into the hedges on either side, and soon uncovered a bulging plastic bag half-buried in broken foliage. Hidden, but hurriedly. 'Hey Dave, I found something here.'

She slid on nitrile gloves, picked up the bag and pulled it out. Inside was Talantire's damaged and muddied jacket, low-rise shoes, broken wristwatch and two smashed phones. It took a further minute to see that the SIM cards been removed.

'There's no doubt about it now,' Nuttall said.

'Shit, *shit*! She predicted this would happen and we were so sceptical,' Maddy wailed. 'Now, she might already be dead.'

'Be positive,' Nuttall said. 'She's tough as hell, and won't go down without a fight. It's too early to start blaming yourself.'

'But what I don't get is how they knew she was out here.'

'A spy in the control room?'

'Maybe, but they would have to be pretty precise to know exactly the route she was taking, and when. When has a police officer ever been abducted on a live op, except by the target of that op?'

'Winterflood's already got the farmer on the phone,' Nuttall said, checking a message on his iPad. 'He's confirmed that there has been no sign of her at the farm. The guy's in his seventies. It ain't gonna be him.'

'We can get a CSI unit here,' Maddy said. 'But they won't find anything. Anyone who's been this professional to be able to find her out here won't have left any dabs.'

'I wonder,' Nuttall said. He went to the boot of their own unmarked Vauxhall. He pulled out a Tyvek suit which he slipped over his own trousers and bomber jacket and then slid on blue nitrile gloves.

'You can leave that for the technicians, Dave; let's get on to the farm.'

'Hold on a sec.' He lifted up the matting from the boot of their car, pulled out a jack from the spare tyre compartment, fitted it in place underneath the rear of Talantire's car and jacked it up.

'What are you doing? The tyre isn't even flat,' Maddy said, hands on hips.

'One moment.' Nuttall took an inspection torch and wriggled under the back of the car. 'Thought so,' he said. He re-emerged a few seconds later, holding a small black object the size of a box of matches. 'That's how the abductor knew where she was.'

'Is that a tracker?' Maddy asked.

Nuttall got to his feet and dusted himself down. 'Yep. Magnetic. Less than a hundred quid off Amazon. Any idiot can use one. Let's stick it in an evidence bag.'

Maddy provided one and Nuttall slipped the object in. 'Once we get that back to Primrose, we might be able to track down the receiving device,' he said. 'However, we've got to realise that the moment we move it from here, the abductor will know that Talantire's car has been discovered and is being moved. They will know we're onto them.'

'I think that's a risk we're going to have to take,' Maddy said. 'This is clearly a very sophisticated operation and, I have to say, lends credence to Jan's theory that Brent West is behind it.'

'Yes. Maybe she isn't so paranoid after all. But we can't possibly go after someone of West's seniority without compelling evidence and the full backing of the chief constable.'

'If Talantire couldn't get it in the months she's been working on it, how are we going to do it now?' Maddy asked.

Nuttall shrugged. 'Follow the fitness tracker. That's the best we can do for now.'

Chapter Sixteen

While Talantire was fighting for breath, Detective Chief Superintendent Rebecca Crossfield was queuing for coffee and a Danish pastry at a hotel cafeteria in the Midland town of Bromsgrove. She was one of 200 attending a police chiefs' conference on organised crime. Amid the clatter of cutlery and the chatter of officers, she was looking through her phone, passing the time by flicking through the latest Interpol newsletter. One article detailed growing evidence that the most powerful European mafia, Italy's 'Ndrangheta, was muscling in on some of the cocaine distribution routes in Europe currently controlled by Albanian gangs.

It piqued her interest because the Albanians supplied some of the Merseyside drug gangs she was investigating. The issue was bound to come up in a class A drugs session that afternoon to be chaired by the head of the NCA, Niall Thompson, and at which she would be presenting her own force's successes and failures.

Once she had paid for her brunch, she sat at a quiet table and looked in detail at a request for information from Interpol's Milan office, which was referenced in the article. It had gone to every police force across Europe and was a series of surveillance photographs of a meeting in September in Austria between two senior 'Ndrangheta operatives, Paolo Scortini and Felix Nunnero, and a third man, thought to be a professional arsonist, and known as Il Bruciatore: the burner. Italian police were convinced he may have been connected to several insurance fraud fires across Italy and Germany, costing hundreds of millions of euros.

But the question Milan had really wanted to know the answer to was: who was Il Bruciatore? Did anyone recognise him? Facial recognition software had drawn a blank against every known member of the mob.

She opened the attached image sequence. At first glance, they looked like holiday photographs. Spectacular mountain scenery, taken in summer with long lenses, showing two well-dressed, fit-looking men, standing by their parked cars at a viewpoint at the edge of an Alpine road. The location given was just above the village of Heiligenblut am Grossglockner in the Austrian province of Carinthia, an hour or two's drive from the Italian border. Later photographs showed a white Audi with what police said were false plates arriving and parking next to them. A tall dark-haired man with a close-cropped beard, wearing mirror sunglasses and a baseball cap, emerged and shook hands with the two. The next pictures were close-ups of the group from behind, the two mafia men and Il Bruciatore peering away at the view. They seemed well acquainted, relaxed, even.

Then a single picture caught Il Bruciatore looking up, half towards the camera. Handsome, with chiselled features and a great smile. He looked a lot like Brent West. A heck of a lot. The beard was a novelty, a three-day growth. And so were the tiny diamante earrings. Could this be him? There was one way to be sure. She flicked back to the very best picture, one taken from behind, a crystal-clear professional telephoto shot. Yes, they were there. Brent had a pair of moles on the back of his neck, one black and round, the other brown and elongated. Together they formed a kind of horizontal exclamation mark, one that she had felt with her fingers when she was kissing him. They would be concealed beneath the high collar of a work shirt but were exposed here on a T-shirt. She zoomed in on the image as much as she could.

Yes, yes! It was. It was definitely him. Brent was a mafia agent. The implications were chilling. When they had last shared a hotel bed in Hertfordshire, just before Christmas, she had told him things about her own cases, her pursuit of drug gangs in Merseyside. Times, places. Everything. She spoke of her disappointment that the price of class A drugs continued to fall, evidence that supply was getting through unimpeded, despite all her efforts.

In the last few days, she had even, foolishly, mentioned that Talantire had come up to see her in Liverpool. She had not, however, detailed the accusations made against him. Nonetheless, he would guess.

It all began to fall, horribly, into place.

If Brent West was Il Bruciatore, the burner, his speciality would be nothing to do with arson. He would be the man who incinerated 'Ndrangheta's enemies, rubbing them out entirely, erasing their DNA. When a body vanished, it put the killers beyond judicial reach. She racked her brains to find a reason to refute her growing suspicions, but could not. No, it could only be him who had orchestrated the crematorium killing in North Wales.

Talantire had accused West of sexual exploitation of female officers, but that was surely only the start. She had been right that he was a criminal, more right than she could ever have guessed. If an officer as senior as West was so corrupt, and so closely connected to the mafia, every operational secret of British policing would be exposed to organised crime. Worse than that, he could have been undermining Interpol for years. He almost certainly was the mole they'd been hunting when she worked in Lyons, five years before.

The Director General of the National Crime Agency was here at the conference, somewhere. She'd seen him earlier in a corridor. She had to find him immediately.

—

Commander Brent West slipped from his car in the car park of the Bromsgrove Parkway Hotel and hurried towards the conference centre. As he strode along the corridor towards the conference room his phone rang. It was Sam Mahoney.

'Make it quick, Sam. I've got a meeting with the head of the NCA.'

'They seem to know where Talantire is,' she said. 'Some kind of tracker. I'm not on the case, but I'm taking a risk for you by looking at the case files. There's a request in for a helicopter and a drone unit. The control room is buzzing with it.'

'What? I can't believe Donnelly screwed this up.'

'Will you protect me, Brent? If this all explodes? I need to know.'

'Of course I will.'

'I put my career on the line for you, remember? Feeding information to you.'

'You were a brilliant double agent, but as I say, I have to go.'

'I love you,' she said, but before she had finished the final word, he ended the call.

Talantire reckoned she'd been in the van for an hour or more, and must be miles away from where she started, but still on minor roads. At least she was now sideways within the bag, still foetal, the zip on her right. The bag was tight across her shoulders and hips, but she was at least not taking her whole weight on her shins. But she was increasingly travel sick from the constant turns, the sharp braking and acceleration, and the total disorientation. A nightmare fairground ride, in darkness, with the taint of diesel fumes which permeated the limited air she had to breathe.

As her stomach convulsed, she felt the gathering terror of throwing up, because the gag would ensure she'd choke on it. She had to get it off. She *had* to.

After a particularly sharp turn of the van, the bag slid sideways, her head connecting painfully with a hard ridge, presumably the side wall of the van. She heaved, and fought to contain her gag reflex, her eyes smarting with the effort as she kept swallowing back corrosive reflux fluids. To distract herself, she tried to picture where she now was in the cargo compartment. Her bottom was against a vertical metal panel, through which she could feel road vibration, and the back of her head against a ridge. Moving the bag significantly was almost impossible. The best she could do was to press her feet away an inch or two, moving like a caterpillar, where she found a niche, in the side of the van, to rest her heels in. Bracing them, she rubbed the edges of the canvas bag against the wall of the van, hoping for a catch on a sharp object, something that might make even the smallest hole in the tough material.

Nothing.

She explored the sharp vertical ridge behind her head. As she was lying, it ran left and right behind her head. Tilting her head back, she managed to catch the edge of the buckle at the back of her head on the ridge. This buckle was on a strap which secured the ball gag. She nodded her head backwards and forwards, and felt the buckle, begin to slide up against her hair. Getting enough purchase was very difficult, so she had to caterpillar back and forth, keeping her heels in the niche. Finally, it slid up above her ears and released the tension which held the ball in her mouth. With her tongue, she was able to push it out. Unable to see, she felt the strap with her mouth. She thought it would be leather, but it was some kind of artificial webbing, the tough kind used on rucksack straps. The metal buckle had a prong, not sharp, but good enough to puncture the canvas of the bag if she could get it down to her hands, tied behind her. But how was she to do that without being able to move any of her limbs?

She knew the ridge could help.

Using her mouth, she dropped the gag, which fell to her left, in front of her shoulder. She then wriggled and rotated that shoulder, gradually sweeping the ball so it was behind her. With knees and feet, she tried to caterpillar along the van floor, so that the ridge slid down her back, trapping the ball behind it. Minutely, she wriggled and writhed and caterpillared, feeling the ball and its webbing descending her spine, until finally her fingers could reach it. Once she found the prong, she tried to manoeuvre it to work away at the cable ties on her wrist. It was quickly clear that she couldn't apply any force from her fingers back towards her wrists. Instead she worked the edge of the buckle at the bonds, but again it just wasn't sharp. Feeling the gag again, the edge of the webbing seemed to be more abrasive, especially one section where it was stiff, having been glued around the central bar of the buckle. She tensed her wrists apart, keeping the cable ties taut, and worked that section backwards against the stiff webbing. The slight vibration in the plastic restraints gave her hope, and she worked away for several minutes, as the vehicle continued to swing from one side to the other. She still felt quite travel sick, but felt that she must be making some progress.

Then all at once, the cable tie snapped. She was immediately able to part her wrists and move them under her body, sliding one arm between her knees down to her bound ankles. She had only just started work with the webbing when the vehicle came to a halt. She could hear wipers. It must be raining.

The engine was turned off, and now she could hear that a phone was ringing. She froze as Donnelly answered it. 'What is it? Wasn't it you who insisted on radio silence?'

There was a pause and then: 'That's total bollocks. I searched her. I *did*, thoroughly. No, there was no fitness tracker, just an ordinary wristwatch, which I ditched. No, it's not the phones either. I smashed and buried 'em. You really want me to go back and undo the bag to double check? She's a bloody handful, a real hellcat, and I can't search her without undoing all the bloody ties, can I? Yeah, I would have stripped her completely, but you said not to. I assumed you wanted first dibs.'

In the distance she could hear the roar of traffic and a faint chorus of sirens. Police? They were some distance away, but the rain helped carry the sound.

'No, no, no, it's not the van, trust me. I changed the plates, as agreed. Should be fine for ANPR, but I'm keeping off main roads all the same. These are a clone of some van in Gateshead, as I mentioned. Should be clean as a whistle. Yeah, the BMW is in a lock-up in Exeter.'

The driver-side door opened, and the slight shift in the vehicle made it clear Donnelly had exited. He came round to the back and opened the rear door. She could feel him enter the cargo compartment. 'I can undo her if you want, but it will take time. I might have to zap her with the Taser again. I've got more ties. It's up to you. But you know what I reckon? They've just found her car, that's all. I can see that on my own tracker. It's been moved, just a few minutes ago.'

Donnnelly then rested his foot on her head, gradually increasing pressure. 'Enjoying the ride, are yer, Jan?'

She tried desperately not to make a noise, but her body jerked.

'She's fine. I don't think she can hear much in there.'

What Donnelly heard next clearly upset him, and he banged his hand against the roof.

'What, now? But we're at the M5. Can't you hear the traffic, down the embankment? We'd *be* there in forty minutes. For fuck's sake!'

There was a long gap with Donnelly just making noises of acknowledgement. Finally, Donnelly said, 'Right, alright. Right, speak to you later.' A volley of swearing indicated the call had ended. Donnelly slammed shut the door to the van's cargo compartment, then made his way back to the driver's seat. 'Fucking panicking micromanager,' he muttered, then turned to address her in the bag.

'Right, here we go, darling, back the same fucking way we came.' He restarted the engine, and put the vehicle in reverse, slewing round angrily so that the kitbag rolled over to the other side. He then gunned the engine and accelerated away hard, making some kind of sarcastic commentary to himself that she couldn't hear in any detail except for the tone. Only when he stopped a few minutes later, cursing roadworks, could she hear what he was saying to himself above the sound of the idling engine.

'Look at this! No bloody traffic waiting the other end, no bloody work taking place, just two wankers in hi vis, holding me up on red while they look at a tree. Why did I ever get involved in this bloody charade, eh? There's easier ways to make a hundred grand and that's the truth. The risks I'm taking for Brent bloody West, Jesus Christ. Maybe I should just drown you, eh love? What do you think of that? There's a nice, quiet river just over the bridge here, and I'll just submerge the bag in for five minutes. Only need a foot of water, don't I? I'll keep me boot on top of yer, until there are no more bubbles. He wanted you to have an unpleasant death, but I reckon that's just as bad as being burned alive. The devil or the deep-blue sea, eh?' He chuckled to himself.

Talantire hadn't made a move for several minutes, but with renewed panic started to work away at the bonds on her ankles again, tiny sawing movements of the stiff webbing.

'Now, *finally*, we get green,' Donnelly said, as he accelerated away angrily, making the kitbag slide a little towards the back. The final jerk did it and the cable ties on her ankles parted. She wriggled around in the tight bag until she could slide a hand over her shoulder to feel the zip and tried poking a finger through the tiny hole where it ended near her head. She could feel the tag on the zip, and with a sinking heart realised it was indeed immovable and padlocked. She could feel the hard weight of the lock it was connected to. Her only way out now was to break the zip apart. This time the prong of the buckle might prove useful. Lying sideways in the bag, she prodded and pushed and worked away with the point to try to find a weak tooth in the steel zipper. She began at the top and worked down, one tooth at a time, pressing and prodding. Finally, she succeeded in pressing the buckle prong between two teeth at the level of her knees, which parted, and once she got her finger through, the entire zipper began to slide apart. The noise of the engine and the rhythmic sweep of the wipers gave her cover. Light then flooded in, dazzling her. She held the bag almost closed, just peering out cautiously. She could now see that the interior of the van had originally been blue. The white repaint job had been hurried, and there were plenty of patches of the original colour showing through near floor level. This looked to be the van that Rebecca had told her about, the one that was implicated in the North Wales crematorium trip, linking Donnelly more clearly to that crime. This did nothing to reassure her.

Part of Donnelly's head was visible in front of the headrest, still talking to himself as he drove, taking out his fury on the gear change as he swung the van left and right through small lanes, muttering to himself about the weather, how hard he had to work for a pittance and his general misfortune.

She peered out and round the van. The rest of the cargo compartment was largely empty. The ridge she had used to free the gag was on the left and seemed to be part of a racking for vertical storage, while on the right side the three washing machine and dishwasher boxes she had seen previously were folded flat and stuffed behind metal stanchions.

For a further minute she massaged her calves and wrists to get some feeling back into them, and to pull in more oxygen to her air-starved lungs.

Now she was ready to emerge from her bag. Ready to tackle Donnelly.

Chapter Seventeen

Back at Barnstaple CID, Fred Winterflood had instructed a police helicopter to follow the fitness tracker signal which was now twenty-six miles away from Talantire's car. The sporadic hits on GPS showed it heading north-east, travelling through country lanes at the speed of a vehicle, getting close to the M5 then doubling back before heading north. Maddy had passed the logon details so that the rapidly expanding enquiry team could all access the data. Digital evidence technician Primrose Chen made sure that everything worked properly.

'Have you seen the body monitor data, sir?' she asked Winterflood. 'Her heart rate is quite high, but her blood oxygen levels are really low. It's registering red.'

'At least she's still alive,' he responded. 'Let's patch in a medic to see what we might learn about her health from this dataset.'

An incoming call from Dave Nuttall was passed through to Primrose.

'Primrose, are you able to retrieve Talantire's dashcam footage from the cloud for us?' He explained how the device itself had been removed but would probably have an image and hopefully the number plate of the vehicle she was taken away in.

'I'll get onto it straightaway,' she replied.

After hanging up, the digital evidence officer looked through the police vehicle database to find the unique number of Talantire's unmarked Skoda, and the corresponding dashcam ID. She then logged on to the cloud and was quickly able to retrieve the video footage. There were dozens of hours of it, but she went immediately to the last few minutes of the file, the most recent images.

What she saw there was so horrifying that she let out a little cry. Winterflood and some of the other officers crowded around her terminal as she replayed the last few minutes.

The dashcam caught a rear view of Talantire heading from the car towards a white van with partially open rear doors, then a man in dark overalls with a balaclava jumped out brandishing a Taser.

'Oh, God, poor Jan!' one of the female officers exclaimed, her hand over her mouth.

Talantire was virtually out of view on the right-hand side of the picture, but the dashcam caught the firing of the device, the twin wires fizzing across the screen and a high-pitched screaming. She slumped sideways, partially over the bonnet at the right-hand side of the frame. The impact of her head on the metal made the dashcam jump. The man seized her, and they fought and wrestled on the bonnet for a seemingly endless half minute. He then backed away to press the yellow Taser repeatedly against her, the screams of agony hard to listen to.

'What a fighter she is,' Winterflood breathed, as she again fought back as the man came for her, trying to grab his wrists.

'I feel so helpless,' Primrose said, her hands steepled over her nose.

The man shouted and swore, and punched at Talantire's now-slumped form, hauling her off the bonnet, dragging her along the road then bundling her into the back of the van. Even then, she regained consciousness and fought back furiously. Another jab of the Taser produced a convulsive jerk of her limbs, then he got to work on her wrists and ankles. Finally, she was bundled into a bag, the van doors were closed and the man ran back to the Skoda. The image jerked and went dead. The dashcam had been removed.

'Does anyone know who this guy might be?' Winterflood asked.

'Brent West?' Primrose suggested.

'He's too broad or at least not tall enough,' Winterflood replied. 'But we need to know West's whereabouts. Detective Superintendent Wells has promised to get a call in to the chief constable so we can get more resources.'

'West is probably at the big chiefs' pow-wow near Birmingham,' another officer suggested. 'He's into gang crime, isn't he? That's what the conference is about.'

West made his way back into the conference centre from the car park. What Donnelly had told him during their call had slightly reassured him. It seemed unlikely anyone could be tracking Talantire. There would only be a sporadic GPS signal, anyway, from inside the metallic shell of the van. It would be too hard to identify a specific vehicle from the signal, and besides, within twenty minutes she'd be somewhere no GPS could penetrate. This was a farm building with a basement, in the Brendon Hills of East Devon. He'd arranged it as a backup plan, made for just such an eventuality.

The farm itself had been used by a cannabis drug gang for three years until last March, when it had been raided by police. Following the court case and conviction of the three trafficked Vietnamese nationals who had run the operation, the ownership of the farm as the proceeds of crime was still in dispute between the Ministry of Justice and HMRC. Fortunately, he had a key to the police padlock. The basement, lined with foil insulation and the windows masked, would be the perfect place for Talantire to be kept after she'd been properly searched. Better still, he'd made sure a legit second-hand Volvo estate was there to which she could be transferred ready for the final trip to Burnham-on-Sea. With luck, it would only be a twelve-hour delay.

West berated himself for breaking his own rules. He'd hoped to avoid having to speak to Donnelly during the journey. Even though he'd used a burner phone, if Donnelly was subsequently caught, then there'd be a link between Donnelly's burner and his own, triangulated right here at a police conference. It could be incriminating.

He checked his watch. He had ten minutes before he had to meet NCA head Niall Thompson. Still enough time to ring Sam, maybe she had more information. He returned to the car park, hurried through the rain and sat in his own car. He tapped out her number and got voicemail. *Can you update me?* It was all he dared ask.

The reply was by text, two minutes later.

> In a meeting. Call you in ten. Big op here. Not looking good.

It was a cagey reply, and suitably ambiguous. If she was ever asked to justify it, she would be able to say she was concerned about Talantire's safety. But he knew what she really meant. He fought his own caution for a moment and then gave in. He had to ring Donnelly. Again.

—

DCI Fred Winterflood had just finished a conference call with Detective Superintendent Michael Wells and Chief Constable Hamid Sharif. He fully expected that, given the mushrooming size of the twin officer abduction cases, some senior officer would be parachuted in to replace him as SIO. So he was pleasantly surprised that Sharif had insisted he had full confidence in him pursuing the case, even though it included allegations against a feted superstar from another force. Sharif had gone off to confer with the chief constable of Avon and Somerset, promising him full support.

So long as he could get compelling evidence.

Only now, as he pulled together all the paperwork, did he realise what might be happening. He was being set up to fail. The bigwigs at Middlemoor, the savviest careerists and arse-kissers, the desk jockeys and long-lunchers, sensing the highly political nature of the case, probably wouldn't want to touch this case with a barge pole. The allegations against Commander West, though unsubstantiated, would be a make-or-break career moment for whoever arrested him. No end of people would expect to see Winterflood fail, his work in the heat of the moment to be picked over at leisure by well-paid lawyers, HR consultants and second-guessers.

Winterflood had never sought the big time. He regarded himself as a straightforward, honest-to-goodness copper. He wasn't one of the political creatures, seeking promotion, trying to worm his way up the ladder. He just wanted to see criminals behind bars, without fear or favour. But he couldn't turn a blind eye. He'd always had an overdeveloped sense of justice, and the stubborn courage to follow wherever it may lead.

Then he looked again at what he had.

Forensically and evidentially, it was a disaster zone. No bodies. No dabs. No DNA. No ANPR. No incriminating CCTV. Just a startling set of allegations.

The Crown Prosecution Service would have nothing to do with it yet – he was sure of that. Everything now hinged on what Jan Talantire could tell him. He was depending on her to provide the evidence that he had been unable to find. Another big reason that he prayed for her survival.

Only she could save his bacon.

–

Peeking out of the bag, Talantire couldn't see Donnelly's face in the rearview mirror. The angle was too low, which should have meant he couldn't see her either. The driver compartment was separated from her by a bench seat, with a large headrest. She slid out of the bag, under cover of the engine noise, and looked around.

The temptation was to bolt from the vehicle through the rear doors when it next stopped, and she was certain that in normal circumstances she could easily outrun Donnelly. But she had no shoes, and might anyway get cramps from her confinement. She couldn't risk being caught. She was terrified of the Taser. She wanted to overpower him while he was driving, but she needed weapons.

There was no toolbox. Nothing she could obviously use. The best she had was her tights, and if she'd been wearing a skirt instead of trousers, she could have slid them off and made them into a garotte. The ball gag was no use; the straps were too thick to really cut in to his neck, and the headrest would make it difficult, and again there was the Taser to think about. Above all, Donnelly was a strong, thick-set man, physically capable and determined. She'd overpowered men of his size before, but not when they had a Taser to hand.

She scrutinised the rear door panels and could see there was a release catch. She recalled that when Donnelly had last slammed the rear door, he hadn't locked it.

Okay, back to plan A: flight, not fight.

She waited, crouching on the driver side of the van out of sight until he next came to a junction. As the vehicle slowed to a halt she took four quick steps to the back, pressed her fingers down to release the catch and pushed the rear door, hard. It swung open with a loud metallic groan.

'Oi!' Donnelly bellowed immediately.

Talantire exploded from the back of the van, onto a deserted country lane. She was out! The road was lined with high hedges on both sides, not a hint of human habitation. The rain was slashing down, and visibility was poor under the grey sky. The tarmac was cold, hard and wet against her stockinged feet, but she ran for her life, arms pumping, lungs greedily sucking in the air she had so long been forced to ration.

The nearest field gate was forty yards away and she sprinted for it. Donnelly was quick to put the van into reverse, and was almost on her by the time she reached the gateway. The gate itself was rusting metal, sagging at the hinge, just above waist height and held in place on the latch with a loop of baler twine. She ran full pelt at the gate, braced one arm on the top and vaulted it effortlessly, landing in a muddy puddle and running on. She was sure Donnelly would struggle to do the same.

He had no intention of trying.

Reversing past the gateway, he simply drove the van at the gate. Talantire had managed to get twenty yards into the field before she heard the gate smashed down, the gunning engine and the slurp of tyres churning the meadow. She was in pastureland, rising sharply to the left, with a thick hedge of holly and blackthorn to the right, and beyond it, woodland. Trees! That's where he couldn't follow, except on foot. She sprinted alongside the hedge, looking desperately for a gap, and saw one, choked with nettles, leading steeply down to a stream.

She had no choice.

With the van almost upon her, she threw herself through the gap. She scratched her arms and face on the thorny branches; her feet were ripped by sharp twigs underneath and the rising sting of nettles. Plunging into the water, only a foot deep, was a bit of respite, and allowed her to make progress upstream through thick shrubs by grabbing branches and pulling herself through, below the sightline from the van. She could see the top of it on the other side of the hedge and could hear Donnelly getting out, and the slam of the door.

'I'll fucking kill you, stupid bitch!' he bellowed into the empty sky. 'You can't escape me!'

She heard the telltale click of a weapon being cocked. *Shit!* A firearm as well as a Taser. She should have guessed. The man was former armed forces, former head of a police firearms unit, probably a crack shot. There were plenty of illicit opportunities to retain a gun over such a career. It lowered still further her chance of survival. Her heart was pounding. This was the biggest test of her life. Keeping as low as she could, she splashed her way upstream, parallel to the van. Her feet were already cold as ice and stinging like hell. Her hands were freezing and ripped by bushes, and her blouse was torn, drenched by the pouring rain. To her right were the trees, thick, dark evergreens, closely planted, that would give better cover. She scrambled up a short muddy bank and threw herself into the woods.

A shot rang out, not far from her. She could hear Donnelly shouting at her, cursing and swearing in rising frustration at her Houdini-like escape. A torch beam flashed in the gloom, across to her right, and she could hear his heavy footfalls. He seemed to be about thirty yards behind, struggling with the undergrowth. She slowed down and crouched lower, trying to move quietly. As she slid forward, she spread mud from her legs onto her face and neck. Camouflage, concealment, survival. The beam flashed again, but there was too much undergrowth between them for her to be seen. She shrank behind a large yew tree, thick and old, and tried to suppress her panting.

Somewhere in the distance she could hear a police siren. Donnelly must've heard it too because he turned off the torch and stopped shouting. He was continuing to move, though, and she could hear his footsteps, the noise of the bushes he was pushing through. She looked behind her and could see that this yew tree was one of many on the edge of an overgrown churchyard, old, unkempt, all tilting gravestones and rusted railings. But between her tree and the graveyard was open ground, and a mown path. She needed to avoid it. She didn't want to put herself anywhere that Donnelly could fix a bead on her. She could hear him getting closer, now with the torch on again, pointing at the ground, following her bloody footprints on the muddy ground. Despair flooded her. She felt there was literally nothing she could do now; shivering with cold, effectively barefoot, exhausted and bleeding from numerous scratches. He would find her and he would kill her.

Executed in the rain, just another victim. Like Alex. Like Nadine.

She cast around for a weapon. A few smallish stones, and a little further away a half-brick. Nothing that was really going to do the job. He was quite close now, stealthily feeling his way around the trees about twenty yards away. His phone rang, and he answered it on speakerphone so she could just about hear the other person.

Brent West.

'Where are you?' West demanded.

'Nearly at the farm, but I've hit a bit of a snag.'

'What kind of a snag?'

'She's escaped.'

'What! From inside a padlocked kitbag! How on earth—'

'I have no idea. But I don't think she's far away. She's got no shoes.'

'You bloody incompetent! How did she manage—?'

'If you'd let me use handcuffs instead of cable ties, it wouldn't have been possible, but oh no, you worried about metal residue at the crem. We could have handled—'

'Rope, you needed to use rope!' West bellowed. 'Jesus, I knew I should have done this myself.'

'Yeah, but you wanted a bloody alibi, didn't you? Let others do the dirty work. Let me tell you something: if I go down for this, I'm bringing you down too. I am not disposable like the others, do you understand? A hundred grand per delivery ain't enough for what I'm doing.'

'You can have a hundred and fifty if you bring Talantire in.'

'No, two hundred grand. She was bloody hard work from the start, fought like crazy, now here I am tramping about in the pissing rain, catching my death. If you'd let me kill her at the beginning it would have been all right, but oh no, she had to be transported alive, like that poor sod who worked at Middlemoor. It's a lot more trouble, a lot more risky. So I tell you this, when I find her, and I will, she's getting the bullet straightaway, and I'm bringing her straight over to Burnham. You can deal with the fallout.'

Talantire could see Donnelly now, his head breaking cover, not looking in her direction. This was a man who no doubt had been on many army courses about quiet tracking and hunting down an enemy, but in his fury had forgotten it all. Letting his anger get ahead of his professionalism.

'Calm down, Colin. Keep your cool, think straight. I'll look after you, I promise.'

'Fuck off,' he said, killing the call and pocketing the phone. 'Wanker,' he added, afterwards for good measure, and looked away, back towards the van.

Talantire risked standing up and threw an egg-sized stone far away to her left. It crashed into bushes and drew Donnelly's gaze. She heard the click of a gun cocking as he sank out of view, but she could hear his movements, heading away from her. She waited another minute, then headed off in the opposite direction, keeping low, skirting the edge of the churchyard, moving from one dark yew tree to the next. A footpath by the side of the graveyard led to a small Norman church about a hundred yards away. She had to go for it. She'd die of exposure if she didn't get somewhere warm soon. She ran, avoiding bushes until she reached the path.

And there, by a gravestone, was an elderly woman under an umbrella. She looked up as Talantire ran towards her, and despite Talantire's insistent finger to her own lips, she gave a shout of alarm at the muddy, bloodied wraith pelting towards her.

'Ring the police, there's an armed man!' she shouted, sprinting past her towards a lane at the end.

The woman looked paralysed with terror, and Talantire felt the best chance to save her life would be to draw Donnelly away. She ran on, her breath coming in deep gulps. A single gunshot and scream confirmed her worst fear. She risked looking over her shoulder and saw the woman slumped on the path thirty yards back, Donnelly standing over her.

The track ran down the left-hand side of the church and ended in a T-junction twenty yards ahead, with a pull-in to the church on the right that had one car parked in it. She jinked as she ran, hoping that Donnelly would pursue, not stop to fire. She'd done almost no weapons training, but had read that a handgun was inaccurate against a moving target at more than ten yards. But she did not want to test that thesis against a professional. She wanted gates, hedges, rough ground, obstacles, anything that made the pursuit more difficult for him. Anything that impeded him getting a clear shot.

'You can't escape,' Donnelly bellowed, his heavy lumbering steps and gasping breath carrying clearly.

At the T-junction, she sprinted left on the narrow lane, out of view. There were no houses, but there was a public footpath sign opposite. She ran for it, vaulting a farm gate. Here the land went very sharply uphill, steep sodden pasture, a tempting route on which her superior fitness could begin to tell. However, there were cattle up there in the field too, so she decided to keep away from them. Any movement she triggered from them might be a clear signal to Donnelly where she was. So instead, she crouched down behind a thick, ivy-covered hedge and moved stealthily to the right, parallel to the road. She stopped and crouched down next to a small gap, which gave a view back towards the church and the lane beside it.

A few seconds later, Donnelly emerged onto the road, gun in hand. He looked left and right up the rain-soaked lane, before returning to a parked car and checking underneath it. She was close enough to hear his ragged breath, worse than her own. He looked worried. No wonder, his prisoner gone, and a fresh murder committed just half a minute ago.

The distant thudding sound of a helicopter made Donnelly look up and then seek cover in the front porch of the church. A siren too, further away. The helicopter seemed to take ages to come into view, circled once, high up, far to her left. With Donnelly less than fifty yards away she was afraid to wave to it. But they would know roughly where she was from the tracker. She edged further along the hedge when she heard a police car approaching at speed, sirens going. She ran along to a low point in the hedge and climbed onto a bramble-entangled wooden fence, back onto the road, so she could be seen.

The police car sped past, the occupants apparently not seeing the arm she waved.

But someone else had seen her.

Donnelly had sprinted out of the church porch and was just five yards away, drawing a bead on her. Her feet and trousers were so entangled in the painfully spiky shrubs that she struggled to free herself. The helicopter thudded low overhead, just as a second police car came into view. Donnelly grabbed her around the neck, and pulled her off the fence, with the gun pointed at the side of her head, standing behind her.

'You're my ticket to freedom, so thank your lucky stars,' he said, as he turned to face the slowing patrol car, brandishing Talantire as a human shield.

'Listen here,' he announced to the two white-faced young officers who emerged from the car. 'I'm a former head of a firearms team, so I know the routines. Get me the chief constable, here in person, I've got a deal to make.'

Chapter Eighteen

Brent West sat in his Ford Explorer and cursed. He couldn't believe that Talantire had somehow managed to escape from a locked army kitbag. How was that even possible? And then to follow it by escaping from a moving van driven by an army marksman who had both a gun *and* a Taser. It simply reinforced the feeling he'd had for many years, that only he really had the thoroughness, temperament and preparation for a complex operation. But on this particular occasion, he couldn't afford to be anywhere near her.

In five minutes, back in the conference centre, he was due in a meeting with the head of the NCA. But it would be hard to concentrate on it until he knew that Talantire had been caught and killed. Perhaps he had been overambitious in trying to keep her alive to experience the full glory of the crematorium. Now he needed to make yet another call, to a backup resource. Something he had hoped he wouldn't have to do.

–

Rebecca Crossfield found Niall Thompson amongst a knot of senior male officers, all staring at their phones, near the entrance to the largest conference room.

'Sir, if I may interrupt. I've made a very important discovery.'

Thompson looked up, peering owlishly at her from behind his red-framed glasses. 'Yes, Rebecca?' The others, mainly white- or silver-haired men in their sixties just glanced at her and then returned to whatever it was that they were looking at. One of them she knew: Nigel Hart, Chief Constable of Staffordshire.

She showed Thompson her iPad, on which she had enlarged the surveillance photograph showing the three men on the alpine road. She then swiped through to a close-up of their faces.

'This man, known as Il Bruciatore and wanted by Interpol, is in fact Commander Brent West of Avon and Somerset Police,' she said.

At this, she had the attention of everyone. A few of them exchanged knowing glances and wry smiles; others grinned indulgently at her. She passed the iPad to Thompson, who gave a slight shrug before handing it on to Hart. Clearly not convinced.

'You mean the bearded fellow?' Hart asked.

'It's really him. I know; I worked with him, in France,' she added, aware that she sounded rather too desperate to get them onside.

'That's an extremely serious allegation, DCS Crossfield,' Thompson said. 'Do you have any evidence?'

Before she could reply, she detected a certain change in the body language of the assembled group. They all looked over her shoulder.

'Perhaps we can ask the man himself,' Hart said, with a smirk.

With a sinking feeling, Rebecca turned her head to see West striding towards the group, looking utterly magnificent: handsome, upright, in a dazzling white shirt, teeth gleaming. This was a man who had future chief constable written all over him.

'Ah, Brent,' said one of the officers, who, judging from his lanyard, was a deputy chief constable, Christopher Morton. 'We were just looking at your holiday pictures.'

The laughter seemed to turn into a rising froth of bonhomie as if they were somehow drawing electricity from West's charisma.

'Good day, gentleman, and lady.' He nodded to Rebecca, adding, 'Are we friends again?'

'What do you mean?' she replied.

He simply grinned at everybody else. She had to hand it to him: the man was the master of the pre-emptive put-down. Alluding to some trivial spat in order to draw the sting of whatever it was she was alleging.

'Take a look,' Hart said, handing West the iPad. 'She reckons it's you.'

'Which one?' West asked, with a laugh.

'You're supposedly moonlighting for the Mafia, burning down buildings in Milan,' said Morton, with a smile. 'Disguising yourself with a beard.'

'Well, if only I had the time for all that,' West chuckled, rubbing a hand over his immaculately shaved jaw. 'Beards make me itchy.'

Rebecca felt herself almost visibly shrinking in the gentle laughter that surrounded her. Almost every fibre of her being was longing to flee, to storm away. But that would give them their victory.

Summoning all her courage, she said, directly to him: 'I know this is you, and I know you're working for the 'Ndrangheta, feeding in operational secrets—'

'Oh Brent, you do seem to have upset a lot of the ladies,' Morton said.

The head of the NCA winced at this. 'Ah, Chris, I think it's unfair to characterise it that way,' Thompson said, holding up his hand. 'All allegations of corruption, however amateurishly presented, should be thoroughly investigated. I'm sure that DCS Crossfield would not have made such a grave charge had she not assembled something quite convincing. But I have to say, this is not the forum for us to discuss it—'

'Because in the meantime, Brent, a kidnap drama is unfolding on your old stamping ground,' Hart said.

Rebecca looked at the assembled group. *So that's what they were all staring at on their phones.* Hart offered his own phone on which a video was playing. It showed a helicopter's-eye view of a country road surrounded by woodland, in which a ring of police cars was gathered around a man who was holding a woman at gunpoint, his arm around her throat from behind.

'This is a former firearms unit officer, Sergeant Colin Donnelly,' Hart said. 'The woman is Detective Inspector Jan Talantire.'

'Oh my God,' Rebecca gasped. 'I know her!'

'—Me too. I worked briefly with Jan last summer,' West interrupted. 'I was never sure her temperament was quite suited to policing, and of course she was recently suspended, but nobody deserves this. Poor woman—'

Rebecca interrupted '—You've got a bloody nerve—'

'Now then everyone, *please*,' Thompson said. Two phones within the group began to buzz. One of them was West's. He ignored it.

Hart, who had retrieved his phone, looked up from it. 'Donnelly has apparently just made an allegation. It concerns you, Commander West.'

West excused himself from the conference, blaming an urgent call. And there was indeed one from his own chief constable. But that could wait.

He retreated to the gents' toilet, and from the privacy of a cubicle sent a coded message on his burner phone on a rarely used WhatsApp group. This was backup plan number two, and he was dubious about whether it was going to work at all. But he had to try. He then booked himself on a flight from Bristol that evening to Milan, departing at 6:45 p.m. He had to keep himself one step ahead.

He then rang back the chief constable of Avon and Somerset police and agreed to the informal interview requested, in the light of the welter of allegations. West promised he would be back at Portishead by seven p.m., he said. By the time he was missed, he'd be on the flight. He'd known that at some stage this would all come tumbling down; he'd just never guessed it would be so soon. His escape plans had been made months ago, though, with help from his friends in Italy. There was already plenty of money stashed away in the Gulf, and in Caribbean tax havens, false passports and a backstory that wouldn't raise suspicions. It was the cosmetic surgery he would ultimately need for his new identity that worried him most. Still.

Talantire was held firmly around the neck by Donnelly, who forced her to kneel down on the road in front of him in the pouring rain, facing half a dozen uniformed constables. He was crouching behind her with one knee in the small of her back. She could feel his hot breath on her neck.

'Don't you get any closer or I'll blow her brains out. I am not kidding.' The tip of the pistol was against her temple, and she felt pretty sure that her captor was desperate enough to pull the trigger.

She was so cold and so wet now that she knew she must be suffering from exposure. Her fingers and toes were numb. Only her throat was warm, encircled by the heat of his arm. Donnelly had already demanded to speak to the chief constable, but she knew that it was a hostage negotiator the uniforms were waiting for, someone who could not make the deal that Donnelly wanted but could only play for time. She had seen a uniformed inspector, clearly out of his depth, skulking away behind a van at the back of the police vehicles. She knew, but couldn't see, that there were officers behind, too, with a couple of vehicles. Once the firearms unit arrived, Donnelly would be very jumpy because he couldn't cover every direction.

And that was presumably why he stood up gradually and began to back them towards the church. 'You lot, just keep away,' Donnelly yelled to the encircling officers. He got her to shuffle backwards, bent towards him, for about ten yards until they reached the entrance porch to the church. There he had a solid wooden door behind him, and they both were protected from the downpour.

'I said, stay back!' Donnelly yelled, discharging the gun into the ceiling of the porch.

The encroaching officers jumped back.

He then whispered into her ear. 'Right, you, don't give me any trouble and you'll get what you want. I'll spill all the details about West, his links to the Mafia, the pet cemetery that he's taken over in Burnham-on-Sea, all that.

But they've got to keep me alive, right? There's nothing on a computer, nothing written down, just what's in my head. So you got to help me if you want to bring him to justice. Understand?'

She nodded as best she could, tapping her finger on his arm. 'Ease the pressure, please,' she croaked.

He eased his arm forward a fraction. 'It's a deal,' she said.

'I need to make a bargain with them, will you help me?'

'After three murders, you won't get much slack,' she said.

'Three?'

'The old lady back there.'

'Oh, yeah, her.' He made it sound like a minor oversight, an accounting slip in some larger balance sheet.

The thud of a helicopter grew. 'Right, this will be it. I want you to back me up, okay?'

'Okay.' Talantire was aware of another vehicle far to her right, and so was Donnelly.

'Here's the firearms boys,' he said. 'Yeah, the Exeter unit. I know 'em. And there's young Zach Townend. You remember him?'

'No.' She couldn't see so well with his arm around her neck.

'He's the lad you complained about on the cliffs, you remember? Best marksman on the unit.'

She recalled clearly the explicit sexual gesture a young man under Donnelly's command had made while she was making an arrest last summer on the cliffs at Portloe.

'Armed police, put the weapon down!' bellowed a firearms officer away to her right. The unarmed uniforms were withdrawing, their places taken by an armed tactical unit, body armour, helmets. The entire atmosphere had got more tense, his arm tighter again around her neck, his body braced.

'I'll release her if you cut me a deal,' he yelled. 'I'll give you the details about Commander West, who is the mastermind of all the abductions.'

'Donnelly, put the weapon down,' shouted the same officer.

For the next five minutes there was a stand-off. Donnelly making demands and the firearms unit yelling for him to lay down his weapon. Talantire's throat was painfully constricted, and she feared for her life as much because of the firearms boys as she did because of Donnelly himself. She reckoned it was 50–50 whether she'd make it out or not. Donnelly, too, seemed to have doubts. He was no longer waiting for the chief constable he had demanded but was starting to throw out demands.

'I want you to listen, see? You want the top man. Only I can give him to you. So hold your fire and she'll be safe. Right, there's a senior officer behind all this, and I can give you the details, can't I, Jan?'

She did her best to nod her head.

The high-velocity shot was silenced, wasping in from the left, just behind her ear. A thud, and a warm spatter on the back of her head. Then a second shot, so close it ruffled her hair. She tried to slip under the arm around her neck, but tumbled to the ground, still embraced, but by a dead and largely headless body.

There were no more shots, just a lot of yelling and a press of armoured bodies sprinting up to her and pulling her away. She sobbed with relief when strong arms lifted her away and onto a stretcher. She felt the exposure blanket, heard the kind words from paramedics before she was lifted into an ambulance. Further back, she saw one of the helmeted firearms officers in the arms of congratulating colleagues. Her view was blocked by the arrival of Hamid Sharif. The dapper chief constable, with his acid-burned face, looked like he belonged in hospital with her. The chief constable asked the paramedics how she was, and they mentioned hypothermia and extensive but largely superficial wounds.

'I'll let you go, Jan,' he said to her. 'The debrief can wait, but I want you to know how proud I am that you are an officer on this force. And I apologise for our neglect of your personal safety. We are going to post an armed guard in your hospital corridor until we get to the bottom of what has been happening.'

Chapter Nineteen

Talantire slept in the ambulance and came round in a thickly blanketed bed in a hospital ICU, hooked up to intravenous warm fluids, a heart monitor and oxygen. Maddy Moran was at her bedside, holding her hand, as nurses bustled around. She gripped Maddy's hand, and had one burning question she wanted to ask:

'Did they arrest him?'

'Brent West? No. But he's been called in for interview by his chief constable.'

'I still don't think they have anything on him.'

'Don't you worry about that now, leave it to us.'

'But...'

'You were in a right mess, Jan,' Maddy said. 'Your feet were slashed to ribbons; you must have walked on broken glass. I brought you a load of fresh clothes, ready for when they let you out tomorrow. I've got you a new phone, too.' She placed it on the bedside. 'There will be a full debrief tomorrow.'

'I want to do it now.'

'No, you can't,' interrupted a nurse. 'You are already too tired.' She ushered Maddy out, leaving her only with the officer at the doorway. He was a tactical firearms guy, with a handgun at his hip and a baseball cap. He was chewing gum vigorously. She recognised him. He was the same one she saw being congratulated by his colleagues as she was being loaded into the ambulance. The man at the cliffs back in the summer. She recalled him cradling his automatic weapon like it was a newborn baby. He had his back to her as she stretched out and took the new phone. She set up the voice recorder app and then slid the device into a box of tissues, by her pillow, and pulled the top tissue up to obscure it.

'Excuse me, officer.'

He glanced at her, then turned away.

'Was it you?' she asked him. 'That fired the shots?'

He nodded, still chewing.

She recalled the name. 'Zach Townend?'

'Yes ma'am.' He still didn't look at her.

'Was it initiative or an order?'

Now he looked at her. He was in his mid-twenties with an uncomplicated boyish look.

'I got a clean shot, from the side.'

'It was inch perfect,' she said.

He shifted uncomfortably. 'Proud to have saved your life, ma'am.'

'Thank you.' She said nothing more for a minute, then replied: 'He wasn't going to kill me; did you know that?'

He rolled his eyes and turned away.

'He didn't need to die.'

He turned cold eyes upon her. 'Those judgements aren't for the likes of me.'

'On the contrary, you pulled the trigger. You took responsibility to take a life.'

'I did my job.' His eyes said more: *Some people have no gratitude.*

'Donnelly was just about to tell us what he knew.'

'Was he?' The man shrugged and turned away, inspecting the corridor, eyes darting left and right.

'But you've saved another person,' Talantire continued.

He glanced back at her, his jaw tensed with the chewing.

'Commander Brent West,' she said.

'I don't know what you mean.'

'Was the second shot meant for me?'

The chewing now was intense. He didn't make eye contact, nervously scanning the corridor.

A nurse came in and bustled around, checking Talantire's drip. There were other medics further into the ICU, just a few yards away, but out of earshot.

'Zach, I know that you post under the name Asteroid on the same firearms WhatsApp group as Brent West. I've seen some of your comments, as well as those of Donnelly.'

He said nothing, which seeing as she was recording him, was frustrating. She continued to work on him.

'The regs stipulate that a firearms officer who has just caused a fatality would be expected to go off duty immediately afterwards. So why is it you that's here, looking after me, and not one of the others?'

'No idea. I was told to be here.'

'I'm guessing that you have considered trying to finish me off here. A pillow over the face, maybe. I don't know how much West promised you. Maybe the same amount for me as for Donnelly. But the big snag, of course, is that killing me now would be much more problematic for you to explain. Whereas the Donnelly assassination was as sweet as could be. Absolutely in your line of work, no blowback at all. My guess is that you're happy with the money you got. A bird in the hand, so to speak.'

He stepped outside the room and closed the door quietly behind him. She reached out for the phone, turned off the app, forwarded the file to Maddy's personal phone, then hid the device under the pillow.

Chapter Twenty

It was more than a year later. Talantire was at the Old Bailey in London, sitting in a wood-panelled waiting room for prosecution witnesses outside Court Two. It was the third day in the murder and conspiracy trial of Brent West, and she had missed everything that had been said that day, having to wait there until she was called. She couldn't even find out what the press were saying that day because she hadn't been allowed to take her phone, and there was nothing to read. The only other person there was a woman volunteer from the Citizens Advice Witness Service, and the occasional usher who passed through. Primrose Chen had been there earlier, but had now been giving evidence for two hours. Talantire was the last prosecution witness and felt uncharacteristically nervous.

She had given evidence in courts dozens of times during her career, but everything depended on what she said and how convincing she was to the jurors. The fight to bring her nemesis to court had been the longest and toughest fight of her career, but putting West behind bars still remained a difficult task. He had been arrested at Bristol Airport and denied access to his flight by an alert security officer, who had seen the arrest warrant notification ordered by National Crime Agency chief Niall Thompson, and which had been sent to Border Force only five minutes before the flight was called. Thompson had finally been persuaded by Rebecca Crossfield's evidence, which now included additional pictures of the West rendezvous in Austria, and a picture she had found on a police sports Facebook page, showing him weight training with other officers, images which clearly showed the distinctive moles. The initial charge was misconduct in public office, a catch-all while more evidence was gathered.

But implicating West in Talantire's kidnap was going to be harder. Right from the beginning the CPS had warned her that the case was finely balanced: the evidence against him was almost entirely circumstantial.

There were no bodies; no proof that those he had supposedly intended to kill were in fact dead. Even the local coroner was unable to proceed with a report because there wasn't sufficient evidence of the deaths of either Nadine Lister or Alex Brown. Moreover, there was not a single incriminating DNA trace or fingerprint which put Brent West anywhere near either pet crematoria where it was alleged that the victims died. The best they had was electronic evidence which indicated that he had connections with Colin Donnelly, the former police sergeant who had carried out the abductions. Donnelly was killed by a single shot from a police marksman while holding Talantire hostage. The CPS lead lawyer, Yasir Khan KC, had described that act as extremely convenient from the defendant's point of view. What Donnelly knew, and had been in the process of saying when he was shot, would have been very useful to the prosecution.

She leaned back and for the umpteenth time gazed at the grand corniced ceiling, following the brown water stain which snaked across until it disappeared near a light fitting. The chair she was sitting on, originally grand, was worn out, the dark green plush almost bald, the material held together with gaffer tape. It had a rather alarming wobble too. One of the other chairs was darkly stained, as if somebody had been caught short. She sympathised. This place was almost designed to make you feel nervous. Speaking of which…

She stood up and told the volunteer that she was going to visit the ladies' toilet. The facilities at London Central Criminal Court were notoriously antiquated, and it was a long walk along a narrow corridor and down two sets of stairs before she entered the green-and-brown tiled bathroom which served multiple courts. It was garishly lit and smelled of stale urine. She made her way past the row of rectangular porcelain washbasins, looking for a cubicle. Three out of the eight were out of order and two were engaged, but she eventually found a vacant one in working order.

While she was in the cubicle, someone came in to the bathroom, crying softly. The voice was familiar, and after she'd finished, Talantire flushed the toilet and eased open the door. There in front of her, dabbing her eyes at a washbasin, was DC Samantha Mahoney. West's current girlfriend and listed as a witness for the other side. She stared at Talantire in the mirror with alarm.

'Are you giving evidence?' Sam asked.

Witnesses weren't supposed to speak to each other, but Talantire could see no harm in replying.

'I will be when I'm called. I've been waiting for three days.'

'I was told the defence case is likely to start this afternoon. They probably won't get to me today; that's what I've been told. I'm here just in case.'

'I had really hoped you would be a witness for our side,' Talantire said. 'After what you said about his behaviour.'

Sam didn't reply, but smiled tightly, as she skilfully reapplied her eyeliner.

'Did he really make you have an abortion?' Talantire asked.

Sam gave a slight shrug.

'Sam, please don't let him get away with it.'

With Donnelly dead, Sam was now the only person who knew enough to put West in jail. She wondered why the woman had been crying, whether it was some casual act of cruelty by West, or the discovery of yet another infidelity. There were so many questions she would like to ask, but she had already said too much; she couldn't risk being reported to the judge.

Talantire washed her hands but tutted on discovering that the soap dispenser was empty. She rolled her eyes at Sam, who gave a small smile of sympathy. This, the only meeting of minds with a woman who, as West's accomplice, would have been happy to see her dead, burned alive.

—

While Talantire was waiting, Maddy Moran was listening to Primrose Chen. The digital evidence officer, wearing a smart business suit and a fawn hijab, swore her oath on the Koran. Under Khan's gentle questioning she described how she traced a call between one burner phone, used by Colin Donnelly and found on his body, and another that cell-site triangulation had isolated to the extreme northern edge of a hotel car park in Bromsgrove.

'That was the very same hotel where Commander Brent West was attending a police chief's conference, was it not?' Khan asked.

'Yes,' she said.

The jury were next shown CCTV coverage of a man walking across the car park to a black Ford Explorer, looking at his phone. As he entered the car, the timestamp on the video was exactly the same almost to the second as a call that was made from somewhere very close to that spot to Donnelly's burner phone.

'Miss Chen, is it your contention that Commander West made this call?'

'It seems very likely to me that he did,' she responded. 'The timings were exactly right, and we can see on the CCTV that it is Commander West who is on the way to his car. The call was initiated from the car park, lasted two minutes, and as you can see from the CCTV, that matches the time that he emerges from the vehicle and comes back into the conference.'

Khan finished his questions and then she was cross-examined by West's barrister, Eleanor Cranham.

'Miss Chen, can I ask you, do the police have in their possession the phone from which this call was made?'

'No. We think it has probably been destroyed.'

'And was there anything recovered remotely from this phone that indicates it might have been owned by the defendant?'

'No, that's the entire point of a burner phone—'

'So it could be anyone's phone?' Cranham asked.

'No, it could only have been in the hands of someone in the extreme northerly end of that car park at the time the call was made.'

'How many cars in that car park fall within the area of cell-site triangulation, would you say?'

'Thirty-seven. It's the last three rows.'

'So correct me if I'm wrong, but someone in any of those thirty-seven cars could have made the call.'

'Most of those cars had no occupant.'

'How do you know?'

'Because we have identified each and every one of them and linked all but two to individuals who were present at the conference.'

'We cannot be sure beyond all reasonable doubt, can we, the that the call in question was made by Commander West?'

'It's very likely it was him.'

'Ms Chen, the burden of proof here, in an English court, is beyond all reasonable doubt.'

Watching this, Maddy seethed at the implied rebuke based on her ethnicity. Khan immediately objected to the line of questioning, which Cranham rephrased.

'I don't think there's any reasonable doubt,' Primrose said.

'But it could conceivably be one of the occupants of the other two cars within the triangulation area?'

'It's not completely impossible,' she conceded.

Talantire was called as the next witness. Maddy held her breath and leaned forward in her seat, as Khan led her through her relationship with West, and then the complaints process at Middlemoor and its frustrating conclusion, right up to her abduction and her astonishing escape from a locked kitbag.

'Detective Inspector Talantire, during that journey, you heard some of the conversations that Donnelly had on the phone, didn't you?' Khan asked. 'What can you tell me about the nature of that discussion?'

'Yes. Firstly, it was clear that Donnelly was not the boss, and that he was undertaking my abduction on behalf of somebody else. He also bitterly complained when talking to himself after the phone conversations were finished that he was taking all the risk, while the mastermind of the operation constructed himself a series of cast-iron alibis.'

'And you took this person at the other end of the phone to be West?'

'Yes. In fact, I recognised his voice in a later call.'

'Why do you think he wanted to get rid of you?'

'Because I was energetically trying to investigate his record of abusing female officers, and would not be bought off.'

Khan finished by praising her courage and bravery, before Eleanor Cranham stepped up to cross-examine for West.

'No one doubts, Ms Talantire, that you have endured a truly horrible experience at the hands of the late Colin Donnelly. However, your attempts to point the finger at man who was 250 miles away at the time seems a little stretched, wouldn't you say?'

'No.'

'Is it not true, Ms Talantire, that you have dedicated the last seven years of your life to trying to bring down my client, in an enduring campaign of jealousy and rage?'

'That's completely untrue.'

'Well, the facts are the facts. Did you or did you not collude with another officer to fabricate allegations against my client?'

'I neither colluded nor fabricated—'

'Really? I would like to offer as evidence a sound file, in which you and Mrs Nadine Lister were overheard discussing how to bring him down.'

Only a small portion of the file was played, and when it was finished, Talantire said: 'Why don't you play it all so you can hear me say to Nadine that we shouldn't have been talking to each other?'

'But you *were* talking to each other, were you not?' Cranham persisted.

'I picked up the phone and she began to speak; what could I do?'

'It's for me to ask the questions, not you, Ms Talantire.'

'I'd like to know why you don't want the whole truth, the context—' Talantire said, gripping the edges of the witness box.

'Oh dear, if you'd like to make a speech, I suggest you go to Speaker's Corner at Hyde Park. A court of law—'

The judge intervened. 'Mrs Cranham, I suggest you stop goading the witness.'

'I'll rephrase,' Cranham conceded. 'Is it not true, Ms Talantire, that you were put on a final written warning by Devon and Cornwall Police and then later suspended because of this continuing campaign to get my client?'

'Yes, but—'

'We don't need the "but"; the "yes" will suffice,' Cranham said.

'My only campaign is for the truth—'

'Oh do, please, spare us the self-serving moral crusade.'

'—to find out why those who complain about their treatment at the hands of Brent West end up dead!'

The barrister looked at her. 'Ms Talantire, would you say you have something of a temper? Anger management issues?'

'That's not how I would describe it,' she said, knowing what was coming next.

'Please read to the court the highlighted paragraphs from your personnel report,' Cranham said, passing across a document.

Talantire held up the paper and began. '"DI Talantire has the best record of crime detection, and the highest conviction percentage of any officer—"'

'Ms Talantire, that was not the highlighted section.'

'If you want to find out about me, perhaps it's best to read the whole document,' she said, turning to the jury.

Clearly nettled by this response, the barrister then herself read out sections which detailed Talantire's shortcomings, and finished by saying: 'The chair of the panel examining your complaint and the collusion against my client concluded, and I quote: "I'm not sure this officer has a future in the police".'

Talantire interjected. 'I'd like to point out that I have been reinstated, my final written warning rescinded and I was given an apology by the Chief Constable of Devon and Cornwall Police.'

'Well I'm sure, Ms Talantire, that nobody wants to be unkind to a woman who was abducted and locked in a bag.'

'I was reinstated before that.'

'Ms Talantire, setting aside your personal animosity to my client, do you have any direct evidence that he was involved at all in this, or indeed any of the supposed abductions?'

'You've already heard the evidence from my colleague Primrose—'

'Ms Talantire, I'm asking you. My client supposedly committed two murders, but we have no bodies. We don't even know if these people are dead.'

'The coroner said they probably are.'

'But the coroner also said, did she not, that the circumstances did not reach the evidential bar required for them to be officially declared dead.'

'Yes.'

'And she recognised, did she not, that we do not have any forensic evidence whatsoever.'

'That's what happens when people are cremated.'

'But we don't know they were cremated, do we? And we certainly have no fingerprints, no DNA, no sightings to show that Commander West was in any way involved.'

Talantire said nothing.

'Please answer,' Cranham continued. 'And can I remind you that you are under oath?'

'I heard Donnelly talking to him.'

'Oh yes, while bound and gagged and locked in a kitbag, in a van rumbling along a bumpy country road, you claim you were able to hear well enough to be certain beyond reasonable doubt who Donnelly was talking to.'

'Some of the conversations I overheard when the van was stopped, when I'd already extricated myself. I also overheard West when Donnelly was pursuing me through woodland. At that time the phone was on speakerphone, and I recognised his voice.'

'Well, I'm sure the jury will have their own opinion on the independence of your judgement. No further questions.'

The lunchtime recess was announced, and Talantire was allowed to join her colleagues in the public gallery. In the afternoon, the defence called their principal witness, the defendant. Brent West, as usual, looked magnificent and imperturbable in a pristine white shirt and a dark suit as he ascended to the witness box. The barrister spent nearly an hour presenting West's police accomplishments and commendations. Eventually, she asked: 'Commander West, in order to answer some of the allegations against you, I need to ask you about your personal life.'

'Go ahead.'

'Would it be fair to say that you have had a number of girlfriends since your divorce?'

'Yes.'

'And how would you characterise your behaviour in those relationships?'

'Consensual and considerate.'

At this point, Talantire noticed a young woman in the jury lean forward and smile at him, her chin resting in her cupped hands.

'Do you have relationships with women in the police?'

'I did occasionally.'

Occasionally? Talantire struggled to suppress her snort of contempt.

'Why did you?' Cranham asked him.

'Because the police is an all-encompassing institution that leaves you with very little free time to meet anyone outside. However, I was careful to always turn down approaches from women who were direct subordinates. It was important not to appear to have conflicts of interest.'

'And it was women who approached you?'

'Generally, yes.'

'Ladies and gentlemen of the jury, I think you can see, without me asking, why it would be that way around,' Cranham said, removing her glasses and gazing at them. There were several knowing smiles in return.

'You have heard the testimony of Ms Talantire, about your relationship seven years ago and her accusations against you.'

'Yes.'

'Is there any truth in them?'

'No. I simply recall her being very upset when I ended the relationship.'

Liar! I finished it. Talantire was fizzing with indignation, but he did not look in her direction.

'What do you think motivated her enmity towards you?'

Khan objected at that point on the grounds that West was being asked to give an opinion of what was in somebody else's head, but the judge allowed Cranham to continue.

West said: 'I assumed that her pride was hurt and that is why she made up these allegations about me.'

Asked about Nadine Lister, he gave very similar story. 'My relationship with her was really quite brief, and I ended it fairly soon because I felt she was looking for a way out of her failing marriage.'

Talantire could see Nadine's husband Roger sitting in a row in front of her in the public gallery. He too was muttering.

'Do you know where Mrs Lister is?' Cranham asked him.

'I don't. She did tell me that she occasionally had suicidal thoughts, so I do fear for her,' he said. He expressed similar bewilderment when asked about Alex Brown.

'According to recovered documents, Mr Brown witnessed you and an unnamed female officer indulging in sexual relations in the office on Easter Sunday last year, indeed, on the very desk of the chief constable.'

West smiled at this. 'That incident never happened.'

'So it was entirely made up?'

'Well, I was in the office at Middlemoor that day, working. But no, the incident never occurred. Mr Brown had on a previous occasion made a pass at me, and though I rather gently declined, I think he too was rather offended.'

'Thank you, Commander West. No further questions.'

Yasir Khan then began to cross-examine West, concentrating on the various relationships that he had had with female officers. 'Commander West, do you consider this to be a professional way to carry on within the police, where an officer of your seniority should be expected to uphold the highest standards?'

Eleanor Cranham intervened to object. 'My client is not on trial for his attractiveness, nor his suitability for high office.'

The judge rejected that and asked the defendant to answer.

West addressed the judge: 'I can't say I'm proud of everything that I have done, but all my relationships have been consensual and respectful.'

'In that case, Commander, why did you offer payment to Nadine Lister in exchange for her silence over allegations against you?'

'Quite simply because those allegations, though untrue, would be highly damaging to my career and my reputation, if publicised.'

'If they are untrue, why did you offer payment? Is that not the behaviour of a guilty man?'

'Not at all. Nadine is a very unstable and vulnerable person, struggling to save her marriage. I persuaded her that joining Talantire in this unjustified campaign would not bring her happiness. In the end she agreed.'

'In the end, actually, you murdered her, didn't you?'

'No, and the accusation doesn't make sense. If I was going to murder her, why on earth would I go to all the trouble of getting her to sign a non-disclosure agreement and start paying her the money?'

At this Talantire noticed a male member of the jury nodding his head in agreement.

'Perhaps, Mr West, because it was a relatively cheap way of removing yourself from the suspect list.'

'That's absurd,' West said, looking at the jury.

This was not going well. Khan continued to chip away, but West remained unflappable. Khan announced that video evidence, found at Donnelly's home, was going to be shown.

Talantire's throat went dry. She knew this would be her and West at his flat seven years ago – the video she had presumed existed but had never found. She'd already been told it would be partially pixelated to obscure genitalia, but the sounds she made were explicit enough, and totally embarrassing. She felt her face hot and red through the seemingly endless tape, but West remained impassive. When it finally finished, the barrister asked him: 'Can you identify either of the people in this video?'

'No.'

'Is it not you and Detective Inspector Jan Talantire?'

'No, it's not me, certainly.'

'So you think it may be her?'

'I don't have a strong opinion either way.'

'Had you seen it before?'

'No.'

'Yet you would agree that the bedding on show is the same Marks & Spencer's duvet cover that was found at your home?'

'No. It's a very common design, I believe.'

'In your statement you said you had no idea how this video happened to be on a data stick in the possession of former firearms unit Sergeant Colin Donnelly. Is that correct?'

'Yes.'

'Unfortunately, as the court will know, the late Mr Donnelly cannot be cross-examined on this, or indeed on any other matter, because he was shot by a Devon and Cornwall Police firearms officer while holding Ms Talantire hostage. However we do have a complete list of the WhatsApp messages shared by Mr Donnelly and Mr West, and indeed many other serving and former Devon and Cornwall police officers. So Mr West, looking again at the list of 236 WhatsApp messages you contributed to that group over five years, we can see that you are were in conversation with Mr Donnelly in what could broadly be termed a misogynistic fashion, on the sexual performance of at least half a dozen serving and former female officers—'

'Those were all consensual relationships.'

'That's not what I'm about to ask you. A relationship may be consensual within certain boundaries. For example, it might be unusual, one might suggest, for a sexual partner to be happy that you, without asking her permission, write what we might call a "Tripadvisor" type of review, and share it freely not only with your friends but with officers who might well turn out to be her colleagues. Consent, for that, was not given.'

'M'lud, I wish to object to this line of questioning,' Cranham said. 'It may be unbecoming and discourteous to share this detail with friends, but it is not illegal unless it is published. There is no comparison in legal terms between consent for sex and the boundaries of privacy.'

'M'lud, I'm merely attempting to delineate the background against which the offences took place.'

Given the judge's approval to continue, Khan asked: 'Message 116 on your list from 2016, in a discussion about the attractiveness of Ms Talantire, is as follows, and I quote, "She gives surprisingly good head". Do you remember sending that?'

'No. It was more than seven years ago.'

'You accept that it was you?'

'Yes, though it's not something I am proud of.'

'And here on message 119, which I must remind the court was deleted by the witness but was still retained on Donnelly's account, you say: "Enjoy." There is a broken link to a video. I put it to you, Mr West, that the video referred to is in fact the one we have just seen that you recorded in your flat.'

'No, you're mistaken.' West smiled indulgently. 'There was no video recorded in my flat. I think the one you have shown was probably one involving one of her other partners.'

As the cross-examination continued, Talantire could feel the chances of conviction ebbing away. West's charisma seemed to bathe the jury in a glow. Of the eight female members at least three were looking at him in a way that could not be regarded as dispassionate. One young woman, who had leaned forward throughout the proceedings, seemed to be viewing him with what could only be described as desire.

Chapter Twenty-one

At the next court recess, Talantire again saw Sam Mahoney. The young detective constable was sitting in a corridor, having an animated but whispered conversation with West's barrister Eleanor Cranham. All that Talantire could catch was 'I can't go through with it,' then 'No', repeated several times. Just a glimpse was enough to see that her eyes were full of tears. Talantire hurried back and knocked on the prosecution barrister's door. One of the juniors opened it, and she saw inside Yasir Khan, in full wig and regalia, eating a baguette. He had a napkin tucked into the top of his collar.

'I've got some important information,' she said. 'Can I come in?'

He beckoned her in as he tried to swallow what looked like an extremely large mouthful. As soon as the doors closed, she said: 'I think defence witness Sam Mahoney is having second thoughts about testifying.' She told him what she had seen.

'This is Detective Constable Mahoney, yes?' Khan said, flicking a crumb off his cheek. 'I was planning to ask about her trip to Morocco and whether she posted Alex Brown's postcard.'

'There's no proof. Her DNA didn't show on the postcard,' Talantire said. 'I would concentrate on her attempts to glean information as a spy on West's behalf. There's something else that she disclosed to me: that West made her have an abortion.'

Khan noted it all down. 'Very interesting. If she's going to change her tune she may be declared a hostile witness, which would be interesting. Thank you for the tip-off.'

—

It was the next day when the defence called Sam Mahoney to the witness box. Talantire gazed at this young woman, conservatively dressed in a trouser suit, with her dark hair teased into a series of waves. She looked much more composed than when Talantire had seen her in the corridor the previous day.

Barrister Eleanor Cranham asked her a little about her career and then delved into her relationship with Brent West.

'When did you begin your relationship with the accused?'

'In March 2023.'

'We have heard testimony accusing Mr West of abusive and controlling behaviour in relationships. Has that been your experience?'

She hesitated, then glanced at the dock, where West was sitting with his arms folded. Talantire could see he had raised his eyebrows, as if prompting her.

'Please answer the question,' the judge interceded.

'No, that has not been my experience,' she said quietly.

'How would you describe his behaviour towards you?' Cranham asked, gesturing with her spectacles towards the defendant.

She glared at West, but said nothing. Khan, sitting in the row behind Cranham, turned to look at Talantire, and gave her a discreet nod. *You were right*, it seemed to say.

'I, er...'

The judge intervened again, to remind her gently that she was under oath, then added, 'Ms Mahoney, if you have any doubts about what you are expected to say, remember it is only the truth and all of the truth that we are expecting here.'

Cranham glared at the judge, and then referred to her papers. 'DC Mahoney, in your statement to the police you said, and I quote: "Brent West has been kind and thoughtful and considerate to me at all times. I do not recognise the account of his behaviour described by others".' She looked up at her questioningly.

'Actually, I do recognise it,' she said, glancing across at the judge. There were gasps across the public gallery.

Cranham looked like she was going to implode. 'My Lord, I'd like to request a short adjournment,' she said.

'On what grounds?' the judge asked. 'The witness does not appear to be unwell.'

Cranham consulted with her colleagues before saying, 'I'd like to declare Ms Mahoney a hostile witness.'

'Then you may continue,' the judge said.

Talantire could see that Brent West was glaring at his girlfriend from the dock, his affable mask finally slipping.

'Ms Mahoney, you said in your statement that you did not recognise in your own relationship with the defendant any of the alleged abusive behaviour described by others. But now you say you do. Can the court believe anything that you say?'

'Yes, they can.'

'Given that you are a perjurer, I would suggest not.'

'I was put under huge pressure by Brent and, just yesterday, by you to side with him. But it's now clear to me I would have to lie to do that.'

'Well, well, Ms Mahoney, I have to say that what comes out of your mouth is your own responsibility, and if you want to keep changing your mind, I would suspect that there is no value in what you have to say.'

The judge intervened. 'Mrs Cranham, that isn't a question. Do you have any further questions for this witness?'

'No, m'lud.'

Khan wasted no time in beginning his cross-examination.

'DC Mahoney, perhaps I can begin where my learned colleague left off. You say that you did recognise the defendant's behaviour as described by others in your own relationship.'

'Yes. He was controlling; I can't deny that.'

'In what ways was he controlling?'

'He liked to choose what clothes I would wear when we went out together, and made suggestions about my hair and make-up.'

'Was there anything else?'

'Yes, there was.'

'Would you care to tell the court about it?'

She seemed really nervous now, and glanced across at the defendant, who was looking daggers at her. She didn't say anything.

'DC Mahoney. Did the defendant control other aspects of your life? Whether or not you had children, for example?'

'Objection, m'lud,' Cranham interjected. 'My learned colleague is shamelessly leading the witness.'

The judge seemed to agree, but even after Khan withdrew the question the hint had already taken root.

'I was asking you about—' Khan said.

'Brent made me have an abortion,' Sam said. 'He told me that it would damage his career if they saw me with a swollen belly, he had a grown-up daughter and said he didn't need any more responsibilities.' At this, the witness gazed at Talantire. Their eyes met. It was clear that Sam now had plenty of things she wanted to say.

'So you went ahead with the termination?'

At this, Sam began to cry. Khan gave her time. She finally nodded, and every female member of the jury stared in rapt attention.

'Did you want a child?'

'Yes, I did,' she sobbed. 'And I thought he loved me.'

'Do you think that now?'

She shook her head and cried again. Khan gave her more time, clearly delighted at this gift of a witness. A female juror blew her nose and wiped her eyes. Many of the men were obviously moved too.

'There's more,' Sam said, thickly.

'Take your time.'

'Brent seemed very interested in bondage, which really isn't my thing. On the day I told him I was pregnant, he got angry. He seized hold of me, dragged me to the bedroom, tied me up and gagged me, then forced me into a large holdall. I was crying, I could barely breathe, and I begged him to release me, which he eventually did. That's when he made me promise I would get rid of my baby.'

'I think everyone in the court will agree that is an act of astonishing abuse. Do you regard that as the reaction of a caring partner?'

She shook her head. 'No. He apologised afterwards, and I forgave him. He later bought me some jewellery to say he was sorry.'

'Why did you accept his apology?'

She didn't answer for a moment, and then said softly: 'I loved him. And I thought he loved me. He did seem to be sorry. He thought I might enjoy being tied up; that's what he later told me. He got me completely wrong on that. He asked me if I thought I could escape from it, and I confessed no, it would be impossible.'

'May I ask, DC Mahoney, how exactly did the defendant tie your hands and feet?'

'With plastic cable tie things.'

'And your gag?'

'That was a ball gag.'

'Were you aware of him using exactly this method of bondage on other women?'

'No, initially I wasn't. In fact, it wasn't until I read the papers yesterday evening that I was aware that a similar method had been used on Detective Inspector Talantire.'

'Objection, m'lud. Evidence already presented and not contested was that Colin Donnelly used these methods when abducting Ms Talantire, not the defendant.'

'I think the court is aware of that,' the judge said.

Khan continued. 'Ms Mahoney, given what you have discovered about the evidence of Ms Talantire, do you now believe that the defendant is guilty of arranging to have her abducted?'

'Yes, I do.'

'Do you believe that West intended to have her killed?'

Sam licked her lips and hesitated. 'Yes, I believe so.'

There was uproar in the court. Talantire restrained the urge to wave her fist in the air in triumph.

'I'd like to ask you one more thing,' Khan said, once calm had returned. 'You travelled to Morocco in September on holiday, I believe.'

'Yes, I did.'

'Did Commander West give you an item to post?'

'Yes. It was a postcard.'

'Was this from him?'

'No. I assumed it was a colleague of his, but it was strange that Brent had asked me to buy a stamp for it in Morocco and then post it to the UK. He said it was a practical joke, so I didn't think much about it at the time.'

'When did you discover that this postcard was from Alex Brown to his mother?'

'Only when I examined the case files after Brent was arrested. I was shocked.'

'Why were you shocked?'

'Because it became obvious to me that Brent had created a false trail to show that Alex Brown was still alive and in Morocco. And that must have meant that, in fact, he was dead. He had also given me a phone to take with me and asked me to turn it on a couple of times, but never answer it.'

'Alex Brown's phone?'

'Yes, I believe so now.'

'Did you bring this to the attention of your senior officer?'

'No.'

'Whyever not?'

'Because I wasn't supposed to access those case files. I wasn't working on the case, and it's a dismissible offence.'

'Is that the only reason?'

'No. I wanted to get the answer from Brent, but he wouldn't talk about it.'

'Did Commander West ever say to you that he wanted to kill Alex Brown?'

'No. He never even mentioned him to me.'

'Did he ever say to you that he wanted to kill anyone?'

'Well, he did once say that he wanted to kill Jan Talantire, but I assumed he was joking. We discussed her many times and what a thorn in his side she was. I still didn't think he was serious, until I heard what happened to her.'

'And what do you think now?'

'He intended to murder her. I realise that now. And just yesterday, I realised that one day he would do it to me too.'

'It's a damn lie!' The shout came from the dock. Talantire looked at Brent West. He was no longer the imperturbable police commander. The snarl on his face, the stabbing finger of accusation directed at Sam and the three burly custody officers who had to restrain him. Finally, they removed him from the court to the cells beneath.

When Talantire turned to look at the jury, they were all staring at where West had been. The indulgent smiles were gone, and no one was leaning forward. The woman who had clearly fancied him had a hand over her mouth. The magic had been dispelled.

Epilogue

Samantha Mahoney's evidence turned out to be crucial. The jury took two days to return a unanimous verdict of guilty on all counts. West was sentenced to life, with a minimum tariff of thirty years. As he was taken down, he pointed a finger at Sam, who was now sitting in the public gallery. He drew a finger across his throat. A clear death threat. Under disciplinary investigation for unauthorised accessing of file, Sam Mahoney left the police soon afterwards, but remained under police protection. In view of her part in bringing West to justice, the CPS decided not to press charges relating to her involvement in covering up the disappearance of Alex Brown.

DCS Rebecca Crossfield had worked hard over the last year to firm up her suspicions that Brent West was working with the Mafia, but proof remained elusive. She and Talantire formed a friendship, and saw each other a couple of times a year, in addition to cooperating through work. The ownership of the Burnham-on-Sea pet crematorium was traced to a shell company based in the Caribbean, but it proved impossible to find out who was the ultimate owner. However, it was closed down by the local authority for licensing breaches.

DCI Fred Winterflood was commended for his investigation. Police marksman Zach Townend left the force. James Garrett was sentenced to five years for his attack on

PC Tim Caldwell, who is now completely recovered from his injuries.

It was several months later when Alex Brown and Nadine Lister were formally declared dead by the coroner. Talantire, Fred Winterflood and a number of their colleagues attended separate memorial services for them.

It was on a summer morning after attending the memorial service in Exeter of Alex Brown that Talantire made the journey to Brixham along with Mary Stuart Davies to visit the grave of Katarina Lezcano. The grave occupied a secluded position under the branches of a cherry tree, within view of the sea, and had been well tended.

Talantire considered the long chain of events that contributed to this unfortunate woman's death. It all came back to Brent West. The estrangement between Katarina and her son would have been temporary, but for his abduction and murder by West. The blunt and dismissive messages sent from Alex's phone by West in reply to her pleas for help simply compounded her fragile mental state and drove her to suicide.

—

It was six months after the case was concluded that Harry Vickers piloted his launch out through the Teign channel and into the waters off South Devon. In a brisk wind, he headed for his creels, still marked by the buoy. This time, as he hauled them up, he found one had snagged on something. It was a brass cylinder, with a chain, partially encrusted with seashells. The chain had snagged on a knot on one of the ropes. As he pulled the creel into the launch, he unhooked the cylinder, which was about the size of a food tin. As he examined it, he could see that it had been engraved:

> *Madre e hijo, unidos desde el nacimiento
> hasta la muerte*

Harry unscrewed the watertight lid and saw inside some papers. He dried his hands carefully before gently emptying the cylinder. Inside was a colourful card, written in a young child's hand: 'To Mummy'. There was a letter from mother to son on his fifth birthday and another for his twenty-first. There were objects too: a commemorative coin, a hank of a baby's soft hair, held together by a clip, and a photograph of a woman cradling a child, beaming to the camera. This he knew must be the woman who had washed up under the pier. Harry took out his phone and photographed everything before carefully returning it to the canister. He thought about bringing it in for Geoff Hutchinson to have a look at. But this time capsule was surely intended to remain in the sea, to which the woman in her last remaining minutes alive had consigned it. Surprised to get a clear enough signal, he then typed the engraved message into Google translate:

> *Mother and son, bound together from
> birth to death.*

He screwed on the lid tightly, made a little prayer and then gently released the canister into the water. It sank immediately, and was lost to sight. Harry restarted the engine of his launch and turned the tiller until the prow pointed towards shore. Then he headed for home.

Afterword

I undertook a considerable amount of research for this book. I would like to thank Hester Russell, Head of Crime at GWBHarthills solicitors in Sheffield for her expert guidance on the court scenes. Lilli Foster at Rinnovare hair salon was a great source of advice on hair extensions. Claire Malcolm and Joy Chambers undertook various experiments with their fitness trackers for me and proved that they worked placed as described in the book. Joy Chambers also guided me on the technicalities of social work. Thanks are also due to Dr Neil Rushton, and my long-time sources Home Office forensic pathologist Dr Stuart Hamilton, and retired detective Kim Booth. I'm also grateful to my beta readers Jo Joseph, Valerie Richardson, Tim Cary and John Selfe. Any remaining errors are my own.

I'd like to thank Louise Cullen, Alicia Pountney, and all the editorial staff at Canelo, plus freelance editors Bonny Macleod and Russel McLean, and proofreader Matthew Robertson. Craig Thomson and Julian Holmes at WF Howes continue to be massively supportive of the audiobooks, superbly voice by Mandy Weston. Thanks also to Julie Davenport, Helen Jennings, Murray and Dani Sharpe, plus Bill and Sarah Allen for friendship and support during my research and publicity trips to Devon and Cornwall.

Last but not least, I'd like to thank my wife Louise, as always for her patience and support.

Finally, in a case of life imitating art, the chemical dye system that I devised for the plot for tracing heating oil thefts, is now being assessed by Devon and Cornwall Police as a tool against rural crime.

Do you love crime fiction and are always on the lookout for brilliant authors?

Canelo Crime is home to some of the most exciting novels around. Thousands of readers are already enjoying our compulsive stories. Are you ready to find your new favourite writer?

Find out more and sign up to our newsletter at canelocrime.com